Praise for Stealing People

'Wilson is a master at creating suspense, but it's his depiction of the evil that men do that is truly outstanding' *Catholic Herald*

'Gripping' *Literary Review*

'Robert Wilson brings all his talent as a supreme thriller writer to bear in this tightly-plotted, fast paced, addictive page-turner'
BitetheBook.com

'Tense, high-concept entertainment masterfully delivered'
Irish Independent

'Clever, complex and compelling. These hallmarks have shot Wilson's thrillers featuring kidnap negotiator Charlie Boxer onto my 'must read' list' *Peterborough Evening Telegraph*

'If you enjoy kidnap thrillers, you'll love this one. Not only is it exciting and unpredictable but it must contain more kidnaps per chapter than any book ever written' *Morning Star*

'The action is fast, complex and at times very, very unexpected'
Crime Review

WITHDRAWN

Robert Wilson has lived and worked around the world, including spells shipbroking, tour guiding and exporting bathrooms to Nigeria. After escaping car crashes, civil wars and angry baboons, Rob turned to writing novels. Since then, he's written thirteen acclaimed crime novels including the CWA Gold Dagger-winning *A Small Death in Lisbon* and the Falcón series, recently adapted for television. His first novel featuring Charlie Boxer, *Capital Punishment*, was shortlisted for the CWA Ian Fleming Steel Dagger award. To find out more, visit www.robert-wilson.eu

By Robert Wilson

The Ignorance of Blood
The Hidden Assassins
The Silent and the Damned
The Blind Man of Seville
The Company of Strangers
A Small Death in Lisbon
A Darkening Stain
Blood is Dirt
The Big Killing
Instruments of Darkness
Capital Punishment
You Will Never Find Me
Stealing People

STEALING PEOPLE

Robert Wilson

An Orion paperback

First published in Great Britain in 2015
by Orion Books
This paperback edition published in 2016
by Orion Books,
an imprint of The Orion Publishing Group Ltd,
Carmelite House, 50 Victoria Embankment
London EC4Y 0DZ

An Hachette UK Company

1 3 5 7 9 10 8 6 4 2

A CIP catalogue record for this book
is available from the British Library.

ISBN 978 1 4091 4819 7

Typeset by Deltatype Ltd, Birkenhead, Merseyside

Printed in Great Britain by Clays Ltd, St Ives plc

The Orion Publishing Group's policy is to use papers that
are natural, renewable and recyclable products and made
from wood grown in sustainable forests. The logging and
manufacturing processes are expected to conform to the
environmental regulations of the country of origin.

www.orionbooks.co.uk

For Bryony

STEALING PEOPLE

1

Rakesh Sarkar came off the Westway driving his twenty-first-birthday present from his father through the back streets of Bayswater as if he was his grandmother. The spliff he'd smoked was giving him eye-crinkling giggles at the absurd image of a be-spectacled little old Indian lady hunched over the steering wheel of a Porsche 911 Carrera. It had taken all his self-control not to open up the throttle on the raised dual carriageway, with London stretched out glittering at his feet while Renault Clios and Opel Corsas overtook him on the inside.

The reason for this reluctant, law-abiding drive back to his flat in Arundel Gardens was that he'd been out with relatives at a restaurant and drunk wine before going to his English girlfriend's flat in Shoreditch to knock back shots of Glenmorangie, smoke a joint and have dispiritingly rapid sex. The following morning he had a five a.m. call to be at his commodities trading desk at Trafigura Limited on Portman Street. He'd been late once before and the only reason they'd allowed him to continue his internship was because his father, Uttam Sarkar, was the owner of India's largest commodities conglomerate, the Amit Sarkar Group.

The alcohol and drugs meant that the Porsche had to be driven at a speed so slow it was almost stalling with outrage. So he was infuriated when an unmarked white car overtook him and switched on blue flashing lights above the rear bumper. The giggles vanished as he pulled into the kerb, lowered the window and hyperventilated the damp night air.

Two police officers got out holding up hands against the head-lights and made a sign that he should turn off his engine. One of them approached the driver's side. The other walked slowly around the car. Sarkar coughed, stuck his head out of the window, sucked in more cold air.

'Anything the matter, officer?' he said.

'Little bit erratic there, sir,' said the policeman.

'Erratic!' said Sarkar, instantly maddened. 'What do you mean, *erratic*? I've never been so careful in my life.'

The officer came down to his level, sniffed.

'Never been so careful in your life?' he said. 'Can I ask you if that's because you've been drinking, sir?'

'No, I haven't, officer. I don't drink and drive. Absolutely not.'

'There's a smell of alcohol on your breath, sir,' said the officer. 'Are you sure you haven't been drinking? You did cross the central road markings on several occasions, and we associate that with driving under the influence.'

'I can assure you I have had nothing to drink,' said Sarkar, heart thumping in his throat.

'Just look this way, sir,' said the officer, shining a flashlight into his eyes.

Sarkar blinked, felt foolish.

'Your pupils are dilated, sir,' said the officer. 'Perhaps you've been using drugs and that's what's made your driving even more erratic than if—'

'It wasn't erratic. I was driving at the … *below* the speed limit. If I crossed the central line, it was only because there were parked cars on either side. We *are* in London, you know.'

'We do know that, sir. We're with the Metropolitan Police,' said the officer. 'I'm going to have to ask you to step out of the car and take a breathalyser test, sir.'

'What the fuck …'

'Just try and keep the language and your temper under control, sir. We're only doing our job. Can't have people driving around under the influence, can we? End up killing people, then where would you be?'

'Look,' said Sarkar, desperate, 'what's it going to take?'

'It'll only take a few minutes, sir … if you're clean.'

'You know what I mean, officer.'

'Do I?' said the officer, frowning. 'Sergeant, just come over here, please.'

The other policeman joined him. Two hard faces peering in at the driver's window.

'You've got our full attention now, sir. Just say what it was you wanted to know. What's it going to ...?'

'I asked you "What's it going to take?"' said Sarkar.

'And I said a few minutes if you're clean, and you replied ...'

'I replied: "You know what I mean, officer." And I think you do.'

'*Do* I understand that correctly, Sergeant?'

The two officers looked at each other, eyes narrowed.

'I think he's offering you a bribe, sir.'

'How much are you willing to offer ... as a bribe?'

'A grand.'

'A grand, eh?' said the policeman. 'One thousand pounds.'

'Make it two. One each,' said Sarkar.

'Do you have this money on you, sir?'

'No.'

'So how's that going to work?'

'I have it at home. In a safe.'

'I think the best thing for you to do is go with the sergeant in the car in front, and I'll follow you home in your little motor. How's that? Best be safe if you're inebriated.'

Sarkar got out of the car, handed over his keys, followed the sergeant to the unmarked police car and got in.

A policewoman was sitting in the back, blonde hair tied up in a bun. As he sat down, closing the door, she leaned towards him and he felt a sharp prick in his left buttock. He yelped with shock.

'What the fuck was that?'

'Sorry, sir?' said the policewoman.

The sergeant got into the driver's seat, pressed the central locking button.

'I felt something sharp go into my backside,' said Sarkar.

'Don't know what you're talking about,' said the policewoman. 'Now would you mind breathing into this?'

'Yes I bloody would,' said Sarkar. 'You stabbed me with something.'

3

'*Stabbed* you?' said the policewoman, shocked, showing him her empty hands. 'Let's just wipe the seat. We get all sorts in here, you know. Drinkers, drug users. They sometimes drop their syringes.'

'Are you telling me I might have sat on a drug user's syringe?'

'Well it's never happened before, but you're complaining so I think it's worth checking.'

'I want to get out of this car,' said Sarkar, ripping at the door lever.

'Just keep calm and breathe into this, and we'll check if your alcohol level—'

'I AM NOT going to be CALM!' roared Sarkar. 'I am NOT going to be breathing into your bloody breathalyser. I might have picked up HIV from a syringe rolling around in your car.'

'We're not bothering with that,' said the sergeant. 'We've come to an agreement … apparently.'

'Oh really, Sergeant?' said the policewoman, ignoring the raving Sarkar. 'What sort of an agreement?'

'He's offered us two grand,' said the sergeant.

The Porsche 911 Carrera roared past them, disappeared into the night.

'Where the fuck is he going?' said Sarkar, staring out the window, digging his iPhone from his pocket. 'I thought he was supposed to be following us, not tearing off down the street … I'm calling my lawyer. There's going to be no two grand now.'

'Just tell us where to go, will you, sir?' said the sergeant.

'The nearest bloody police station,' said Sarkar. 'I'm not putting up with this. That fucker's run off with my *car*.'

The policeman checked the back seat in the rear-view, raised an eyebrow at the policewoman, who slipped off her shoe, leaned back, raised her foot and kicked Sarkar so hard in the side of the face that his head ricocheted off the window.

Silence. The policewoman took the iPhone from Sarkar's slack hands.

'I do hate it when they get shouty,' she said.

'I thought you'd given him enough trank to take an elephant down.'

'We're not in the movies, you know.'

4

Klaus Weber, chauffeur to the Deal-O supermarket heir Hans Pfeiffer, was sitting in the reclining driver's seat of an S65 Mercedes listening to Mahler's Symphony No. 5 played by the World Orchestra for Peace, conducted by Valery Gergiev. He had grown to like classical music driving Hans Pfeiffer around Europe. Pfeiffer lived in Switzerland and didn't like flying; only did it if absolutely necessary. He also didn't like talking very much, and certainly not to people like Weber, with whom he struggled to find anything in common, so there was plenty of time for listening to music.

'How's it going, Klaus?' said Jack, who'd just drifted over from his limousine, peaked chauffeur's cap in hand. 'Hey, like the music.'

'*Alles gut*,' said Weber, leaning across the seat. 'Mahler.'

Despite this being his third consecutive night outside Chinawhite, all the other chauffeurs had ignored Weber. He'd walked past their cars smoking a cigarette but none of them had lowered their windows. Like Jack, they were mostly carrying celebrities around from club to club and rarely spent more than an hour at any one location. Jack was the only one who'd been friendly.

'Fancy a coffee, Klaus?'

'Sure, but where at this time of night?'

'Tinseltown, Great Portland Street. Just round the corner. Two minutes' walk. Stays open till one o'clock.'

Weber checked his watch, weighed it up.

'OK, just a coffee.'

'They do food as well. Nachos. Burgers. Don't turn your nose up at it.'

'Don't what?'

'Don't worry, mate. Let's go.'

Weber was one of six drivers on the payroll. But tonight he wasn't waiting for Hans Pfeiffer. This time he was sitting up the road from one of the fanciest nightclubs in London, hanging on the whim of Pfeiffer's nineteen-year-old daughter, Karla. When she'd finally had enough, she would text him to pick her up. He would ease down to Winsley Street, open the door at Chinawhite's and she'd hop in off her Jimmy Choos to be taken back to the Pfeiffers' Chelsea town house.

Weber's precisely engineered German brain reckoned he wasn't going to hear from Karla until at least two o'clock, as tonight she was in the company of Wú Gao, the very beautiful son of the Chinese real-estate heiress Wú Dao-ming. This was the couple's third evening together at Chinawhite, and each night had been about an hour longer than the last.

'So how's it been with Herr Pfeiffer in London these last few days?' asked Jack.

'Oh, you know, the same thing every day,' said Weber, putting on his Hugo Boss uniform raincoat but not the peaked cap. 'We drive around. Look at property. They talk. I don't hear anything. I just drive the car.'

The rear passenger seats of the Mercedes were completely glassed in and hermetically sealed. Weber never heard a word of any of the discussions between Pfeiffer and Wú Dao-ming. He'd been driving them around London looking at potential development sites for luxury apartments, for which there was a huge demand in China. Pfeiffer already had more than forty Deal-O supermarkets around the capital and understood the investment opportunities, while Wú Dao-ming had the clients. Communication with Weber was via an intercom and consisted of the word 'Stop' and not much else. He was careful not to mention Wú Dao-ming to Jack. Pfeiffer was very strict about commercial security. He didn't want anybody knowing who he was talking to.

Karla and Wú Gao hadn't known each other for long but they got on. They spoke in English, which was their only common language. Wú Gao was in the first year of an economics degree at the LSE and it was he who'd proposed they go to Chinawhite. Karla was in her first year at Central St Martin's College of Art and Design. Wú Gao was mad about art. His mother had an extensive collection of Chinese artists. Karla was mad about Wú Gao.

'You know who I'm waiting for tonight?' said Jack.

'Somebody different to last night?'

'Always different.'

'I don't guess very well,' said Weber, stiffly.

'Scarlett Johansson,' said Jack. 'She's over here to see Jonathan

Glazer, you know, the director of *Under the Skin*.'

Weber looked blank. Jack shrugged, and as they walked past the Market Place Bar he took Weber's arm and pulled him down a narrow alleyway, a cut-through to Margaret Street.

'Quicker this way,' he said. 'You like German movie directors?'

'I prefer football.'

'Don't tell me ... Bayern Munich.'

'How did you know?'

'It's written all over you, Klaus. Arjen Robben, Franck Ribéry, Thomas Müller. Top bloody notch.'

As they walked past Ryman, a tightly gloved hand flashed out of the shadows and hit Weber hard on the side of the neck. He stumbled, fell on to all fours and found himself staring into the grey slabs and joins of the paving stones, his vision dark-edged and pulsing.

The man who'd chopped him across the carotid stepped out of the dark and stuck a hypodermic into his left buttock, ramming the plunger home. He straddled Weber, who'd collapsed on to his elbows, grabbed him around the chest and lifted him to his feet. Jack found the car keys in his trouser pocket, along with a wallet. They stripped off the Hugo Boss coat, which Jack put on, and removed his mobile phone from the inside pocket, checked it. A car pulled up on Margaret Street, reversed on to the pavement as far as the single post in the middle of the alleyway. The boot sprang open.

They walked Weber, toes trailing, to the car, folded him in and shut the lid. The gloved man handed Jack a small canister before getting into the passenger seat. Jack walked back down the alleyway and returned to Weber's Mercedes. He opened the rear door, stripped off a piece of tape from the canister and stuck it below the seat. He got behind the wheel, turned on the Mahler and put Weber's mobile phone on the armrest. Waited.

At 01.45 Jack received a text from Karla telling him she was ready. He put on the driver's cap and rolled down to Chinawhite, where she was waiting with Wú Gao. He pulled up, started to get out of the car. Karla told him not to bother and they climbed into the back.

Jack pulled away heading west. He took out his own mobile

7

phone and pressed the dial button, which triggered the canister to release nitrous oxide into the passenger area. Within a minute the couple started giggling, heads thrown back. They were holding hands and their faces rolled closer to each other. Jack checked them in the rear-view, saw the euphoria sweeping over them. Their lips touched and parted, their tongues flickered, but they were laughing too much to sustain a kiss for very long.

Jack wheeled the Mercedes round, heading east. His passengers were oblivious. He rounded Russell Square, aiming for a small side street off the Gray's Inn Road where there was high-walled off-street parking by a small warehouse. He pulled in, unlocked the rear passenger doors. Two men opened them from the outside. Karla and Wú Gao turned to see the masked men reaching in. They nearly smiled before their faces were engulfed by chloroformed rags. The masked men got in the back, closed the doors. Jack pulled out on to the Gray's Inn Road.

'Call this number,' said Siena.

'Who do I talk to?' asked Jerry.

'Dunno. Someone. They'll have stuff. We need more *stuff.*'

'You're already fucked up, Si.'

'Get outta here,' said Siena. 'I haven't even started.'

The music thumped in the walls, fizzing up from the basement through the floors. They were sitting in a bare room at the top of a house on Leonard Street in Hackney. Lighting came from the orange street lamps below through uncurtained sash windows. Siena had her knees up to her chin. Jerry was lying at her feet. He rolled over and noticed that she wasn't wearing any knickers.

'What happened to your pants, Si?' he asked.

'Don't be a perv, Jerry.'

'Couldn't help it. I'm just lying here and—'

'I don't know,' she said, dismissing it, waving him off. 'I must have fucked somebody. Can't remember. Call the number. We need something.'

The door opened. A head of long blonde hair looked round, saw them.

'Hi,' he said.

Silence.

'Mind if I time out in here?'

The music was cartwheeling up the stairs behind him.

'Just need some space is all.'

Siena and Jerry looked up, said nothing.

'Got some weed if that helps?'

'We done weed,' said Jerry.

'All right, I got some pills. Different colours.'

'We done Smarties too,' said Siena.

'Got some lines of blow, but it don't look like you got the ... surfaces for that.'

'We can *make* surfaces for that,' said Siena, suddenly enthusiastic, nudging Jerry with her foot.

'This stuff's very pure, got to be careful with it,' said the blonde guy. 'Don't want to have to peel you off the ceiling at six in the morning.'

'Like how pure?' asked Siena.

'You Aussies?' asked the blonde guy. 'I'm just hearing a little twang there.'

'She's Aussie,' said Jerry. 'I'm from Dalston.'

'Go get some glass, Jerry. We need surfaces like the man said. What's your name?'

'Joe,' said the blonde guy.

'I'm Siena. He's Jerry,' she said.

Jerry got up, brushed past Joe and left the room.

Joe squatted down opposite Siena. He was young and fit. His blonde hair was central-parted. He tucked it behind his ears, stroked his goatee.

'So how come you got such pure blow?' asked Siena.

'I have friends,' said Joe. 'My weed you turned down. That's not just any old weed. My tabs're not just any old tabs.'

'What's so special about your weed?'

'It's called AK-47. Grow it myself. Maybe not quite up there with Super Silver Haze but it's close. The seeds are flown in from California.'

'And the tabs?'

'I got me a guy with access to a university lab. He does things like isolate the powerhouse drug from kratom. You know kratom?'

'Heard about it in Thailand. Never tried it.'

9

'Well this lab tech can isolate the 7-hydroxymitragynine from the alkaloids in the kratom leaves.'

'Whatever the fuck that means.'

'It means he's found a way to extract a drug ten times stronger than morphine, but with no addictive qualities, you hear what I'm saying?'

Jerry came back in with a piece of plate glass.

'So what's with the blow, Joe?' he said, happy that he wasn't going to have to chase down any more stuff.

'I have a Mexican guy who supplies me with uncut product,' said Joe.

'Can we meet him?' asked Siena.

'I'd introduce you, but he's unpredictable. Has a habit of killing people he doesn't like, and there's no telling.'

'You're fucking with me,' said Siena.

'He was born and raised in Ciudad Juarez,' said Joe. 'Thirty thousand people a year get killed there. It's like a war zone but with a death rate ten times higher.'

'Shall we, like, get on with it?' said Jerry, bored by Siena fancying yet another guy who could get her high.

Joe produced a tiny bag and a razor. He uncapped the razor, sliced the top off the bag and poured the small quantity of white powder on to the glass. He made three thin one-inch lines with the razor and handed a stainless-steel tube to Siena. She snorted a line and the effort knocked her back into the wall. As Jerry snorted his line Siena's neck became longer and she let out a little cry as of a distant child playing. Jerry fell back slowly and lay there with his groin slightly raised.

'Oh, ma-a-a-an,' he said.

Joe snorted his line, took the hit in his stride, dropped his head back.

'Oh my God,' said Siena. 'Let's go party.'

They went down into the basement, threw themselves into trance music so dense they could almost chew it. Siena got in close to Joe. The sweat soaked through his T-shirt, showing the edges of his pecs. She slapped his chest, wrapped her arms around his neck. They went back upstairs to the empty room with the orange light. She knelt down, let him know that she was available, looked back at him. Joe clocked the lack of knickers, slipped on a condom. Afterwards they sat with their backs to the wall.

'You going to let me try one of your kratom tabs?'

'They're not cheap.'

'I got money.'

'Doesn't look like it.'

'That's how I play it,' said Siena.

'So ... where's it come from?'

'My mother owns Casey Prospecting Limited in Western Australia. We keep China in iron ore.'

'Whoa,' said Joe. 'She know you're in a dive like this?'

'She's knows I'm in London.'

'Right. So let's make sure we don't have an ugly OD scenario on our hands.'

'You can OD on kratom?'

'This mix you can,' said Joe. 'Strictly one tab ... no more'n that.'

'Yes, sir.'

'How old are you?'

'What do you think?'

'I hope you're over sixteen.'

She punched him in the arm for taking the piss.

'Well?' he asked.

'I was seventeen last week,' she said, kissing him on the mouth. 'You?'

'Twenty-four in October.'

'Then let's do some kratom.'

He gave her a tab, which she knocked back with Coca-Cola.

'You going to take one?'

'It's better I keep an eye on you the first time.'

'You're different,' she said. 'Not many guys give a shit.'

'Don't want your mum coming down on my head.'

'You ever seen my mum?'

'No.'

'She's over two hundred pounds,' said Siena. She gasped.

'You OK?'

'Just getting something from the kratom.'

He waited. They stopped talking. She fell asleep. Ten minutes later he picked her up and put her over his shoulder, tugged her

11

dress down over her bare bottom and walked downstairs. He didn't meet anybody.

Outside, he walked down the street and a car pulled up alongside him. He lowered Siena Casey into the back seat, got in with her. The car pulled away.

'Everything OK?' asked the driver.

'Perfect,' said Joe.

'Great. That's four in the bag for tonight. Just a couple more to go.'

'Tonight?'

'One later this morning, one tomorrow and we're done.'

2

Irina Yermilov was up early. Sergei, her husband, always liked her to be dressed and ready to see him off whatever the time. And dressed meant dressed up, not just jeans and a T-shirt. It had always been like this, even in the days when he'd been a lowly mafia soldier in Prague living in a hotel on Wenceslas Square. She'd always had to get up in the morning, put on full make-up, her best spray-on minidress and high heels to accompany him down to the roped-off breakfast area where they would eat in conspicuous isolation in front of the tourists and other idiots who thought that Prague was still working in the spirit of Vaclev Havel. At least he treated her with respect. None of his cronies could bring their prostitutes to the table. And some of them came down with three girls to show what real men they were.

The cook was laying out the breakfast: blinis, sour cream, caviar, syrniki, rye bread, sausage, cold cuts and scrambled eggs. Irina was looking her devastating best as Sergei came downstairs. He was flying to Moscow for a high-level government meeting and was in no mood for conversation. The breakfast room overlooked the St George's Hill golf course. Yermilov didn't see it, didn't care about it, didn't even play golf.

'Is Yury coming down to say goodbye?'

'He's just getting dressed,' said Irina. 'You know what he's like in the mornings.'

'Is he playing today?'

'Yes, the under tens are playing Downsend this afternoon.'

13

'You will go and watch?'

'Of course,' she said, giving a little hurt pout.

'Sometimes you have your other things,' said Yermilov, as if they were trifles.

Irina said nothing, served him his black tea in a glass in an ornate silver holder, which was just about the only thing she did for him in the mornings.

Sergei tucked a napkin into his neck, covering his tie, shirt and jacket. He ate. A lot. He weighed in at two hundred and fifty pounds. His eyes had got smaller, pig-like, as his face had grown around them. He breathed heavily through his nose. He looked at his 18-carat gold Rolex, which pinched into the skin of his wrist, assessing the time he could devote to this meal. He wolfed blinis, sour cream and caviar, followed by several syrniki, before starting on rye bread, eggs and sausage. He washed it all down with the strong, sweet tea provided by Irina, who was a little under half his weight and still had the figure of the promising tennis player she'd been when she'd first bumped into him.

She'd got to the point where almost every day she regretted that extraordinary meeting in a Moscow nightclub. She knew his type from the company he was keeping and the way the nightclub owner was falling over himself. In fact it was the nightclub owner who'd asked her if she would care to join Sergei at his table. She refused and the sweat came out on his face. No, she wouldn't go to him. She wasn't some whore. He had to come to her. Which he did. On the dance floor. He was young and beautiful in those days, and loaded with money, which he was keen to blow on her at every opportunity.

Then they went to Prague and she saw what he was doing. He beat up people who didn't pay his extortionate protection rates. He had his men smack the girls around who weren't getting enough customers. She'd heard he tortured people whose relatives had run up casino debts and that he killed debtors if they couldn't come through with the money. But by then it was too late. There was no way out and somebody else had come along to make sure she would never leave. Yury.

There was the thunder of small hooves as her nine-year-old son hurtled down the stairs. He was washed, brushed and dressed in the Danes Hill School uniform of black trousers, white shirt, tie and grey pullover with a blue V. He went to his father, who hugged him and kissed his neck, stroked his head. Sergei loved his son with an intensity that surprised Irina. She'd never felt anything like that passion from him in the twelve years they'd been together. In fact he'd kept her at arm's length in almost every aspect of their lives, and lately, thank God, that included sex.

She had no real idea what he did for a living now. She knew it was business and that he had powerful connections in government. She also knew that it wasn't the straightforward brutal stuff that he'd been doing in Prague. He was in that strange middle ground that only modern Russia specialised in, somewhere between industry, government and crime.

She fussed over Yury, got him eating and happy, which she knew Sergei loved to see: a healthy appetite and humour were the essentials. Sergei responded by making funny monster faces, which made Yury giggle but only convinced Irina that he was revealing the aberrations of his inner life.

Finally the company car rolled down the drive to the neoclassical pedimented building that had recently been valued by a local estate agent for insurance at £14.5 million. It was an armoured Mercedes with a heavyweight driver and a bodyguard in the back. The same way Yury would travel, except the boy's Mercedes wasn't reinforced. Sergei stood up, ripped the napkin from his neck and wiped his mouth. He beckoned to Yury, who hopped off his chair and gave his father a huge hug, arms stretching around his full girth, face buried in his stomach. Sergei kissed the boy's head. They parted. Irina was given a dismissive flap of the hand over his shoulder.

'See you Tuesday,' he said.

Irina and Yury went to the window, which made the picture Sergei Yermilov demanded to see – mother and son waving goodbye. The Mercedes pulled away. There was a palpable relaxation in the room. The troublesome monster had departed. Now they could start enjoying themselves.

Fifteen minutes later, a VW Passat arrived with driver and bodyguard. They parked by the garage, opened the door and drove out in the family Mercedes, stopping in front of the house. The bodyguard got out and looked around warily, as if he was on a Moscow street rather than outside a luxury house in St George's Hill. He rang the bell. Irina busied herself getting Yury's laptop and books together and the case of clean games kit that the maid had washed and ironed. Yury held his iPhone to his chest with both hands. Irina gave him a big kiss on the lips. His eyes shone back at her.

Yury was unfazed by the fearsome bodyguard, who smiled at Irina revealing a gold tooth and a grin so lacking in humour she was concerned at letting her son go into his care. The boy threw himself across the back seat, followed by the bodyguard. The car pulled away and headed for the road outside the perimeter of the exclusive estate. Yury's thumbs danced over his iPhone.

In a few minutes they came out on to the Byfleet Road and headed for Oxshott and Yury's school. They were early so as not to get caught in the school rush. Sergei Yermilov did not like his son's car being stationary in traffic, where there were fewer options for escape, and so Yury was sent to school about forty minutes before all his school friends.

As the driver pulled away, a truck eased out into the road behind the Mercedes and stalled across both lanes. The Mercedes travelled fast along a stretch of road with no traffic in either direction. As it passed the turning to the Silvermere Care Home, a police car pulled out from a side road on the left and the driver was forced to stop. At the same moment another police car pulled out behind them, blocking their rear. Two officers got out of the car in front. They were dressed in peaked caps and flak jackets and had holstered weapons on their hips. The driver checked the rear-view, saw two similar officers coming from the other car. He looked at the bodyguard, who shrugged. Yury looked up from his iPhone to find that real life had become more interesting.

The driver stared at the approaching officers with eyes narrowed, full of suspicion. His legs were squeezed shut with a PSS Silent Pistol between them. The bodyguard had access to an MP-443 Grach. The four officers drew level with the car. In each case one was slightly ahead of the other and the rear officer had his hand on the Glock 17 in his holster. The lead officer in each pair asked the occupants of the car to open their doors, making a gesture so that it was understood.

Even the driver wasn't a hundred per cent sure what triggered his next move – some intuition bred from frequent assaults– because he suddenly kicked open his door, which knocked over the lead officer, and produced his PSS. He had no time to fire. The rear officer drew his Glock 17 and put three bullets in his chest and one into his head before he'd even fired a shot.

At the same moment the lead officer at the rear yanked open the door and fell away so that the shot that came from the MP-443 Grach shattered the window but didn't touch him. The officer behind already had his Glock out and shot the bodyguard in the head. The blood spray speckled the bewildered Yury's face. He was still holding his iPhone. The lead officer recovered, reached in, knocked the iPhone out of the boy's hands, grabbed him by his pullover, shirt and tie and hauled him over the inert bodyguard's legs. Yury started kicking and screaming. The rear officer produced a handkerchief, put it over the boy's face and he immediately slumped. The lead officer walked back with him draped over an arm while the other officers kicked the doors shut and trotted back to their cars. They moved off. As they approached the Silvermere Haven Pet Cemetery, they flashed the truck, which pulled into the lane so that they could pass.

The police car in the rear turned and drove back, flashing the truck stalled across the road. It manoeuvred out of the way and they drove past heading for the M25. The operation had taken three and a half minutes.

By midday, DCS Oscar Hines, the new head of the Metropolitan Police's Kidnap and Special Investigations Unit, had made all his decisions. He had told no one. Since his appointment, which had come with the news that DCS Peter Makepeace was now the new head of the Organised Crime Command, he'd realised that the offices were rife with rumours of cuts and redundancies. Under those circumstances nobody liked to see their new boss working in total secrecy on new plans.

He looked through the numbers on his contact list and made his first call of the day to DI Mercy Danquah, who was away giving a course on Special Investigations techniques.

'This is DCS Oscar Hines,' he said.

'Hello, sir. How can I help you?' said Mercy tentatively.

'I'd like you to come back to the office and present yourself here first thing tomorrow morning.'

'Can I ask what it's about, sir?' she said. 'As you know, I'm giving a course here. I can't just walk out. Something has to be said.'

'You don't have to worry about that. I'll see to everything,' said Hines. 'Just make sure you're here tomorrow morning. Thank you. Goodbye.'

Mercy clicked off her phone and looked around the people sitting with her in the canteen. They all stared back, some with food on the way to their mouths.

'Got to go,' she said, standing. 'Sorry.'

She went into the lobby and out into the rain, where she stood under the canopy of the entrance and made a phone call to her lover, Marcus Alleyne.

'It's me,' she said. 'What are you doing tonight?'

'It sounds like I might be doing something with you, whereas I had been thinking of having a quiet night in on my own,' he said. 'You all right, Mercy?'

'No, I'm all wrong,' she said. 'I'm booking a table and we're going out to dinner. You come round to mine and we'll catch a cab. We are *drinking* tonight.'

'You're sounding very ... purposeful, Mercy.'

'This might be the last time we go out for quite a while,' she said.

'And why's that?'

'I think I'm about to lose my job.'

18

3

'I want you to find my father,' she said, in a deep voice with a little croak in it, sexy.

'How long ago did he disappear?' asked Boxer.

'Three days,' she said, sitting back in the white leather chair.

'Only three days,' said Boxer. 'You know the LOST Foundation doesn't—'

'Yeah, I know it doesn't.'

'So what are you doing here, Siobhan?' asked Boxer. 'The nearest police station is where you want to be.'

'I don't want to go to the police.'

'Any reason?'

'I know my father wouldn't want them – or anybody else – nosing around in his affairs.'

Boxer leaned back from the bare table in the initial meeting room: no phones, no computers, no interruptions for the families they saw there. The young woman stared at him. Her broad shoulders relaxed inside a pricey grey leather jacket with oversized fur collar and zips going every which way. Her elbows rested on the arms of the chair with strong hands hanging down over a high-waisted long black leather pencil skirt, which had ridden up to show muscular calves enclosed by black ribbed tights. She crossed her legs with no protest from the leather.

'Why come to me?' he asked, trying to work out how old she was, the expensive clothes going a long way to disguising her youth.

'I was advised.'

19

'Who by?'

Silence. Her foot started nodding with her thoughts.

'Going to give me a name?' asked Boxer.

'That's my business,' she said.

'Just out of interest, where are you from?'

'Not relevant.'

'Not strictly, I know. It just helps me … culturally. You sound English but with a slight American accent and you have the look of a South or Central American. Venezuelan maybe. *Habla español?*'

'*Si, mi madre era Cubana*, and my father's English. I did some schooling in the States … my father has business interests there.'

'How did they meet? Your parents.'

'On my father's yacht.'

'You said *"era"*. Does that mean your mother's dead?'

'She died just over six years ago. Breast cancer followed by liver cancer.'

'And how old are you?'

'Twenty-eight.'

'I don't think so,' said Boxer, taking a stab: not easy to age people in their twenties.

'Then why ask?'

'Don't make me fight for every answer,' said Boxer. 'It tires me out and I lose interest.'

'Twenty.'

Boxer raised his eyebrows.

'Ish,' she said.

A knock. The door opened without waiting for a reply.

'Sorry,' said Amy, backing out. 'I didn't know you had people.'

'What's up?'

'The heating engineer working in your flat says he's finished but wants to talk to you.'

'I'll call him back.'

'Hi, I'm Siobhan,' said the young woman, swivelling in her seat, stretching out her hand, which caught Amy off guard: unexpectedly formal. She stumbled reaching forward to shake it.

'My daughter, Amy,' said Boxer.

'I'll leave you to it,' said Amy, retreating under Siobhan's unswerving gaze.

The door closed. Siobhan turned back to Boxer.

'Where's she from?' she asked, eyes wide.

'Very funny,' said Boxer. 'Her mother's Ghanaian ...'

'And you're English,' said Siobhan. 'We should get along just fine. Nice looking girl. How old is she?'

'Were the police looking for your father at the time of his disappearance?' asked Boxer, ignoring her, not comfortable with the look she'd given Amy.

'Not actively.'

'Look, why not go to them? They've got far more resources than me.'

'My father's a very private kind of guy. The sort of information I'd have to give the police is not what he'd like to have out there,' she said, flinging a hand at the window. 'The people he does business with wouldn't like that kind of ... scrutiny. Is that the right word?'

'It'll do,' said Boxer. 'You've seen my colleague Roy Chapel, he's ex-police—'

'But I'm not talking to Roy Chapel,' said Siobhan. 'I'm only talking to you, Charles Boxer. Nobody else.'

'There are plenty of people a lot more qualified than I am to find your father,' said Boxer. 'Private eyes with contacts everywhere, even in the criminal world if that's what you're hinting at. I'll give you some names. You can tell them I sent you.'

'I'm not interested in anybody else. I only want you.'

'What if I'm not available ... or interested?'

'My father and I were staying at the Savoy Hotel,' said Siobhan, riding over that little wave. 'Since my mother died we've been very close. He takes me with him everywhere. He doesn't go for a walk in the park to smoke a cigarette and leave me behind sitting in a hotel room with no communication for three days.'

She was leaning forward now, elbows on the table, her hands clasped, resting her chin on them. She had long, thick, dark, glossy hair falling in waves to her shoulders, framing her face, which was both strong and beautiful. She had a wide red lipsticked mouth and a slight gap between her very white front teeth. Her light brown eyes under a pair of long, darkly gabled eyebrows transfixed him, held him to account.

21

Something about her left Boxer hanging in the balance. He couldn't make his mind up one way or the other and wasn't sure about what. She was a danger to him, he'd intuited that, but he could feel an irresistible pull into some innate darkness.

'This doesn't mean I'm taking on the job, but let's have your father's name,' he said. 'Preferably his *real* name and his age.'

'Conrad Jensen,' she said. 'But everybody calls him Con ... not for the obvious reason. As I understand it, you've got to be straight-talking if you want to get anywhere in the security business. And he's seventy-two but doesn't look it. He's tall at six foot three, lean and fit. He's got a beard at the moment, which I don't like.'

'Photo?'

Siobhan played with her iPhone, handed it over.

'That was taken four days ago in Green Park,' she said. 'He dyes his hair.'

Jensen was in a wool coat, a burgundy scarf and a black trilby. His beard was brownish mixed with grey, but well clipped and shaped like a shovel. Boxer zoomed in on the face, which did not look as careworn as he might have expected. Jensen's dark hair was touching the collar of the coat. He had high cheekbones and his eyes were an intense blue and stared into the camera, giving the face a mesmerising charisma.

'How long did it take before you called someone about Con disappearing?'

'Three hours,' she said. 'He told me he'd be gone for an hour. I try not to panic.'

'And who did you call?'

'His girlfriend Tan ... short for Tanya. Her surname's Birch, although you could switch the r for a t and get a more accurate picture of what she's like.'

'And?'

'She was pissed ... annoyed, I mean. And possibly drunk, too. That would not be unusual,' she said. 'She was always annoyed if she found out we were in London and Dad hadn't called her.'

'So why *did* you call her?'

'Just in case Dad had gone over there for a ... you know ... fuck, and not told me.'

'Was that the nature of Con and Tan's relationship?'

22

'Fuck pals, you mean?'

'If you like.'

'I suppose so,' said Siobhan, sitting back, hands clasped over her stomach,' I mean, he didn't call her up for philosophical or literary discussions or to go out to the theatre, the opera or even the movies. It was always dinner in somewhere like Locatelli's or the Wolseley and then back to her place.'

'Did you ever go?'

She frowned and pouted.

'Tan and I didn't get along. Ever since a couple of years ago when I went to stay with her while Dad flew off to a meeting in Amsterdam.'

'Want to tell me about that?'

'None of your business. You haven't even taken on the job and you want all the dirt,' she said, reclaiming her iPhone.

'You got any siblings?' asked Boxer.

'Not that I know of.'

'Half-siblings?'

'None that have ever been talked about.'

'Who did you call after the angry Tan?'

'Dad's lawyer, Mark Rowlands.'

'I don't know that name.'

'It took me a while to track him down. He was on a trip down the Amazon.'

'What did he tell you to do?'

'Sit tight until he called me back.'

'And that took a while?'

'A couple of days,' she said. 'But when he did, he gave me your name.'

'Does Mark Rowlands think your father has been kidnapped?'

'If he has, then nobody's thought to ask me for a ransom.'

'That doesn't answer the question,' said Boxer. 'Did Mark Rowlands give you my name because I'm a freelance kidnap consultant or what?'

'I think it's probably more along the lines of "or what", because he didn't tell me you were a kidnap consultant.'

'What *did* he tell you?'

'He told me that you ran this charitable foundation called

LOST, that you were skilled at finding people. And yes, he mentioned that you were a negotiator but he didn't relate it to kidnapping.'

'That's interesting.'

'Why?'

'Because I'm known primarily as a kidnap consultant. I am not particularly skilled at finding people. I run this charitable foundation for personal reasons.'

'What are they?'

He looked at her long and hard with a stare that should have had her shifting in her seat. Siobhan smiled back, her tongue flickering in the gap between her teeth.

'I'll tell you mine if you tell me yours,' she said.

'My father went missing when I was a kid, seven years old. I never heard from him again,' said Boxer. 'I like to help people who've suffered the same sort of loss.'

'Tan came back from work early and found me fucking a boy on the sofa.'

'I thought you were going to tell me the real reason Mark Rowlands recommended my services.'

'The *real* reason?'

'I'm not a PI. He didn't mention my kidnap consulting skills. I used to be in homicide and Amy's mother is a detective inspector. So why, given my lack of primary skills and all my police connections in this burning metropolis overflowing with investigative talent, should you come to me?'

Silence.

She knew. He could tell she knew the one thing nobody was supposed to know about him. He could also tell that she'd been told not to mention the unmentionable.

'How old were you?' he asked, switching the subject.

'When?'

'When Tan caught you with the boy.'

'Not quite sixteen,' she said, relieved to be off the hook. 'But that wasn't it.'

'What *was* it?'

'I think it was because we were on her best white leather sofa.'

'So if Con didn't meet Tan, and kidnapping doesn't seem to

be a concern, where else could he have gone?' asked Boxer. 'Your father presumably has business associates, and Mark Rowlands will have—'

'Dad doesn't work with anybody. He might team up with someone for a contract but never on a regular basis. He keeps himself to himself. But he has plenty of businessmen and other ... types he deals with.'

'So what's his game?'

'He supplies security to the US military.'

'But he doesn't work for one of the known private security companies?'

'He's a private contractor ... that's all I can tell you. He hasn't sat me down and talked me through his business. I listen to his phone calls when he's in the room. I pick things up. That's all.'

'Any names?'

'Some, but you don't get to hear those until you've taken on the job.'

She was impressive, had learnt a few things listening to her father, not a common trait in the young.

'Do you know the value of any of these contracts? Have you heard figures?'

'They're not peanuts.'

'If you're in the Savoy ...'

'You don't have to worry about my ability to pay.'

'I'm not. I'm interested in levels. Hundreds of thousands, millions, tens of millions or more?'

'More,' said Siobhan. 'What does that tell you?'

'It's just an indication of risk.'

'Are you risk averse?'

'Is that one of your father's expressions?' asked Boxer. 'I'm a kidnap consultant. I don't take risks with other people's lives. That's the extent of my aversion. What about Con?'

'My father was *never* risk averse, but that doesn't mean he was reckless. He just ... pursued his interests.'

'Does that mean financial or business interests or just what fascinated him?'

'He tried to avoid being bored even for money.'

'Where do you live now?' he asked, finding her caginess

tiresome, but impressed by the way she played her hand. 'Are you still in the Savoy or of no fixed abode?'

'I moved into a flat in Islington this morning. Lofting Road. A short-term rental.'

'OK, that's good. Don't want you out on the streets,' said Boxer. 'So where do you and your father live normally?'

'These last few years he's had his work cut out in the Middle East,' said Siobhan. 'We have a flat in Dubai, been spending time there.'

'All right,' said Boxer. 'Give me your mobile phone number and I'll let you know.'

'Why can't you let me know now?' she asked, dropping her guard for a second, showing her need.

'Because now I'd have to say no, whereas later I might say yes ... depending.'

'On what?'

'On how my enquiries go.'

She got up to go, keeping her eye on Boxer as she collected her things, trying to think of something that might persuade him to say yes. As she headed for the door, Boxer couldn't help looking at her: the long silver zip that travelled the length of the skirt with its winking pull tab hanging below the hem, her black stilettos with the silver detail above the heels, her narrow hips, her broad shoulders, her hair cascading over the grey fur collar, which didn't look fake.

At the door, she turned, caught him looking at her and interpreted it right. Not sexual, just curious. Puzzled even. She reached for the handle and revealed a chunky Breitling Galactic stainless-steel watch and bracelet on a wide caramel wrist. If anything persuasive had occurred to her, she'd decided that saying nothing was more powerful. She nodded to him, closed the door quietly.

Boxer stared after her, still dazed, definitely not at his best after an all-night poker game in which he'd lost £120,000. He'd returned home at first light, collapsed into bed. He'd woken up at three in the afternoon remembering the dangerous thought he'd had only the previous morning (one of those that no one should ever be tempted to think) that life was good. His relationship with Amy, built on the solid rock of trust, was getting better as they worked more closely together. He was in love with Isabel, who he'd consulted for on the kidnap of her daughter a couple of years ago, and the passion had not abated. Mercy had turned her attention to her new boyfriend, Marcus Alleyne, and had eased herself into a friendship with Boxer rather than insisting on being his lover manqué. He was even getting on better with his mother, Esme. Amy, who was very close to her, had been instrumental in that. All this had meant that he was careful about the consulting jobs he took, travelled less and was as close to being happy as he'd ever been.

And then he'd lost heavily at poker. No cards and all his bluffs had failed, and yet he couldn't tear himself away from the table. Now Siobhan had stepped into his world. He knew that this job was something he shouldn't even have to think about. The answer was a screaming NO! The kid looked like trouble on stilts. And yet ... there was something fascinating about her, and Conrad too.

The first thing he had to find out was how she knew about his willingness to kill people who'd done wrong. As far as he was concerned there was only one man in London with that knowledge: Martin Fox of Pavis Risk Management, who'd given him free-lance work since he'd left the salaried security of the top kidnap consulting private security company GRM. He hadn't worked for Pavis since the job he'd done for Isabel and her ex-husband Frank D'Cruz, negotiating the return of their daughter Alyshia. There'd been offers but he'd turned them down, didn't like Fox's intimate knowledge of his past. Fox had been clever enough not to press him, understood his sensibilities. Now, as Boxer's thoughts rumbled on in the aftermath of Siobhan's powerful charisma, he began to wonder whether this was just Martin Fox making an indirect approach.

Boxer made the call.

'It's been a while,' said Fox, coming on the line.

'I think we should meet,' said Boxer.

'I'd given up on you.'

'I'll see you at our usual bench.'

'Now?'

'I'll be there in twenty.'

He hung up, put his coat and scarf on, tucked his Canadian

trapper's hat under his arm and went out into the main office, where he saw Siobhan still there fitting a black furry Cossack hat on to her head and finishing up a conversation with Amy. She slipped her hands into some black leather fur-trimmed gloves, hunched her shoulders and walked out, one hand in the pocket of her calf-length raincoat, the other yanking out an umbrella from the coat stand. She swaggered a little and returned Boxer's unflinching gaze. He waited until he heard her heels on the stairs.

'What was that all about?' asked Boxer.

'My earrings.'

'Your *earrings*?'

'And she asked me out.'

'To what?'

'A Sarah Lucas show at the Whitechapel Gallery.'

'Sarah Lucas?'

'Not your kind of thing, Dad.'

'How do you know?'

'Instinct,' she said and shrugged.

'You going to go?'

'If I don't get interrupted any more and I can finish my work.'

'What do you make of her ... Siobhan?'

'She's cool.'

'You want to expand on that?'

'Why? She want us to work for her?'

'Me. She wants *me* to do something for her.'

'Like?'

'Find someone,' said Boxer, walking to the window, looking down on Siobhan as she came out into the mews. 'Her father.'

'So what's the problem?'

'That's where I was hoping for some help from you,' said Boxer. 'There's something ... not quite right about her. I was hoping for some intuition of the female kind.'

'Not quite right?'

'I can't explain it,' said Boxer. 'At one point I asked her how old she was and she said twenty-eight.'

'That's how she dresses.'

'Then she said she was twenty ... ish.'

'Same as me ... ish.'

'It's not her age that bothers me. It's her instinct for lying, which is never good in a client. And ... there's something else.'

'Maybe she wanted you to take her seriously.'

'I took her seriously all right,' said Boxer. 'I had no problem with that. Never for a moment struck me as someone to take lightly. You?'

'What?'

'Come on, Amy, get your head in gear,' said Boxer. 'That girl's trouble and I can't see why. Let's have some youthful insight.'

'Like?'

'She seemed attracted to you.'

'Lesbian?' said Amy, scoffing. 'Don't be ridiculous, Dad. Male fantasy.'

'Not mine,' said Boxer. 'You came in, she introduced herself and when she turned back to me she was ...'

'What?'

'In a heightened state.'

'Of what? Excitement?'

'Looked like it to me.'

'I didn't get anything like that off her,' said Amy. 'We just talked.'

'Are you going to go to the Sarah Lucas show with her?'

'Like I said, if somebody lets me get on with my work.'

'Call me. Let me know how it goes. What's she do ... Sarah Lucas?'

'You don't need to know.'

'Did Siobhan give you her mobile phone number?'

Amy nodded. Boxer beckoned it out of her. It was different to the one she'd given him.

'One other thing,' he said, from the doorway. 'Call the Savoy and just make sure for me that Siobhan Jensen was staying there these last few nights.'

29

4

17.55, 15 JANUARY 2014
Marylebone High Street, London W1

Boxer walked down to Oxford Street automatically checking his back, making sure he wasn't being followed. He was clean. As he took the escalator down into Bond Street tube, he looked up, saw Siobhan standing at the railing looking down on him. She tinkled a wave, raised an eyebrow. Con had taught her a few things.

In Green Park he made his way to the bench where he always met Martin Fox. It was empty. He was glad of his fleece-lined hat as he sat waiting in the freezing dark.

Martin Fox approached from Constitution Hill. His office was in Victoria, on the other side of Buckingham Palace, which was now lit up behind him, making the park feel darker. His silhouette, with fedora, raised collar and flared trench coat, gave him the look of a professional cliché. His shoes with steel heel tips rang out on the wet tarmac between the high bare trees and the gleaming grass. He hovered to see whether a handshake was forthcoming. It wasn't. He sat on the bench leaving a good space between them. Silence, apart from the distant roar of the metropolis.

'Been working, Charlie?'

'I've been playing a quiet game since that D'Cruz job a couple of years ago.'

'I heard about your daughter's … travails,' said Fox.

'Who from?'

'Your mate in MI6, Simon Deacon. We meet in the Special Forces Club once a month. He says he hasn't seen much of you either.'

'Been keeping a low profile,' said Boxer. 'In fact I've been spending as much time with Amy as I can. I've done some "re-prioritisation", as you'd probably call it.'

'I can understand that after what you went through,' said Fox. 'How's Mercy these days?'

'She's still with the Met's Kidnap and Special Investigations Unit, but not quite as driven as she was before,' said Boxer. 'She's done some ...'

'Some what?'

Boxer decided against it. Fox knew far too much as it was.

'What can I do for you?' asked Fox, feeling Boxer dry up. 'I haven't got any work, if that's what you're after. You've drifted off the scene since D'Cruz.'

'I'm all right on that score. I did some jobs in South America to keep my hand in.'

'Who gave you those?'

'My US contacts,' said Boxer, no names, Fox always digging.

'Well we haven't come out in the cold and wet for a drink,' said Fox, 'so what is it?'

'Do you know a lawyer called Mark Rowlands?'

'No.'

'Do you know a security contractor called Conrad Jensen?'

'I know that name.'

'But nothing about him?'

'Not off the top of my head other than that he has contracts with the American military,' said Fox.

'For what?'

'Security and IT, I think. Not sure of the specifics,' said Fox. 'Why do you want to know?'

'There's been an approach.'

'To work for *him*?'

'You sound surprised.'

'As far as I know he doesn't touch kidnap negotiating,' said Fox. 'Unless he's making a move into that part of the market, which seems ... unlikely.'

Silence again. A helicopter scudded above the stripped trees, lights winking.

'Or,' said Fox, 'is this a roundabout way of telling me he's been kidnapped and you're looking for intelligence? Except …'

'What?'

'Nobody would come to you direct with a job like that. They'd go to GRM. Are we going to lay our cards on the table or are you going to play me the whole night long?'

'The person who made the approach knew something about me.'

Fox turned his head slowly in Boxer's direction.

'Right,' he said, 'and you think because of what came out about your "additional service" in the D'Cruz case that I'm responsible?'

'It occurred to me.'

'Let's get something straight about your "special service", Charlie. *You* started it. You left GRM. I gave you a job. The first one passed off without incident. Then there was the case of Bruno Dias's daughter, Bianca, which went horribly wrong. You got her back, but badly damaged. It had an effect on you. Then you did the Russian job with the Ukrainian gang and that's when you offered your special service. Not me. *You*. The Russian gave you the intelligence and you followed it up. When the Russian offered you money, you told him you'd prefer a donation to LOST.'

'How did Bruno Dias know about the LOST Foundation and that I'd be open to him making a contribution for the work he wanted me to do?' asked Boxer. 'You know I can't afford those offices we've got in Jacob's Well Mews. They're Bruno's donation.'

'That was just coincidence. As I remember it, Amy was supposed to go with you on that trip. If she'd been there, none of that would have happened.'

'The coincidence is *you*, Martin. He knew about my special service from you. I've become your niche in the kidnap consulting business. Why would anybody go to Pavis when GRM are just down the road?'

Nothing back from Fox.

'*You* were the one who started offering my special service, Martin,' said Boxer. 'And *that* was not your prerogative. You told Dias. Just admit it, for God's sake.'

'All right, yes, I told Dias. He was mad with rage …'

'And now it's out there, which is why this girl came to see me

32

this afternoon. I know she knows. I can see it in her eyes. And she's been told to be careful. Not to say it to my face.'

'Which girl?'

'Conrad Jensen's daughter.'

'And she heard it from her father's lawyer, Mark Rowlands.'

'Who got it from where?' said Boxer.

'Not me,' said Fox. 'Are you trying to find out if I'm making an indirect approach to you to recover Conrad Jensen?'

'Are you?'

'No. Rowlands could have got that information from …'

'Where?'

Silence.

'This is what I don't like,' said Boxer. 'It's getting to be common knowledge.'

He could hear Fox thinking.

'Has Conrad Jensen been kidnapped?' he asked eventually.

'Nobody's asked his daughter for a ransom yet and it's been three days.'

'So what exactly is the job?'

'To find him.'

'But why you?'

'That's what I want to find out,' said Boxer.

Amy turned right out of Whitechapel tube station and, walking through the vestiges of the Bangladeshi market, which was being packed up for the night, headed for the glittering helix lines of the distant Gherkin.

There was a very long, stone-cold sober queue outside one entrance to the Whitechapel Gallery, while a gaggle of less sober people were steaming out of another. Two bouncers manned the door, rebuffing chancers who could see where the party was. Amy sent a text to Siobhan, who told her to ask for Kev at the door. Kev took out his mobile phone, checked it, compared Amy's face with what he had on the screen and carved her away from the scrum outside.

Siobhan was striding down the corridor with two glasses of pink champagne. Before Amy could ask how Kev could possibly have had a photo of her on his mobile, Siobhan handed her a glass, chinked it with her own.

'Let's take a look,' she said, and grabbing Amy by the arm led her into the main gallery, which had the feeling of bedlam about it, as wildly dressed couples circled exhibits: a vest stretched over a table with two Galia melons hanging in the neckline, next to a filthy, torn mattress with two fried eggs and a coat hanger with a kipper dangling below.

'The Full English Nightmare,' said Amy.

Siobhan laughed and they wandered underneath Zeppelins with masturbating arms upstairs through a room of photos of a male dangling steak above his genitals, opening a beer can as if it was his cock and the predictable foamy spurt. Siobhan only slowed as she came to a couple of vast bleached male members, which appeared like the abandoned driftwood beams of an ancient galleon, where she emptied her glass. They went downstairs to the bar where she poured more champagne.

'What do you think?'

'Glad my dad didn't come,' said Amy.

'Modern art not his scene, or just embarrassing to stand next to your pa looking at a tumescent three-metre cock on the floor?' asked Siobhan. 'Sarah's obsessed.'

'You know her?'

'Sure?'

'How?'

'I'm interesting,' said Siobhan. 'Fancy one of these?'

She flipped the lid of a small tin box to reveal some white pills.

'What are we talking about?'

'Ecstasy ... nothing wild.'

They socked back a pill each. Siobhan refilled the glasses.

'So what makes you so interesting?' asked Amy.

'You'll see,' she said. 'Lucian Freud wanted to do me when I was thirteen, but my father wouldn't have it.'

'*Do* you?'

'Paint me.'

'He had a bit of a rep for the other.'

'My father's objection wasn't that he might have fucked me,' said Siobhan. 'More to do with wanting me to sit for five hours a

34

day for a year. We weren't in London that much and, shit, I mean that's like two thousand hours of your life.'

'My father would've probably killed him.'

Siobhan stared at her for a beat.

'But if he was *painting* you,' she said, 'trying to see into you? I mean, looking at you as if you were an animal. Don't you think that would be fascinating and ... seductive?'

Amy had her back to a white brick wall. The drug was making her more alert to the people around her, mellowing her insides too, making them treacly. Siobhan loomed over her. She was taller on her high heels. Amy sipped her champagne, wouldn't look her in the eye, not sure what she'd find there.

'A friend of my father's seduced me like that,' said Siobhan. 'Didn't just take an interest in me as a kid, asked me what I thought about stuff ... like my mother dying. Nobody would talk to me about that. Most people just glide past each other. They don't dig. Too afraid of what they'll bring to the surface.'

'How old was your father's friend?'

'Sixty-eight.'

'God.'

'Does that disgust you?'

'So how old's your father?'

'Seventy-two,' said Siobhan. 'My mother was twenty-three when she met him. There was an age difference of twenty-one years. Age doesn't mean that much to me. Nor gender.'

She kissed Amy on the lips, her tongue darting between her teeth, sliding over her tongue, the roof of her mouth, quick, electric. The charge slammed into the back of Amy's head, ran down her spine and legs, earthed into the tiled floor.

5

A call. Boxer remembered he hadn't spoken to the heating engineer who was installing a new radiator in his Belsize Park flat.

'How's it going?'

'All done, Charlie. Now all you need is a decent boiler. The one you got in there would make them go quiet on the *Antiques Roadshow*. And by the way, who's Charles Tate?'

'Me.'

'Not according to *my* invoice.'

'Yeah, I know, too complicated to go into, but … it's me. Why?'

'I found a package addressed to Charles Tate under the floorboards when I was putting in the new pipework. Feels like a video cassette. I've left it on the kitchen counter.'

Boxer hung up. He had been about to go round to see Isabel, who'd just flown back from Mumbai after six weeks with her daughter, but now he had to investigate that package, couldn't resist it. He called Isabel, who said she was still groggy with jet lag and would rather he left it until later.

Crammed into a rush hour tube, he stared into the coated backs of the passengers pressed against him. The time he'd spent as a boy and an adult searching that flat for a letter, a card, any tiny scrap of a note from his father. Something that would tell him, personally, why he'd had to go, to abscond, why he'd had to bloody leave him, his only child. It was the main reason he hadn't sold the flat. Couldn't bear the idea that he might have missed something.

He'd persisted in the belief that his father was a straight guy. He was an accountant, for God's sake, trained at Price Waterhouse no less. Studied PPE at Oxford University. A judo champion. One of the four judokas the British team was going to send to the 1964 Tokyo Olympics until he'd torn his knee ligaments. A man who didn't smoke, hardly drank, hadn't even got any points on his driving licence. They didn't come straighter than his dad, David Tate.

Then, as a homicide cop, Boxer had looked into his father's cold case, the John Devereux file, which had been the only reason he'd become a detective. Devereux was the TV commercials director his mother, Esme, had produced for until he'd been found murdered in his Bibury home on 13 August 1979. The next day his father had absconded before the police could interview him. Boxer had been determined to prove his father's innocence, but the investigation hadn't been quite so straightforward and had been the main reason he'd left the police force to become a kidnap consultant. Sod history. History had never done him any favours.

And now here he was again. Hunting after history.

He got back to the flat in Belsize Park by seven o'clock. The package was addressed to him in his father's handwriting. *CHARLES TATE* in big capitals. It was Esme who'd changed his surname to her maiden name when it was clear her husband wasn't coming back. On the reverse side, again in his father's hand, were the words: *To my only son, Charlie. Lots of love, Dad xxx*. He remembered the madly scribbled note that Esme had shown him nearly two years ago, when Amy had run away using the same words in her note that his father had written on the day of his disappearance: *You will never find me*. This time the writing was not as erratic as that note to Esme, but not as neat as other letters he'd inspected over the years.

Boxer had a sudden vision of his father sprinting up to the top of the house during those last, mad minutes before vanishing into oblivion, picking up a holdall, stuffing clothes into it as he went. But then he couldn't quite picture him with the time or presence of mind to find a cassette tape, fit it into an envelope, write his son's name on both sides, rip up the carpet, claw a hammer into the crack of a floorboard, wrench it up, throw the package into the cavity, hammer the pins back and kick the carpet over the grippers. No, this was done well before that awful day.

It touched Boxer to think of his father doing this for him. All those years living in hope that he would have secreted a note to him and yet it had never occurred to him to look under the floorboards. Why would he? Why would Mr Straight Tate leave a package under the floorboards? He realised now that this must have been planned and that there was some calculation involved. He wasn't supposed to find it immediately. Maybe it was inappropriate for a seven-year-old's eyes. It struck him, too, that this was supposed to be found only by happenstance or not at all. It was curious to feel his father's mind at work. Perhaps not so different from his own as he thought of his safe with his poker winnings, the piles of cash in different denominations, the gun under the kitchen floor with the spare magazines and his secret numbers. As if he, too, knew that one day he might have to get out of his life with only moments to spare. Maybe we're all like this, he thought, fingering the package.

He turned it over and over in his hands, imagining his father's touch and care all over it. It was a buff envelope with a butterfly fastening, which had been taped over as well. The glue had aged and dried so the tape came away easily. He pinched open the butterfly and a video cassette slid out. Boxer recognised the old Betamax tape that had enjoyed brief popularity before the VHS format took over, because his mother's production office had been full of them.

He had a surge of excitement that this was a video message and he was going to see his father talking directly to him. Tears came into his eyes. Something like eggshell cracked in his chest as he felt the emotion welling up from his stomach. On the other side of the cassette was a faded sticker from Dex-Box Productions and, in his father's hand: *Found May 17th 1979.* Found? The date was three months before his father had absconded. Perhaps, thought Boxer with some delusory joy, this had nothing to do with Devereux's murder and his father's disappearance. It was just a communication with *lots of love, Dad xxx*. But then why 'Found'? Why hide it? He shook the envelope and a folded piece of paper fell out.

*

38

Marcus Alleyne was sitting in his second-hand white Peugeot Bipper, which was still emblazoned with the daft cartoon logo of the cleaning company that had sold it to him. He thought it made him less obtrusive. He was parked next to some garages opposite a block of flats in East Walworth. The van was full of cigarettes he was going to deliver to a bigger supplier. He was nervous about the way the business had come to him. Although he'd worked with Harvey Cox before, it had been a while ago and he didn't know his sidekick, but at least he'd been vouched for by Glider.

Then again, this was the first job he'd had from G in the last eighteen months. There'd been a breach of trust between Alleyne and the north London gangster. When Amy had gone missing a couple of years ago, Mercy remembered that Alleyne was the receiver of some cigarettes Amy had smuggled from the Canaries. It had been a bit of fun for Glider. Mercy had forced Alleyne to give her Glider's address and had sent Boxer round to visit. Since then Glider hadn't given Alleyne any work.

This business hadn't come direct from G. When he checked back, Glider's mobile number went through to some woman called Jess, said she was G's new security boss and was acting on his instructions. She told him it was a regular bit of business, ten grand a month, with Harvey Cox and his sidekick Delroy Pink. Ten grand was too much for Alleyne to ignore and he wanted to get back in with Glider. But was it a set-up? Had the cops got to G? Fear slipped the leash and the thought that he might be part of a deal for a lighter sentence galloped through his mind. He saw himself from above sitting alone in a police cell waiting for his telephone call, the one that would drop Mercy to her knees.

'Calm the fuck down,' he muttered.

He was smoking a cigarette with a few strands of grass in it to take the edge off. He had the window open a crack to let the smoke out and the cold, damp air was blowing in. He turned on the engine, cranked up the heating. A white transit pulled up and a young black guy got out of the passenger side.

'You Marcus?' he asked.

Alleyne blanked him. That was not supposed to be the opening gambit. The young black guy leaned back, looked into the transit, shrugged. A rail thin black guy got out and came to Alleyne's window walking in what seemed like exaggerated slow motion.

'Sorry,' he said, looking in with a bloodshot eye. 'What he mean is: Glider sends his best regards.'

Alleyne shunted him back as he opened his door. The younger man shuffled to the front of the Bipper.

'We going to do it here?' asked the rail thin man, looking around at the dead end made up by garages on either side, a wall joining them.

'You Pink?' asked Alleyne, thinking what a ridiculous question to ask a black guy.

'That's me.'

'Who's driving?' asked Alleyne.

Pink nodded the younger man to the driver's side.

'Who's he?'

'Jarrod.'

'Move your van forward, Jarrod. I don't want you parked up in front of me. Take it between the garages.'

'How we going to do this?' asked Pink. 'You want him to *reverse* in there?'

'You and I are going to start with the money, my friend,' said Alleyne, looking at him warily.

'Yeah, right. Ten grand is what we agreed.'

'He reverses between the garages and you get in the passenger side of my van.'

The man nodded to the driver of the transit, wound his finger round and pointed to the garages.

Alleyne waited, sniffing the air, wondering if this was going a bit off or were they just being thick, these two?

The transit pulled away, turned and reversed up between the garages. Pink got in the passenger side of the Bipper. Alleyne eased himself behind the wheel. The man handed over a brown envelope packed with two blocks of fifty-pound notes. Alleyne counted through one and measured it against the other, put them in his inside pockets. He pulled out and reversed up alongside the white transit.

'You take the two boxes out the back and I'll get the other two out the side door,' he said.

He slid the side door back, unloaded the two boxes and brought them down to the back of the transit. When all four were loaded, he nodded to Pink and turned to shut the rear doors of the Bipper.

And that was when Jarrod appeared from behind his van, his arm swinging sideways.

A hard jolt to the back of his skull. Alleyne's forehead thumped into the rear door of the Bipper. White sheet lightning flashed behind his eyes and he was falling into the black abyss.

'I'm not really into that,' said Amy.

'You don't sound very certain of yourself,' said Siobhan, sipping her champagne, grinning her little gap-toothed grin.

She wasn't. She'd never had a kiss like that before in her life. Even in the heat of the bar her nipples had gone hard and her breathing rapid. There was some kind of current fizzing in her coccyx and the treacliness in her stomach meant that she had to consciously resist the desire to run her hands over the black T-shirt straining over Siobhan's breasts under her grey leather jacket.

'Was it the tab you gave me?' asked Amy.

'I doubt it,' said Siobhan. 'That was just a placebo … mini aspirin. Maybe we should get some fresh air.'

She took Amy's glass, put it on a table and walked her out of the bar with her arm around her waist. Amy tripped down the steps and staggered into the street. Siobhan caught her, cupped her breast. Amy felt the strength in Siobhan's arm, the roundness of her bicep pressed into her side.

The cold air sharpened up Amy's mind but she couldn't help herself. She slipped her arm under Siobhan's jacket, around her ribs and caressed her breast. She wanted another one of those electric eel kisses and pushed her face into Siobhan's neck, felt its cords under her lips.

'Let's go somewhere and relax,' said Siobhan, smiling.

They sat on a crowded overground train opposite each other. The distance in the aisle felt huge, but when the woman next to Siobhan left her seat, Siobhan put her finger up forbidding Amy to join her. They got off at Highbury and Islington and walked down Upper Street, hands clasped like lovers, as a homeless couple prepared themselves for the night in the doorway of a travel agent.

Siobhan pulled Amy off the main road and led her down dark, glistening streets of Georgian terraces.

They arrived at Lofting Road, to a house just down from a big old red brick Victorian school, and Siobhan let them into the warmth of a ground floor flat, where they fell on the sofa kissing madly. Siobhan kicked off her heels, pulled Amy up and pushed her into a dark bedroom at the back of the house, where she undressed her, sucked on her breasts and put her into bed. Amy heard the zip travelling the full length of Siobhan's black leather skirt.

'Turn the light on. I want to see,' she said, massaging the saliva around her nipples.

'It's sexier in the dark.'

Amy spread her arms and legs out, felt the smooth texture of some expensive new white cotton sheets and duvet on her skin. She'd never been possessed by such powerful sexual anticipation in her life. The thought slid into her mind: maybe she was gay. Maybe this had been the problem: she'd just naturally assumed she was het without ever trying women. Certainly the boys she'd been with hadn't triggered this kind of excitement. Was that really a mini aspirin Siobhan had given her?

There was a noise somewhere else in the house.

'Come *on*,' said Amy.

'Did you hear that?' asked Siobhan.

'It's just someone upstairs.'

'The house is supposed to be empty. I was told I would be the only—'

A beat of silence before a tremendous crack. Feet rumbled into the living room and the bedroom door crashed open. The lights were slashed on. Amy sat up in bed, eyes slitted against the sudden glare. Men with tights over their heads, one with the loose leg hanging down his back like a long plait. Siobhan naked apart from her bra. But that wasn't all ... A penis was hanging from the pubic hair between her legs. Amy shook her head as if the 'mini aspirin' might be responsible for the hallucination. But no, it was definitely a long, slim penis between narrow hips above muscular thighs.

The first man in lunged forward and slapped Siobhan on the

side of the head. She went down fast, without a word, stunned, eyes fluttering at the edge of consciousness. Amy sprang up out of the bed holding the duvet by two corners and hurled herself spread-eagled at the two men. The three of them crashed to the floor. A grunt as one of their heads made contact with the wall. Amy was up and heading out of the room until she felt her trailing ankle gripped, her hip practically wrenched from its socket. She fell, clawed at the carpet as she was dragged back. A hand closed around her throat, gripped her windpipe, rammed her into the corner of the door jamb, shook her.

'This isn't about you,' said a voice, London accent. 'You keep it shut and you won't get hurt. Orright?'

She nodded. The thumb loosened off her throat. She sucked air into her rasping lungs.

Siobhan was on all fours, still groggy from the slap. She went for the sash window but the catch had to be unscrewed. One of the men got to his feet, grabbed her by the hair, hauled her back and threw her to the ground. He lashed her twice across the face with his hand.

He came back to the door, laid the duvet out, rolled Amy over, stuffed something into her mouth, and smoothed tape over her lips. They lined her up on the duvet and, as they wrapped her up, she saw Siobhan, eyes rolled back, blood coming from her mouth. They tied Amy up tight, trussing her with cord they'd brought with them, and lifted her on to the bed. She heard the muffled moans of Siobhan getting it together.

'Right,' said the voice. 'Let's get this one sorted.'

More slaps. Gasping and crying. They left the room dragging Siobhan between them. Amy heard them haul her into the bath-room and the sound of a struggle, of a body bouncing around in a glass cubicle. The terrible smack and thud of blows and then a male grunting as if making some hideous effort, and Siobhan's cries, muffled and struggling for breath. The shower came on. There was indistinct questioning. More blows, slaps as of a wet towel making cruel contact, and crying out, but always muffled. More questions, harsh and whispered, as if being ripped out rather than spoken. Then the horrible rhythmic male grunting and the process repeated.

43

After forty interminable minutes, Amy heard the men conducting a manic search of the flat. They came into the bedroom, turned out drawers, ripped open cupboards and then finally left. Silence resumed except for the consistent noise of the shower hissing water on to an inert body.

6

Alleyne started to come round, confused to find himself on a cold concrete floor. Water was being squirted on to his face. It dripped into a drain hole close to his mouth from which came a cool but morbid stench. His arms were tied behind his back. He struggled to bring them forward and realised he'd been hogtied, with wrists connected to his ankles. Everything was black. Not a scintilla of light coming in.

'What the fuck you hit him with?' asked a voice, London accent.

'A SAP glove.'

'Show me.'

''S only a glove.'

'Fuck me, this must weigh a pound. What's in it?'

'Steel shot.'

'Bloody hell, the idea was to put him out, not knock him into next fucking week.'

'I just cuffed him on the back of the head. He fell forward and banged hisself on the van door on his way down.'

'It's going to be fucking jelly in there, you bloody moron.'

'Look, he's coming round now.'

'Marcus,' said the voice. 'You all right, Marcus?'

His tongue felt foreign in his mouth, good for shoes but not for talking. He winced at the water on his face, tried to follow it with his lips, to get some moisture. His eyelids were too heavy to open, or maybe taped shut.

'Look, he's after it. Squirt it in his mouth. Maybe that'll help.'

45

The coolness of the water in his hot, dry mouth felt good but his tongue didn't know where to go and the water shot down the wrong way. He coughed, which set off blinding flashes in his head. He sucked in air, groaned against the nauseating pain.

'Get him sitting up,' said the voice. 'We don't want the bastard drowning on us.'

They disconnected his wrists from his ankles, sat him on a chair. Alleyne knew for certain that he'd been stripped naked as the chill of the metal seat spread over his buttocks, made his scrotum cringe. They lifted his arms over the back of the chair. He had to breathe down the vomit, could feel it gathering, didn't want that, thought it would kill him.

'Ease up. Let him be. Give him a chance to pull hisself together,' said the voice. 'You with me, Marcus?'

'Yeah, I'm with you,' he said, panting, head lolling. 'I don't know where, but I'm with you.'

'Right. Looks like he's alive and sensible. Put him in the back of my van and we'll sort the money.'

Alleyne felt himself lifted off the chair, carried horizontal and laid down on the cold floor of a van. They secured his wrists and ankles with ties to the side of the vehicle. There followed a long, vague discussion and a parting.

Someone got into the van next to him.

'This'll keep you relaxed for your next trip,' said the voice. 'No SAP gloves here.'

The last thing Alleyne heard was some large doors opening, as of a warehouse. The van jolted him as it moved off and he blacked out.

He came round with no idea of time and a poor recollection of what had happened, only that he knew he'd been kidnapped. He was sitting on a metal chair again, arms over the back. He was in pain and more things came back to him.

'Who are you, what the fuck do you want?' he asked. 'Let's get on with it. You been sent by Glider?'

'Slow down, Marcus. We're going to take this one step at a time,' said the voice. 'This phone of yours, what sort of a phone do you call this?'

'A mobile phone?'

'Don't get clever, or we'll have to knock you about some more.'

'What am I supposed to say? A Nokia 109. A *cell* phone. I don't know what answer you're looking for. It's just a phone, for fuck's sake.'

'It's not a *smart*phone. There are no numbers on it. No apps. Nothing.'

'It's my business phone. I don't carry any numbers on me when I'm doing business, that way there are no ... what do you call them? Repercussions. That's it. If I get caught, nobody goes down with me.'

'So you remember all your numbers, do you?'

'Not all of them, no. There are too many. I just memorise the ones I'm doing business with on that particular night. It's a precaution.'

'And you've got another phone with all your numbers on it?'

'No.'

'I mean, like your private numbers.'

'Private numbers?'

'People close to you. Like your family, friends ... your girl-friends,' said the voice. 'Boy like you, good-looking black bastard, bit of money about you. You must have plenty of girlfriends. Hard to keep track of them all.'

'What are you driving at? Is there a question in there? I don't know what to tell you.'

'Where's your other fucking phone?'

'I haven't got one. They're all in my head.'

'All right, let's have your girlfriend's number then.'

'Which one?'

'Don't fuck me about, Marcus.'

'You're the one who said I had plenty of girlfriends.'

'It was a test to see if you're a *lying* black bastard.'

'Well I'm not up to tests. Somebody whacked me over the head. I'm blank in here ... just going with the flow, hoping for the best.'

'You mentioned Glider.'

'Yeah, he was the contact for this job. He vouched for you.'

'That tell you anything?'

Silence from Alleyne, thinking now. Glider had served him up, which meant he must have made some connections.

'No,' he said.

'No what?'

'It doesn't tell me anything.'

'I know he hit you hard, but you're talking all right, you're not slurring your words, you're together. Now think about it. Glider gave you the job and look where you are. He doesn't like you, and Glider's got a lot of time for black bastards. Now why's that?'

'I think you'll find Glider's got a lot of time for black *girls*.'

'You see, Marcus, you're sharp. Things are coming to you. So what is it about you that Glider doesn't like?'

'Give me a clue. I'm still a bit mushy in here.'

'Your girlfriend. Singular,' said the voice. 'You had a bit of a rep before. Lad about town. Three or four on the go at once. But now you've only got eyes for one, haven't you, Marcus?'

Marcus felt a chill in his chest. The voice was standing closer now, had his knees between Marcus's legs so he couldn't close them. He shuddered as one hand strangled his genitals, gave them a nasty tug, while the other gripped him around the neck and horrible garlicky breath came close to his face.

'You want to retain these family jewels, don't you, Marcus?' said the voice. 'Now let's have Mercy Danquah's number.'

Boxer unfolded the sheet of A4. At first glance he saw there was definitely some tension in his father's handwriting.

Dear Charles,

I hope you're happy, my dear boy. It's the only thing I would have wanted for you because the truth is I have not been happy. I can honestly say that you have been the only light in my life, the best thing that has ever happened to me. You've given me purpose. Without you it would have been so much money earned, so much material bought and nothing much else until the relief of death. I'm forever in your debt and you don't even know it.

I leave you this tape. It is not for the faint-hearted. I would advise you to destroy it without investigating further, especially if you have achieved the happiness that has so eluded me.

It is not an excuse, only an explanation.

I hid it under the floorboards thinking that you would find it only if you were desperate for some answers. I do not want you to find it. I think it will be very damaging for you. You must take this warning seriously. It is a destructive story you will be embarking on if you decide that you have to watch this tape.

If I were you I would smash it to pieces and walk away. If you feel your life will not be able to progress without the knowledge contained in this tape then so be it. You could, of course, watch the tape and decide that the investigation it demands is not for you and that would be a fine thing as far as I'm concerned. That is why I am not going to tell you of its significance.

All I will say is that you will get your answer just as I got mine.

It is going to lead me to do something that cannot be undone and in the process I will lose the one person I value above all others. You. It is a very high price but there is nothing I can do about it. I cannot resist what has grown inside me. It is after all the weakness of most men.

Do not let the same happen to you. Be strong, my wonderful son. Be strong enough to walk away.

Your ever-loving father,
Dad xxxx

He read it through ten times, maybe more. He didn't just read it, he fed off it, ravenously. The love within it was what he'd craved these last thirty-five years. It contained nourishment, but he also knew it wouldn't be enough. He was never going to be able to take his father's advice. At the very least he was going to have to watch the tape. The only good thing about it was the format. He didn't have a Betamax player, nobody did. The time it would take for him to locate one would give him the necessary space to contemplate his actions, give him some detachment from his terrible need.

His mobile vibrated in his pocket. Amy.

'You have to come here, Dad,' said Amy, her voice on the trembling brink of collapse. 'It's Siobhan. She's … she's been … Just come here … fast.'

*

It had taken time for Amy to emerge like a giant chrysalis from her tight white duvet cocoon. She tore the tape from her mouth, spat out what proved to be her pants and went naked through the wreck of the living room to the bathroom. She hesitated before opening the door, panic-stricken at what she might find under the running shower.

The cubicle had cracks running up one of the glass walls; its door was open. Siobhan was jammed up against the tiled wall, her head slumped forward on her chest covered by a towel, which had been white but was now stained pink. She still had her bra on but was naked apart from that. She sat with legs splayed on either side of the plughole, feet braced against the walls of the shower cubicle, her penis shrunken back into the pubis. The water running down the plughole was reddish against the white ceramic base.

Amy turned off the cold shower, ran back to the bedroom, called her father, got dressed as she spoke and went back to Siobhan.

She peeled off the towel. Siobhan's face had taken some punishment. She was looking at Amy out of the corner of a wild, swollen eye full of fear until she realised who it was. Her hands were tied behind her back.

'Help me,' she said.

'Can you bend your legs?' asked Amy.

'Yuh,' she said, and coughed up some bloodstained spittle from puffy lips, which ran down her chin.

She brought her legs up. Amy rolled her into the foetal position, back facing out of the shower.

'Where are you going?' asked Siobhan.

'Get a knife, cut your wrists free.'

'Don't call anybody.'

'I've already called my dad.'

'All right,' said Siobhan. 'But no police.'

Amy came back with the knife. Fresh blood leaked out of Siobhan's behind, down her buttock and the back of her leg.

'Oh God,' said Amy as she cut through the nylon cord. 'What did they do to you?'

'Fucking perverts,' said Siobhan, rolling on to her back, rubbing life back into her wrists. Tears leaked down the side of her face. 'Help me up.'

Amy got her standing. She limped to the sink and looked at her face in the mirror, hair in sodden rats' tails.

'Not so pretty,' she said. 'Get this sodding bra off me.'

Amy unhooked the clips. Siobhan ripped it off her shoulders and hurled it into a corner with rage. She turned to the full-length mirror on the back of the door. Bruises had already come out on her upper body, hips and thighs. She rubbed the contoured muscles of her arms. Touched the rack of her visible abdominals, tentatively fingered the blue-black marks on her ribs and checked her small breasts with red nail-polished fingertips.

'What a mess,' she said, investigating her shrivelled genitals and wincing at the pain. 'Now you know ... I'm not quite what I appear to be.'

'So what are you?' asked Amy.

'Intersex. XXY. Bit of Siobhan, bit of Sean.'

She had a sudden loss of strength and dropped to her knees.

'Run the bath for me, will you?'

'You should see a doctor before you have a bath,' said Amy. 'You don't want to lose any ... evidence.'

'Just run the fucking bath,' said Siobhan viciously. 'None of this is going outside these walls. Be grateful for that, unless you fancy going down the nick to explain your involvement?'

'But you ... you've just been *raped.*'

'And?'

'Nobody should get away with that. Fucking nobody.'

Siobhan cocked her head up like a savaged pit bull and eyed Amy as if she were her dog-fighting owner, sized up her leg, in two minds whether to take a chunk out, unsure whether she was saviour or tormentor.

Amy reached for the taps, ran the bath, got Siobhan to her feet and lowered her into the water.

A knock on the front door to the house. Boxer called out. Siobhan shooed Amy away, sank down into the bathwater to her lips. Amy shut her in.

Boxer surveyed the damage to the flat's front door.

'I've just called someone to come and repair this,' he said. 'How is she?'

'That's the first hurdle,' said Amy. 'She/he? He/she?'

Boxer nodded as he grasped the import, put it together with what had puzzled him about Siobhan. Amy explained further, told him about the attack and all its violence, but with some omissions about their state of undress at the time. Boxer pulled her to him, hugged her, and she clung on, determined not to cry with relief.

'What's the damage?' asked Boxer, looking over her shoulder at the tossed living room strewn with cushions and clothes, a couple of emptied suitcases. 'You don't sound as shaky. How bad is Siobhan?'

'She's been beaten up,' said Amy. 'They must have water-boarded her or something like it. She had a sodden towel over her face when I first went in. The worst was the rape. She's got blood coming from down there.'

'Did they touch you?' he asked, holding her away, looking her over. 'What's that mark on your neck?'

'They just grabbed me by the throat, said it wasn't about me and to keep out of it. They tied me up in the duvet.'

'Will Siobhan talk to the police?'

'Nope.'

'How long were they here?'

'Three quarters of an hour.'

'So it was an interrogation, not just a beating?'

'More like torture.'

'But the idea was to get information,' said Boxer. 'Did you hear any of it?'

Amy shook her head.

'Did you check whether she was staying at the Savoy with her father?'

'There was a room booked in the name of Conrad Jensen from the twelfth until this morning.'

'Ask her if she'll talk to me,' said Boxer, releasing Amy, looking in on the state of the bedroom. Amy had a word with Siobhan, nodded him into the bathroom.

'Just me and Siobhan for the moment,' he said.

He sat on the toilet. Siobhan eyed him over the rim of the bath with a puffy lid.

'Don't start talking to me about police,' she said.

'You should get some ice on that eye,' said Boxer.

'Thanks, Doc.'

'I can get you one of those if you want ... and she won't ask questions.'

Siobhan shook her head.

'Amy said they raped you and that you're bleeding,' said Boxer. 'That's not something you should ignore.'

'Like I said ...'

'Are you going to let me help you, or what?'

'Are you going to accept the job, or what?'

'Did this attack have anything to do with that?'

Siobhan looked at her nail-varnished fingers. Boxer wondered if she'd manipulated this situation: not the savage assault, but drawing Amy into her world in order to put pressure on him. If she had, it had worked.

'All right,' he said. 'I'll take the job ... on one condition.'

'What?'

'Amy stays out of it.'

'Some things are not in my hands,' she said, shrugging. 'Consenting adults and all that crap.'

'That's my only condition,' said Boxer. 'Do we have a deal or am I out of here?'

'What's your daily rate?'

'I don't have one for finding missing persons. All I ask is that you make a contribution to the LOST Foundation.'

'Like what? I don't do charity. Don't get it.'

'It depends on your level of gratitude when the job's done.'

'And what if I'm not here by the time the job's done?'

'I normally like my clients to be more positive at the outset,' said Boxer.

'We don't know who we're dealing with yet. We just know the world my father works in.'

'OK, if you're dead, you won't be in any shape to feel satisfied, so ... no charge,' said Boxer. 'If on the other hand this turns out to be a kidnap situation, then that will change things. I can't operate under those circumstances because the Metropolitan Police will have to be informed and they have their own kidnap unit.'

'Would somebody kidnap a person and make no demand for three days?'

'In this case it would have been more likely that *you* would have been kidnapped in order to exert pressure on your father to release funds that he has control over,' said Boxer. 'So for your father to be kidnapped is unusual but not totally out of the question. What access do you have to any significant funds of your father's? How easily could they be released?'

'I have access to data on some but not all, and no right to release on any.'

'I presume he keeps funds offshore.'

'Like ... who doesn't?'

'The other ninety-nine per cent of people in the same world,' said Boxer. 'Has there been any unusual movement in the accounts to which you have access?'

'No.'

'So you've been checking?'

'I've been waiting in a hotel room for three days and Mark Rowlands told me to keep an eye on them and to tell him if anything happened.'

Silence.

'Don't think for a moment that I've forgotten: you still haven't given me your word,' said Boxer.

'All right, for fuck's sake, I promise to leave Amy alone,' she said, trotting it out. 'We didn't do anything except snog ... that's all.'

'She's only just got her life back together,' said Boxer, logging the revelation of a kiss.

'After what?'

'Too complicated.'

'Look, it was only sex, we weren't about to elope or anything,' said Siobhan. 'I can't help it if people get a thing about me, can I?'

'People do, do they?'

'Well *you* haven't,' she said. 'Which is probably just as well.'

'You're trouble and you and I know it. You've taken this beating as if it's happened to you before.'

'People don't like confusion when it comes to sex.'

'That was a heavy beating. Forty-five minutes according to Amy,' said Boxer. 'What did they want?'

'To know where my dad was ... what do you think?'

'How did they know where to find you?'

'Followed me, probably.'

'You've had some training on that front,' said Boxer. 'If you know how to follow you must know when you're *being* followed.'

'Not when my mind's on other things,' she said, trying a grin but wincing away from it.

'Be serious, it's important,' said Boxer. 'Do you think they already knew you were living here?'

'They didn't follow us from the gallery. So they definitely knew I was here.'

'How did you book this place?'

'Online. A holiday rentals site.'

'How did you get the key?'

'The owner of the flat met me here, told me the other two flats were empty but tenants were arriving tomorrow.'

'And you took a cab from the Savoy with your luggage.'

'This morning around eleven o'clock.'

'Any tail?'

'Not that I could see.'

'What did you bring with you?' asked Boxer. 'Your own things and presumably whatever your father left behind?'

'Yes,' said Siobhan, thinking.

'Was there any of his business paraphernalia in his stuff, like a laptop, papers ...?' asked Boxer. 'I mean, they've tossed the place completely. Were they looking for something specific? What questions did they ask you in their interrogation? And Amy says the one that spoke to her was a Londoner. Is that significant?'

'You're asking too many questions for somebody who's had the shit beaten out of them,' said Siobhan.

'Sorry, take your time.'

'First of all my father does everything on his phone. He doesn't like information being left around in computers or filing cabinets. He likes it all next to his chest. All his deals – the legal ones at least – are done on his phone.'

'And the illegal ones?'

'In person.'

'You could expand on that if you wanted to.'

'There's not much to expand. I was never invited ... as you can imagine.'

55

'Who was he doing illegal deals for?'

'Not illegal exactly ... just stuff below the radar, as he called it.'

'OK, but for who?'

'The Americans were the only people he worked for. If he was doing stuff for anybody else I didn't know about it.'

'Did you ever see any of these Americans?'

'People would come to the flat in Dubai. Some of them were American.'

'Anybody recently?'

'A guy came to see him twice before we left. That's the tenth and the eleventh of January.'

'Name?'

'Mike with a weird surname like Klink or Klonk ... something onomatopoeic.'

'Do you know what they discussed?'

'*Nada.*'

'You talked about seeing data from these offshore accounts. What about payments made into or out of them?'

'There wasn't anything from the US Department of Defense if that's what you're asking.'

'Just answer the question, Siobhan.'

'Of the offshore companies whose accounts I've seen, there were three: Xiphos Technologies Inc., Hoplon International Ltd and Kaluptein Trading Inc.'

'And where were these companies based?'

'Christ,' she said, closing her eyes. 'Xiphos was in Belize, Hoplon in Bermuda and Kaluptein in the British Virgin Islands.'

'And these companies paid into which of your father's accounts?'

'He didn't *receive* anything. My father paid *into* these companies from accounts he had in the same territories. So his Belize company, called Interceptor Trading Ltd, paid Xiphos; the Bermudan company, called Ferguson Consulting Ltd, paid Hoplon; and the BVI company, called Sunbeam International Ltd, paid Kaluptein.'

'Why did your father name his companies after Jensen cars.'

'Don't know what you're talking about.'

'The Jensen brothers made sports cars after the war until the seventies.'

'My father doesn't give a shit about cars,' said Siobhan. 'I would say he's only interested in people. Yeah, money and people and how they work together ... and how the one fucks up the other. And power, too, or is that the same thing?'

'So you told these two guys that your father had walked off into the night three days ago and you hadn't seen him since,' said Boxer, 'and they didn't believe you?'

'I didn't end up like this because they were happy,' said Siobhan. 'They wanted to make sure I didn't go to the police. They showed me what to expect if I did and threatened me with worse.'

'Any indication what they wanted from your father? Money ... expertise? Had your father stolen something?'

'They just wanted to know where he was.'

'It could, of course, have nothing to do with his business and be something ... personal.'

'It felt like it.'

'I mean you don't beat and rape a man's child unless you want to make a very personal point.'

7

The call came through at 20.16. Mercy remembered the time, a professional tic, as she clicked the receive button to what she thought was going to be a call from Marcus Alleyne.

Until that moment she'd been sitting at the kitchen table in her dark blue jeans, a black roll-neck cashmere sweater (a present from Amy), navy blue high heels and full make-up, waiting for him to show. Normally this would not have been an unusual situation. Alleyne, the laid back Trinidadian, felt that punctuality was uncool, while it was Mercy's duty, as the cop, to always be on time. But given the circumstances of the phone call earlier today, and the fact that they hadn't seen each other for four days, she thought he might, for once, have been on time.

Mercy decided not to let it bother her. It was his nature. She slipped back into a reflective mood. January did this to her. The cold and wet, which she loathed, and the possibility of losing her job made her retreat into a dazed state of comfort rumination. She'd been seeing Marcus for nearly two years now. The only man she'd seen for longer was Charles Boxer, and it had just started occurring to her, with some surprise, that she was now over Boxer. She didn't think about him any more. He naturally cropped up in her mind because he was Amy's father, but she no longer thought about him in the addictive way of the unrequited lover of the last twenty-odd years.

Her mind was full of Marcus. He occupied her, but not in the all-encompassing, oppressive way that Boxer had. With Marcus,

58

she was so confident of his love, there was no room for anything else. They talked every day about everything. Well, almost. He loosened her up, made her laugh and they still had great sex.

So what was the problem?

That word: 'almost'. They talked about lots of hard things: Mercy's relationships with her family, her difficult daughter, Boxer, Isabel, even Isabel's daughter and ex-husband. Marcus Alleyne had an incredible appetite for people and their difficulties. It was as if he had an empathy muscle that needed a daily workout.

The one thing they couldn't talk about was Alleyne's ... occupation.

He was a fence: receiving stolen goods and selling them on. It was how they'd met. In Amy's horror phase she'd brought a suitcase of cigarettes over from the Canary Islands with a group of girls and Alleyne had met her at Gatwick airport. One of the rooms in Alleyne's Railton Road flat was given over to flat-screen TVs, tablet computers, coffee machines, high-end trainers, cigarettes and other contraband. Even Boxer's mother was wearing a pair of trainers from 'Santa's Den', as Alleyne referred to the room.

This was more than awkward for a detective inspector with the Kidnap and Special Investigation Unit. It meant that they lived their relationship in a bubble. Mercy couldn't afford to introduce Alleyne to her family and friends and especially not to any of her colleagues, and she certainly didn't want to meet any of Alleyne's acquaintances, who ranged from small-time crooks, rap artists and twerk specialists to debt collectors, gun dealers and well-known gangsters.

How much longer could they live in this bubble before it burst? She'd already asked Alleyne if he could go straight, but had no idea how he would be able to make £50,000 a year (after tax) going legit. Especially as £20,000 of that money made its way back to Trinidad as his contribution to the family's investment in a tourist development.

Mercy had asked Boxer's advice and he'd been bleak about her options. If Alleyne couldn't quit being a fence, she would have to quit the kidnap unit, quit the relationship or, as she had done over the last two years, ignore it and hope for the best. She took the third option every time.

And now it occurred to her for the first time that maybe they'd found out about her relationship with Alleyne and this was why DCS Oscar Hines was demanding her presence in his office tomorrow morning. Her eyes widened at the possibility. How could she have been so slow?

And where *was* Marcus anyway?

That was when her phone rang. 'Marcus' came up on the screen, but not his voice into her ear.

'Mercy Danquah?'

'Who is this?'

'Just answer the question,' said the voice, London accent.

'Yes, this is Mercy Danquah,' she said, keeping it bored and predictable.

'We're holding your friend Marcus …'

'Above your head?' she said, not taking it seriously. 'I'm not impressed.'

'He said you'd be a cool customer.'

'Let me speak to him,' she said, instantly annoyed, not liking the idea of Marcus taking the piss out of her profession with his dubious mates.

'He's indisposed,' said the voice. 'I think that's how you'd put it.'

'Don't give me that crap,' she said. 'We're supposed to be in the restaurant in less than half an hour.'

'I'd change your reservation to a table for one if I was you.'

'Not funny. You hear that?' said Mercy, giving him a beat of silence. 'I'm not laughing. Put Marcus on the line … now!'

'I'm sorry, but he won't be able to make it to the phone,' said the voice, very polite. 'We've had to soften him up a little.'

Silence. Things sinking in. Her professional mode smacked down the fluttering fear in her stomach.

'So far all I know is that you've got his mobile phone,' said Mercy.

'In that case you don't know him very well,' said the voice.

Silence. She'd told Marcus not to carry her number in any of his phones.

'Right. Now you're thinking, aren't you, Mercy?'

'There'll be no progress without proof of life.'

'That's more like it. Very professional. Glad to hear you're taking this seriously now.'

'Let's have it then. No more bullshit.'

'We'll just have to wait for him to come round,' said the voice. 'Maybe you could give us a question we could ask him?'

'What's the name of my father's village?'

The line went dead.

She dropped her phone on the table. Her cool deserted her. She was up and pacing the kitchen floor. Her hands gripped the close-cropped hair on her head as she came to a halt at the sink and looked at her reflection in the window to the big, dark outside. Her fingers trickled down her cheeks as she realised that this was the ultimate disaster.

There was only one person she could call.

As soon as she opened the door to her mock Georgian house on a luxury estate in the middle of Kensington, he knew something had changed. She'd put on weight for a start, which was an achievement after six weeks in Mumbai.

'Did you get my text?' asked Boxer, hanging up his coat.

'Yes,' said Isabel, standing behind him, waiting.

'I'm sorry. I had to go. Amy had a tricky scenario with a client,' he said, turning to her.

'She's all right, though?'

'She's fine. And you?'

'Just tired,' she said. 'Jet lag always gets me coming back from Mumbai.'

He hugged her to him, felt the warmth of her contours pressing into him, a difference in shape, and with a trembling vulnerability underneath. He kissed her neck. He'd missed her. Six weeks she'd been away. Something she'd planned over a year ago, wanting to spend quality time with her daughter and her boyfriend, Deepak Mistry. She and Boxer had talked every day, but a physical craving for her had started up within a week, something that had never happened before with any other woman.

'So how was Mumbai?' he whispered into her hair. 'Did you get into the street food?'

'Oh, you know, Frank was exhaustive and exhausting, as you

can imagine,' said Isabel, pulling away from him. 'Alyshia and Deepak were lovely. I didn't travel as much as I wanted to. We did that Kerala trip and the week in Goa was great, but I was taking it easy.'

'Is something the matter?' asked Boxer. 'You ... feel different.'

'Alyshia's come back with me.'

'Was that the idea?' asked Boxer, convinced that it wasn't. 'She's all right, isn't she?'

'She's fine,' said Isabel. 'Let's go into the kitchen.'

They sat on either side of the table. She poured Boxer a beer, and herbal tea for herself, which he glanced at. She stretched her hands across the table and took hold of his. She looked straight into his eyes so that he felt compelled to stare back.

'I'm pregnant,' she said.

The surprise and elation spread through him.

'Well at least that's settled,' she said and squeezed his hands, released him.

'What is?'

'You're happy. I had to see that to make up my mind.'

'About what?'

'Whether to keep it or not.'

'But ...'

'At my age it's not a light decision.'

'Then let's talk about it.'

'I could see you were pleased.'

'I am. I can't deny it. It's ... it's great.'

'Then I will have the baby,' said Isabel. 'If you'd been a bit iffy ... well, I'd have ... That's why I had to look you in the eyes.'

'You'd have what?'

'I'd have terminated it.'

'Does that mean you don't really want to have it?'

'I do, but if you hadn't been keen, that would have decided me. It's not the right age to be having a child. Alyshia should be having one, not me.'

Boxer leaned back, gripped the edge of the table.

'I'm sorry, it was stupid,' she said. 'Not to think about it. I just assumed I wasn't fertile any more. My periods have been erratic for the last five years and I thought I was weighing into the menopause. I mean, we've been sleeping together for two years without contraception ...'

'So how pregnant are you?' asked Boxer. 'I mean, you didn't look pregnant before you left.'

'Over five months ... twenty-four weeks, they reckon.'

'And you didn't know?'

'I thought something was going on, but that it was me being menopausal,' said Isabel. 'I'd missed two periods, but that's not so unusual.'

'And how did you find out?'

'I wasn't feeling great so I went to Alyshia's doctor in Mumbai. I thought it was a stomach bug. I was feeling sick. First thing they found was that my blood pressure was raised. Then they did a blood test and it came back positive.'

'Have you spoken to your GP here?'

'Not yet. I had an amniocentesis test while I was in India and it was clear. Did you ever ...'

'What?'

'Doesn't matter.'

'Come on, Isabel, let's get it all out.'

'The question mark over Amy ... who her father was. Did you ever get that checked out?'

'No. It didn't matter to me. We're closer now than we've ever been.'

The discovery of the tape left by his father flashed through his mind and he decided that he wouldn't bring that up now. He'd wanted to ask her advice. She had such sound judgement. But now, he realised, was not the time.

'What's going on in there?' she asked.

'Nothing.'

'That's why I didn't want to tell you over the phone from India. I wanted to be looking into your eyes when I told you,' she said. 'You have two modes: professional and personal, and they're instantly interchangeable. Your job demands that you hide your emotions, which you do ... very well.'

'If I'm honest, for the first time in my working life, the job has faded away in importance. I used to love it because it put me in a place where I believed things really mattered.'

63

'And now?'

'You matter to me now. And Amy, Mercy, even Esme has started to matter.'

And as he spoke, the emotion came up in his throat and he thought his voice might crack and betray the intensity of what he was feeling for Isabel and his new life in which she'd been so instrumental. She reached a hand across. He took it and kissed the soft skin over the small knuckles.

'Say it,' she said. 'Nobody ever says anything these days.'

Her face leaned over the table: the straight dark eyebrows above the velvet brown eyes that always completely undid him, the high cheekbones with the faintest declivity beneath where his lips had found their most preferred resting place. Then there was the full mouth with the pronounced Cupid's bow, which had whispered close to his ear so many words that hadn't just disentangled the unanswerable knots of a lifetime of confusion, but repaired him too, rendered him whole.

'I love you,' he said, and something quickened in her. Her neck flushed, the cords tightened and her blood ticked into his fingers. 'Nobody has ever paid me a greater compliment than wanting to bear my child. You've rescued me ...'

She knew it was true. She'd noticed changes in herself, realised now that the shadowy allure of her unknowable first husband no longer intrigued her. All it had done was hide a terrible emptiness, in fact worse, his ruthlessness. She'd been excited but frightened when she'd sensed the same draw in Boxer, and had found the courage to reach in, but this time had discovered something different. He seemed determined to escape from his inner darkness and was willing to strive for any possible light.

Boxer's phone vibrated against his chest. After the night he'd had with Amy and Siobhan, it was not a call he could ignore. Isabel told him to take it.

'Mercy,' he said, wondering why she was using her landline.

'Are you alone?' she asked.

'I'm with Isabel.'

'This might be a conversation for us to have alone.'

He looked up at Isabel, who was sipping her tea. She pointed him into the living room. Mercy filled him in on what Alleyne's kidnappers had told her.

'Have they given you a proof of life?'

'I've asked a question and I'm waiting for the reply.'

'How long ago?'

'A few minutes.'

'And I'm the first person you've called?'

'There's no one else who knows about my involvement with Marcus.'

'In your office, you mean, but not in the outside world,' said Boxer. 'Any indication what this could be about? I mean, it's not going to be money, unless ...'

'No, they've said nothing.'

'Are you working on anything sensitive at the moment? You or others in your office. People in powerful places?'

'I've been away on a course. I haven't caught up with what's going on,' said Mercy. 'I was wondering about Glider. I was thinking that maybe he'd worked out how you turned up at his door when we were trying to find Amy.'

'That was nearly two years ago.'

'It wouldn't have been difficult for him to trace the source back to Marcus, and you know what these guys are like. They hold a grudge, keep it nicely incubated until the right time comes along and they can make use of it for their own benefit.'

'You want me to go and talk to Glider again?'

'Don't make it sound like it's something I ask you to do every day of the year.'

'Just a question, Mercy. I ... I'm thinking,' said Boxer. 'How are you going to play this with your colleagues?'

'We don't know that they're going to be involved yet.'

'Is there something in your life that I don't know about?'

'I hope so. I wouldn't like to think that Charles Boxer knows everything there is to know about Mercy Danquah.'

'As far as I know, you have your work, Amy, Marcus and your family,' said Boxer. 'Is there anything interesting going on with any of them?'

'Nothing special,' said Mercy.

'So it's got to be work.'

'Except that I'm not working on anything at the moment,' said Mercy. 'Where's Amy, by the way?'

'She was in the office until late and then went to an art show with a friend,' said Boxer, smoothly.

'She hasn't come home and isn't responding to my calls and texts.'

'I think she's staying with the friend.'

'Who is?'

'Her name's Siobhan,' he said, fluffing it slightly.

'You don't sound so sure about that.'

'I am.'

'I don't know any Siobhans.'

'She's a client.'

'Isn't that a bit weird?'

'Her father's gone missing. She needed a bit of support so Amy went to the show and stayed with her afterwards.'

'LOST supposedly doesn't handle current cases, which means you're telling me something but holding back on some nasty stuff.'

'Don't wind yourself up, Mercy,' said Boxer. 'I know it's in your nature but you don't have to know everything, especially tonight with your particular situation.'

'All right, will you go and see Glider ... do a bit of rooting around in there?' asked Mercy.

'When?'

'How about now?'

'I'm having a conversation with Isabel and anyway, why would I be going to see Glider? We have no idea whether he's involved.'

'Marcus was nervous of him.'

'I'll go and see him ... but tomorrow if that's all right. Tell me if the gang makes contact again. Don't talk to anyone else unless you're coming clean to your colleagues.'

'It's a bit late for that, and don't treat me like an idiot.'

'It's never too late, and you're under a lot of stress.'

'Which you're doing what to alleviate?'

'Good night, Mercy.'

'At least you didn't tell me it was my own stupid fault.'

'Some people think I'm sensitive.'

'Only Isabel.'

'Good night, Mercy.'

He hung up, went back to the kitchen, saw through the partly open door that Isabel hadn't moved. She sat at the table, her shoulders hunched, bringing the *tisane* to her lips. He watched her thinking about their child inside her and realised for the first time that he'd found a woman who was everything to him: lover, friend, mother, sister, partner and now, although not officially, his wife.

The image of the envelope, the tape inside and the letter from his father came to him again. He'd let Isabel penetrate the last line of defence and all the hurt that had so consumed him after his father's disappearance had bled away to be replaced by something that had eluded him all his life: happiness.

He decided there and then to take the advice his father had given in his letter: destroy the tape and forget the part of his personal history that had only ever brought him pain.

Isabel turned and smiled. He could see that she was happy, too, and that this was a unique moment for them. He seized it. He took her face in his hands and kissed her eyebrows, her perfect mouth.

He stopped and looked into her eyes.

'We're on the sunlit uplands,' she said, 'running free. Nobody can touch us.'

'I can hear you thinking,' said Siobhan croakily from the bed, tapping her head. 'What?'

'If you must know, I was thinking that penises aren't exactly things of beauty.'

Amy had pulled an armchair into the bedroom and was watching Siobhan dozing in the bed. A table lamp on the floor provided some dim light. Siobhan had asked her to sleep with her, not to 'do' anything, as she was in no condition, but just to have someone close. Amy demurred, a word she'd only ever associated with Jane Austen types, but now found herself, a nineteen-year-old Londoner with street cred to spare, doing just that.

'So now you're spooked about me?' said Siobhan.

'Not spooked, just unsure.'

'I like to shake people up,' said Siobhan. 'I know I shouldn't, but think about it, your life's been pretty predictable while I've had to live with the uncertainty of being neither M nor F. All I'm doing is sharing some of that uncertainty, and sometimes it fucks me up.'

'My life's not been that predictable, you know. I've been trouble, but my father thinks you're off the scale.'

'He's probably right. That's all I've had all my life. It's just gotten to be the norm. I never used to seek it out because it had no problem finding me. Now I save it the bother and just reach for it.'

'So why do you dress and behave like a woman when you're more evidently a man?'

'I'm both, remember, but women have nicer clothes.'

'But you prefer women to men?'

'You got a high opinion of yourself, girl,' she said. 'I like both but mostly one more than the other at any given time.'

'How does your father feel about that?'

'I'm lucky, given that I'm an "aberration", that my father didn't insist on corrective surgery. A lot of parents of intersex kids take that decision for them, decide that you're more of a boy or more of a girl and ask the surgeon to be decisive. The only problem being that what's evident down there is not always the same as what's going on inside. And you end up with something cut off that you really needed to make you into the person you think you are.'

'How does your father feel about you?'

'Good question. Most of the time there's too much going on in his head to know what he feels emotionally. He doesn't communicate. He keeps all that stuff deep in his English reserve. Occasionally, though, he's shown me something and it was always when I was smaller and being more boyish. He preferred that. I think he always wanted a son, but he's never said so.'

'So why define yourself on the outside as a woman?'

'The same reason you do,' said Siobhan, rolling on to her back and groaning. 'Now shut up and get me some more painkillers so I can sleep.'

Amy fed her another paracetamol and she sucked the water through her damaged lips, dabbed them with the duvet cover.

'Don't forget how you felt when I kissed you in the gallery,' said Siobhan.

'How did I feel?'

'Your hair went Afro from the steam coming out your ears.'

'Very funny. Don't flatter yourself.'

'I saw what I saw,' said Siobhan. 'Nobody will ever kiss you like that again in your life.'

Mercy was on the Railton Road, ringing the doorbell of Alleyne's young neighbour, Tonell, who he used for keeping an eye on his car when he was loading up before going on a job. Mercy and Tonell got on now. He curtailed his language for her. Didn't use the word 'bitch' any more.

'Yo, Mercy,' said Tonell.

'Have you seen Marcus today?'

'Yeah, I seen him. Loaded his van 'bout six fifteen this evening. He goin' on a job.'

'Did he say where?'

Silence.

'Tonell?'

'Just thinkin', Mercy.'

'No rush,' she said, looking at the time on her mobile phone.

'He was doing a deal with somebody he'd worked with before but new crew. Jamaicans he thought 'cos of the accent. Caribbean anyhow,' said Tonell. 'He was nervous. Yeah, that was it. He was nervous 'cos the contact name was Glider what he had a run-in with on account of you. He didn't much like where he had to go 'n' all. East Walworth.'

'No street name?'

Tonell shook his head.

'Did Glider give him the contact or did the buyer say Glider would vouch for him?'

'Glider and him don't speak no more, so I guess ...'

'What did you load into the van?'

'Thousand cartons of smokes.'

'What does he get for that?'

'Pro'ly ten gees, 'bout a poun' a pack.'

Mercy's mobile went off. She walked back to her car, taking the call on the way.

'You took your time,' she said.

69

'Marcus says your father's village is called Anfoeta, in the Volta region of Ghana,' said the voice. 'And it took a long time because Marcus is very protective of you, Mercy. We had to take out our frustration on him. He took a very severe beating on your behalf. I hope you realise that.'

Silence from Mercy as anger and fear battled away. She got in the car, dropped her head on to the steering wheel. She was not prone to tears, never cried in her professional life, whatever the horrors of the case. Her job demanded a cool head at all times. But in this situation she couldn't help herself: professionalism went out the window, the tears flowed as her imagination ran riot with images of Marcus's bloodied face. She had to grip the wheel and remind herself of the basics of kidnap negotiation. The mind game. The power of the unseen.

She breathed it all back down, found that savage streak within her.

'Just get on with it,' she said. 'You've had your fun. Let's get down to business. If it's money you're after, you've got a long wait. I've got a four hundred and fifty grand mortgage and two cash ISAs, which might cover my Christmas credit card bill. I have a net worth of zip. So what is it?'

'I'd heard you'd be a hard nut to crack, but that's my speciality and crack you I will,' said the voice. 'And not just the outer shell. Right the way into the middle. The first thing you'll hear is the crushing of your bones and the crumpling of your heart. Good night, my little Mercy.'

8

Alleyne was back in the chair. He didn't like it there. At least when they left him lying on the concrete floor they weren't hurting him. The chair was metal, cold and unstable, and in his struggles he'd fallen backwards so that his head had flicked back on to the concrete and he'd knocked himself out. They'd brought him round eventually and asked him about Mercy's father's village, which he'd struggled to remember. Now they were on him again. This time they'd said they were filming him and he was to speak nicely and look good for his audience.

'So, we've been successful, Marcus,' said the voice. 'We've got over the first hurdle: Mercy's taking us seriously now. She's satisfied that you're with us. Now we're going to up the pressure.'

'You told her what you want yet?' asked Alleyne, confused. 'Can't think what that would be. I mean, she's broke. I've got more available cash than her. You want her to do something for you, I don't know how that goin' to happen, because she works in a team. They looking over each other all the time, supervising their arses off, assessing each other's performance. She start acting strange, doing things different, poking her nose in places where it should not be poked, she will get found out. She will not survive in that environment. You get me?'

'How many of her colleagues know about you?'

'None,' said Alleyne. 'If she told them, she'd have to quit her job. Too much of a liability. It's sensitive work.'

'What's that say about you?'

71

'It doesn't say anything about me.'

'Think again, Marcus,' said the voice. 'She's still in her job because ...'

'Because she loves her work.'

'Yes, and ... what's the logical progression of that sentence?'

'She's good at it, too.'

'And?'

'All right, she loves me.'

'And how do you feel about her?'

Silence.

'I love her. We're lovers.'

'How much do you love her, Marcus?'

'It's not quantifiable,' said Marcus.

'Try.'

'It's not to your advantage to know.'

'Why don't you let us be the judge of that?'

It was strange to find himself in this situation. He'd spent quite a few mornings thinking about the woman lying in bed next to him. Mercy Danquah. He even loved her name, had to stop himself from whispering it in her ear when they made love to each other. Mercy, Mercy, Mercy. He knew that she was the one for him. The only one. Had known it from the moment he'd first seen her standing on his doorstep being demanding. And yet it wasn't until now, under the peculiar stresses of this kidnap, that he realised the full extent of his involvement.

'I'd lay down my life for her without a thought,' he said.

Boxer was up early and on his way to Perth House on the Bemerton estate, just off the Caledonian Road, to see Glider. Mercy had called him back with some additional intelligence, which he was thinking how to use. He wasn't looking forward to this meeting, as it would probably call for some violence, and, having left the warmth of Isabel's bed, he was steeling himself for the task.

He'd first met the tattooed thug that was Glider a couple of years ago. Mercy had sent him there after she'd persuaded Alleyne that his life as a fence would be over unless he gave her the address.

As Boxer came off the Cally Road, he was aware that even at 6.30 a.m. he was not alone. He'd earned a couple of outriders who were bringing him in. In the square of muddy greenery with its broken-hearted children's playground outside Perth House where Glider had his flat, there were others. By the time he reached the stairs, he had four behind and two in front and he came to a halt.

'Can I help you boys?' he asked.

'I know you,' said a voice from behind.

'Then you'll know I've come to see Glider.'

'Let's have your name again?'

'Charles Boxer.'

Someone peeled off and made a phone call. Boxer looked at each gang member, saw the nerves in their faces: the shiftiness in the eyes, tension around the mouths. One of them was a girl.

'No reason to be on edge,' he said. 'It's just a social visit.'

The man with the phone came back, nodded. They grabbed his arms, two kicks to the back of his legs and he was kneeling with his arms up behind his back. The girl came down on to the first step and dropped to her haunches so that they were eye to eye.

'A little body search,' she said and went through his pockets, took everything out, ran her hands down his flanks, under his jumper, coat up over his head, hands all over his back, round his crotch and arse, down his legs. Shoes off. Not just a weapon search but a wire check too.

They walked him up the cold concrete stairs in his socks to the third floor and along the walkway to Glider's flat, where the door was opened from the inside and he was handed over to two men. Only the girl followed from the welcoming committee, carrying his shoes. They took him into the living room, where there was now dark blue furniture and the walls were a bright, buttery yellow like fields of rapeseed. The carpet looked new and was the sky blue of a clear Arctic day. They pressed him into a solitary armchair on the other side of a coffee table from a three-seater sofa. It was warm in the room.

'Your shoes are by the front door,' said the girl, in bare feet now. 'He doesn't like shoes on his new carpet.'

They waited. She was still holding his possessions.

'The security's stepped up since I was last here,' said Boxer.

'That's my speciality,' said the girl. 'He brought me in after your last visit. I could see he was too exposed, didn't have the right personnel. We're tight now. So do your business and leave quietly and everything will be fine.'

'Why's everybody so nervous?'

'Not for me to say.'

The door opened and Glider came in. He'd let his hair grow out so that it was now *en brosse*, and he was wearing a dark blue suit with a white shirt open at the neck. None of his tats were visible and his nose looked as if it might have been remodelled into a better shape. A red tie hung from his left hand. He looked like a successful businessman rather than the north London thug he'd been the last time. The girl put Boxer's things on the coffee table. Glider sat down in front of them.

'Thanks, Jess,' he said. 'Behave himself?'

'Dream guest, boss,' she said, and left.

'How d'you like it?' asked Glider.

'Your new set-up or the equal opportunities for women?'

'She's a diamond, that Jess. Break your arm soon as look at you. Black belt in tae kwisine or something like that. Wipe the smile off your face with her left foot, kill you with her right. Body made out of ship's hawsers. Lovely.'

'You've gone pro, Glider,' said Boxer. 'Been making a living?'

'Gone very well since I last saw you,' he said. 'Lots of crusty pies, not enough fingers.'

'You know why I'm here?'

'Can't say I do,' said Glider. 'I don't do black girls any more, if that's what you're asking. I moved on. Had to change my tastes. So if your daughter's done another runner, you better start some other place.'

'Not my daughter this time,' said Boxer. 'You were a big help on that. Thanks. She's very well now.'

Glider was riffling through Boxer's wallet, asked for the PIN number on his iPhone, worked it over.

'Your new security outfit seem very nervous,' said Boxer. 'You expecting trouble?'

'It's not a trouble-free business I'm in,' said Glider. 'I've learnt that. Learnt that from you. Have to expect it from all sides.'

'You've got to that point where you're doing favours for people?'

'Favours? You make it sound like I never done any favours,' said Glider. 'Did you a favour, didn't I?'

'And I thanked you for it.'

'I noticed. Sounds like you've got another favour lined up for me,' said Glider. 'And the answer's no.'

'That last time I came here,' said Boxer. 'You know how I got to you?'

'No idea,' said Glider.

'I think you do,' said Boxer. 'You don't organise a security set-up like this without good reason and one of your security detail let slip that this all started because of my last visit. So let's try again. How did I get to you the last time?'

'I don't know and I don't care,' said Glider, hardening up now, some steel in his look.

'You're on their radar now, you know that, don't you?'

'Whose radar?'

'The Organised Crime Command.'

Now he was listening.

'You've heard about the National Crime Agency?'

He nodded.

'The OCC and the kidnap unit are under the same roof.'

'So?'

'I could give you a bit of free consultancy seeing as we had such an amicable relationship the last time we met.'

'I don't remember the amicable bit,' said Glider. 'You threatened to ram an ashtray through my teeth ... that wasn't very fucking amicable, was it?'

'We were talking about my daughter and you weren't taking the situation very seriously. I had to get your attention.'

'Who or what are we talking about this time? You're going in circles. You're not getting to the fucking point.'

'You still using Marcus Alleyne to fence stolen goods for you?'

'No.'

'Marcus Alleyne's a friend of mine and he said you gave him a job.'

'He's a friend of *yours*?' said Glider as if this was the most unlikely thing he'd heard in a while.

'To be a bit more accurate, he's a friend of my ex-wife ... Amy's mother. She's a detective inspector in a special investigations unit attached to the kidnap and extortion department of the Organised Crime Command.'

'And Marcus Alleyne is her *friend*?' said Glider. 'What the fuck is she playing at? Nobody in their right mind ...'

'Come on, Glider,' said Boxer, wearily. 'Don't make this sound like it's news to you.'

'What goes around comes around,' said Glider, with cold blue eyes.

'You want the OCC on your back?'

'I wouldn't be able to help them even if they humped me nicely,' said Glider. 'You've got to get it straight in your head. I don't know what's going on with Marcus Alleyne. I don't use him any more.'

'So when did you last give him a job?'

'That's not how it works,' said Glider. 'I don't have jobs to give. I don't have stuff that needs to be fenced. People ask me who they should use. I give them a name. If they use the name, I get a cut from the deal. I'm just a ... whaddyacall'em ... facilitator. That's the word.'

'So when did Marcus Alleyne fall off your list of fences?'

'All right, I'll spell it out for you seeing as you know without fucking knowing it,' said Glider. 'I stopped using him when I found out he'd sent you to my door. That, in my world, is a fucking betrayal. And once you betray me, you're off my books.'

'Was that it, Glider? All of it? Someone betrays you like that and you don't want to get your own back?'

'If I'd suffered, yeah, I would have done. If that ashtray *had* gone down my throat I'd have made Marcus take the same, but it didn't. Lucky for him and your ex, come to think of it. All his lovely white teeth splintered to fuck.'

'So when did you drop him?'

'Got to be eighteen months ago now.'

'How did you find out it was him?'

'Traced it back to how your daughter got involved. Her friend. Don't remember the name.'

'Once you've facilitated an intro, is there anything to stop your client using your recommendation again and again?'

'They'd still give me a cut … if they knew what was best for them,' said Glider. 'What's this all about, Mr Boxer? You're feeling me up like airport security.'

Boxer thought about it, decided to come clean.

'Marcus has been kidnapped.'

'And what do they want?' asked Glider. 'His family aren't short of a bob or two, you know.'

'It looks like they want to put pressure on Mercy.'

'That's who they're talking to, is it?'

Boxer nodded.

'And you know he went out on a job and didn't come back?'

'His helper loaded up his van with a thousand cartons of smokes, expected him to make ten grand from it. Marcus was going to East Walworth and the buyer, who had a Jamaican or at least a Caribbean accent, had given your name as contact.'

'I don't know much south of the river,' said Glider, 'and Marcus never called me to check. That's the point of a contact, you know. You make sure the guy you're doing business with is vouched for.'

'Maybe Marcus was still nervous of you, but your name was good enough for him to go ahead,' said Boxer. 'Perhaps he didn't call you because he knew you'd still be bearing a grudge.'

'I've got bigger fish to fry than Marcus Alleyne,' said Glider. 'I was annoyed, which was why I took away my business, but that was the end of it.'

'What about leads? People you've done business with in the past who might call him up again on a pretext.'

'Now you're asking for a favour … another one. And you still haven't seen me right for the first one,' said Glider.

'What are you looking for?'

'How about a little less attention from the OCC?'

'That would be a difficult promise to keep.'

'At least you're fucking honest,' said Glider. 'I'll think of something, get you some leads.'

9

Eight-year-old Sophie Railton-Bass was standing at the window of the lower sitting room of her mother's house in Wilton Place looking down into the street, waiting. She was wearing the uniform of Francis Holland Junior School. A navy-blue pullover, white shirt, blue and grey checked skirt, navy-blue tights and sensible black shoes. The only thing she was holding was a rag doll frog called Zach. Her blonde hair was tied back in a ponytail, apart from one long wisp that hung from her forehead and which she sucked in the corner of her mouth. A black Jaguar XJR SWB pulled in to the kerb below. The driver, a man in his sixties in grey trousers and a purple pullover, got out, looked up at the window and opened his arms as if the love was radiating forth. He smiled. Sophie waved at him.

'Pat's here, Mum. I'm off now.'

'Have you got your coat?'

She shrugged into the thick grey coat with dark collar and buttoned it up.

'Yes.'

'Don't I get a kiss?'

'If you insist on a kiss I'll resist till you miss so desist or I'll hiss.'

'Why do you talk such rubbish?' said Emma Railton-Bass.

'It's not rubbish. It rhymes.'

'Come here.'

Sophie walked a tightrope to her mother and held her face up, eyes closed, lips pursed. Her mother took hold of her little face in both hands and kissed her on the cheek and forehead.

'Now don't go distracting Pat,' said Emma, opening the door, guiding her daughter down the stairs. 'I want you there in one piece.'

'Which piece?' Sophie said, turning at the front door and holding up her hand and foot. 'This one ... or that?'

'All of you.'

'Love you, Mum,' she said, waving Zach at her, and disappeared down the final flight of stairs and out of the door.

She trotted towards the Jaguar. Pat Gould opened the passenger door and gave her an exaggerated Elizabethan bow.

'Where to, ma'am?'

'I think I'd like to go to Versailles today,' said Sophie.

'Traffic's abominable ... coaches and horses all the way out of the Channel Tunnel, ma'am.'

Sophie sighed.

'In that case you'd better just whisk me away to Sloane Square, and don't spare the nags.'

Gould pulled out, took his normal route to Sloane Square. The streets were all empty of people at this time of day.

'The crowds are terrible this morning, ma'am,' he said. 'They've all come out to see you.'

He cut down Lyall Street and was surprised by a couple of workmen in white hard hats, yellow goggles and dayglo jackets standing by a red and white barrier in front of a pile of rubble, pointing at him and urgently waving him off to his left. It was so quick he didn't have time to think. He just turned the wheel, coasted up the ramp of the pavement, under an arch and into a mews.

A huge white plastic scaffolding sheet broke away from the building on his right and descended over the car so that he had to jam on the brakes. In seconds the driver's door was opened and a rag was closed over his face. His eyes widened, which was all the reaction he could muster to the sting in his neck from a needle. He slumped across the gearstick. Exactly the same thing happened on Sophie's side, except as the rag closed over her mouth and nose, she felt herself being torn from the car. She clung on to

Zach. The scaffolding sheet billowed as her vision collapsed into absolute darkness.

Boxer was standing in front of the almost empty One Hyde Park, whose penthouse apartments with views over trees and greenery to Speakers' Corner and Marble Arch changed hands at £140 million. He called Amy, asked if Siobhan was stable.

'She's still sleeping.'

'What about you?'

'What about *me*? I'm all right.'

'You had a bit of a shock last night.'

'The rape ... was terrible,' said Amy, 'but the way she took it was almost worse. It was as if she ... as if she thought she deserved it or that it was to be expected.'

'She's used to extreme reactions to her gender,' said Boxer. 'And she's no shrinking violet, but maybe all that charisma attracts the wrong kind of people.'

'People like me, you mean?'

'No, Amy, in fact I think you've been a positive influence,' said Boxer. 'What I meant was: she craves the attention even if it comes with violence. She doesn't want anybody to be indifferent to her.'

'I find her kind of fascinating,' said Amy, distracted, unintentionally verbalising a thought.

'She told me, by the way.'

'Yes, she kept telling me how interested people are in her,' said Amy. 'Lucien Freud wanted her to sit for him, you know that?'

'I'm not sure we're talking about the same thing,' said Boxer. 'Siobhan told me you'd kissed last night. That must have been ... confusing?'

'She told you *that*?'

'I told you she likes the attention. I didn't have to prise it out of her. Be careful what you tell her and what you show her.'

'*Christ*,' said Amy, mortified. 'Did she blurt anything else out?'

'Was there anything else to blurt?'

Amy had a flashback to the intensity of last night's sexual anticipation and decided that was too much information for her father even with their new relationship.

'We were having a drink in the gallery bar after seeing the show and she just snogged me ... I couldn't do anything about it.'

'I'm here if you need to talk,' said Boxer. 'Your mother's worried about you. And you should call her because, and don't get annoyed with me for not telling you this, Marcus was kidnapped last night and—'

'Holy shit, Dad. What the fuck's the matter with you?' said Amy. 'How can you be so cool about something like that? Mum'll be in a total state.'

'She is, and I didn't tell you for very obvious reasons, but now that I know you're OK, I think it would be a good idea for you to call her,' said Boxer. 'I've just been talking to Glider, see if he was involved.'

'Was he?'

'Doubtful,' said Boxer. 'Anyway, call your mother. She could use some support. I'm going to see Tanya Birch now.'

'Isn't it a bit early?'

'Mark Rowlands cleared the way. She's got a meeting up north this afternoon and she's leaving early, so we agreed an 8.15 meeting,' said Boxer. 'Call me when you've spoken to your mother, and remember, nobody in her office knows about Marcus.'

He hung up, rang on Tanya's doorbell in the arched porch of a five-storey Edwardian mansion block on Hans Crescent, not far from Harrods. He went up to her second-floor flat. Tanya was a petite blonde with skinny legs under a very short black miniskirt, a tight black cashmere V-neck sweater and a fine gold chain around her neck from which hung a small gold cross. Her hair was shoulder length and close to platinum in both price and colour. Her hands were surprisingly large, almost manly, and sported complicated rings with brown diamonds, semi-precious stones and twisted gold and silverwork that looked like plant life. She led him into her living room, where she indicated the white leather sofa that had featured in Siobhan's little tale of sexual *flagrante*.

'So what's happened to Con?' she asked, sitting in a white Arne Jacobsen egg chair with her legs joined tightly at the knees.

'He's disappeared. We're trying to find him. You're the obvious starting point.'

'He didn't even call me,' she said, icily.

'Perhaps he was here strictly on business.'

'He's always here *strictly* on business. That's never stopped him calling me before. Makes me wonder how many times he has been here and not called. Mind you, that little ... Siobhan,' she said, biting back something nastier, 'always seems to take delight in calling me whenever she's along for the ride just to let me know he's not getting in touch. Bitch or ... whatever you'd call that sort of thing.'

'You don't get on with Siobhan?'

'That's probably the understatement of the decade,' said Tanya. 'She's a trollop or whatever you call someone of her sex who throws themselves at anything that moves. I suppose slut would cover it. There's even been a *disgrazzia* here in my own home.'

'She mentioned that.'

'Did she?' said Tanya.

'Any particular reason why Siobhan would take against you?'

'Jealousy,' said Tanya, with no doubt. 'It was like that from the outset. I tried to be ... nice. I offered to take her shopping and she didn't show up. I had her here to stay and she behaved appallingly. I went out of my way to be accommodating and she was just plain nasty in return. So ... she's banned now. We barely speak, although she did call a few days ago to make sure Con wasn't with me but, as usual, I just thought she was taking the opp to rub my nose in it. I only really took it seriously when Mark Rowlands called.'

'When did you last have contact with Conrad?'

'On the sixth of January. We'd spent Christmas and New Year together ...'

'Where?'

'Con had rented a house in the Cotswolds.'

'Was Siobhan there?'

'Only over Christmas.'

'Were any of Con's friends or business contacts with you at any stage?'

'I'm not sure Con has any friends as such. We socialise with my circle. As for business contacts, he keeps that separate, although somebody did turn up on New Year's Day. An American with one of those really unlikely names that only Americans have – Walden Garfinkle.'

'Did he stay?'

'He joined us for lunch but didn't say much. He was very polite and revealed nothing. He was very hairy. I mean a really dark five o'clock shadow. Hands like a chimp's, eyebrows and ears sprouting all over. He even had hair on the outside rims of his ears,' she said, shuddering. 'He was in a dark blue suit, white shirt, a red bow tie and looked very Ivy League. Oh, and he had huge and utterly perfect white teeth that looked as if they'd torn many a steak and possibly human beings apart.'

'Did Conrad offer any explanation?'

'That he was a business associate,' said Tanya. 'After he'd gone, my friends all thought he was CIA and Con didn't bother to persuade them otherwise.'

'And that's the only person you've ever met?' said Boxer. 'Did Conrad talk to you about his work?'

'Never.'

'Did you ever overhear conversations, phone calls?'

'Bits and pieces when he was talking in English, nothing that would give me or you any idea of the sort of thing he was up to,' said Tanya. 'There were definitely times of great intensity: the Arab Spring at the end of 2010 and beginning of 2011. Libya and Syria still get talked about even today. And then that guy, the whistleblower ...'

'Edward Snowden.'

'Yes, him. When he came out into the open in June last year, the phone calls were endless. A lot of Hong Kong Chinese, Russians and Spanish as I remember it.'

'Was Con good at languages?'

'Yes, which was why I didn't pick up that much. He is fluent in Arabic, Russian, Spanish and French and can get by in Mandarin but not Cantonese. He has a whole bunch of other lingos that he knows enough of to eat, drink and be merry in, as he put it.'

'Did you talk about the Arab Spring or Snowden? Did he reveal any sympathies to you?'

'He was pro the Arab Spring and anti Snowden. Or rather, that's my generalised reading of his feelings. He thought these oppressive Arab regimes had it coming to them. As for Snowden, he seemed to find his actions brave but foolhardy. He was astonished at the outraged reaction of the world. He thought everybody must have been delusional if they believed that governments hadn't been accessing private data since the internet began.'

'Did you know that Con was a private contractor to the US military?'

'Those words have never been said to me in that order, but I've gathered as much.'

'How would you describe his behaviour before and after the visit from Walden Garfinkle?'

She sat back in the chair, crossed her legs, toyed with her gold chain.

'You know, Con wasn't the sort of man you could read very easily,' she said. 'He was attentive without ever being intimate, which was fine by me. I'm sixty-two years old and I've had my fair share of intimacy and not much of it did me any good. So Con was refreshing in that respect. I always felt there was a whole other world going on that none of us knew about, but Con did, and he was working some of the levers. So to answer your question, there was no *apparent* difference, certainly not at the lunch when Walden was still there. But after he left, Con went into the library room at the house and sat there on his own staring out of the window for probably an hour. I went in there and called his name and he didn't even turn, let alone answer. Later on we had supper with the guests who were staying and he was back to his usual self. When everybody had gone to bed, he went back into the library with a glass of Springbank, his favourite whisky. I heard him talking on the phone but I didn't see him until morning. No explanation, but that was Con. After that, he was fine.'

'What happened on the sixth of January?'

'We came back to London. I dropped him at Heathrow where he was meeting Siobhan to fly back to Dubai. He called me a few days later. He made no mention of coming back to London. He asked after me, my son and two daughters, the grandchildren. Yes, he always liked a sense of family. That was strange, but then again, given that he only had Siobhan and she's sterile, I suppose he hasn't got anything like that to look forward to.'

'Can you think of anything that would make him want to walk out of his current life?'

'If I was Con, the only thing that would make *me* want to walk out of my life would be Siobhan.'

'Just out of interest, how old is Siobhan?'

'You'd never get a straight answer out of her,' said Tanya, shaking her head. 'She's a myth-maker, a fantasist, a fabricant. She's twenty-three, born on the twenty-fourth of November 1990. I saw her passport when I went to get her a visa.'

'Have you got any idea of the sort of people she was mixing with in London?'

'Con said she was pretty wild. Off the leash, was how he put it. She's so sexually voracious it's as if she defines herself by her ability to pull. She eats like a pig, drinks like a fish and fucks like a rabbit ... Con's words again. The only friend, or rather "person", I met her with was the guy she was screwing on my sofa. He had a back full of tats and didn't seem bothered in the slightest that he'd been caught being sodomised on my sofa by ... a man/woman. So I think Con's reading of the situation was accurate or at least not exaggerated.'

'Siobhan came to see me three days after Con disappeared, on the instructions of Mark Rowlands. Last night she took my daughter, who works with me, to an art show. They went back to Siobhan's place ...'

'Uh-oh,' said Tanya, warily. 'She'd only take her home for one reason ... I'm sorry, but it's true.'

'And two guys broke into the house, tied my daughter up and interrogated, tortured and raped Siobhan over a period of three quarters of an hour.'

Tanya sat silent, hands over her mouth, eyes wide open.

'Is that what you'd call a normal night out for Siobhan?'

'No, but ... I really don't know,' she said, shocked. 'Oh my God ... tortured?'

'They beat her up while they interrogated her.'

'And raped? Are the police involved?'

'She didn't want them involved. She wouldn't let my daughter call them in the immediate aftermath or me when I turned up on the scene later,' said Boxer. 'She insisted that my daughter run her a bath, got into it and by doing so compromised any evidence.'

'Look, I don't want you to get the wrong idea about me. I know

85

I sounded vindictive about Siobhan earlier. I know what I look like to most people: a silly, blonde rich bitch with too much time and money on her hands.'

'You haven't come across like that to me.'

'What I'm going to say might sound really terrible: the fact is, you can't believe everything you see and hear where Siobhan's concerned.'

'What does that mean?'

'I'm not saying it *is* the case, and I certainly wouldn't say this about anybody else, but now that you've told me about the bath, I think ... Siobhan could have cooked it up herself.'

Mercy could see Amy sitting in a clear circle wiped from the steamy window of the Portugal Coffee Deli on the South Lambeth Road, a short walk from her office near Vauxhall tube station. She waved and got a lift when Amy waved back. They hugged and kissed and the hug was so strong, Mercy gasped against the emotion. Even now, two years later, she still couldn't believe the transformation in her daughter.

They sat, ordered coffee and a couple of custard tarts. It was just after 8.20.

'I'm sorry ... I didn't find out about Marcus until this morning. Dad kept it from me.'

'Why?'

Amy put her hands across the table, grasped her mother's.

'Promise this is just between us. Mum and daughter. No police.'

'I promise,' said Mercy, rolling her eyes, squeezing her daughter's fingers.

Amy gave her a quick recap of last night's incident, leaving out the kiss and the sexual anticipation.

'That's a serious—'

'That was just so you know why Dad didn't tell me. He knows what happened. She's his client and we're looking for her father. And don't ask me why it's us covering a current missing persons case and not the Met.'

'Your father wouldn't tell me either.'

'Because it's client confidentiality,' said Amy. 'And I'm not here

86

to talk about me. It's Marcus we should be talking about. What's happened?'

'They called, told me they had Marcus and that they'd had to work him over to get my number. I asked for proof of life. They gave it to me and I haven't heard another word.'

'What about work?'

'I haven't told anyone.'

'Who knows about you and Marcus?'

'Nobody.'

'Impossible,' said Amy. 'You think people don't know when you're having an affair, but everybody can tell. They might not know who with but they know you're in love.'

'No they don't.'

'Mum,' said Amy, kindly. 'Join us in the real world. Believe me, they can see it in your eyes, your body language, your whole demeanour.'

'All right,' said Mercy, conceding nothing, 'but they absolutely don't know *who* it is. If they did ...'

'So you don't spy on each other?' said Amy, doubtful. 'There must be some kind of internal investigation team.'

'Yes, but only when there's been an accusation or there's a genuine suspicion of corruption, malpractice or whatever.'

'So how are you going to handle this? Are you going to come clean to your boss, whatshisname? Makepeace.'

'Makepeace has been promoted,' said Mercy. 'And if I come clean I'll be taken off all operations. Marcus's kidnap will become the property of the unit, which will put him in immediate danger.'

'Does that mean what I think it means?'

'It means I'm waiting for developments.'

'Before you come clean?'

'Before I make a decision.'

'This doesn't sound like you, Mum.'

Mercy made blinkers with her hands around her eyes, stared at Amy down the tunnel.

'Everything is on the line: my lover, my job, my whole ...' she stopped to consider. 'No, that's not true, *that* has changed.'

'What?'

'It's not my whole existence. It used to be, but it isn't any more,' said Mercy, giving her hands over to her daughter.

'Me *and* Marcus,' said Amy, kissing her mother's hands. 'You love him. He's the only guy you've ever cared about apart from Dad.'

Mercy looked off out of the window, knew it was true.

'You've got to work out the best strategy for his survival,' said Amy. 'Whoever these guys are, they're going to come back and ask you to do something for them. You haven't got any money worth talking about so they're going to want you to compromise yourself in some way. And I know you. You won't be able to do that.'

'I don't know that it's about work. It could be my family.'

'Like who? I'm trying to think of somebody with money, influence and charisma, and since Uncle David died two years ago in Accra, I haven't come up with anyone,' said Amy.

'So what would your survival strategy be?'

'You won't believe this,' said Amy, 'but I think you should come clean. Get the whole of the Met behind you. Can you imagine the power of that – the whole force behind one of their own? The only drawback is ... you'd lose ultimate control, but you'd still be in the picture because the kidnappers would have to come to you with their demands. On the other hand, if you don't tell them and you get found out, and especially if you get found out compromising your position, you're finished for life ... with jail. And I wouldn't like to be a black ex-copper in HMP Holloway.'

'Have you been speaking to your father about this?'

'Not about this kidnap, we haven't had time, but about Marcus, yes, I have.'

'And?'

'You should have told them about him a year ago when you knew it was getting serious between you.'

'That's my little problem. I no longer have Makepeace to rely on. The boss of the unit is an unknown quantity. And if anything happened to Marcus I'd never forgive myself.'

'Don't play their game, Mum. It goes against everything you stand for. Marcus could be in just as much danger if you try to handle it solo.'

'I just want to know what they're after. If they told me that, I could make a decision based on facts.'

'You and Dad have told me an awful lot about kidnaps over the years, and the one thing that's stuck in my brain is that the gang's main strategy is to bring to bear as much emotional pressure on the victim's loved ones as they possibly can.'

'It's started. They've already said they're going to break me, but nobody's broken me yet and there's not going to be a first time.'

'You know it could be days before you find out what they want. Coming clean now looks a lot better than coming clean three days after he was taken,' said Amy. 'I don't know why I'm telling you these things. You know it perfectly well already.'

Mercy's phone vibrated against her hip, she ripped it out, took the call.

'I hope you're only discussing this situation with your daughter and nobody in your office,' said the voice. 'You do … and she's next.'

10

Back at the office, Mercy sat in a toilet cubicle, elbows on knees, hands steepled over her face, staring blankly into the tiled floor as a ruthless calm settled in her stomach. This always happened when the real pressure came on. She recognised the seismic change: fear and anxiety being processed through white-hot anger to emerge transformed by some strange heat exchange into Arctic composure. She had always been able to switch off the personal and revert to the professional as if nothing was happening inside her.

But this time it was different.

She was making decisions, profound and deeply personal decisions, of the sort that had to be made alone. No colleague could help her, no sage advice dissuade her. She was wrestling with all her professional instincts. Her moral compass in which she'd always been able to trust had suddenly lost its bearings. She was in unknown territory.

If she hadn't been sure how much she loved Marcus Alleyne before, now she was absolutely certain. She couldn't tolerate his suffering. The threat against him, and now her daughter, had brought out some innate impulse she'd never known was there. She'd had an inkling when Amy had disappeared, believed murdered, and she thought she'd lost the best love of her life. But with Amy remoulded to her and this new passion in her life, she was now utterly convinced that she would meet any threat to either of them with total ruthlessness.

The only thing she couldn't decide was whether to do this from the inside or out. Should she risk compromising the actions of her colleagues or put the welfare of the two most important people in her life in the hands of others?

The main door to the ladies' opened. Voices from outside drifted in and released her from the grip of her thoughts. She stood, flushed the toilet, went to the sink, nodding and smiling at two sergeants talking about their big night out. She returned to the office and sat at her desk opposite George Papadopoulos, who was looking at her anxiously.

'What?' said Mercy, unable to hide her irritation, knowing that what was going on in his mind had to be more mundane.

'I've just been told at the coffee machine,' he said. 'There's been a leak. You heard anything your side?'

'Clearly not or I'd be looking as haemorrhoidal as you. Relax, for God's sake.'

'The new DCS is talking redundancies. Further sweeping budget cuts. We're down to the bone operationally, so that only leaves people, which means us. I mean the unit, not just us two. Could be anybody.'

'But we're the best performing double act in this whole cabaret. I saw them in half and you put them together. You make them vanish and I bring them back. We're brilliant.'

'He doesn't know that. Maybe he just sees the Greek and the African and thinks let's get shot of the immigrants.'

'Calm down. He's not *allowed* to think like that.'

'It doesn't mean he won't,' said Papadopoulos.

The phone went on Mercy's desk. Papadopoulos jumped.

'What *is* the matter with you?'

'Josie and I have got a two hundred and fifty grand mortgage, Mercy,' he said. 'A social worker and a copper with a combined income of bugger all. I've got shit in my pants all day, every day.'

'For God's sake, cork it, George, and I mean your mouth.'

She picked up the phone, listened, put it down.

'He wants to see me.'

George dropped his head on to his desk, leaving his hands up in prayer.

She walked the corridor, amazed at herself. How could she keep up this banter with such a monumental decision, made slightly more awkward by George's desperation, hanging over her? She clenched her fists, looked up to find that Makepeace's name had been removed from the door and replaced by 'DCS Oscar Hines'. She breathed deep, felt her mind swerve one way: come on now, let's get this out right. Talk him through it, take the hit, home by lunch-time.

She knocked and went straight into the familiar office with the stranger behind the desk. Hines stood up, leaned over and shook hands, did all the pleasantries with charm, pointed her into a seat.

The DCS was monstrously handsome, with tremendous shoulders and a full head of white hair, which was swept back from his forehead while grazing his collar at the back. He had very long, luxuriant black eyebrows above gimlet green eyes, which reminded her of Boxer's. His face was broad, with a powerful nose and flared nostrils above a red-lipped mouth, which was frequently wetted by the quick flash of a tongue tip. But it was his hands that fascinated Mercy. She could still feel their dryness, their firmness without being crushing, and their length and width. There was something of the concert pianist about their expressiveness. She wouldn't have minded being anointed by them.

'There have been rumours,' he said, steepling his forefingers, resting them against the slight cleft in his chin, 'and I wanted to put your mind at rest. Nobody from the special investigations unit will lose their job. I guarantee it.'

Now was the moment. Interrupt. Get it out and over with. Feel the release.

'I'm glad to hear it,' said Mercy. 'George has just bought a flat with his partner and he was getting nervous.'

'I've looked at the reports on your work over the last three years and all I can say is that you've been relentlessly impressive, DI Danquah. Peter Makepeace and your colleagues think you're nothing short of magnificent, and in taking DS Papadopoulos under your wing, you've created an extraordinary team.'

'Thank you, sir,' said Mercy, trembling inside at the praise being heaped on her, hungry now to hear what was coming her way. 'I learnt a lot from DCS Makepeace and I wouldn't have been able to perform at this level without the support of my colleagues.'

'I understand that since your private life has ... normalised over the last two years you've reached new heights, but what particularly impressed me was how you've managed to perform under the most intense pressure of all. I'm referring to the Bobkov case when your daughter was *in extremis*, shall we say. You're a remarkable woman, DI Danquah. There aren't many people who could have retained their intelligence, humour, focus and analytical elegance under those circumstances.'

'Now it sounds as if you *are* going to fire me,' said Mercy.

Hines roared with sudden laughter, held his arms open as if he was going to hug her and slapped the edge of his desk with his gorgeous hands. Mercy looked down on herself, incredulous at her behaviour.

'Bloody marvellous,' said Hines. 'Which brings me to the next point. I've got a job for you, or rather several jobs all rolled into one. Yes, a bit more demanding than usual and it's no accident that I mentioned Bobkov, because the nature of it means you will be coming into contact with the secret services. Ours, the CIA, and I wouldn't be surprised if we get a showing from the the the Russian Foreign Intelligence Service, the SVR.'

'In London?' said Mercy, amazed.

'All in London,' said Hines. 'My task at the moment is to give you an initial briefing before we head off to Thames House, where we'll be getting together with MI5 and MI6 et al.'

'We're still talking kidnap rather than terrorism, aren't we, sir?'

'Possibly both,' said Hines. 'I'm going to begin at the end, so to speak. Because the last kidnap has transformed the political landscape. Have you heard of the US company Kinderman?'

'They're an American-based corporation doing oil field services and equipment as far as I remember. Deepwater platform rigs, pipelines, refineries and chemical plants, that sort of thing?'

'Right, that's their mainstream business,' said Hines. 'So the hostage is an eight-year-old girl called Sophie Railton-Bass. Her mother, Emma Railton, is the ex-wife of Kinderman's global CEO Ken Bass, who is currently working out of Dubai. The girl was being chauffeured from the family home in Belgravia to Francis Holland Junior School in Sloane Square. At ten minutes past eight this morning the car was diverted into a mews off Lyall

Street using fake roadworks. The chauffeur was just a driver, not an experienced operative, and it seems he was quickly overwhelmed. The girl was transferred to another vehicle, whose colour, model and registration are unknown. The police were called by several of the residents of the mews when the chauffeur's car remained in its awkward position and they found him slumped back in his seat, no keys in the ignition and the doors locked. The chauffeur has been released from the car, which has been removed for forensic inspection.'

'What shape is he in?'

'Still unconscious in the Chelsea and Westminster Hospital.'

'Anything from the kidnappers?'

'Emma Railton received a call at 08.35 from a male voice telling her that they had kidnapped her daughter and would require a payment of twenty-five million pounds in cash, but not for her release. This is not a ransom, they said, this is just for expenses. Time and location to be nominated. Ken Bass has been informed. Sophie is his only child and he adores her, as he still does his ex-wife. He bought her the house in Belgravia, gave her a lump sum of one hundred and twenty million dollars and ten million a year, and he's still worth in excess of a billion dollars.

'Now for the really complicated stuff,' said Hines. 'You know about Kinderman's oil activities, but they're also involved in other sorts of building work, like military bases in Iraq and Afghanistan. Some of them are secret; most of them are not open to public tender. They've also developed a private security company, Anchorlight Services, to protect their construction workers and convoys. You may remember there was some trouble when a platoon of their employees opened fire and killed seventeen innocent Iraqis. What you might not know is that they were using a consultant for these security operations in the form of a famous, or infamous, depending on how you look at it, British ex-army officer who'd been with the Staffords and later became a mercenary. His name is Colonel Ryder Forsyth.'

Mercy's eyebrows went over a hump.

'Do you know him?' asked Hines, missing nothing.

'That was my ex-husband's old regiment. He fought with the Staffords in the 1991 Gulf War.'

'As did Ryder Forsyth until he quit the army in 1994 and went into ... well, let's call them "activities" in Africa. It also appears he never made it beyond captain in the Staffords, but calls himself Colonel.'

'You're making him sound a bit dodgy, sir,'

'Well, he isn't squeaky clean. How can you be if you're a mercenary in Africa who then slipped off the radar and reappeared in strange places like Colombia and Central America, where he specialised in "planned operations for the release of kidnap hostages"?'

'How did he get involved with Kinderman?'

'He pulled off an extraordinary rescue operation of Kinderman oil employees who'd been kidnapped in Mexico, one of whom happened to be the son of the then CEO of Kinderman Services and Logistics in South and Central America. By all accounts it was a real Chuck Norris job. The boy was being held by a very nasty drug baron, and Forsyth went in there and not only killed the gang hierarchy but rescued the hostage unhurt. He was secretly given a medal by the Mexican president and God knows what by Kinderman. Right man, right connections, right time.'

'And he's involved in this job?' asked Mercy.

'I'm afraid so. Such is the reach of Kinderman into the British government that they have been able to force, or should I say coerce us into a joint operation. So in this particular case the kidnap consultancy will be run by Ryder Forsyth, the special investigation unit will be ours – i.e. you – and the CIA will be doing whatever they do and feeding us any relevant intelligence.'

'Sounds like a nightmare,' said Mercy.

'At least they've recognised that they need our help on the ground, that London is our turf, but even that was touch and go,' said Hines.

'Do we, or the CIA, have any reason to believe that the kidnap has been undertaken by anyone other than a criminal gang seeking financial gain?'

'Not in any obvious way, but when the Kinderman corporation is involved in anything, the US government sits up and takes notice. That means, given the sensitive nature of a number of their projects in the Middle East, Iraq and Afghanistan, the CIA will at the very least be listening in, and more than likely extremely active.'

'This being an organised kidnap with evident planning, can we assume that the gang would know what they're taking on and be prepared for some intense heat?'

'They'd be mad not to,' said Hines.

'You said "in this particular case", sir. So there've been other kidnaps?'

'Six in the space of thirty-two hours,' said Hines. 'Three in the early hours of the fifteenth, four hostages taken. We're not entirely sure of the timings. Siena Casey, daughter of an Australian mining heiress, went missing from a party in Hackney. Karla Pfeiffer, daughter of Deal-O supermarket heir Hans Pfeiffer, was kidnapped along with Wú Gao, the son of Chinese real estate queen Wú Dao-ming, after attending a nightclub in the West End. And finally Rakesh Sarkar, the son of Uttam Sarkar, the head of commodities conglomerate Amit Sarkar Group, has disappeared but they're not quite sure when ... or how. The parents in all cases have received phone calls asking for the same demand for expenses, which in each case is the first they knew of their child's disappearance. There was a further kidnap yesterday morning on the outskirts of the St George's Hill Estate in Weybridge, when a car taking nine-year-old Yury Yermilov to Danes Hill School in Oxshott was held up. This time the driver and bodyguard were murdered. Driver shot four times in the head and chest, bodyguard once in the head and the boy kidnapped. Irina Yermilov, the boy's mother, received a phone call this morning again asking for twenty-five million pounds, not for ransom, just for expenses. Time and location to be nominated.'

'Is this where the SVR come in?'

'Sergei Yermilov, the boy's father, is, to put it bluntly, ex-mafia. I say ex, but I don't think you ever leave the Russian mafia. I think your role is just redefined. He works very closely with Anatoly Zykov, who is the A to Z of the president's personal finances. So we're talking about someone who is well plugged in to the Kremlin and is a member of one of the largest and most brutal mafia groups, called Solntsevskaya. He started off working in Prague as a *krysha*, some kind of enforcer, and gradually worked his way up to brigadier, eventually becoming the *sovietnik* or adviser to the boss. The precise nature of his current activities is not well known. Research is going to have to be done, or we're going to have to rely on information from the SVR.'

'Have they nominated someone like Ryder Forsyth to run this kidnap?'

'Not yet. I think they're waiting to see what we'll put in place, and because we haven't got to the half of it yet, we're still in the planning stage.'

'So what's going to be my role in all this?'

'I want you to run and co-ordinate the special investigations teams for all the kidnaps and make sure that the relevant information is fed to the consultants handling the negotiations,' said Hines. 'We're going to Thames House now. Apart from the Home Office, the Joint Intelligence Committee, MI5 and MI6, there will also be Peter Makepeace of the OCC and various bods from the Joint Terrorism Analysis Centre.'

'What about the kidnap consultants?'

'I will be co-ordinating them,' said Hines, handing her a sheet of paper. 'Here is your contact list. You know all our consultants, but I would suggest you and DS Papadopoulos introduce yourselves to Colonel Forsyth and let him know how you're going to proceed with the investigation into the Kinderman girl. He'll want to know.'

'Does that mean you want me to run that investigation personally as well as co-ordinating the rest?'

'With DS George Papadopoulos, yes. You will have a team collating all the intelligence from the other investigations and feeding it out,' said Hines.

'Do I have to take orders from Forsyth?'

'You have to … accommodate him and report to both of us,' said Hines. 'You know how it is with the Americans when it's one of theirs. I've managed to retain my position as director of operations overall, but I'm under no illusions as to when I might get carved out of the Kinderman process.'

Silence while Mercy's mind writhed.

'Anything else, DI Danquah?'

This was the moment to come clean. Now was the last possible time. Tell him and walk away from the biggest investigation of her career. No contest.

'Only that DCS Makepeace always called me Mercy, sir.'

It was a short walk from Tanya Birch's flat to the Special Forces Club where Boxer had arranged to meet his old friend from MI6, Simon Deacon. He left his coat in the cloakroom, went upstairs to the bar, saw Deacon waiting for him by the window looking out into the street. The grey light glanced off his hard, lean, scraped face and prominent cheekbones. He turned, held up a hand. The small nick of a scar under his left eye was his only blemish apart from the two deep lines above the bridge of his nose, which gave him a permanent frown. It made him look perplexed at what was going through his own mind, while being curious about what was going through yours.

'Been a while,' said Deacon, standing, giving his old friend a hug. 'Can't stay for long, there's a big pow-wow due at Thames House. How's my god-daughter getting along? Haven't seen her since last summer. Still on the straight and narrow?'

'I'm not sure the straight and narrow is a path that Amy's ever going to successfully tread,' said Boxer. 'You know she chucked in her course at Bristol University? Couldn't justify the debt. But she's happy working for me now at the LOST Foundation.'

'She told me, and likes the work too. I can understand her not wanting to start life forty grand down and she's a kid who likes to get her hands dirty. She said it's not just finding the missing persons that she likes but persuading them to go back to their families. So things must be working out well between Mercy, you and her.'

'Yes, they are. Not easy, but we're in a new era where we actually talk and everything seems possible.'

'And Isabel?'

'Great,' said Boxer, swerving away from revealing the pregnancy, wanting to give Amy and Mercy the news first face to face with nothing else on their minds.

'A man in love, I'd say.'

'You could be right,' said Boxer. 'No, you *are* right ... why be cagey about it? I'm crazy about her.'

They looked at each other. Deacon smiled.

'Good to see you happy, my friend,' he said. 'Coffee?'

Boxer nodded, sat back and asked after Deacon's wife and children. The barman brought the coffee, left them in peace. They were alone in the long, dimly lit room lined with special ops team photographs. Boxer gave Deacon the Conrad Jensen story. The only reaction he got was a repetition of that extraordinary American name.

'Walden Garfinkle?'

'Mean anything to you?'

'He's a CIA troubleshooter. He doesn't specialise in any particular geographical area so you're as likely to see him in South Korea as you are in Argentina. He deals with personnel problems. Agents gone rogue, suspected doubles, people with mental problems: full breakdown, inability to differentiate their front from reality, total betrayal. That kind of stuff.'

'And why would he go and see Conrad Jensen, who as far as I know is a contractor not an agent?' said Boxer. 'Then again, his girlfriend told me he was very active around the Edward Snowden debacle. Could he be operating on both sides of the fence?'

'Conrad Jensen? That name *does* ring a bell somewhere. I know I've seen it before, or heard it, just can't think where,' said Deacon, tilting his head back, searching his mind. 'Got it. Not surprised it didn't jump out at me. One of those career episodes I'd rather forget. For your ears only, Charlie. He was on the list of interrogators in one of the black sites they used for extraordinary rendition.'

'Sounds ugly.'

'It's not something I'm proud of. I had to go to the Temara interrogation centre, in a forest outside Rabat, after the London bombings in 2005 to oversee an interview with a terror suspect. We wanted the opportunity to put some questions to him and I was sent with a colleague from MI5.'

'Not one of our finest moments,' said Boxer.

'When you're interviewed for MI6, they ask you how you feel about interrogation techniques and in theory you find yourself able to accept that sort of thing for Queen and country, but the reality is very … sullying. When I flew back to London I bought a new set of clothes, dumped the old ones, didn't want even the smell of that place in my own home.'

'And Temara was where you met Conrad Jensen. Was he an interrogator?'

'Yes, he was an active member of the interrogation team. We watched the process through an observation panel, wrote down our questions, which were handed to the guys doing the work, and listened to the answers they ... extracted. Our CIA counterpart told us afterwards that the team we'd seen were not CIA. They'd been contracted to do the job, as if that might make us feel better about what we were doing.'

'What did Jensen look like then?'

'I didn't see that much of him. He wore a surgical mask during the interrogation and only flipped it off when he came out for a breather,' said Deacon, looking into his head, trying to recall. 'He was in his sixties, but didn't look it. Hair dyed dark. A good-looking man with a strong face, one that you would trust. His eyes ... we both remarked on his eyes on the flight back because it was the only part of his face we saw properly in the harsh light of the interrogation room. They were intense, because they were so blue, but somehow not cruel; in fact rather sad, as if this ugly business was painful to him, but had to be done. The CIA guy told me he'd been working with him since the War on Terror kicked off in 2001. He spoke fluent Arabic.'

'Had they known him before?'

'*He* hadn't, but the agency had. He didn't say in what capacity.'

'His daughter says he makes a lot of money from these military contracts. When I said tens of millions, she replied: "More." It seemed like a lot for a guy working as a lone operator. No office, no partners. She also said he was doing illegal stuff, or rather, work that the US military wanted done below the radar.'

'Don't get involved, Charlie,' said Deacon. 'Call the police. Let them sort it.'

'You know me. I find it difficult to walk away from this kind of thing.'

'Just when you've reached a point of real happiness for the first time in your life?' said Deacon. 'I can see it. It's written all over you. Why fuck it up?'

'It's in my nature. I mean ... not to fuck it up, but to want to help people in distress.'

'I'd agree if I was sure you were in touch with the truth, but you're not,' said Deacon. 'There *are* private security companies with contracts worth hundreds of millions, but they're big security operations with, for example, the US Embassy in Kabul, or creating massive IT systems for tracking terrorist networks. But that kind of money doesn't get spread around to one-man bands for anything illegal or covert. Too difficult to hide.'

'Unless he was subcontracted via a larger private security company,' said Boxer. 'Any ideas how I could get in touch with Walden Garfinkle?'

'If you think you're going to get any more truth from him than from this Siobhan character, think again. He's a player. You're not equipped to deal with the likes of Garfinkle.'

'Who said I had to deal with him? I just want to talk.'

'There's no such thing as talking with these guys. Everything is a negotiation. It's their currency.'

'He's the only other lead I've got who's actually seen Jensen this year. You're next, but nine years adrift,' said Boxer. 'Then, of course, there's always Martin Fox.'

'I thought you'd finished with him,' said Deacon. '*He* thinks you've finished with him.'

'I don't want to work with him any more,' said Boxer. 'That job two years ago, he got too close to me, Mercy and Amy. He knows you too. I don't like that mixture of private life and work.'

'But you'll tap me for intelligence.'

'You're my brother and not just in arms.'

Boxer could see how pleased Deacon was to hear that.

'I thought Martin Fox might have been behind this,' said Boxer. 'Thought he might be trying indirectly to tempt me back into the fold. So I saw him last night.'

'Why did you think he'd have a hand in it?'

'Instinct,' said Boxer, quickly. 'I don't think it's totally out of the question that someone like Conrad Jensen could have been working for the US military through Pavis, do you?'

'But not below the radar,' said Deacon. 'That's not Martin Fox's modus operandi. He's always been totally above board.'

Silence. Boxer looked out of the window.

'So how did it go with Fox?' asked Deacon.

'I didn't change my mind about working for him, if that's what you mean,' said Boxer. 'I've heard you're very pally with him these days ... he said.'

'I've known him a long time and not just through you,' said Deacon. 'He's always been a reliable source of quality information. I've put him forward for security jobs in Afghanistan by way of reward and he's always performed better than expected. My relationship with him is as good now as it was fifteen years ago, which is why I'm surprised not only that you don't trust him, but also that you could think him capable of, what shall we call them, dark acts?'

'You're right,' said Boxer. 'Maybe I've let something get out of control in my own mind.'

'But what? You must have had good reason to doubt him or to intuit his involvement. Did Siobhan say something that pointed you towards Martin?'

'Yes, you're right, the truth gets messy in Siobhan's mind,' said Boxer. 'I shouldn't have paid so much attention to her. Forget it.'

'You're holding something back,' said Deacon. His phone rang, he checked the screen. 'I've got to go now.'

'Don't forget about Garfinkle.'

'I won't,' said Deacon. 'Remember who your friends are, Charlie.'

11

09.10, 16 JANUARY 2014
Thames House, Millbank, London SW1

The seriousness of the situation was immediately apparent, not only from the number of people in the boardroom but also the quality of the personnel. For a start, the Minister for Policing and Criminal Justice was present, flanked by two civil servants. Mercy was relieved to see some faces she knew. Simon Deacon immediately came over to say hello.

'Just had a coffee with Charlie,' he said, kissing her.

'What are you and Charlie cooking up?'

'Just the usual info exchange. He wants me to track down some CIA guy for him,' said Deacon, surveying the room. 'Looks like I'm in the right place.'

'Are you the only rep from MI6?'

'They're not going to send five regional heads,' he said, nodding. 'I've got to go back and brief them all.'

'Does anybody know what we're talking about yet?'

'No interest has been declared by the kidnappers. MI5 haven't picked up anything. Must be a tight ship to get past them. So we wait and see,' said Deacon.

Peter Makepeace came over and they were interrupted by a call to the table. Mercy and Makepeace sat with Hines, while Deacon went over to the intelligence side. A senior officer from MI5, Mike Stanfield, chaired the meeting.

'I think you've all had preliminary briefings about these five kidnaps, which were conducted over an estimated period of thirty-two hours between around midnight on the fifteenth to about

8.30 a.m. on the sixteenth of January. We've concluded from the time frame and the nature of the ransom demand – or should I say "expenses" demand – that all these kidnappings are connected. One of the reasons we have gathered this extraordinary meeting is that in every case the victim's parents are in some way connected to the government of the country from which they come.

'Rakesh Sarkar's uncle is the Minister for Commerce and Industry in the Indian government. Hans Pfeiffer's sister is married to the German finance minister. Wú Dao-ming's brother is one of the eighteen members of the Chinese politburo as vice chairman and secretary general of the National People's Congress. Anastasia Casey has just bought into one of Australia's largest media organisations, is on first-name terms with the prime minister and her grandfather was governor general. Ken Bass is a close personal friend not only of the vice president of the United States, but also of the prime minister of the UAE. His ex-wife is an old school friend of our prime minister's wife. And finally Sergei Yermilov is intimately connected to the Russian president through his links to the president's banker.

'The only other thing that connects the parents in these kidnaps is that they are all billionaires – it has to be said that estimating Yermilov's personal wealth wasn't easy, although he did buy a luxury apartment in the Shard last year for fifty million, which must somehow qualify him.

'We have, as yet, not found any clear, all-embracing reason why a terrorist organisation would target these individuals. While Kinderman is an obvious candidate for Islamic terrorism because of its work for the US government in Iraq and Afghanistan, Yermilov's connection to the Kremlin might be of interest to a Chechen or Georgian organisation, Wú Dao-ming's reach into the politburo might be of interest to rebel communities in Xinjiang, Anastasia Casey's mining operations could antagonise conservationists and Aboriginal tribes, Hans Pfeiffer's connection might excite rebellious elements in southern European nations who've grown to dislike the Germans, and the Sarkar family could be vulnerable to Pakistani terrorism just by being Indian. There is nothing they have in common that could make them the target of a single terrorist entity. And we at MI5 and GCHQ have not picked up on any new organisation that's specifically targeting billionaires.

'So in the absence of any obvious terrorist motive, until perhaps a more subtle one is revealed to us by the kidnappers, our first task is to try to establish the nature of the group who've planned and carried out these abductions. What we do know is that they have pulled off a series of expensively arranged and very well-executed kidnaps.

'We have no idea how Rakesh Sarkar was taken. His car was eventually traced to a street off Ladbroke Grove with no CCTV cameras, so there is no record of how it got there or how he was removed from it. He was last seen by his girlfriend in Shoreditch at around 11.30 on the fifteenth of January. Hans Pfeiffer's chauffeur, Klaus Weber, woke up dazed and confused at seven in the morning of the fifteenth in his Mercedes, which had been parked in a street in Plaistow. He has a recollection of going for a coffee with a fellow chauffeur, whose name was Jack, and who was waiting with him in a street near the Chinawhite nightclub, supposedly for Scarlett Johansson, but while we've been able to establish that she was in London, we know she was not in the club that night. Siena Casey's friend Jerry Hunt says she disappeared from a party with a guy who'd given them some top-quality cocaine, but he was unable to come up with any name other than "Joe" and gave a sketchy description of the man he assumes she left with as "long blonde hair, goatee, very fit". We might get more intelligence from the Sophie Railton-Bass kidnap once the special investigations unit gets to work on it. At least it happened in daylight, although it was in a mews and occurred under cover of a scaffolding sheet. Only in the first daytime kidnap, when the Yermilov boy was taken, are there possible breaks. Two police cars were spotted leaving the scene. The traffic on the Byfleet Road was stopped by two trucks and we have a description, but not of the drivers and no registrations. We are hoping for some clues from the ballistics.

'What this particular kidnap shows is the organisation and confidence of the team carrying it out. The traffic was stopped for less than five minutes while the operation was in progress. In that time drastic decisions were taken to kill the driver and bodyguard, possibly because they would be able to identify their assailants, but also because, as mafia henchmen, they were probably prepared to take them on. Their Russian-made weapons were found at the scene.'

'You seem to be implying that the level of planning and preparedness to take action would mean that these people are professionally trained,' said the minister. 'Possibly army or special forces?'

'As you know, Minister, there are now thousands of private security companies in the world. Most of their personnel *are* professionally trained. Some of the top security companies can attract people from special forces, for instance Anchorlight, who are the PSC under the umbrella of the Kinderman Corporation, have ex-Navy SEALs, Rangers and special ops people on their books. Many London-based PSCs have ex-SAS and SBS personnel on their staff. It's also well known that the US military are making more use of private contractors than ever before, some of whom they train or retrain to perform the tasks they want them to do. There are over a hundred thousand of them in Afghanistan alone at the moment.'

'So someone with an idea could easily recruit the personnel to carry it out?' said the minister.

'May I?' said an American opposite Mercy.

'Clifford Chase, London station chief of the CIA, please go ahead.'

Chase had straight blond hair, which flopped over his forehead so that he had to constantly brush it back. He had blue eyes under eyebrows that disappeared into his face and a mouth with no lips which made a fierce dark line below his nose. He was the epitome of the clean-cut American with the stamp of Ivy League on him.

'I'd like to introduce Ray Sutherland, the head of counter intelligence for Europe and Russia, in the UK,' said Chase.

Sutherland leaned forward, straightened his back. He was wearing a dark blue suit, white shirt, red tie. His hair was side-parted and dyed black. The only remarkable thing about his face was that his right eye winced permanently, as if he'd spent too much of his life looking through keyholes. Behind Chase and Sutherland were two men in identical dark blue suits, one with a red tie, the other with a blue tie. The red-tied man was shaven-headed and built like a US Marine; the blue-tied man was slim, with limp brown hair and green eyes. Mercy thought that all four men looked impervious to humour and incapable of charm.

'It's true that there are a lot of highly trained personnel out there,' said Sutherland. 'It's also true that they go in and out of employment on contracts. So they could have done six months in Iraq, six in Afghanistan, a few months in Africa, South America. Not many PSCs have permanent staff other than administrative. But what we do know about this community supplying the PSCs is that it's tight. All these guys talk to each other about what they're doing. It would be difficult to set up a series of kidnaps like this without people hearing about what's going down. Especially as most of these guys are motivated by money, and as I understand it, the "expenses" demands stand at one hundred and fifty million pounds, which sounds like a profit-motivated enterprise. So we at the CIA have put in motion within the US a deep investigation amongst all private contractors to the US military. I would suggest the same could be done here in the UK.'

Mike Stanfield nodded as if this had already been thought about, discussed, and agents were taking action.

'Has anybody thought to calculate approximately how many people might be involved in a series of kidnapping like this?' asked the minister.

'It's difficult to say with the night-time abductions,' said Stanfield. 'But the daytime ones we reckon would have required at least ten people to accomplish. We assume that because they happened on different days, the same team carried out both kidnaps. We're not sure what happened with Sarkar, but his car was involved and the only way to get it to stop would have been by the police. We know they had access to police vehicles and uniforms. Klaus Weber has mentioned this other chauffeur, Jack, who would probably have had an accomplice to overwhelm Weber. We think it happened at about the same time as the Sarkar kidnap, meaning separate teams. The Siena Casey kidnap was performed by a lone male, maybe with backup. So that's, say, three for the Sarkar kidnap, the same for the Pfeiffer and maybe just two for Siena Casey, plus ten for the two daytime ones and a further seven to ten perhaps involved in sourcing cars, trucks, spray-painting, co-ordinating and intelligence gathering. So maximum thirty people.'

'And have the lines of communication already been agreed between, say, MI5 and MI6 and the CIA?' asked the minister. 'Has anybody heard from the SVR yet?'

'Nothing from the SVR so far,' said Stanfield. 'And we already have good lines of communication with our allies in the intelligence field.'

That drew a weighted silence from the community around the table, which was broken once more by the minister.

'And what's happening with all these families who've lost their children?' he asked.

'I think DCS Oscar Hines can help with that,' said Stirling.

'In the case of Hans Pfeiffer and Wú Dao-ming, who are in the UK, we've sent two kidnap consultants to the Pfeiffers' house in Chelsea, one of whom is Chinese-speaking. They are in the process of setting up crisis management committees for both parents. Rakesh Sarkar's mother is on her way over from Mumbai and the father will follow. Anastasia Casey will arrive tomorrow. I believe she has her executive director and an Australian consultant standing by. I have a Russian-speaking team at the St George's Hill Estate advising the Yermilovs; they have told me that Sergei Yermilov has ignored them and spent every moment on the phone since his return from Moscow, pulling together all the resources of the mafia and the SVR, with permission from the president himself. I understand that the Kinderman Corporation have appointed their own kidnap consultant to run the negotiations for Emma Railton.

'I will be director of operations and I have appointed DI Mercy Danquah as the co-ordinator of the special investigations teams. She will also take personal charge of the Sophie Railton-Bass case. I have given orders to four other special investigation teams, who will be looking into the other kidnaps. We also have a communications team setting up in our Vauxhall offices who will co-ordinate all the information gathered by the special investigation teams and disseminate it to all the consultants. I have a contact list here that I would like everybody to have, and for them to open lines of communication with the relevant personnel.'

One of the civil servants leaned in to the minister and whispered something.

'Are we agreed on a media blackout for the moment?' said the minister.

Everybody nodded. The minister stood and left the table with his small entourage. The discussion carried on for a further twenty minutes as contacts were established, and then the meeting dispersed. Deacon was talking to the CIA men when Mercy came over to say hello to Ray Sutherland, who in turn introduced the red-tied bull of a man as Hank Mitchell and the blue-tied blond as Troy Novak. She instantly intuited from their handshakes and eye contact that none of them were comfortable with two unalterable facts: that she was black and a woman.

'As you've just heard, I'll be running the special investigation units on the ground,' she said. 'I just wanted to let you know that if you have any questions about London or need any local knowledge, please don't hesitate to call.'

They all nodded, but she knew she wasn't going to hear from any of them, nor would they be a source of help for her teams. The three men said their goodbyes and moved away.

'Genial trio,' said Mercy.

'They're very edgy,' said Deacon.

'About what?'

'The Kinderman involvement, the expertise, and the possibility that one of their own is involved. You know, an ex-CIA guy or a contractor.'

'I didn't get the feeling there was going to be a free flow of intelligence coming from them.'

'Nor did I,' said Deacon. 'So much for the special relationship. Did you register the silence when our allies were mentioned?'

'Heard the mice farting.'

'By the way, Mercy, are you all right?' he asked, appearing squarely in her vision.

'What do you mean?' said Mercy, thinking this man missed nothing.

'You just look a little ... preoccupied, that's all.'

'Me?' she said. 'When I'm just about to embark on the biggest case of my career? Preoccupied? You've got to be kidding.'

'Where are you?' asked Mercy.

'Knightsbridge,' said Boxer. 'What's this number you're calling me on?'

'Disposable phone,' said Mercy. 'Can we meet? I'll explain.'

'Are you around here somewhere?'

'I'm about to start a very complicated job in Belgravia.'

'I thought—'

'That's why I want to talk,' said Mercy. 'Give me the name of a place and I'll be there in ten.'

'Gran Caffe on the corner of Basil Street and Hans Crescent.'

Boxer hung up, turned back from Knightsbridge tube station and went to the café. He ordered an espresso and called Amy.

'Did you speak to your mother?'

'Yes.'

'And?'

'I told her to come clean to her new boss.'

'Where are you now?'

'Islington. I went home, changed, packed a few things and I'm on my way back to look after Siobhan.'

'Any news from her?'

'I doubt she's gone anywhere in her state.'

'Be careful of Siobhan,' said Boxer. 'You seem fascinated and I can understand why, but she's difficult, by which I mean economical with the truth. She's also had the benefit of some training from her father, and I've just spoken to Simon Deacon, who tells me that Conrad's long career has not always been pretty.'

'What does that mean?'

'There's been some spying and it's clear to me that some of those techniques have been passed on to Siobhan. He's also been involved in the uglier side of interrogation,' said Boxer. 'I've spoken to Tanya, too. I know there's no love lost between them, but I've seen and heard enough to know that Siobhan is at best unpredictable and at worst dangerous.'

'All right,' said Amy. 'You've made your point. I'll be careful.'

Boxer saw Mercy appear out of the crowds in front of Harrods. He hung up, ordered her a flat white.

'What's with all the secrecy?' he asked. 'And where's George?'

'Do you know Colonel Ryder Forsyth?' asked Mercy, sitting down opposite, tearing her gloves off.

'Colonel?'

'Maybe, maybe not. Anyway, Ryder Forsyth ... from your time in the Staffords.'

'Yes, I know him,' said Boxer. 'But let's start at the beginning, Mercy. As in ... what the hell's going on?'

'I'm on a job,' said Mercy.

'You said it was complicated.'

'It is. Kidnaps ... lots of them, a whole series. And you know me. Got to keep the brain on the go.'

'I just spoke to Amy. She said that she'd told you to come clean.'

'I weighed it up and decided against,' said Mercy. 'What did Glider tell you?'

'Not much. I don't think he's involved, if that's what you mean. He's promised me some leads,' said Boxer. 'But Mercy, let's just talk this through. Your head's not on straight.'

'Tell me about Ryder Forsyth.'

'We fought in the same unit in southern Iraq in the Gulf War.'

'Was he an officer?'

'Not then. He was an NCO. He annoyed people by always volunteering our unit for the most dangerous possible missions,' said Boxer. 'He applied for a commission afterwards and was made captain.'

'Did you keep in touch?'

'We weren't friends but I knew about him. Simon Deacon kept up with him. He used Ryder when he was on the Africa desk then lost touch. I came across him through one of my American contacts and we worked together once in Colombia rescuing hostages from FARC rebels. I was the consultant and he did the gung-ho stuff.'

'Was he any different to when you knew him in the Staffords?'

'He'd been through a lot. He was a recovered alcoholic. And when running the security on a film shoot in Ecuador, he ended up having an affair with a famous and married American actress, which ended badly for both of them. He'd also had a triple bypass and a hip replacement and had lost an eye, which he covered with a black patch in those days. He's that sort of person. Never

111

does anything by halves. But what's Ryder Forsyth got to do with anything?'

'He's the consultant on one of the kidnaps,' said Mercy.

'But he's freelance. Since when did the Met … ?'

'It's no different to how you and I ended up working together on the D'Cruz case,' said Mercy. 'Forsyth's kidnap is the most important one, politically speaking. So I'm acting as his personal special investigations unit and co-ordinating all the other SI teams.'

'Don't do it, Mercy. Come clean and get out now while you still can without hurting anybody.'

'As soon as I know why they're holding Marcus, I'll make my final decision.'

'You'll be in too deep by then and you know it. They'll make sure you won't be able to extricate yourself. It's a set-up. It's been planned.'

'We don't know anything until we know it.'

'Have the gang holding Marcus been in touch again?'

Silence.

'I'll take that as a yes,' said Boxer. 'Tell me.'

More silence as Mercy stared hard out of the window.

'Another threat?' asked Boxer.

'They're watching me,' said Mercy. 'They must have seen me with Amy because they said she'd be next if I talked.'

'This is out of control,' said Boxer. 'You can't go into a job with this background music. Who is Ryder Forsyth working for?'

'Strictly P and C?'

'Of course, you don't even have to ask.'

'I do, because it's the Kinderman Corporation. The CEO's daughter has been kidnapped.'

'There'll be money in that, political pressure and Christ knows what else.'

'Money's all they've asked for … so far. Not a ransom, but … expenses.'

'Expenses?'

'Twenty-five million's worth.'

'Is Forsyth employed directly by Kinderman or through a private security company?'

'I think it's direct. They have a history.'

'Find out for me.'

She suddenly reached across the table and grabbed his hands, looked long and hard into his face.

'You want me to do something for you, I can tell.'

She dropped her forehead down on to the union of their hands.

'I can't ask you to do this,' she said, whispering into the tabletop.

'Look at me,' said Boxer. 'You can ask me anything you want and I'll do it for you. You know that.'

'If I find the people holding Marcus, will you … deal with them?'

'*Deal* with them?' he asked, frowning.

'They've threatened Marcus, they've threatened Amy and they've threatened to break me … crush my bones and crumple my heart, to use their words.'

'And you think this is a better way to proceed than through the legal channels of the Met?'

'They're watching me. I don't know how. They must have someone on the inside. They knew I was the unit's top investigator.'

'And that you would be given the Kinderman job.'

'It's even bigger than the Kinderman job. There've been five kidnaps and six victims. We don't know what it's about. I've just had a meeting at Thames House and they've no idea … any of them MI5, MI6, JIC, not one of them,' said Mercy. 'All I know is that if I deviate from the gang's line, at the very least Marcus will die.'

'You can't be seen to be behaving strangely.'

'And that's the point … you can.'

'What exactly did you mean by *deal* with them?' said Boxer. 'And why would you think I'm the man to do that for you?'

'I know you have a gun, which you keep under the floorboards in your flat,' said Mercy. 'And no, I wasn't snooping. Amy told Marcus years ago. So she knows, too.'

'Amy?' said Boxer, nodding, things making sense, remembering his mother telling him how Amy had gone through her flat when she'd been left alone there. 'I've never had to use it, you know.'

'I knew what you were going to do to El Osito in Madrid.'

Silence as he recalled the baseball bat blows to the Colombian's knees and the more lethal one he'd planned to the man's head.

'Makepeace asked me what that was all about. I told him you were alone and under particularly stressful circumstances,' said Mercy. 'What I didn't tell him was that in your shoes I'd have done the same.'

'I don't think so.'

'What am I doing now?' said Mercy.

'There's one big difference.'

'No, I don't think so. I've found enough anger to step over a moral boundary,' she said. 'It surprised me. I don't know where it's come from. Do you?'

More silence from Boxer as he held her hands and stared out of the window, the layers of the past stacking up in his mind and the sense of equilibrium he'd felt stabilising his life only hours ago spinning out of control.

'Do you?' asked Mercy, eager to have the benefit of his experience in such extreme matters; worried, too, that he'd have no idea, that it might be something psychopathic in a man who'd been the first she'd ever loved.

'I wanted to tell you something important,' he said, stumbling through the nightmarish landscape of his subconscious. 'Something that might help you understand. Isabel is pregnant.'

It stunned her. The impact of the news and its incomprehensible relationship to what they'd been talking about.

'What does that mean?'

'She's going to have the baby.'

'I know what being pregnant means,' said Mercy. 'When's it due?'

'All being well, May.'

'Congratulations, but … what does that have to do with … with what we were talking about?'

'That's what it takes for a human being to morally transgress,' said Boxer. 'If any harm came to Isabel, I would not hesitate.'

A relief spread through her and she felt reconnected to the person she'd loved for more than twenty years. Her phone beeped and she looked at the text, said she had to leave.

'Give me any leads you can get from Glider,' she said, and kissed him on the cheek.

He watched her go, glad for the break, relieved that she hadn't questioned him further, because it was a place he hadn't visited for quite some time. In fact ever since he'd aimed that blow at El Osito's accusing face, he'd managed to avoid answering the questions raised by the Colombian's enquiring mind.

Amy knew the flat was empty the moment she opened the door. In the bedroom she found the duvet turned back and brownish stains on the pillow where Siobhan had dribbled in her sleep. She looked for a note. Nothing. She called Siobhan's mobile and heard its ringtone elsewhere in the flat. She called her father, told him Siobhan had gone and not taken her mobile.

'No sign of a break-in or a struggle?'

'Difficult to say. The flat's still a bit of a mess but the doors are intact and the locks were changed by your guy last night, so if they'd come back, they'd have had to bust the door down again.'

'There's nothing you can do, no way of contacting her. You'll just have to sit tight and wait.'

'Is that what you want me to do? There's other stuff back at the office.'

'I don't want you to go back to the office,' said Boxer. 'Your mother didn't come clean. After your meeting with her this morning, the gang made another threat in which you featured as the victim if she dared to talk to her colleagues. She thinks they've got someone on the inside. At least you're not moving on normal lines. They'll have difficulty finding you. So wait there and text me when Siobhan gets back.'

Amy started in the sitting room, worked her way methodically through the things that Siobhan had gathered up and thrown in the two suitcases. She sorted out the clothes that clearly belonged to Conrad Jensen, checked them, seams and all, for anything strange. She folded and packed his clothes into the Samsonite and went to work on Siobhan's. Then she crawled around the room tilting back armchairs and the sofa, looking underneath. Nothing. She moved into the bedroom and collected Siobhan's dirty clothes, stripped off the bloody pillowslip and tidied the bed. Underneath

115

she found a small piece of paper with a UK mobile number on it.

'Found what you're looking for?'

Amy screwed the paper up in her fist, turned and sat on the floor looking up at Siobhan, who was in skinny black jeans and the multi-zipped leather jacket. Her hair covered her puffy eye. The only visible damage from the night's attack was her bruised mouth, cut lip.

'You recovered quickly,' said Amy. 'Where've you been?'

'You're not my mum,' she said. 'I go where the fuck I like.'

'Without your phone?'

'Too easy to track.'

'So what were you doing that you didn't want to be tracked?' asked Amy. 'If we're working together, we've got to know your movements.'

'I was out buying something a little stronger than paracetamol.'

'Like?'

'Percocet. Paracetamol but with some oxycodone thrown in,' said Siobhan. 'I went out like a cripple and I've come back healed.'

Amy sent a text to her father.

'Reporting me to your superior?'

'He's trying to help you ... if that's what you want.'

Siobhan shrugged.

'What the fuck does that mean?'

'It means I've done what I've been told to do by Mark Rowlands. What else is there?'

'Don't you care about your father?'

'D'you care about yours?'

'Yes,' said Amy, looking at her steadily.

'Why? What did he ever do for you?'

'He put himself in danger for me,' said Amy. 'I didn't know him until that moment. What do you know about Conrad?'

'He's a spook ... or something like it. What can you ever really know about a spook?'

'Even spooks need love ... probably more than most if they're living in an artificial world.'

'You're clever for a kid,' said Siobhan. 'I can tell you listen. Most people don't. As far as love is concerned, my father doesn't want anything complicated. I told you, he doesn't show his feelings. It's probably a professional requirement, as well as the fact that the poor bastard's male and English.'

'So what's your motive for finding him?' asked Amy. 'Are you just being professional under instruction from Mark Rowlands?'

'Don't try and get inside *me*,' said Siobhan, pointing at her chest. 'You'll find a big NO fucking ENTRY sign right here.'

'But you're allowed to go around kissing me, winding me up sexually and emotionally, and fucking off without telling us?'

'That's my Cuban side. I'm mixed race as well as mixed gender.'

'We *should* get on, but we don't because you won't talk to me. You just give me a whole load of riddle-me-ree.'

'Riddle-me-what?'

'My gran's expression for nonsense,' said Amy. 'I'm not interested in riddle-me-ree, so if that's all you've got to give, I'll keep my distance.'

'*I'm* the one who does everything for *him* and he tells me nothing in return,' said Siobhan. 'Do this, do that, do the other. I'm like his ... his skivvy. Then he just walks off into the night without a fucking word and I'm left picking up the pieces, as per fucking usual.'

'Has this happened before?'

'No, he's never left me without a word of where he's going, but he has left me with a mess to clear up.'

'What about this time? Was that why you had to get out of here? Was it just for the Percocet, or something else?'

12

'So what was the vanishing act all about?' asked George. 'Is that another part of the cabaret you didn't tell me about?'

'I was gathering intelligence on Colonel Ryder Forsyth,' said Mercy. 'I was told that he was flying in on a Kinderman jet from Zurich, where he happened to be at the time of the kidnap, and that he wouldn't get here until, well, now, and he'd need some time to sort things out, so I thought I'd take the opportunity to do a bit of digging. Always good to go into an unusual scenario forewarned.'

'Maybe we should have taken a look at the crime scene,' said Papadopoulos. 'And why didn't you want me there for the intelligence-gathering bit?'

'I wanted you to be able to observe without preconceptions,' said Mercy. 'We're going into a much more complicated situation than usual and this guy Forsyth is a big personality working for a company with powerful connections in the US government. We have to get off on the right foot. But when I'm acting I don't always have the best powers of observation, which is where you come in. I'll be concentrating on forming a relationship with Forsyth, but there'll be a crisis management committee, which I'm sure will consist of some important people, given the nature of the child's mother's ties to Kinderman.'

They pulled up outside 31 Wilton Place, next to the grey brick Victorian church of St Paul's Knightsbridge. Mercy pressed the buzzer on the intercom, which was answered immediately. She was told to hold up both warrant cards to the peephole before they were admitted. A man in a dark blue suit, who did not introduce himself, took their coats, led them up to the first floor and showed them into a small sitting room, which was empty. He withdrew without offering anything.

The wealth on display in the conservatively decorated room silenced them. They sank into their respective armchairs and did not speak. Thick dark blue velvet curtains kept the gunmetal sky at bay. The grey fitted carpet gave background to a silk weave Tree of Life rug that was so sharp it looked as if it had been painted on the floor. Two prancing statuettes – a bronze of a hoofed Pan playing his pipes, and a fleeing girl – occupied the mantelpiece on either side of a Van Cleef & Arpels gold clock. There was a bookcase with leather bound volumes, which did not look much read, and four paintings, one on each wall.

'Know anything about art?' asked George in a whisper.

Mercy shook her head.

'Above your head's a Degas, that one over there is a Cézanne and the nude in the bath is a Bonnard,' said George. 'This one behind me is a Seurat, I think. That's about three mil just on these walls.'

'I'm impressed,' said Mercy. 'By you, not the paintings.'

'I did a history of art option at uni.'

The blue-suited one returned and took them upstairs to another, bigger living room. Sitting on the sofa was a man who seemed to be dressed in clothes he did not wear very often: dark blue worsted trousers and a white shirt under a grey jacket. His shoulders strained against the confinement and his feet looked awkward encased in black brogues. His hard, lean tanned face, which was borderline haggard from too much exposure to the sun, made him look as if he wore a wetsuit most of the year. He had one blue eye that seemed to work but the other eye, fixed in its socket, was made of glass and was brown. He had a number of head scars, as if he'd made the mistake of looking over the parapet just as the bullets started flying. He had long grey hair combed back in rails that rested on the collar of his jacket. The top of one ear was missing and the scar, from a machete blow, went to the corner of his glass eye. He stood, and at six foot four made the room feel small and crowded.

'Ryder Forsyth,' he said, in a voice that had had gravel raked over it.

They shook hands. Mercy noticed he had a finger missing. Despite her extensive life experiences, she felt like a teenager in this man's company, while Papadopoulos looked on the brink of taking an aeroplane out of his pocket and flying it around the room.

'You taken a look at Lyall Mews yet?' asked Forsyth. His accent, no longer entirely English, had developed a Texan drawl.

'I went to Thames House for a meeting and then came straight here for our briefing,' said Mercy.

'You'll see why it was chosen,' said Forsyth. 'I dropped by on the way here. There was scaffolding covered with plastic sheeting over the house on the right side and the street level window of the flat on the left has security shutters and a blind permanently drawn. I'm told that both places were unoccupied at the time. You might be lucky and find a witness in the mews, but I doubt you'll find anyone who overlooked the action. I reckon it took 'em less than a minute.'

'We're waiting for the forensics from the car, and it would be good to talk to the chauffeur.'

'I think you'll draw a blank on both,' said Forsyth. 'The gang was very well organised and the girl's chauffeur was just that: untrained in anything other than driving. Didn't even lock the doors, according to Mrs Railton-Bass.'

'Would it be possible to talk to Emma this morning?'

'Why?'

'As an investigator I like to have as much information as possible about the victim and the parents: a sense of their relationship, the mother's view of her child, the girl's personality, her strengths and weaknesses. All that right down to the clothes she was wearing, any illnesses, teeth missing ... you know, everything.'

'I'm not sure I understand the point,' said Forsyth. 'How's all that going to help you find her?'

'The point is we never know the detail that'll help us make the connection to where the girl is being held. We just need to know everything possible,' said Mercy. 'The last time we investigated a highly sensitive case of this kind we found that the kidnapped boy played trick football, and that gave us a crucial line of inquiry.'

'I'll talk to Mrs Railton-Bass,' said Forsyth. 'I'm trying to keep her mind as uncomplicated as possible … you read me?'

'We also like to form an emotional connection to our subject. It inspires us,' said Mercy. 'Have you heard from the gang again since this morning?'

'No, Mrs Railton-Bass just took that one call. We've had no proof of life, just a money demand.'

'Are you, the family or Kinderman expecting anything other than a money demand?'

'What do you mean by that?' asked Forsyth, with an edge to his voice.

'Kinderman is a big corporation and there's been a shift in public sentiment against them. They've been perceived as gaining unfair access to government contracts. There's been talk that they actively promoted the Iraq war for their own benefit. They also seem to have dodged a bullet in the oil spill scandal in the US Gulf. Since we've been in the austerity years, they've come under the spotlight again, as a number of their higher-profile employees are perceived as outstanding examples of the unequal distribution of wealth that might cause people to rise up and start a revolution. On top of that, Anchorlight have killed people in unstable parts of the world. So I'm sure there are people out there who could be looking for some sort of revenge: the Taliban, other religious extremists or maybe just destroyed families.'

'You're making some unfortunate implications,' said Forsyth.

'Unfortunate?' said Mercy, frowning. 'I'm just voicing some of the attitudes that prevail around the world. You don't have to take them as coming from me.'

'Whatever. We have people looking into that.'

'You mean the CIA?'

'I mean them and people contracted to the CIA.'

'You knew my ex-husband,' said Mercy. 'Charles Boxer. You were in the Staffords together.'

'I don't remember that name,' said Forsyth, shaking his head, which Mercy could see was a lie. 'Let me go and talk to Mrs Railton-Bass.'

Forsyth left the room. Papadopoulos looked at Mercy, eyebrows in his hairline. Mercy put her finger to her lips. They waited;

neither took a seat. Ten minutes went by. Papadopoulos walked over to a painting, stood there nodding at it.

'Now you're not going to tell me you don't know who this is by?' he said.

'I am, George. I don't have time for galleries.'

'Picasso? Heard of him?'

'I thought that was a car,' said Mercy, flat with irony.

'Very funny.'

Papdopoulos transferred his attention to some drawings on the wall.

'Goya,' he said. 'Nice.'

Mercy rolled her eyes. Forsyth came back into the room.

'She'll see you,' he said, pointing at Mercy, 'and only you.'

Mercy followed him out into a dark corridor. He shut the door behind them and turned.

'I understand I'm reporting to you,' she said. 'Am I going to meet the other investigators, those CIA contractors you mentioned? Or are we not going to pool our resources? I've just met three CIA guys this morning and I'm not sure they were very excited at the idea of any collaboration.'

'Don't worry about that. They're operating at a different level,' said Forsyth. 'You're on the ground, using your London knowledge. They're putting out their feelers in the spook world looking at terrorist networks, criminal organizations, that kind of thing. If they give me intelligence that I think would be useful to you, and vice versa, I will facilitate it, but I doubt your paths will cross.'

'This has all the feeling of a military operation about it,' said Mercy. 'You've got separate entities progressing towards a common goal with commanders in charge. I always think kidnaps work better with a more creative dynamic. That way we—'

'Kinderman don't care what you think. They just want you to do your job.'

'You sound like you don't trust me,' said Siobhan.

'My dad warned me, said you were at best economical with the truth.'

'So you listen to your dad,' said Siobhan, curious, 'and obey everything he says, like a good little girl?'

122

'He's had to deal with some difficult people: nasty, violent, manipulative, untrustworthy, cunning, lying, treacherous little bastards ... and that was just me when I was a teenager.'

'Thank God for that,' said Siobhan, spurting with laughter, 'I thought you were going grim on me.'

'I listen to him because he's not an idiot like most other dads I know, and I learn stuff from him, a lot of stuff. My mother, too.'

'Can't wait to meet *her*,' said Siobhan. 'Dinner must be a hoot around your place.'

'So where did you go?'

'I was following up a lead.'

'Without telling the people you've asked to help you?' said Amy, hardening. 'Maybe you should tell me about this lead.'

'I went to see a guy my father knows, someone from his world.'

'Why wait until now?'

'Because he's not the sort of person you find very easily,' said Siobhan. 'You have to go through others, tell him what it's about and be patient.'

'When did you kick this off?'

'After I'd called Mark Rowlands.'

'Does he know about this guy?'

'No. He's just the lawyer, he doesn't know anything about the everyday work,' said Siobhan. 'My father always told me to call Mark Rowlands if there was a problem. He also told me where to find a telephone number I could use, but only in a crisis. Once the days went by and I found myself calling Mark for the fourth or fifth time, I knew it was a crisis, so I went to get the number.'

'Where from?'

'A dead drop. Know what one of them is?'

'Got an idea. Sounds a bit olde worlde. Finding shit in bird boxes in parks.'

'This is buried in code on a computer website, which they change every week,' said Siobhan. 'Anyway, some guy answered and asked for my name and number and told me I would hear from them. A few hours later somebody called me back and asked me the nature of my business. I told them Dad had disappeared and they said they'd get back to me ... which they did, this morning.'

'So, talk me through it.'

'I had to go to a park bench on Highbury Fields, sit and wait. Eventually a guy came along, walked up behind me and asked me not to look at him. He sat at the other end of the bench, glanced across at me as you do, and then talked straight ahead, barely moving his mouth. I'd also told them I needed Percocet and he'd seen the damage to my face in the glance and asked me what had happened. I told him ...'

'Did you tell him it was something to do with your father? That they'd questioned you about him? Raped you?'

'I said nothing about the rape, but I told him the rest. He said he would drop a glove when he left; the Percocet was inside, and I should take it and then come after him with the glove as if he was a stranger.'

'Did he have any idea who it might have been who assaulted you?'

'No, but I could see he was ... not exactly showing concern, because these types don't show anything, but there was a flicker. As if he knew who they were or who'd sent them or something like that.'

'Did he have any news about Conrad?'

'Nothing. He said: "It's gone very silent out there." As if normally there'd be something, like white noise at the very least, but this time there was a total blank.'

'So what are our chances of finding him if these "friends" of Conrad can't pick up anything on the airwaves?' asked Amy.

'I would say the chances of you finding him are small.'

'Did they say they'd get back to you if they heard anything more? And ... who are *they* anyway?'

'They didn't say they'd get back to me, but they did ask where I was living, as if they might be keeping an eye on me. Who are *they*? God knows. Dad worked with a lot of people and I suppose he built up a network of highly trusted amigos and these are the guys he can rely on when something goes wrong.'

Boxer caught a bus to Green Park, took a call from Simon Deacon, who told him that Walden Garfinkle would be in touch. He was crossing the road to get the tube up to Highbury and Islington when a call came through from Garfinkle.

'I'm told we should talk,' said Garfinkle.

'I'm on Piccadilly, if that helps.'

'You know the Haymarket Hotel on Suffolk Place?'

'No, but I can get there.'

'Go to the concierge and tell him W. G. Grace sent you.'

Boxer walked up Piccadilly to the Circus and down Haymarket to Suffolk Place. He spoke to the concierge, who called a porter and mumbled in his ear. He followed the porter through the hotel to a small private room in which there was coffee and cakes. He poured himself some coffee and some minutes later a man fitting Tanya Birch's description of Garfinkle came into the room. They shook hands. Garfinkle's was large, padded and soft, more like an animal's paw that could produce claws if the occasion demanded. He poured himself some coffee and before taking a sip picked up a cake and put it whole into his mouth. He ate ruminatively with crumbs tumbling down his suit from his mouth. He sipped coffee again and repeated the process. Only then did he sit down, brushing flakes and crumbs from his suit.

'No breakfast,' he said, to explain his greed. 'What can I do for you, Mr Boxer?'

'Conrad Jensen disappeared on the twelfth of January and his daughter has asked me to find him,' said Boxer, who'd decided to come clean; no clever stuff with this kind of operator. 'You went to see him on New Year's Day in a rented house in the Cotswolds. I was wondering if you could help me.'

'In what way?'

'I understand Con was a contractor to the US military and that among other things he was involved in black site interrogations, the Arab Spring and Edward Snowden. I was wondering if any of these activities could have made him feel the need to disappear,' said Boxer. 'You are someone who works in his world. I understand you solve personnel problems in the CIA. You saw him just over two weeks ago. I would be interested in any insight you could give me.'

'You're a kidnap consultant.'

'That's right. I also run a foundation called LOST for finding missing persons. Normally they are cold cases that the police have given up on, but Con's daughter was sent to me by his lawyer, Mark Rowlands, and she persuaded me to help her.'

'So you're sure he hasn't been kidnapped?'

'The daughter has not had any such communication,' said Boxer. 'And if he had been kidnapped I would not be able to run the negotiation. That would have to be done by the Met's kidnap unit.'

'Why did the lawyer send Conrad's daughter to you when, forgive me for saying so, there must be far more effective investigators in London?'

'Possibly because I have a wide-ranging network of people I can draw on,' said Boxer. 'I would not be sitting here if I didn't.'

'I'd have thought Conrad would have some buddies he could rely on who would be far better connected than you and much more likely to be able to track him down. I mean, he knows some experts in their fields: espionage, terrorism, IT, interrogation, security, firearms, you name it, Conrad's done it,' said Garfinkle. 'You thought about that, Mr Boxer?'

Now he understood what Deacon meant about Walden Garfinkle.

'I have,' said Boxer. 'The lawyer researched his possibilities and came up with me. Siobhan came to see me in some distress at being walked out on. She didn't want the police involved, which told me something ...'

'What exactly?'

'That we were talking about an individual who is operating below the radar part of the time and doesn't want the authorities looking there because the people who pay him wouldn't want the police looking there either.'

'You mean us,' said Garfinkle, tapping his chest, 'when you say "the people who pay him"?'

'Only you would know if you have an exclusive arrangement.'

'So you think Conrad's lawyer chose you because you're not averse to operating outside the law of the land?'

'I think he chose me because I have a reputation for getting things done,' said Boxer. 'And I don't have any agenda other than finding him.'

Garfinkle looked at him with the eyes of a man used to assessing complicated people: hooded diamonds of light looking out from under the exuberant growth of his eyebrows, which were tweaked upwards at the ends. Boxer had the feeling that his assessment was crucial as to whether he would get answers or leave empty-handed.

'A conscience is a difficult thing in our business,' said Garfinkle. 'We need agents with conscience because to have them without would be like trying to shepherd a pack of psychopaths. Most of my problems with agents occur as a result of conscience. They reach a moral boundary too far.

'When they took on the job as young men and women, they were happy in their blissful ignorance to swear by Almighty God that they would do anything for the president and our great country of the United States of America. But as time goes on, these agents get older and they become men and women of experience. They develop relationships and some of them produce children. Whatever happens, gradually their conscience comes into play with their work. They are no longer just thinking about themselves and how they appear to their employers. They are conscious of how they might appear to others. It's not always easy to lie in bed next to someone when you've just killed a man or interrogated someone and be the same loving individual you were, especially when you cannot tell anyone what you have done.

'Sometimes agents cope by using delusional strategies. These have the short-term benefit of getting them through their day but the long-term prognosis for a delusional is not good. They become unstable. They don't know who they are any more. They lose sight of themselves. They behave strangely. They become unpredictable. They are oppressed by feelings of guilt that they don't understand.'

'Is this a state that Conrad Jensen had reached ... in your opinion?'

'The interesting thing is that he is not a young man. I would expect this kind of behaviour from an agent in his late thirties or early forties, but Conrad has already gone seventy.'

'Did he start late?'

'That's an interesting point. The first time we made use of him was in Cuba in 1989. We wanted information on how Cuba was going to cope with withdrawal of Russian economic support. How unstable it might become. And Conrad had just started a relationship with a woman who worked on the sugar board. We approached him and asked if he could help, and he was a natural. He was in his mid forties then. So yes, a late starter.'

'Do you know what he did before that?' asked Boxer. 'I mean, he was a man with a yacht, which means he'd made some money somewhere.'

'Of course we checked him out and made sure that he hadn't made his money from trafficking drugs or anything like that, and he was clean. He had a history of running businesses in the US, Europe and the Middle East and selling them on. He ran a number of IT companies developing database management software, which was big at the time. He spoke a lot of languages, including Arabic and Russian, which impressed us and made us wary too. We checked out his relationships to make sure there were no communist sympathies and again he was in the clear.

'He was very friendly with a couple in Damascus, a Syrian businessman who ran flour mills all over west Africa and the Middle East and was married to a Russian woman, which we assume is how he learnt those two languages. He made a lot of connections through the Syrian and was trading chemicals out of Libya and oil products out of Tunisia, and he even spent a few years trading sheanut out of Ghana and Benin. But that still doesn't mean I know precisely what he was doing before he was engaged. We didn't have a complete life history. That's what we're looking at now. All I know is that when he was employed he was not a communist and he was a businessman with no criminal record in any country prepared to tell us. When the War on Terror started back in 2001 he was in the perfect position to help us, which was when he set up his company, Jensen Security, and became an official CIA contractor.'

'Have you always employed him directly or have you ever used his services through another contractor?'

'That's a strange question, Mr Boxer.'

'I'm talking particularly about a company called Pavis Risk Management, run by a guy called Martin Fox.'

'I'll look into it. I don't associate the name with Conrad, but you have to understand I am not his operations officer.'

'You were talking about conscience in relation to Conrad. Was that what you went to talk to him about on New Year's Day?'

'Why do you ask?'

'I spoke to his partner, Tanya Birch, who told me that he seemed thoughtful after your visit. He sat in a room on his own for quite some time in a contemplative state,' said Boxer. 'I learnt from my friend Simon Deacon that Con had worked in a black site outside Rabat conducting interrogations in 2005. If anything was going to stimulate your conscience I'd have thought it would be something like that, but nothing happened for, what, another nine years? Was there something else that tipped him over the edge?'

'I understand from his operations officer that he wanted greater US involvement in Syria. When things really began to go off the rails in late 2011, he started getting angry because of US inaction. He could see that if something wasn't done, the whole country, whose people define themselves by their religion, was going to break up and splinter into factions, which would give the Islamic extremists their opportunity. *But*,' said Walden, holding up a fat, hairy finger, 'he also understood our position after the horror of Iraq and Afghanistan. He knew there was little appetite for it from either the government or the American public. He could also see the alarming possibility that it could develop into something confrontational with Russia. So he wasn't happy about it, but he accepted the US position.'

'And Snowden?'

'Look, I think he admired Snowden for having the guts to come out about something he felt was deeply wrong, but you have to understand that Conrad had been instrumental in putting together software teams to write the programs that would ultimately give the US government these internet surveillance powers. Conrad made a lot of money developing IT systems for the US government. He was part of the problem that had made Snowden angry enough to blow the lid on it.'

'That doesn't mean he couldn't develop a conscience about it,' said Boxer.

'No, that's true,' said Garfinkle.

'But clearly what you're saying is that none of these areas of difficulty were why you went to see him on New Year's Day.'

'My aim on New Year's Day was to find out what was on his

mind,' said Garfinkle. 'I'd been warned by his operations officer that something was troubling him. I'd met him a number of times over the years. I was especially active when we were operating the black sites, as this was clearly a step over a moral boundary that even the operations officers weren't happy about. We've had lengthy discussions over the years covering all areas of potential anxiety. Conrad was never a concern to me. Perhaps it was his maturity. I'm only a few years younger than him. We saw eye to eye on a lot of things. But I take it seriously when someone like Conrad appears to be unhappy. He knows a lot about our operations and some of them would be classified by the media as unsavoury to say the least.'

'You mean you're worried that he might be about to blow something open in the media?'

'When somebody does a disappearing act like this, we're always worried.'

'So how did you get on with him on New Year's Day?'

'We got on fine, as always. He just didn't tell me anything. I've understood more from you telling me that Tanya said he was very contemplative after I left,' said Garfinkle. 'That makes me think that he might be about to embark on something risky.'

13

Three is never an easy number around a table, especially when one of them was Ryder Forsyth. They'd had the awkward introduction, the commiseration and an initial chat, and Emma Railton, while revealing her frantic worry, had also shown herself to be intelligent, strong, focused and not given to sentimentality. She was a very attractive woman in her mid to late forties with blonde hair cut gamine style, minimal make-up around her grey eyes, a small red rosebud mouth and an hourglass figure that seemed both old-fashioned and yet incredibly sexy. Mercy was now trying to conduct the initial interview and neither of them was relaxed with the oppressive presence of Forsyth's personality.

'Ryder,' said Emma, finally, 'would you mind leaving us to have our talk by ourselves?'

'I don't think that would be advisable, ma'am.'

'I know you have your instructions from Kinderman, but first of all don't call me ma'am when I know you're English. My name is Emma. Secondly, just leave us alone. We're women, we know how to talk this out.'

Forsyth got up and left without a word.

'Thank God,' said Emma. 'Don't get me wrong, I think Ryder is tremendous, but you don't know what it's like. As soon as Kinderman is involved in anything, a colossal weight comes down on all the proceedings. Nobody can say a word without referring to some higher authority.'

'Was that one of the reasons why you left your husband?'

'I loved my husband...'

'Past tense?' said Mercy.

'Yes. We did love each other, but huge demands were made on Ken's time and our lives together. In the beginning he tried to leave the corporation but every time they made a big fuss. The vice-president ... of the United States, I mean, would make personal phone calls to him, urging him to reconsider. The remuneration packages went through the roof. And Ken found it very difficult to resist. There were other things too and he accepted that I couldn't carry on. I mean, there are some people who would kill to live in a four-bedroom apartment on the hundred and eighth floor of the Burj Khalifa with all the amenities of a luxury health spa, but it ain't me.'

'Was that it?' asked Mercy. 'You left him because you didn't like the lifestyle?'

Emma cast about the room looking for inspiration and gave up. 'No.'

'Nothing goes out of this room, but I do have to know everything. All the detail. The smallest things matter.'

'This wasn't a small detail,' said Emma. 'I found it increasingly difficult to live with the decisions that Ken was making on behalf of the Kinderman Corporation. I didn't like a lot of the things they were doing. I hated the subterfuge, the politics and the bare-faced lying that went on. Ken had worked all his life to be the CEO of a major American corporation, and at forty-nine years old he wasn't going to walk away from the top job in his world because I was miserable about some of his business ethics. He made his choice. Now he's got one of those trophy wives that come free when you buy a Lamborghini Veneno.'

They looked at each other, registered the seriousness of the revelation, and then laughed. On the back of that release of emotion tears suddenly came and Emma reached for the tissues.

'Sorry, I can't control it.'

'Don't worry. I know what it's like. Always there, trembling just below the surface.'

'You mean you're a kidnap investigator with a daughter who's been kidnapped?'

'A couple of years ago,' said Mercy, 'but she was older, more able to look after herself.'

'Oh, Sophie can look after herself all right. She's eight going on eighteen. She's an extraordinary girl. I wish I'd had her confidence at that age. She's almost more at home with the Kinderman board members than with her class at Francis Holland.'

'So she wouldn't have had dolls or teddies or anything like that?'

'Not exactly. Her only toy is a rag-doll frog called Zach. It's like an alter ego. Sometimes she has dialogues with Zach and other times she becomes Zach. It can be quite unnerving. I'd be driving with a friend sitting in the front and suddenly Zach would appear between us and look slyly from one to the other and say in a deep voice: "Hu-llo, la-a-adies." As if he was some gigolo or pimp. My friend would have to check behind just to make sure it was Sophie holding up the frog. It was that freaky.'

'Interesting,' said Mercy. 'You wonder where it comes from?'

'She's a very inventive little girl,' said Emma. 'We'd go on holiday and she'd take a girlfriend with her and they'd sit on rubber rings in the pool and play out these dialogues as if they were old women in a tea shop, or two old guys playing bowls, or the worst was a couple of teenagers sunbathing and going through their night on the town together, the boys they ended up with. Ken would tell me I had to do something about it. And I'd say in my best American: "Like what?" I mean, am I about to crush all creativity out of my child just because she's a bit weird? She might be a budding screenwriter and I'd have hammered it out of her. Forget it.'

'How did she get on with the chauffeur?'

'Yes, the chauffeur. I got rid of the Kinderman driver around about day two. He was one of those ex-marines, shorn back and sides with a crew cut on top, eighteen stone of pure muscle. He could run through doors, but only because he'd never remember it was easier to open them. Cars would bounce off him, but only because he would go and play in the rush hour traffic. He'd shake your hand with one finger because he'd put you in hospital if he did it properly. No conversation. Pre-programmed for total efficiency. Impossible.

'Now Pat Gould. He was *my* choice. A wonderful man. Irish. Loved a bit of banter and play-acting. Sophie adored him. They'd sit together up front, she never went in the back, and have these rip-roaring conversations with Pat pretending to be her music producer while Sophie was some idiotic child pop star. When he dropped her off at school she'd run through the gates as if she was being mobbed by paparazzi. After school one day I saw her waving at the window and looked out to find no one in the street. When I asked her what she was doing, she said, "Just waving at my adoring fans. You've got to, haven't you, Mum?"'

They laughed again and the tears came straight after.

'So you see,' said Emma,' she really is the light of my life. She makes me laugh like a drain.'

'Is she physically resilient?' asked Mercy. 'Does she have any illnesses, take any medication?'

'Since my separation from Ken she's developed what I call anxiety asthma. She has one of those pumps if she gets into trouble. It's never been an issue but I don't know how she'll react to the stress of being kidnapped. She appears to be self-reliant but she misses her father and relies a lot on me for emotional sustenance. She'll always call me during the day to ... to ...'

The tears came once more. Mercy reached over and squeezed her shoulder. Emma held on to her hand. Mercy asked her to describe the clothes Sophie was wearing (school uniform), any jewellery (pearl studs in her ears), lucky charms (a fossil of a bug embedded in a piece of rock), bracelets (two strings, orange and green, around her wrist), a watch (not one that she wore), and the mobile phone number. Emma handed over some photographs. They talked about teeth, hair and skin. It made Emma feel calm.

'I want to talk a bit more about your husband now,' said Mercy. 'I understand he was very generous to you in the divorce settlement and despite that he is still a very wealthy man. Has all that wealth been accumulated through his work for Kinderman?'

'His father was a very successful businessman. They were good Republican boys and always competed against each other until the day his father died suddenly of a stroke nearly ten years ago,' said Emma. 'He'd always said that Ken had to make his way in the world and that he wasn't going to inherit, that he didn't believe in handing wealth down because it spoilt the next generation. But Ken was already very well set up by the time his father died, leaving him a New York property portfolio and stocks and shares worth around four hundred million dollars.'

Mercy couldn't stop a reaction from her eyebrows.

'I know,' said Emma. 'The sums are fantastic. His father died in 2005 and Ken divested himself of that property portfolio over the following two years and reinvested in gold. He then bought into the banks after the credit crunch and reinvested in property in London, Shanghai and Sydney and made that four hundred million worth eight hundred million in seven years. At the same time his Kinderman shares were doubling and tripling and he was being awarded more and more so that he was very close to becoming a double billionaire by the end of last year. I know because he told me recently that Forbes had got it all wrong. They were nearly eight hundred million bucks out. Whatever ... it's completely obscene.'

'Has Ryder told you about the other kidnaps that took place yesterday?'

'Yes. He mentioned that in each case there was a political connection,' said Emma. 'You must know that Ken was at Princeton with about half the political class of the USA. And the VP of the US was a big pal of his father's and they've known each other for years.'

'Did he also tell you that in each case the parents are billionaires?'

'Ryder thinks that's relevant only from the point of view of motivation for the kidnappers.'

'How does he view this demand for expenses?'

'He thinks it's a joke. I mean he thinks it's just something to show that all the kidnaps are connected and how clever the gang has been to pull them off. In the end he reckons it will come down to negotiation. He's determined to bring Sophie back safely, but I can detect some pride in there. He wants to do it for less than anybody else. And I've told him not to put her at risk for anything as silly as money.'

'Can I ask whether you're in a relationship at the moment?'

'Of course. Yes, I do have a boyfriend ... seems ridiculous to call him that. He's ... er ... somewhat older than me. We met in Dubai. He has business out there. Then when I split from Ken we re-met here in London.'

'Can you give me his name?' asked Mercy. 'We're going to have to check him out, as I'm sure you'll understand.'

'You're going to check *him* out?' said Emma, astonished. 'He used to *work* for Kinderman. He's already been fully vetted by the US military, Kinderman human resources and probably the CIA, but ... by all means. His name is Conrad Jensen.'

Isabel was upstairs lying on the bed, exhausted. She'd put Alyshia off for lunch, said she was going to have to sleep, told her to come round in the late afternoon. She was wrapped in the duvet still fully clothed, no energy to get undressed. She held on to her belly, felt its swelling, imagined the small life doubling and redoubling inside her. She was so happy, even happier than she'd been when she'd had Alyshia because she'd already begun to feel the quality of Frank's particular darkness by then. She'd seen him mixing not only with all the right people but also with undesirable types, the sort you looked at and they strangled something inside you, made your goodness feel laughable.

She thrust it out of her mind. Couldn't understand why she was allowing such doom-laden thoughts to enter her consciousness on a day such as this. She drifted back in time to a party she'd been to with Charlie. It had been a formal affair until after the dinner, when there'd been some dancing. Charlie had cut in and soon they were dancing in an aura of empty space as everybody around them could see from their unswerving gaze into each other's eyes that here were two people madly in love.

It was at this point that she started to find air in the bedroom difficult to come by. She thought it might have been the memory, which had induced excitement and slightly impaired her breathing, but the feeling of breathlessness intensified. She threw open the duvet in the hope that this would help her breathe, but it got worse. She rolled over and fumbled on the bedside table for her mobile phone, trying to suck air into lungs that didn't seem capable of inflating. Her throat protested as her hand lashed out, dashing everything to the floor, and her brain told her that she'd left the phone in the kitchen. She coughed and was alarmed to see a spattering of blood on the white sheet. Where had that come from?

She staggered to her feet, the room reeling so that she clutched at invisible handrails trying to stay vertical. She tripped forward, swerving towards the door, whose jamb seemed to shift so that her shoulder careened into it and she ricocheted into the corridor and somehow managed to grab the wooden sphere on the top of the banister post. She hung on, trying to focus on the stairs, aware now that whatever the cause this was serious and she would have to get help.

The stairs seemed immensely steep and high as she pointed her foot towards the first step. Another cough; blood speckled her hand as her foot stretched out and connected with nothing while her supporting leg collapsed and she dived head first, hands grasping at air. Her vision filled with incomprehensible, disordered images: chest, carpet, feet, light, banister, wall. Her body made jarring contact on the shoulder, coccyx and knee, finishing with a sickening cranial thud against the wall, which relieved her of consciousness and left her face down on the granite tiles of the hallway to the front door.

14

On the way to Lyall Mews, Mercy called Conrad Jensen's mobile but got no response. Papadopoulos was driving and listening to a preliminary report from the forensic team who had done most of the work on the front doors and seating area of the Mercedes. They had just been sent Pat Gould's and Sophie Railton-Bass's prints and so far had found nothing unusual.

'Once we've checked this out, I might leave you and pursue this Conrad Jensen lead at the Savoy,' said Mercy.

'You think that smells of something?'

'Don't know why,' said Mercy. 'Maybe it's because he's a guy moving in on a vulnerable woman with a huge amount of money.'

'You didn't make Emma Railton sound very vulnerable,' said Papadopoulos. 'And Jensen practically works for the CIA.'

'That's never been a recommendation in my book,' said Mercy. 'The CIA were cagey with me this morning. My friend in MI6 reckons they're worried that some of their personnel or contractors might be involved and they want to keep cards tight to their chests. And even intelligent, capable women are emotionally vulnerable when their marriage busts up.'

Mercy left Papadopoulos to investigate the mews and do a door-to-door in Lyall Street, and drove to the Savoy to investigate Conrad Jensen. She quickly discovered that he'd been staying there with his daughter, a woman in her twenties, whose name they did not have as her passport had not been required for the booking. Emma had made no mention of the daughter. Jensen had left the hotel suddenly with no luggage and had been followed by his daughter some days later. Mercy asked to look at the room, a two-bedroom suite, but it was occupied and had already been completely cleaned twice. She asked to speak to the cleaners and to anybody who had interacted with Conrad Jensen or his daughter.

The Portuguese cleaners had never been in the room with Jensen and his daughter present. They had not noticed anything unusual in the rubbish nor in the things littered about the rooms. Mercy moved on to the waiters in the various dining rooms that Jensen and his daughter had frequented. The only interesting thing to emerge from these interviews was that no waiter had ever picked up even a snippet of conversation. Whenever a waiter approached their table dialogue ceased and would only resume once they were out of earshot.

'Was that intentional?'

'We thought it was weird,' said one of the girls. 'He always used to say: "My daughter will have the steak tartare." As if he was trying to establish something. We began to think, even with the forty-odd years' age difference, that maybe they weren't father and daughter, but lovers. We played a game one night taking it in turns to pass by their table pouring wine, cleaning crumbs, trying to catch them out, and we noticed they used sign language. Eventually they just shut up and we left them alone. But there was something about them, you know, not right.'

A call came through to tell her that they had found the receptionist and doorman who were on duty at the time Conrad Jensen left the hotel.

They sat in an office behind reception.

'So Mr Jensen didn't check out?' asked Mercy.

'No, his daughter checked out about three days after we last saw him and put the bill on her father's credit card,' said the receptionist.

'Did you get her name?'

'No.'

'Is that odd,' asked Mercy, 'for people in an expensive two-bedroom suite to check out separately?'

'Not so unusual for the very rich.'

'Anything you can tell us about his stay here? Visitors? Unusual requests?'

'According to his computer file he asked us to admit one Walden Garfinkle to his room on the eleventh of January at six p.m.'

'Did you see Jensen on the night he left?'

'He nodded at me on his way out. That's all.'

'Did you see the daughter during the following three days?'

'Occasionally.'

'How would you describe her demeanour?'

'She was almost constantly on her phone, and when she wasn't, she would sit in the lobby staring into it intensely, her face only inches from the screen, as if she was expecting news from a lover. As far as I know, she only went to her room to sleep.'

'That's very observant,' said Mercy.

'She was a striking woman ... even for the Savoy.'

'What about you?' asked Mercy, turning to the doorman. 'Did you have any contact with the girl?'

'She used public transport every time except on the last day, when she ordered a cab to go to Islington.'

'No street name?'

'Just Islington.'

'Can you remember the cab driver?'

'He was a regular,' said the doorman, nodding.

'I'd like to talk to him,' said Mercy. 'What about Mr Jensen?'

'We chatted about football. He was a Chelsea fan. I ordered him cabs most days. He went twice to Wilton Place, and to a restaurant called Moro in Exmouth Market on the tenth of January at around eight p.m.'

'And on his last night?'

'He gave me a tenner, didn't ask for a cab. He just walked up to the Strand, turned left and that was the last I saw of him.'

'Find me that cab driver,' said Mercy. 'And someone who can give me a physical description of Walden Garfinkle. What about room service? Once Mr Jensen had left, the daughter probably ordered up room service rather than sit in the dining room on her own.'

The receptionist tapped into the computer, looked at the bill and made a call. The doorman left to find the cab driver. A few minutes later a young oriental woman from room service came into the office. She spoke perfect English with an accent that made Mercy think she'd learnt it from the BBC World Service. She remembered delivering food to the Jensens' suite on three consecutive evenings. She'd been struck by the tension in the room and how lonely Jensen's daughter seemed to be.

'I didn't exactly feel sorry for her because she seemed too strong for that and too rich, being in a three thousand pound a night room. I thought it might be a lover problem. I've seen plenty of that in my time. Bust-ups, coming-togethers, disappointments, even fights with punching and biting. I talked to her as I laid out her food. Nothing special, just to see if she wanted any contact.'

'And did she?'

'She made a pass at me. More than a pass. She asked me if I wanted to go to bed with her. And I told her I wasn't that way inclined.'

'How did she react?'

'She shrugged as if I'd turned down an offer of a Coca-Cola or something, like it was nothing,' said the young woman. 'The strange thing about it, for such a beautiful woman, was her approach. It was very masculine. She sat there playing with her phone, legs slightly apart, elbows on knees, and said: "Fancy a fuck?" I remember being confused by her.'

'Were you nervous when you delivered food to her again?'

'No. Like I said, it was nothing to her. I wasn't interested. No problem. We just talked for a bit ... that's all. She told me her dad had left a few days ago without telling her where he was going.'

'Was she worried about him?' asked Mercy. 'Did she talk about her father at all?'

'She was tense, but maybe from waiting for her phone to ring. She never let it go. I asked her what her father did and she just said he was a businessman. She gave me the impression that he'd disappeared before. She said he was probably chasing skirt.'

'Did you get her name?'

'Yes, it was Siobhan.'

Boxer was on his way back to his flat in Belsize Park. As he came out of the tube he had a message from Glider to call him.

'Got a lead for you, haven't I,' said Glider. 'But don't get your hopes up, it's not cast iron.'

'What does that mean?'

'It means I've gone back through my old records to see what business I put Marcus's way and tried to find somebody in that lot who Marcus might still trust if he got a call from them promising decent returns.'

'That doesn't sound very exciting.'

'I checked them out 'n' all,' said Glider. 'And they're still active doing a lot of cigarettes to pubs. Thousands of pounds' worth. And they're south of the river. Bermondsey. That's right next to Walworth.'

'Let's have it, then.'

'His name's Harvey Cox and he operates out of a warehouse off the Old Kent Road at the end of Latona Road, not far from South Bermondsey railway station. And you can use my name as long as you're not going to kill anybody. You'll have to find your own way in. Your best bet is to find a need for some cigarettes or maybe a supply. Lots of them.'

Glider gave him a number and hung up. Boxer called, gave his name and Glider as contact. He asked to speak to Harvey Cox. The voice on the other end said he'd call him back in five. It took ten.

'Cox,' he said. 'You Boxer?'

'That's me.'

'What you got?' asked Cox. 'Buying or selling?'

'Buying,' said Boxer, who reckoned this was the best way to meet Cox face to face in his warehouse in Bermondsey.

'What you looking for?'

'Five hundred cartons a month.'

'We can do that.'

'I'd like to come and see you.'

'We deliver.'

'I prefer face to face. I want to see your set-up.'

'Glider's name is normally good enough, my friend.'

'He said he hasn't done much business with you, and not in that line. I need to see that your operation is … functioning.'

'Yeah, it's functioning,' said Cox, flat with irony. 'All right, you know where we are. We'll be expecting you. You could bring the first instalment. What sort of time?'

'Between five and six?' said Boxer. 'Money?'

'The money is one fifty a pack.'

They haggled to £1.25.

'Make sure you get here before six,' said Cox. 'We let the dogs out after that.'

They hung up. Boxer opened the safe behind the Italian painting and took out £7,000. He went into the kitchen and lifted the floorboards at the back of one of the units and extracted his lightweight Belgian-made FN57 semi-automatic pistol and loaded it.

'You going to come with me this time?' asked Siobhan, consulting her mobile phone.

'Where?' asked Amy.

'They don't say. They just said get going, instructions to follow.'

'What's it about?'

'I don't know, but I imagine they've got news of my father or they wouldn't be calling me out.'

'So it's the same people you met before, your father's network?'

'I don't know if I'll be meeting the same person but it will be someone from the network.'

'I'll have to call my dad.'

'Get on with it then,' said Siobhan. 'When these people say jump, you jump.'

Amy went into the bedroom, called her father, who was just going into the tube.

'Stay put,' said Boxer. 'Don't go with her. That's not for you.'

'What about you, why don't you go?'

'I'm on something else at the moment and there's a time limit.'

'So let me go?'

'You're not trained, Amy. You're dealing with professionals here. Even Siobhan has been trained. You won't know what to look for.'

'What do you mean?'

'The signs that things are going wrong, not unfolding as they should do.'

'Why don't I follow her?'

143

'You won't get anywhere near. They'll lose you on the first street corner if they're any good,' said Boxer. 'You stay in the flat, let Siobhan do her thing. I'll talk to you later. I've got to go now.'

He hung up. Amy went back to Siobhan, who had her coat on ready to go.

'Huh!' said Siobhan. 'Daddy's little girl's going to do what she's told. Sit on the sofa and look at your nice little goody two-shoes.'

'I was thinking I'd follow you.'

'I'll have to tell them you're coming or they'll see you and cut you out like a limping wildebeest.'

Silence.

'See ya later,' said Siobhan, slinging her bag over her shoulder.

'All right, I'll come,' said Amy.

Siobhan punched a text into her phone.

'We'll have to wait now, see if we've got permission.'

At five o'clock, Alyshia D'Cruz was ringing on the doorbell of her mother's house and not getting any answer. She called Isabel on her mobile and frowned as she heard it ringing in the house. Then she got worried, remembering her mother's tiredness, the news of the pregnancy. The long flight back from Mumbai even in business class had been hard for her; maybe she'd picked something up in India. She couldn't stop herself from doing what everybody did in these situations: she dropped to her haunches and looked through the letter box, thinking she'd have to find a way into the house, regretting that she'd given her key back to her mother.

The hall light was out but the light above the stairs was on and that meant she could see her mother lying on the granite tiles, her feet still up on the last steps. Alyshia fell back in shock at the sight. She called an ambulance sitting there on the hard, cold pavement, and then took off for the estate office, thinking it might close and she needed to get a key to the house.

The woman in the estate office caught her mood immediately. The look of horror on Alyshia's face transmitted everything. The woman dropped her handbag and, with the words 'unconscious', 'pregnant' and 'ambulance' resounding in her head, found the spare key to Isabel's house. They tottered on heels too high for urgency past the parking area and the perfunctory gardens. Sirens whooped in the distance. A strange wind gusted around the court-yard in front of the house buffeting them, making them unsteady on their feet and lifting the woman's flared skirt, which Alyshia knocked back down.

Only the Yale key was necessary. The woman fell through the door as Alyshia barged past her, stepping out of her heels and throwing herself down the hallway, landing on her knees and skidding over the granite tiles.

The woman shouted that she would go to the front gates and open them so that the ambulance could get as close as possible. Alyshia didn't hear her as she came to a halt at her mother's crumpled shoulder and was seized with panic as to what to do. Should she move her? It was clear she'd fallen down the stairs. She could see the bruise, broken skin and blood on the side of her forehead. Had she damaged her neck in the fall?

Vital signs, check for vital signs. Isabel's hand was flung over her head and Alyshia grabbed the wrist, which was still warm, and tried to find a pulse. She saw the speckle of blood on the back of her mother's hand and got her head down on the tiles and saw more blood around her mouth and leaking out in a string of mucus to the floor. She reached over and opened an eyelid, remembering something about pupils reacting to light being another indication. The eye stared sightlessly into the sparkling tiles.

The loud whoop of a siren made Alyshia start. Blue lights flick-ered on the walls. Paramedics in fluorescent jackets came crashing through the gardens, one with a bag over his shoulder and an oxygen tank while the other dragged a wheeled stretcher.

'Stand back, love,' the first one said.

Alyshia rolled away helplessly and sat hugging her knees, propped up against the wall, looking at the paramedic's shoulders and back as he rapidly assessed the body, applied oxygen. The other paramedic pulled the trolley in.

'Anything we need to know, love?' he asked Alyshia.

'She's five to six months pregnant, late forties, high blood pres-sure and she's just flown back from Mumbai,' said Alyshia, on automatic. 'There's blood coming from her mouth and the back of her hand is speckled with it as if she's coughed.'

'What does that sound like to you, Dave?'

'Pulmonary embolism,' said Dave. 'Let's get her out of here. We spend time immobilising her neck, she'll be DOA.'

'DOA?' asked Alyshia.

'Don't worry, we'll do everything we can.'

'Call ahead and prep them for an emergency C-section,' said Dave. 'There's life …'

They had her on the trolley and were lifting her out through the door in less than a minute. Alyshia followed, pulling the door to and taking the spare keys with her. She got into the back of the ambulance. The siren whooped once and the ambulance reversed out into the street. She asked where they were going.

'Chelsea and Westminster.'

Alyshia called Boxer. No answer. She left a message. 'This is Alyshia. Call me urgently. Mum's had a fall. I'm in an ambulance on the way to the Chelsea and Westminster. It's 17.23.' She called her partner, Deepak, told him the terrible news. He said he was on his way. She called her father, who immediately tried to divert the ambulance to an even better hospital.

'That your old man?' asked Dave. 'What's he on?'

'He doesn't like things out of his control,' said Alyshia.

'She'll get the best care … probably in the world,' said Dave. 'This is what the NHS is really good at. Dire emergency. Life or death.'

'Is that what this is?' she said, panicking.

'First thing we got to do is get the baby out. Everything that should be keeping your mum alive is going to the baby. We get the baby out and the anticoagulants in to disperse the pulmonary embolism and there's a chance, but I'm not exaggerating when I tell you it's touch and go.'

Alyshia clamped her hands to the sides of her head.

'I'm not … I'm not ready for this.'

'Nobody is ever ready for this,' said Dave, 'except us. The good news is she's still going. She didn't break her neck and we didn't damage her by moving her so quickly. And they're all ready for her at the hospital. Hang on to that, love.'

The ambulance was driving at a terrifying speed for central London. The sirens whooped as the blue lights slashed through the night. The front lights blasted out, driving into the traffic like a snowplough, parting the cars. Alyshia and Dave hung on as the body of the ambulance rocked back and forth, the driver working the steering wheel with furious energy. They pulled into the A&E bay of the Chelsea and Westminster and there was a whole platoon of people waiting. The trolley was unloaded and Isabel was swept into the hospital, drip held high, oxygen bottle by her side, but the clear mask over her nose and mouth was barely fogged.

15

Boxer had turned his mobile phone off in the tube. He was preparing himself and didn't want any interruptions in what was going to be a very difficult negotiation with Harvey Cox.

He found the warehouse at the end of Latona Road. The dogs were still in their cage: two Rottweilers, each around eighty kilos. They barked savagely at him as he walked past. A door to an office by the large warehouse opened and a young black guy beckoned him in.

'I's Jarrod,' he said, and asked Boxer to put his case on the desk and to stand with his arms out and legs apart. He frisked him for weapons and went to take hold of the case.

'That's *my* money in there,' said Boxer. 'I'll take care of it until Harvey and I have done the deal.'

'Thought you done that over the phone.'

'Nothing's done until I've seen the set-up and we've shaken hands on it,' said Boxer, and beckoned the case from the young man's grasp.

Jarrod weighed it as he handed it over, told Boxer to follow. Boxer was glad the FN57 in the secret compartment in the bottom of the case was an especially lightweight gun. Even fully loaded it was well under a kilo.

He was interested to meet Harvey Cox. He'd detected some kind of an accent when they spoke on the phone and he wondered if he might be a Jamaican. As it was, there were two men in the room, one a tall, rail-thin black man and the other a heavily built white guy with close-cropped grey hair and a matching goatee. He turned away from the window as Boxer entered and held out his hand.

'Harvey Cox,' he said. 'And this is my partner Delroy Pink.'

The black man made no move, just nodded. He had the look of someone who'd done people harm. Harvey looked as if he'd ordered it.

'I thought you might be Jamaicans from your accent,' said Boxer.

'We're Bahamians. Black as they come, white as they come,' said Cox, pointing at Pink and then himself.

'Glider didn't tell me much about you, just said that he'd done business with you over eighteen months ago,' said Boxer. 'I hope you don't mind me coming to take a look.'

'From our side, too,' said Cox. 'Glider just said you were cool, no more 'n that.'

'Your man still searched me for weapons.'

'He search everybody, no matter what,' said Cox. 'What's your business?'

'I sell cigarettes in market towns in the south of England,' said Boxer, keeping it vague, not wanting to give them anything that could be checked out. 'I lost a supplier. I need someone to keep the flow going. You?'

'We mostly import American brands through suppliers in Dubai. Occasionally we buy locally if we get peaks in demand,' said Cox. 'We only deal in real brands, no fakes, no Chinese rubbish.'

'It's a big warehouse for cigarettes.'

'I have a collection of wartime motor vehicles that I rent out to production companies for movies and commercials.'

'Who was the supplier you lost?' asked Pink.

Both men looked at him. One of Pink's eyes was bloodshot.

'Somebody in Bristol with a connection in the Canaries,' said Boxer.

'You want delivery outside London, you gonna have to pay extra,' said Pink. 'It's free only inside the M25. You get me? You wanna take a look at the goods ... make sure they're to your liking?'

'Sure,' said Boxer, picking up his case.

They left Cox in the office and walked through the dimly lit building, past dust-sheeted cars, trucks, some British, others American, until they came to a Sherman tank.

'What's this all about, Delroy?'

'Man crazy about war movies is all,' said Pink, opening a door beyond the tank. 'The Sherman's for him. He don't rent that out.'

There was another twenty metres of warehouse space, which had been walled off, where the atmosphere was noticeably drier. There was a small forklift and the boxes were piled in three levels almost to the ceiling. They were stored by brand.

'We keep the humidity under control,' said Pink, pointing to machines around the room. 'The place been insulated to fuck. We don't send out no damp smokes, you get?'

'Looks good.'

They went back to the office. Cox was at his desk, reading glasses on and smoking a strong-smelling cheroot. Pink took up his position leaning against the wall behind him. Boxer opened the small holdall with the money.

'This is six thousand two hundred and fifty for the first five hundred cartons.'

'You want delivery to Bristol, that gonna be another two hundred,' said Pink.

'I wanted to ask you about another London supplier I'd arranged to see,' said Boxer. 'We had the meeting all set up and then he disappeared. I wondered if you'd ever heard of Marcus Alleyne?'

'We heard of him,' said Pink. 'Small dealer. Fencing other goods. Smokes just a part his business.'

'You know what happened to him?' asked Boxer, putting the money on the table.

'Maybe he got picked up by the po-lice,' said Pink.

Cox had turned to look at Pink as if he'd noticed some change in tone.

As Boxer reached in for the last pack of banknotes, he released the catch on the false bottom and retrieved the gun, which he pulled out of the bag and pointed at Pink. Cox stiffened in his chair.

150

'Thought you too good to be true,' said Pink.

'I knew you weren't,' said Boxer. 'Now look, Delroy, I'm not interested in anything except what happened to Marcus Alleyne. Clarify that and I'm out of here.'

'You know what he's talking about, Pink?' asked Cox.

Pink nodded slowly and with eyes gone so dead that Boxer thought he might have had some kind of seizure. His instinct told him otherwise and he took three fast steps to one side of the office door, which slammed open. First thing across the threshold was a Walther P99 held in a black hand. Boxer gave the wrist an upward chop and the gun went off, putting a large hole in the ceiling before falling from the now paralysed hand. One step across and a sharp punch to the solar plexus and Jarrod went down. Boxer picked up the Walther P99 and pointed it at Pink and the FN57 at Cox. Jarrod crawled around on the floor in circles trying to persuade air back into his lungs.

Cox was rigid in his chair, hands flat on his desk, the cheroot still smoking, ears ringing.

'You were saying, Pink,' said Boxer.

Pink had come off the wall, eyes widening to visible whites, which was the closest he ever got to an expression of surprise.

Cox turned to him, suspicious, questioning.

'You doing things behind my back, Pink?'

'Just a little business on the side 't's all.'

'Talk us through it,' said Boxer.

'I get a call from a woman called Jess. She running security for Glider. She offering me twenty-five thousand if I can deliver this Marcus Alleyne to a disused warehouse in Clapham. She telling me he's a fence, does smokes. So I set up a deal where I buy a thousand cartons from him. I's worried about him calling Glider to check. She telling me she's using G's old phone, said she'd set him straight.'

'How did it work?' asked Boxer.

'I set up the deal with Marcus. We take delivery of the smokes. Jarrod here,' said Pink, looking down at the floor, 'he hit the man on the head with a SAP glove, take him out. We deliver him to the warehouse. Some white guy there make sure the man all right, paid us our money, we split.'

'Tell me about the white guy.'

'What's there to tell? He white, shaved head, I mean to the skin, maybe six foot tall, looked like he could handle himself. London accent. Took Marcus away in a white van, didn't catch the plates.'

'Where's the warehouse in Clapham?'

'On the Clapham Road. Borg and Ranelli the name, can't remember the number.'

Boxer looked at Jarrod still groaning on the floor. He leaned forward and hit him hard on the head with the butt of the Walther P99, knocked him right out.

'Tell him that's for hitting Marcus,' he said. 'He's a friend of mine. Now I'm going to walk out of here and you're never going to see me again unless I find that you called Jess. I hear that and I'll be back and I won't be alone and you'll be out of the cigarette business for a long time. When I find Marcus, you'll return his cigarettes to him plus ten grand. How's that sound, Pink?'

Pink gave one of his imperceptible nods, wary of Boxer, like he was the bear in the room. Boxer packed his money back into the bag, with the FN57. He checked his watch.

'Let's take a walk, Pink,' he said, and waved him forward with the Walther.

They went out of the office and into the reception area. Pink stood there waiting.

'Keep going, Pink. You know where the door is.'

The rail-thin body started to shake. Boxer shoved him forward so that he hit the door, bounced off it, blood on his cheek.

'Don't like dogs, Pink?' said Boxer. 'Maybe you don't feed them enough. Give them a nice bit of leg. Mind you, they'd come away hungry from your skinny arse. Now show me the way out.'

Pink shouldered past him, fierce with anger at having his cool exposed as fake. They went through another door and into the warehouse, worked their way through the cars to a steel door on the other side, which had four bolts and a heavy lock. Pink let him out into the cold night air.

'Don't let me down, Pink, or I'll be back with a platoon of me,' said Boxer, tucking the Walther P99 down the back of his trousers.

He found his way around the warehouse and back on to Latona

Road. He turned his mobile phone back on as he started to think about how he was going to deal with Jess, direct or through Glider.

He listened to his messages and started running.

'You're on,' said Siobhan. 'We have to leave our mobiles like I did the last time. They're a nervous bunch.'

'How do we know where to go?'

Siobhan shrugged, put hers on the table. Amy did the same, but underneath it she hid the screwed-up piece of paper with the mobile number on it that she'd found under the bed when Siobhan had disappeared the first time. They left the flat, heading for Upper Street and the Highbury & Islington tube. On the crowded pavement someone brushed past Siobhan, knocked her shoulder back. She was about to remonstrate until she found a mobile phone in her hand, which rang.

'Cross the road, take a bus down to Angel.'

Off the bus they were told to head past the York pub and beyond some gardens, down some steps, to the towpath of the Regent's Canal. They stumbled along in the pitch black with street lights high above them, cars occasionally flashing overhead. A lone figure looked down on them from a bridge. A dog walker on the other side of the canal flicked a cigarette into the water.

They came off the towpath and walked up to Canonbury in a big circle, almost back to Highbury & Islington until they were directed into a park - New River Walk. A path led them along a narrow river and it was as if they were no longer in London. A silence descended. Traffic disappeared. City life backed away. Beyond the park were large houses with extensive gardens in front of unpeopled streets. Yellow-lit living rooms revealed book-lined walls opposite expensive art and gilt-framed mirrors.

'Where are we?' asked Amy.

'Hampshire,' said Siobhan. 'Let's take a seat.'

They waited on a bench for the next instruction. Siobhan took Amy's hand.

'What are you doing?' asked Amy.

'Comforting you on your first mission.'

'Don't be ridiculous,' she said, starting to tug her hand away, but Siobhan held on, pulled her in, kissed her.

153

Amy struggled. Siobhan hugged her tight and she was stronger. Amy gave up all resistance.

'That's more like it,' said Siobhan. 'You know you want to.'

Amy lashed out with a fist. Siobhan took the blow on the side of the head just as her mobile went off. She took the call, glaring.

'What the fuck is going on?' asked the voice.

'Lovers' tiff,' said Siobhan.

'Well stop it,' said the voice. 'You're drawing attention to yourselves. Now walk up the river, cross the gardens and wait on the road for a cab to pick you up.'

Siobhan cut the phone, nodded to Amy, who was ranting.

'Calm down, drama queen,' said Siobhan. 'Let's move it.'

They crossed the river, came out on the other side of the park. A cab pulled up and they got in. Amy rammed herself into the corner, feet up ready to kick out.

'You were so keen before,' said Siobhan. 'What happened?'

'I don't like being attacked.'

'I get horny when I'm on edge.'

'Fuck you.'

'Whatever,' said Siobhan and stared out the window.

She leaned over to the intercom and asked the driver if he had anything to tell them.

'Told me to drop you at Clissold Park. That's it.'

The cab turned on to the Essex Road and headed north, dropping them at the corner of a very flat, huge dark open space where only the occasional jogging trainers beneath fluorescent jackets were visible in the gloom. They crossed the park taking the diagonal tarmac path. Some lads came off the steps of a building in the middle where a board advertised afternoon teas, followed them, muttering low words, until Siobhan stopped and turned.

'Can I help you boys?' she asked.

'I reckon you could,' said one.

'Don't be shy then,' said Siobhan. 'Just come out and ask for it.'

Low, shifting laughter from the three men.

'Let's go,' said Amy.

'No,' said Siobhan. 'I want to know what they're after. I'm sure I can help.'

'Walking alone in a park, two girls, mean only one thing,' said one of the men.

'And what's that?' asked Siobhan. 'Don't be coy.'

Some uncertainty crept into their swagger as they saw her lack of fear. The bold, talkative one stepped forward.

'How 'bout a fuck?' he said.

'Not with you ... surprisingly,' said Siobhan. 'You've got work to do on those chat-up lines. Now piss off back to school.'

He went for her, ducking low, aiming to drive her off the path and on to the grass, get her on the ground. Siobhan brought her knee up sharply, and crowned him with both fists on the back of the head so that his face ploughed into the tarmac. His arms and legs twitched, which freaked out the other two, who turned and ran.

'Where are you going?' Siobhan shouted after them.

'For Christ's sake,' said Amy. 'You've really hurt him.'

'And he wasn't going to hurt me?'

'You can't just *be*, can you?' said Amy. 'Something always has to happen.'

'Only because people have been so fucking nice to me all my life,' said Siobhan.

'Let's go. He's coming round.'

Siobhan took two steps and hoofed him in the groin.

16

B oxer ran into the hospital reception. He hadn't called Alyshia back. He didn't want to hear things on the phone. He wanted to see Isabel. He wanted to hear her voice. He wanted the reality of her flesh, to hold her close. He was out of breath, a wildness in his eyes, and he had his case still in one hand with the money, the FN57 and the Walther P99. He got the words out: Isabel Marks, admitted to A and E, emergency C-section. He asked for a room number.

The receptionist tapped the name into the computer.

'According to this she's still in ICU, fifth floor, lift bank B.'

Boxer was running before she'd finished. Visitors, porters, administrators flitted past him in a delirium on his way to the lifts. He waited, barely able to contain his suppressed rage at the slightest delay. He filed into the lift with people looking cheerful, bored, resigned, indifferent and checked his mobile phone. There were messages, some from Mercy. He didn't want to answer, turned his mobile off.

He was the only person to get out at the fifth floor. He ran to ICU, blathered her name so that the nurse had to ask him to repeat it. She'd just come on shift. She entered the name and frowned.

'She's not here any more ... if she ever was. She's in room 574, which is just down the corridor here on the left-hand side.'

He set off again, hurtling down the corridor, checking the numbers until he got to 574. Only then did he slow down. He straightened his shoulders, caught his breath, brought his head up and examined the laminate of the door and the steel numbers. He knew he had to prepare himself, as if what was beyond the door was going to be enormously demanding. He could feel himself changing, physically and mentally: diminishing in size, narrowing psychologically, conscious of his vital organs, his inflating and deflating lungs, his thundering heart, his quivering legs. It took great personal courage for him just to reach for the brushed steel door handle. Pushing it down seemed like an act of valour. The door swung open. The first thing he saw was a huddled form on the other side of the room like a sculpture, frozen in time. His mind reached tentatively for the title of this sculpture. It struck him as something universal. What came to mind was the word *Pietà*.

The sculpture moved, disassembled itself and rising out of the folds of cloth and limb came two distinct bodies. A man and a woman. Boxer knew them, but struggled to compute from where because his senses were so overwhelmed by what was pending in the room.

'Oh Charlie,' said a woman's voice.

Alyshia stepped out of the deconstructing sculpture and stood before him. Deepak Mistry got to his feet behind her. They looked at him as if he was on a ledge about to jump off.

'Oh Charlie.'

It was Alyshia who'd said these words, and they were so plaintive that they held him, locked him in place, paralysed him. He was unable to cross the threshold, as if to do so would be to admit that something terrible had happened.

They looked to their left and he was aware now that there was a bed in the room and that what was pending was on it. His feet wouldn't move. He could only lean forward and look in. There was someone on the bed, a head on a pillow, staring up at the ceiling but with eyelids closed. No drips, no oxygen. Nothing. Boxer looked back to Alyshia, who had suddenly dropped to her knees and seemed to be retching. She rested her forehead on her fists and her body jerked uncontrollably. Mistry fell to her side, put his arm over her back, looked up at Boxer, beseeching.

He couldn't work it out. Nothing was making any sense. With

cataclysmic effort he managed to put his foot in the room as if he too was emerging from marble.

Looking to his right, he realised that the woman in the bed had dark brown hair. He managed to move closer even though something in his brain was telling him not to go there. He recognised the eyebrows. They were dark and very straight. Then he saw the slight declivity beneath the cheekbone. He was unaware of the delusional powers of the human brain at this point and still had not connected these well-known features to his pregnant lover. He reached her bedside and looked down on her face, which was so still and waxen he wasn't sure whether he was looking at something human.

'Who is this?' he asked.

'It's Isabel,' said Mistry, still kneeling, disconcerted, astonished.

'No,' said Boxer. 'This isn't her. She's … she's … not here.'

Alyshia pulled herself up and went to Boxer's side, put her arms around him.

'It's Mummy,' she said, looking up at him. 'She died on the operating table during the emergency C-section. Her heart stopped …'

'But they said she was in ICU. Are you sure this is …?'

'She never went to ICU. I think they reserved a place for her, but she never made it there.'

Boxer put his case down and leaned over the figure in the bed. He put both fists on either side of her head and looked deeply into her face. He could see vestiges of the woman he loved but the lack of animation was startling. He realised that he'd never seen anyone really close to him dead. Even his mother when she was comatose after her suicide attempt had had more vitality in her than this … this carcass.

'He's in shock,' said Mistry.

Boxer straightened, stared at him, transfixed.

'I didn't mean anything by it, Charlie,' said Mistry. 'We're all in shock. She was so alive only yesterday, and now …'

Boxer stuck his hands into his pockets and looked down at her as if she was a job of work. Then he cast about the room as if the vital bit of her must still be around and all that was required was to get it back in there. Push the genie back into the bottle was the silly phrase that came to mind.

A nurse came into the room with a paper in her hands, which she gave to Alyshia. She squeezed her shoulder and said:

'Stay here as long as you like.'

'This is Charles Boxer,' said Alyshia.

'Oh, right, I'll tell the doctor. She'll want to come and talk to you.'

Alyshia thanked her. The nurse left, closing the door. Alyshia looked at the paper.

'Cause of death: pulmonary embolism,' she said. 'It's a blood clot ...'

'I know what a pulmonary embolism is,' said Boxer, quietly.

Alyshia gave him the paper. He looked at the details. There was no doubt now. Isabel Marks, date of birth, address; everything was as it should be except that this was the paper he should never have had to hold.

A doctor came in. A woman. Impossibly young for such responsibility. She shook hands with Boxer, introduced herself.

'We did everything we could,' she said. 'It's difficult to know how long she'd been lying at the foot of the stairs ...'

'At the foot of the stairs?' said Boxer.

'She fell down the stairs. She'd been in bed and had obviously felt distressed and had tried to get downstairs, presumably to call for help. She fell and was knocked unconscious. Under those circumstances all the mother's powers go to protect the baby. If she'd been found immediately, things could have been different. As it was, we think she'd been there a few hours, and that proved fatal to her.'

'To her?'

'We performed an emergency C-section, and while the mother did not survive it, the baby did,' said the doctor. 'Would you like to see your son?'

'My son?' said Boxer, swallowing hard. He blinked as if this might jolt him out of this particularly strange dream. He picked up his case and followed the doctor, very conscious of putting one foot in front of the other. They arrived at the neonatal ICU, a room full of incubators, computers twitching with data about oxygenation, temperature, cardiac function and brain activity. Nurses in scrubs were observing the monitors, while others had their hands in the

159

incubators seemingly caressing the tiny froglike bundles.

The doctor asked Boxer to wash his hands and then led him to an incubator. He looked down on an impossibly small creature, one no larger than his scrubbed hand. A tube was taped into his nose. His face bore the slight frown of one concerned at his own state. Boxer was allowed to touch the downy, porcelain head, feel its warmth, measure it between his thumb and forefinger. A nurse tried to relieve him of his case but he clung on to it.

'His lungs seem to be quite mature,' said the doctor. 'The prognosis is good.' They all looked at Boxer, but he was incapable of showing emotion. What he had growing in his chest was nearly uncontainable. He managed a nod.

'I think I'm going to have to go out now,' he said.

The doctor nodded as if this was to be expected given the traumatic circumstances. They withdrew from the room and stood in the corridor.

'You can't be on your own,' said Mistry.

'No, Charlie, you have to come with us,' said Alyshia, holding him to her.

'I *want* to be on my own,' he said, extricating himself, moving away. 'I'll be all right. That's just what I need … some time alone.'

He managed a wave as he walked back to the lift. He was comforted by its ordinariness and a porter with a patient sulking in a wheelchair, oxygen mask attached, who looked up at him with eyes that said: 'You should try this … see how you get on.' They left at the third floor and Boxer continued alone to the ground, where he crossed the lobby to the entrance. It was raining outside, angled rods in the orange light. He had no umbrella. He stood outside under the thundering canopy, breathing in the glistening streets, the traffic honking and hissing. A busload of people went past, staring out of the fogged, warmly lit interior on their way to a certain destination. Boxer zipped up his coat, hunched his shoulders and stepped out on to the pavement. He walked without stopping with one hand rammed into his pocket and the case hanging in the other. The heavy rain quickly soaked into his hair down to his scalp. He breathed the darkness into the black hole that now occupied his whole interior.

*

'How much longer do we need to do this?' asked Amy, well soaked by the heavy rain.

'Until they know we're in the clear,' said Siobhan. 'This can go on for hours. They have to be sure. It's like leading someone to your door.'

They were standing out under the bandstand in the middle of a wet and windy Clapham Common. A message came through telling them to proceed to Orlando Road in Clapham Old Town. They walked through the rain to Clapham Common North Side. Siobhan had an earplug in now, connected to the phone.

'Keep close,' she said, taking Amy's arm. 'We're getting to it now. We're going to have to move fast. You ready?'

They entered Orlando Road and about halfway down the empty street Siobhan dragged Amy through a gateway, behind a privet hedge and down the side of a Victorian house, through an open wooden door, which she closed behind her, and into the garden. They walked to the wall at the end and climbed over into the adjoining garden. They waited until a light came on in the basement, ran down the steps into the doorway, through a kitchen, down a hallway and out into the street, where a white transit was waiting with a sliding side door open. They got in. Siobhan slid the door to and they collapsed on the floor. The van took off.

'Stay lying down,' said Siobhan.

The van drove a tortuous route for over half an hour until it pulled up and there was the sound of an opening electric shutter.

'Put this on,' said Siobhan, handing her a black hood, pulling one over her own head. Amy did as she was told.

The van eased forward and pulled up. The driver stayed put. The sliding door opened and the two women were hauled out and marched stumbling over concrete flooring. They were now inside a slightly echoing space. They were not being handled lightly.

They were split up and Amy was taken into a room and slammed down in a chair to which she was tied. All her questions went unanswered. The hood was raised and tape stuck across her mouth before it was lowered again. They left her alone. As the door closed she heard Siobhan's voice:

'You took your time.'

'It was complicated,' a male voice replied.

17

'We're still trying to track down Conrad Jensen,' said Mercy. 'He has a daughter, Siobhan, did you know that?'

'He never mentioned her,' said Emma.

'Why do you think it's important to find Conrad Jensen?' asked Forsyth.

'We always like to track down people who've spent time with the victim and her family. We just need to clarify all relationships, especially the close ones, and—'

'Conrad Jensen has been vetted by the US military.'

'We'd also like to find an American called Walden Garfinkle,' said Mercy, purposely not addressing that remark. 'He might be able to shed light on Jensen's whereabouts, as he saw him in his hotel room five days ago. I don't know if your network can help with that?'

'Anything interesting at the crime scene?' asked Forsyth.

'I'm getting to that,' said Mercy. 'We've found the cab driver who picked up Jensen's daughter Siobhan from the Savoy. He says he dropped her at a flat on Lofting Road in Islington. No answer. We're working on the owner of this flat, which is a short-term let, to see if we can get a phone number for Siobhan.'

'I'm not sure this obsession with Conrad Jensen is healthy,' said Forsyth.

'It's not an obsession,' said Mercy. 'It's routine. We've covered all the other friends and visitors to this house, who've all been available for questioning and we've been able to eliminate them

162

from our inquiries. Jensen has disappeared. He's been in a relationship with Emma and yet he's never mentioned that he has a daughter. Those two things count for more in my book than his being vetted by the US military.

'As for the crime scene, the forensics have turned up a big zero on prints in and outside the car. We found no one in the mews at the time of the kidnap. My colleague discovered from residents in Lyall Street that there must have been eight people involved. There were three men seen in the street putting up the roadworks, all in hard hats, goggles, dayglo jackets and trousers. It would have taken two on the scaffolding to drop the sheet, two on the ground to sedate Pat Gould and kidnap Sophie, and one driver in the white transit that, we've had confirmed, was reversed under the arch to the mews for the girl's removal. There was also a BT Openreach van that was used by the three workmen for their escape. So it was a highly organised operation with considerable care taken. I'd be tempted to call it a military-style exercise were it not for your confidence in their vetting procedures. Have the kidnappers called again?'

Mercy didn't know why she was doing it. Riling Forsyth. Maybe his denying knowledge of Charlie had annoyed her.

'Still nothing,' said Forsyth. 'We haven't had proof of life yet. So if they keep up this level of frequency, there's a long way to go before we start negotiating. It's going to be interesting to see how they cope with simultaneous negotiations with multiple consultants. Never seen that before.'

'Is there anything particularly political that Kinderman are involved with that could complicate this kidnap?'

'That doesn't concern you. You're here to investigate,' said Forsyth, cutting her dead. 'There's another branch of operatives working on that side of things.'

'But why can't you tell her?' said Emma. 'It might help her to know.'

'I'd need clearance, and not just from Kinderman.'

'So there *is* something and it's at a very high level,' said Mercy. 'That's enough for me at the moment.'

'Not even I have clearance,' said Emma.

163

Mercy's phone went. She looked at the number, which she didn't recognise, answered it.

'We have your daughter Amy now,' said the voice. 'We'd like you to wrap up your discussion with Ryder and leave the house. We'll be in touch.'

Boxer had walked all the way home from the Fulham Road to his flat in Belsize Park. He was soaked through. He stripped naked, showered, and dressed again in clean, dry clothes. He unpacked the case, put the money back in the safe and sat at the table, arms folded. He stared at the two guns, whose barrels pointed at the empty package addressed to Charles Tate and the Betamax tape.

He couldn't believe what had happened to him in just over twenty-four hours. He'd tried to assimilate it as he'd walked home, hoping that his rhythmic pacing would help him comprehend the enormity, but it had been too big. Trying to disentangle the emotional fallout of the loss of the only woman he'd truly grown to love, who'd been carrying his child and had probably died as a result, was proving to be too much. In fact he couldn't even grasp the loss. When the image of her lying on the bed flickered into the darkness of his mind, he shook his head at its impossible lifelessness. Twenty-four hours ago she'd held his hands across the table, looked into his eyes and told him she was pregnant. She hadn't just been alive, but doubly alive. Doubly animated. And now?

He tried to think of his son, the impossibly small baby in an incubator whose head was lost in the palm of his hand. He'd never seen such a small living human and he feared for his survival. Was that why he'd walked away? He couldn't bear to make another emotional connection only to lose it?

He sat back, looked into himself, wanting to find an emotion, a reaction, but there was no grief. It stunned him, this incapacity to feel. Two years ago, when he'd thought that Amy had been killed, even though he hadn't seen a body, he'd had some premonition of doom. Something had told him that things had gone wrong. He'd been mentally prepared for disaster and, when he was confronted with the evidence of it, an access to grief had opened up in him. He remembered being in the chief inspector's office in Madrid and shunting the desk across the room with his sobs. But this? He

164

was suspended from all emotion. It was as if, in being unable to find an expression for the complexity of his feelings, his mind had flipped a switch, turned it off until later, when there might be a better chance of managing a reaction.

The inertia frustrated him. The suppressed turmoil of his inner life made him want to move enormous things: buildings, bridges. He hammered his fists on the table, wanting to, needing to get something out, but it refused to come. He paced the room. Each time he turned, he glanced down at the table – the guns, the tape – and he knew that he wouldn't be able to bear the rest of his life without knowing what was on that cassette. But he had to do something *now*. The tape needed a special player; he would have to track one down, he had an idea where. But that wouldn't resolve his need for action.

His eyes fell on the Walther P99: a brutal gun, a lawmaker's weapon whose nine-millimetre potential would stop villains in their tracks. Ironic that it had been in the hands of a criminal, but good for Boxer if he found the need to use it. The thuggishness of the weapon suddenly appealed to him. He reached over and hefted it in his hand, continued his pacing. It came to him that now was the time to go and see Jess.

He put the FN57 underneath the floorboards and slipped the Walther P99 into the pocket of his jacket.

The rain had eased off to a blustery spit. He walked to Haverstock Hill and hailed a cab to take him to the Caledonian Road. On the way he thought about how he was going to play this, given Jess's evident security consciousness. He asked the driver to let him out at the railway bridge, where, in the dripping darkness, he unloaded the gun, putting the bullets in his pocket, and moved it to the small of his back. He walked down the Cally Road and turned right into the poorly lit Bemerton estate towards Glider's building. Again he was picked up by outriders, who tailed him to the foot of Glider's stairs, where Jess was there to meet him.

'Didn't know you had an appointment,' she said.

'I don't,' said Boxer. 'I've come to see you. Is there somewhere we can talk?'

'What's it about?'

'A little money-making business.'

'Do I look like I need to make money?'

'Everybody can use a little extra, and this is very easy.'

'Why me?'

'I think you've got the right qualities for the job.'

'Follow me,' she said, dispersing her team.

He'd been right. The flattery had worked. They went up the stairs to the first floor and along an open walkway to a flat. She unlocked the door, pushed it open and motioned him inside. As Boxer walked in, she reached under his jacket and pulled the Walther P99 out of his waistband. Boxer carried on, flipping the light switches as he went. The flat was almost empty apart from some rudimentary furniture, two battered armchairs, a table with an ashtray containing four upstanding cigarette butts, and two stools on either side.

'Keeping it simple,' he said.

'What's this?' she asked, holding the gun out, pointing it at him.

'It's a Walther P99.'

'Looks like you're expecting trouble.'

'Not from you,' said Boxer. 'It's not my gun.'

'Whose is it?'

'Know a guy called Jarrod?'

She shook her head.

'How about Delroy Pink?'

She went very still. Her dark hair was scraped back so painfully tight into a ponytail that it had almost given her eyes some chinoiserie. She was very well built. Her shoulders were square under a short leather jacket from which a length of belt hung down to her thigh. She wore a tight dark grey roll-neck jumper, which revealed an almost flat, hard chest. Her legs were long and strong, encased in dark stretch jeans, and she was wearing brand-new black and grey trail shoes.

'How do you know Pink?'

'Our paths crossed tonight,' said Boxer. 'He kidnapped a friend of mine called Marcus Alleyne and sold him on. Know anything about that?'

'Sit down in that armchair,' she said.

'He told me you paid him twenty-five thousand. How much did that leave you with?'

'Sit down,' she said, shaking the gun at him.

'You pay someone twenty-five grand, it would make me think you'd come away with fifty at least,' said Boxer.

'Sit the fuck down,' said Jess.

Two steps and he was on her; she fired the Walther P99, which clicked loudly, and it meant she had no time to defend herself. He hit her hard in the side of the head with a fist full of bullets and she dropped to the floor faster than a sack of rubble. His hand hurt a lot, but he didn't care or notice. He didn't even try to shake it out. He was engrossed by the action. He removed the gun from her grasp, reloaded it with the bullets. He went to the kitchen and filled a bowl with water, came back and tipped it over her face. The only reaction from her was a quivering of her eyeballs under their lids. He'd been too wound up, hit her too hard. He slapped her lightly back and forth on the cheeks, raised her eyelids. She murmured. He refilled the bowl, flicked water into her face, and finally she came round, looked up at him blinking.

'Bit of a glass jaw on you, Jess,' he said. 'Got to make sure you get your retaliation in first.'

'Fuck off.'

'Don't take it badly. I've got a lot more experience than you,' he said. 'Didn't mean to hit you so hard. I've had a stressful evening. But you've got to learn something: stealing people is wrong.'

'I didn't steal anybody.'

'Talk me through it. Who put you up to the job?'

She licked her lips, couldn't keep the hate out of her eyes.

'We'll get there in the end,' he said. 'I don't want to humiliate you even more, but I've got no problem hurting you. You've got to understand that I don't like kidnappers and I believe in gender equality. So you will get the same punishment as any man. Now look me in the eyes.'

She looked at him and he saw fear worm its way in over the hate, knew that what he had in his own eyes was beyond her comprehension. He grabbed her by the ponytail and her ankle and rolled her over. He sat on her buttocks and put his foot in the back of her knee, yanked the ankle back and started twisting it.

'You ever had torn ankle and knee ligaments?' he asked. 'It'll take the swing out of your high kicks.'

167

He upped the pressure and she slammed her hands into the floor with the pain.

'OK, OK. Let's talk,' she said.

'Start with how you were contacted.'

'Can we do this without you sitting on me?'

'Sure, but don't make me get you down on the floor again, or that knee won't work the same for the rest of your life,' said Boxer.

He frisked her thoroughly, took her mobile phone.

'Sit in the armchair,' he said. 'Hands on head.'

He pulled her up, pushed her back into the armchair so that her head flicked back. She looked a bit groggy. He sat on the arm of the chair opposite her and waved her on with the gun.

'I used to work for an old boyfriend, a drug dealer, who taught me a bit about running security,' she said. 'We bust up. I heard Glider was looking for someone and he took me on. Then about three months ago the old boyfriend contacted me again, invited me to a party. The idea was for me to meet some guy he'd been doing business with. I'd tell you his name but I'm not sure it would help.'

'Try me.'

'Todd Bone,' she said. 'Yeah, I thought it was made up too. Older guy. Medium height. Stocky. American, in his fifties, grey beard, long grey hair. Kind of hippyish. Green waistcoat, yellow shirt, bead bracelet, that kind of shit. Not my type at all. But he knew his stuff.'

'What do you mean, knew his stuff?'

'About security, tracking people, bringing people in, dealing with people. I learnt a lot from him. He said he'd worked with an American security company.'

'Did he tell you a name?'

'He might have done, I don't remember.'

'Kinderman?'

She looked blank.

'How about Anchorlight?'

'Yes, that was it,' said Jess. 'Who are they?'

'A company that runs security operations in places like Iraq and Afghanistan. They work for embassies, oil installations, that kind of thing,' said Boxer. 'So you didn't just meet him once. You got to know him. How did that happen?'

'I had an affair with him,' she said, shrugging her shoulders.

'I thought he wasn't your type.'

'He wasn't, but I dunno, I couldn't help myself. It just happened. He's twenty-five years older than me, for fuck's sake. Mind you, he knew a thing or two about that stuff too. And he was strong, really powerful, the arms and chest on him, amazing.'

'So you're talking to each other ... in bed. He's telling you how to run Glider's operation and you're telling him how Glider works. How did Marcus Alleyne come up?'

'He asked me if I knew him.'

'*When* did he ask you?'

'A couple of months ago,' said Jess. 'I said I didn't know him but I'd heard the name. Glider had it in for Alleyne but I didn't know why and he asked me to find out.'

'Did you think that was odd?'

'Yeah, but harmless too, and I wanted him to be happy so I found out.'

'You in love with this guy by now?'

'Pretty much ... I mean in lust, in love, who knows? All I know was I didn't want the fucking to stop. One of the very few guys I've been to bed with who really knew what he was doing.'

'So how did he persuade you that kidnapping Marcus Alleyne was a good idea?'

'He's working freelance, this guy Todd, and he told me he'd met a guy who's owed money, a lot of money for some tourist development, by Alleyne's family in Trinidad and he wants to apply pressure. There's a lot of money in it for us, he says.'

'Like how much?'

'A hundred gees.'

'Didn't you think that was crazy money for a small-time fence like Marcus Alleyne?'

'The tourist development was worth tens of millions.'

'Why involve Delroy Pink?' asked Boxer. 'Why give away twenty-five if you don't have to? Todd Bone sounds like a capable guy.'

'He said Pink was the key, that through Pink we could bring Alleyne out into the open, take him,' said Jess. 'I would give the go-ahead on behalf of Glider. Alleyne would be glad to be doing

169

Glider some kind of service. Pink would make the offer, do the deal. We'd be out of it. All we had to do was take delivery of Alleyne and collect our money.'

'Is that what happened?'

'Pretty much.'

'So you haven't had your money yet?'

Jess said nothing.

'When was the last time you saw Todd Bone?'

'Last night.'

'You seeing him again tonight?'

She nodded.

'Where do you meet?'

'My place.'

'What time?'

'He just turns up.'

'What do you do?'

'We have a few drinks and go to bed.'

'And you still call him Todd?'

'Why not?'

'I'd have thought after all these months you'd want to know his real name.'

'What's to stop him giving me another bullshit name?'

'Let's go,' said Boxer. 'And don't bring your people with you, because if I get a sniff of them, you'll get a nine millimetre in your leg.'

They left the flat. Boxer put the gun in his pocket, took Jess by the arm. They walked to the Caledonian Road and Barnsbury overground station and took a train to Kentish Town West. From there it was a short walk to the huge red-brick facades of the Peckwater estate where Jess lived. Her flat was on the fourth floor of a block set back from the road; it had a small balcony that overlooked a kids' playground.

In the flat he told her to lie on the floor of the bedroom with her hands behind her head. He searched the chest of drawers, wardrobe and bedside table. There were two sets of handcuffs and a roll of duct tape in the drawer.

'Whose are these?'

'Does it matter?'

'Are you into it or is he?'

'They're his,' said Jess.

'Do you just go along with it?'

'I didn't like it at first. But he got a kick out of it and that was good enough for me.'

'What time does he usually show?'

'After ten.'

It was close to that time now.

'Does he have a set of keys?'

'Yes. Sometimes if I have to work late with Glider he lets himself in.'

'You keep any weapons in the flat?'

'Just my feet and hands ... and kitchen knives if you count them.'

'When you hear Todd come in, I want you to call him into the bedroom,' said Boxer. 'Don't try anything clever or you'll both get shot.'

The bed had a metal frame. He told her to strip to her underwear and lie face up on the bed, and used one set of handcuffs to secure her arms above her head. He pocketed the others. He checked to make sure that he could see her from the galley kitchen and then closed the bedroom door, placed her mobile phone on the table in the living room and retreated to the optimum viewing point.

It was a thirty-minute wait and all of it agony. The mental effort required to prevent negative thoughts from entering his brain was brutal. He couldn't help it. The sight of Isabel in the hospital went through him like an infection. He was desperate to remember the animated version of her, the one that had held his hands across the table, but it wouldn't come. All he could see was the waxen, lifeless skin around the features that had become so dear to him: the straight eyebrows, the beautiful mouth, the fine declivity. And then there was the stillness of her, the terrible absence of her. He waited for the swelling membrane of some emotion or other, but none came. All that emerged from the murkiness of his mind was an awkward guilt that left him feeling in some way responsible.

A key squirming into the lock of the front door snapped him out of his unbearable thoughts; the shutter slammed down over memory. He tightened his grip around the Walther P99, took a deep breath.

Todd Bone came into the living room from the hallway. He wasn't wearing hippy gear. This time he was in black jeans, a black waterproof jacket and a black woollen hat with none of his grey hair visible. And this version of Todd Bone, if it was him, had no beard. From the darkness of the kitchen Boxer could see him clocking the mobile phone on the table. He also noticed that this Todd Bone was wearing latex gloves.

'I'm in here, Todd,' said Jess.

Bone went to the bedroom door, opened it, stood with his hands behind his back, saw her lying on the bed, handcuffed. She didn't smile.

'See anything you like, mister?' she said in a poor American accent, turning her head to look at him. She seemed shocked, uncertain, perhaps puzzled by his different appearance.

'Sure do,' said Bone, but the accent was off.

'Who the fuck are you?' she said.

Bone moved forward much faster than Boxer had expected, as if there was some urgency. His hands came from behind his back and before Boxer had a chance to move or Jess had time to even scream, he was on her. Boxer saw her legs kick up as if trying to scissor Bone's head, but he was prepared and her disadvantage under his advancing weight was just too much. His body came down on her powerful legs as his hands locked themselves around her throat. Boxer moved at pace across the living room, knocking into the table as he went. Todd's head turned and Boxer knew in that moment that he was dealing with someone highly trained.

It had been a while since Boxer had been in hand-to-hand combat. He still went to training but that was no substitute for the real thing. Bone was fast. He intuited Boxer's reluctance to fire his weapon with Jess behind him on the bed, and his need for Bone's survival. He lunged forward, hand outstretched, and locked on to the Walther P99. Boxer aimed his left fist at his opponent's throat, but Bone's head twisted away and it slammed into the side of his neck. He could feel an expert hand working on the joints of his own holding the gun and he jammed his thumb into Bone's right eye, rammed his hip into his chest and tried to wrench his

172

gun hand free, sending the Walther P99 spinning across the room towards the door.

A powerful arm closed around Boxer's neck from behind and he realised he was no match for this brute, that he needed help, which was still secured to the bed. He drove backwards with both legs and there was a cracking sound and a grunt of pain as Bone's back made jarring contact with the metal bed frame. He was momentarily hurt and Jess was quick enough to wrap her thighs around his neck. He tried to bring his arms up but she put the squeeze on his carotids and his arm around Boxer's neck went limp. Boxer pulled out the handcuffs as Jess rolled Bone over, still between her legs. He secured Bone's hands behind his back and finally Jess released him. Boxer massaged the semi-conscious man's neck and his eyelids fluttered.

'Is this Todd Bone?' asked Boxer, gasping for breath.

'No it's not,' said Jess, leaning over the edge of the mattress, her arms still secured to the bedhead. 'I've no idea who this guy is.'

18

'Is that you?' asked Amy, still hooded up but with the tape removed, her hands secured with plastic cuffs to the chair.

'Could be,' said Siobhan.

'I don't know how you've got the nerve to come and talk to me,' said Amy. 'You fucked me over. I heard you when they brought us in. You're … you're *part* of this.'

'That old line,' said Siobhan. 'Nothing personal, just business.'

'You mean *everything*?' said Amy. 'It was all … business?'

'Ah, the kiss?' said Siobhan, stroking Amy's thigh. 'You liked the kiss after all.'

Amy ripped her leg away.

'I'm not talking about the stupid kiss,' she said. 'What about the guys beating you up?'

'They were part of the crew.'

'And the rape?'

'Theatrical blood between the buttocks,' said Siobhan. 'But I did take a beating. That had to be real. Your father wouldn't have bought make-up and it would have come off in the bath.'

'What about Tanya Birch?'

'She's real … if you can call that manky bitch real. Con's got one in every port. They call him the Golden Dick. Fuck a frog if it'd stop hopping.'

'And are you really Conrad Jensen's daughter?'

'Well, daughter/shmaughter … know what I mean?' said Siobhan. 'But for my pains I am from his lusty loins.'

174

'And has he really disappeared or is that ... ? That must be fake too.'

'No, Con has had to disappear ... nobody knows where he is.'

'You mean you *knew* he was going to disappear?'

Siobhan said nothing.

'OK, I'll take that as a yes,' said Amy. 'But why involve my dad? What's he got to do with this? You already had Marcus, which I assume was to get inside information on some special investigation from my mother. So why pull my dad into this? And what is *this*?'

'It's a series kidnap,' said Siobhan. 'The first of its kind.'

'Who?'

'Rich kids. An Indian layabout, a German art student who'll never have to create anything in her life, a Chinese economics undergrad who hasn't had to understand it from the ground up, an Australian druggie, a Russian mafia adviser's little boy and a young girl called Sophie Railton-Bass. Daughter of the CEO of Kinderman, an American military corporation.'

'All those nationalities,' said Amy. 'Is this political?'

'We're nothing if not ambitious.'

'All right,' said Amy, sensing some resistance, 'so you kidnap Marcus because you know my mother will be one of the investigators, but why do you need me?'

'Icing on the cake?'

'But you didn't need to bring my dad into it. Why do that?'

'Don't ask me. I'm not the mastermind. I just do my job,' said Siobhan. 'Now your starter for ten is to tell me what you and your mum got up to when you were a kid. We're talking proof-of-life shit. You know what that is by the sound of things.'

'She was a lousy mum.'

'But you must have done things together like ... kidnap investigations maybe?'

'Not funny,' said Amy. 'Because, if you really want to know, she used to show me how to take fingerprints.'

'That *is* sad.'

'It was something.'

'And what did you do with your dada?'

'You know how to annoy people.'

'Just one of my specialities.'

'My dad was out of the country most of the time.'

'You've got to give me something.'

'El Osito. That should do it.'

'Teddy bear? OK.'

'A Colombian drug baron who was going to kill me until my dad stepped in.'

'Really?' said Siobhan. 'I wonder whether Con would do that. The more I think about it, the more I realise that it's not so much people my father's obsessed by as their secrets. He has to know what's going on inside. But as soon as he finds out, it's like seeing the inside of a magic trick, very mundane, a bit of jibber-jabber, some sleight of hand, laughable, and he moves on.'

'A secret's only interesting while it's still a secret,' said Amy. 'Once it's out in the world ...'

'That's the problem: you can't share a secret,' said Siobhan. 'It's either yours or mine but never ours.'

'But you can bind yourself to someone with a secret,' said Amy, 'as long as there's trust.'

'Well, that's us finished,' said Siobhan. 'Now that I've *betrayed* you.'

'You can always rebuild the trust,' said Amy, easing back on the anger, remembering now all those overheard conversations between Mercy and Charlie, recalling the demands of her situation.

'Truth and reconciliation,' said Siobhan, with a scoffing laugh. 'And I can tell you we're very short of the first commodity around here. Bunch of fucking spooks.'

'Is that was your crew consists of?' asked Amy.

'Friends of Dad,' said Siobhan. 'I don't think he's got a normal friend. I mean someone who isn't operating, if you know what I mean. Someone who'd just come round to watch the football and have a beer with you on the sofa.'

'Where do they come from?'

'All walks of life. No, that's not quite true, because that would include normal people, and none of them are that. There's special forces nutters, paranoid spooks, private security company bods, ex-military maniacs, a few busted cops, some business types, silver-tongued lobbyists, think-tank nerds, an eerie economist or two … it goes on. Fingers everywhere.'

'Do you … they … call themselves something?' asked Amy. 'If you're aiming at something political, then you've got a cause. Most people with a cause have a name.'

'If they have, they ain't told me,' said Siobhan. 'I'm too lowly. A dogsbody. Expendable.'

'What did you used to do with *your* mother?' asked Amy, casting her rod again.

'Now that would be telling you … something,' said Siobhan, picking up on the trick. 'But I will tell you one secret if you want.'

'Don't bother unless it's real.'

'The kiss,' said Siobhan. 'That was real.'

Mercy paced her kitchen, her police phone in one hand and her private mobile in the other, waiting for another call from the kidnappers. The landlady who'd rented the flat out in Lofting Road to Conrad Jensen's daughter Siobhan had called to give the contact number, which Mercy had tried. It was no longer available. She wondered if the landlady had been given a wrong number, but apparently she'd used it earlier and spoken to Siobhan. Mercy was also trying Amy and Boxer, leaving messages and texts on their unresponsive phones. The lack of contact from all sides was making her desperate.

Her private mobile rang. She slapped it to her face.

'Amy's been telling us that when she was small, you taught her how to take fingerprints,' said the voice, male, the same as the last time. 'Sweet. Not exactly cupcakes and tinsel, Mercy. You were one tough-love mother, weren't you?'

'She wasn't interested in cooking. So you've got the proof of life. What else?'

'How's it going with Ryder?'

'Nothing much happening on that front. You're not communicating with him, and—'

'I meant your relationship.'

'Does it matter?'

'Everything matters when your daughter and your lover are at stake.'

'Well our relationship is frosty. He's very protective of his information. He's keeping everything separate. I investigate the London scenario and he's got a whole bunch of other people looking into the political and Kinderman side of things, which I know nothing about and will never know ...'

'That's fine. Don't worry about the CIA and Kinderman. We'll deal with them. You just give us what we want and you'll see Amy and Marcus alive and well again at the end of all this.'

'So what *do* you want?'

'I want you to make Ryder love you.'

'That's not going to happen.'

'You don't have to fuck him, just make him think that *you* think he walks on water.'

'He's already there splashing about on Galilee.'

'You're weird, Mercy Danquah.'

'You're hitting me on my professional side. It's taken a lot of punishment over the years. It can ride with the punches. I've done rope-a-dope.'

'Another thing: tell your friend Charles Boxer that we've got Amy.'

'I've been trying to. He's turned his mobile off.'

'Tell him it's time to back off now,' said the voice, 'unless he wants to get himself hurt.'

'Back off from what?'

'Trying to find Conrad Jensen.'

'Hold on a sec, *I'm* trying to find Conrad Jensen.'

'Everybody keeps their distance while this plays itself out.'

'What plays itself out?'

'As far as you're concerned, it's just some kidnaps.'

Boxer released Jess from her cuffs. She got dressed. He picked up the Walther P99 and pulled the woollen hat off the man's head, which was shaved. He looked to be late thirties/early forties and not American, unless he was a new arrival. He was still blinking, taking things in from the new perspective lying on his back on the floor with his wrists cuffed.

'Anybody else have keys apart from Todd?' asked Boxer.

'Like, *no* ... what do you think I am?'

178

'Just a question,' said Boxer, looking down. 'So, who are you?'

The guy stared back up, said nothing.

'You been sent by Todd Bone?' asked Jess.

Nothing.

'Boil a kettle,' said Boxer. 'You got a hammer? We've got to get this guy talking.'

Jess went to the kitchen. Boxer sat on the bed turning the gun in his hand.

'Where are you from?' he asked.

Nothing.

'Somebody hire you to kill her?'

No reply.

'You understand English?'

A basilisk stare that made Boxer think he was going to be remembered for eternity. There was only one way out with guys like this.

Jess came back in with the steaming kettle and a claw hammer. He took the hammer, put the kettle on the bedside table. He kicked the man's legs apart and trod on his ankles.

'Undo his trousers,' he said. 'Pull down his pants.'

Jess straddled him and undid his belt. The guy started struggling and Boxer tapped both knees with the hammer. She pulled down his trousers and pants, stood up and backed away.

'Definitely not Todd,' she said.

Boxer took the kettle, stood over the man, still with his feet on his ankles, and held it over the groin area.

'Now keep still or there could be an accident.'

He jogged some boiling water over the man's stomach. There was a sharp intake of breath.

'Now you know,' said Boxer. 'I'm not messing around. Who sent you here?'

'I don't know his name,' said the guy, his accent eastern European.

'Where you from?'

'Ukraine.'

'Who taught you to fight like that?'

'Spetsnaz.'

'You were sent to kill her?'

He nodded.

'You been paid for the job?'

'Not all of it.'

'How much?'

'Thousand before, thousand after.'

'Two fucking grand,' said Jess. 'To off *me*?'

'Not worth having your tackle steamed off for that, is it?' said Boxer. 'Where do you go to collect your thousand after?'

The Ukrainian struggled with that, writhed with his head, being careful not to upset Boxer and the kettle.

'You want to get out of this alive ... get back to Kiev?' asked Boxer.

'Not Kiev,' he said. 'Yalta.'

'Of course. Russian Spetsnaz. Crimea. Sorry. Well, what's it to be?'

'I tell you that, they'll find me, kill me.'

'Who's they?'

'A group. I don't know what they called. They got something ... what you say ... a cause. They fighting for something. I don't know what.'

'Boiling water on your groin *and* killed later. Or no boiling water and killed later,' said Boxer. 'I know what I'd choose.'

'When I finish the job I send a code to a phone number. We meet half an hour later under a bridge over the canal near King's Cross. Caledonian Road.'

'I know it,' said Jess.

'What do you have to take with you to prove you killed the girl?'

'She got a chain around her neck with a ring on it.'

'That's my mother's engagement ring,' said Jess. 'She gave it to me when she died. I told Todd that.'

'No need to feel betrayed,' said Boxer. 'It's just work. You got some kind of a vehicle the three of us can use?'

'Only a motorbike, but I can get a car if I go back to Glider's.'

'Then go.'

Mercy was outside the flat on Lofting Road in her car, waiting for the landlady to show. A BMW Mini pulled up in front of the house; a woman got out and looked around. Mercy crossed the road, flashed her warrant card.

'She sent me new sets of keys,' said the woman, as she let them into the flat. 'Said there'd been a problem with the locks. I haven't had time to get round here to take a look.' She paused at the door, inspected the work.

Mercy saw the two mobiles on the table.

'Don't touch anything,' she said, pulling on some latex gloves and inspecting the iPhone. It was dead. The landlady came in, looked over her shoulder.

'It's been erased,' she said. 'Or the SIM's been removed.'

Mercy opened it up. No SIM. She turned on the other phone without picking it up and looked in the photo section, saw shots of herself, Boxer and Esme, knew that it was Amy's phone.

'What can you tell me about the tenant?' she asked.

'Not a lot. We didn't meet. She paid me in advance.'

'Online transfer?'

'From a company with an offshore bank account in Bermuda called Ferguson Consulting.'

'Get me the details of that account and send them through to my phone, will you?' said Mercy. 'I want to get forensics in here too.'

'What ... now?'

'Tomorrow morning. Can you be here to let them in?'

She walked around the rooms, put in another call to Boxer, still no answer. Came across Amy's bag, knelt down and went through it. Nothing unusual. She looked up and saw from her vantage point that Amy's mobile was slightly tilted. She went back to the table, flipped the mobile, found the screwed-up, flattened piece of paper that Amy had left and teased it open. A UK mobile phone number. She called the operations room at the kidnap unit HQ in Vauxhall, asked them to check the number for her, do a trace on it and call her back. She stared into the table trying to stem a rush of thoughts and emotions about the last time Amy had gone missing, the terrible sense of loss even after years of not getting on. But now ... she winced at the memory of that hug Amy had given her in the coffee shop, her new grown up girl.

*

Jess called Boxer, told him she was outside with the car. Boxer took the Ukrainian down. As they drove to the rendezvous point, Jess handed over the chain from her neck. They parked outside some seventies blocks of flats down a side street, crossed the Cally Road and went down the steps to the Regent's Canal towpath to perform the recce. They looked towards King's Cross and decided that there were too many buildings overlooking that stretch. They went under the bridge formed by the Caledonian Road and walked along the canal, past the ramp up to Muriel Street and as far as the western portal of the Islington tunnel.

On this side there were no overlooking buildings and the narrow boats moored on either side of the canal were silent, unsmoking, uninhabited. The nearest one was twenty metres away from the bridge and had a canvas cover over the rear deck and entrance; its centre was weighed down by a tarn of leafy water. On the way back to the bridge, Boxer unclipped the canvas, making sure he didn't tip any of the water over the side. He told Jess to go back to the car and wait for his text, be ready to mobilise.

'If it's Todd coming to this meet, I want to be here,' she said. 'We've got things to discuss.'

'That's not how it's going to work. There'll be no confrontations. We want to find out where he's going. You wait in the car,' said Boxer. 'You know this area?'

'Lived around here all my life.'

'We don't know where he's going to come from or his mode of transport, so we have to be prepared for everything. I want you to park the car where you can see both access points down to the towpath. If you see Bone arrive or leave, you text me the word Bone.'

'What about me?' asked the Ukrainian.

'You're going to go back up on to the Caledonian Road to send the coded text message that will bring Todd Bone here. I'll be watching you from across the road. You come back down here, stand in the light and wait. When Bone arrives, you hand over the chain and ring, take your money and split,' said Boxer, taking a shot of the Ukrainian with his phone. 'Make it quick. If you tell him anything about us, I'll find you.'

'I want the chain and ring back,' said Jess, stepping forward.

'Don't complicate the issue,' said Boxer. 'Let's just get it done. I'll be under the canvas of the narrowboat. Take your positions and let's keep it relaxed.'

Jess and the Ukrainian trotted up the steps to the Cally Road while Boxer slipped under the canvas at the stern of the boat, careful to maintain the puddle of leafy water. He took up a position with a view of the towpath, making sure his back didn't make contact with the canvas.

Minutes later, the Ukrainian walked slowly out of the deeper darkness under the Caledonian Road and held up his phone. He retreated back under the bridge. Traffic heading into King's Cross crashed overhead.

They waited. Boxer changed position after ten minutes. Too uncomfortable. He lay on his back, listening with the Walther P99 on his chest. He tried to keep his mind blank, but the images of the night kept streaming through his brain. He saw himself stuck on the threshold of the hospital room, not wanting to go in, knowing that what he would see would change him forever. He toyed with the words: Isabel has passed away. Isabel is no longer with us. Isabel is dead. Isabel has died. He said them to himself over and over until the words achieved a wonderful meaninglessness, one that released him from their terrible reality. His mind drifted to the struggling infant in the incubator. That tight, purposeful frown. He tried to think what he should do with this little life that had been left to him, and that was when he heard footsteps on the towpath coming from the direction of the Islington tunnel.

He eased over on to his front, peeked out from under the canvas awning. Nothing. No one. Silence. The footsteps started up again. They were coming up alongside the narrowboat and stopped again at the stern, right next to where he was hidden. He heard the man breathing through his nose. Still couldn't see him. The Ukrainian appeared in the low light shed from the Caledonian Road on to the towpath and made a signal with his hands. The footsteps started up again more confidently and the man finally eased into view, walking slowly but decisively towards the Ukrainian. He was wearing a wide-brimmed hat and a calf-length coat with his hands in the pockets. He was medium height, stocky, with powerful shoulders, which fitted Jess's description of

Todd Bone. Boxer reckoned he'd spent some time assessing the scenario from a distance.

Bone cruised up to the bridge, shook hands with the Ukrainian and they squared off in the dim light. The Ukrainian produced the chain and ring from his pocket. Bone took out a small flashlight, checked it, nodded. He reached into his inside pocket for what Boxer assumed would be the money and produced a SIG Sauer with suppressor attached. No words preceded the four sharp clicks that were the shots that put the Ukrainian down on the towpath. Bone finished him off with a head shot before disappearing into the darkness under the bridge. He came back into the light with weights in his hands, which he must have stowed earlier. He pushed them down the Ukrainian's jacket, rolled him over the edge and into the canal. He straightened his coat and hat and walked back under the bridge. Boxer saw him turn right and go up the steps to the west side of the Caledonian Road. It had taken no longer than ninety seconds.

Boxer sent a pre-prepared text to Jess and got out from under the canvas, clipped it back into place. He ran up the steps, but took the path to the east side of the Cally Road much more slowly, holding back in the darkness of the trees. Bone was already heading south, hands in pockets, relaxed pace. Boxer waited, let him get a good fifty metres ahead before he stepped out on to the pavement and followed him on the opposite side of the busy road.

After a few hundred metres Bone crossed at a zebra crossing and disappeared down a side street. Boxer waited again, watched him, certain that he was trained and would feel a tail at a hundred metres. He called Jess, told her to turn her car around and ease down towards Muriel Street, park, turn the engine off and see if Bone came past on foot. Bone turned left down Muriel Street. Boxer hung back still on the Cally Road, checking the map of the area on his phone and what the options were. The street ahead of him was empty of people; he didn't want to risk going down there. Nothing from Jess. He crossed the road, took the first turning on the right and waited by a concrete pillar in front of an ugly block of flats opposite the Thornhill Arms. He texted a question mark to Jess. She came back with a zero.

Just as Boxer felt his nerve stretched to snapping point, Bone came out of Muriel Street, glanced down towards him and carried straight on. Boxer turned and ran down a parallel street, took a left turn and crossed the road, hid behind a brick pillar by the gate of a kids' playground, which had a view of the street Bone had taken. He sent a text to Jess telling her where Bone had gone, but not to move. He looked at the map again; saw his problem. Bone had all the options, and Boxer realised he was going to need some luck.

Bone appeared at the end of the street, turned into it and started heading towards Boxer, but on the other side of the road. Boxer crossed over, veered away from some steps to a blue-tiled building and the Café Niko; Bone passed in front of him, slowed and got into a blue Ford Focus parked on the corner. Boxer took the registration number, carried on walking, called Jess, told her to pick him up.

Jess pulled up alongside him forty seconds later. They cruised along Bone's route with Boxer looking right and left trying to find the blue Ford Focus. Nothing. They came to a T junction, where they saw the Ford Focus turning left on to the Pentonville Road. They followed. By the time they got to the main road, there were five cars between them and the Focus.

'Keep your distance,' said Boxer.

'Bone taught me how to follow in a car,' said Jess. 'How about that?'

'Useful,' said Boxer. 'Let's hope he doesn't spot his own distinctive style.'

At the traffic lights with Penton Street, the Ford Focus stalled. There was some honking from behind. Then the lights changed to red and it pulled away, turning left.

'That was one of his tricks,' said Jess.

'The old ones are the best,' said Boxer, and switched his mobile phone on.

19

'That phone, Mercy, it's a disposable but it's turned on and we've done a trace on it to an address in Tower Hamlets. Corner of Duff and Grundy Street. Do you want us to send someone round there?'

'No, leave it with me. Too sensitive for that.'

Mercy and the landlady left the flat. Mercy headed east around the City, down the Commercial Road, which was brutal with traffic even at this time of night, to Poplar. She found a big Victorian house at the address she'd been given, drove past it, looking it over. Must have been a pub and a survivor of some Blitz bombing, as all around were terraced houses built in the seventies. There was an empty lot next to it, fenced off, with a beaten-up car in the undergrowth. Mercy did a circuit and parked outside one of the terraces just down the street from the house. Now she saw in the orange glow of the street light an old sign on the side of the building, paint well faded: *The African Queen*. Her phone vibrated. Boxer. Finally.

'What happened to you?' she asked.

'Just tell me where you are.'

'You know they've got Amy now.'

Silence.

'Did you hear me?'

'I heard you,' said Boxer. 'She must have gone with Siobhan. I told her not to, but she's let her get into her head somehow.'

'That's Conrad Jensen's daughter,' said Mercy. 'Now that I

186

know who the Siobhan is you were talking about before.'

'And how's that?'

'One of those kidnaps I was telling you about. The Kinderman girl. The mother, Emma Railton-Bass, is the ex-wife of the CEO. Her boyfriend is Conrad Jensen. I wanted to talk to him to exclude him from our inquiries, but he couldn't be found. And now the kidnappers holding Amy have just told me that *you're* looking for him as well. And that they want you to back off too.'

'I've been set up,' said Boxer. 'I just don't understand why. Tell me where you are.'

Mercy gave him the address.

'Are you armed?' she asked.

'I could be.'

'Well bring it with you and don't drag your feet,' said Mercy. 'I'm ... I need you here.'

'Amy'll be all right,' said Boxer. 'She's learnt some stuff since she's been at LOST.'

'We don't know what we're dealing with here,' said Mercy. 'It feels big and ... just come, will you?'

'I'm on my way.'

'And come alone. Nobody else should know about this.'

Jess turned off the Pentonville Road, trying to pick up the trail of the blue Ford Focus.

'We've lost him,' she said.

'Pull in over here,' said Boxer.

He wrote the registration number he'd memorised on a piece of paper, gave it to her.

'Drive around for half an hour or so,' he said. 'See if you get lucky. If you do, follow him. Don't try to confront him. He's armed. He shot the Ukrainian. And he's expecting you to be dead, which is what will happen to you if you get anywhere near him. Just get the address where he ends up, call me. Nothing else.'

'You wonder why he didn't kill me himself?'

'Maybe he liked you too much.'

'Are all men that weird?'

'Would you have been interested if he wasn't?'

Jess stared out of the windscreen.

'Don't get excited,' said Boxer. 'But he's just gone past us on the other side of the road. So turn round. Follow him. Try and get through the lights with him this time.'

Boxer got out of the car, walked to the Angel and got a cab to the East India Dock Road. He walked up Duff Street, saw Mercy's car, got in the back, sitting low in the seat.

'That was quick.'

'You made it sound urgent,' said Boxer. 'So what are we doing here?'

'We're waiting. In this house is a mobile phone whose number was written on a piece of paper, not in Amy's handwriting, but it was left screwed up under her phone in the flat Siobhan was renting. I gave the number to the trace guys in Vauxhall and here we are.'

'What do you want to do?'

'I want to go in there, take a look.'

'How long have you been watching?'

'About forty minutes. Nothing's happened. No traffic whatsoever. Just that crack of light in the upstairs window on the first floor. Nothing on in the top or ground floors. No cameras that I can see.'

'It's an old pub.'

'And?'

'It'll have a basement with a trap for the beer barrels.'

'You think you're clever.'

'Sometimes.'

They walked round the house, found where the trap had been. It was concreted over.

'Not so clever,' said Mercy. 'Now what?'

'Front door by way of a change?' said Boxer. 'Gun in hand?'

'I can't believe I'm doing this.'

They rang the doorbell, which surprisingly worked. Waited.

A guy in his late twenties answered, hair flicked up at the front, thick-rimmed glasses, a loose-necked jumper, black skinny jeans and yellow Converse trainers. He was smoking a roll-up. Geek. The threat level was so minimal, the idea of producing a Walther P99 seemed ridiculous.

'Huh? I thought you were the pizza guys,' he said. 'Can I do for you?'

'We're in the area ...' said Boxer.

'Seems like you are.'

'... and we thought we'd drop by and say hi.'

'Right,' said the guy. 'And you are?'

'Friends,' said Boxer.

'Friends of ... the Earth?'

'Todd.'

Mercy looked perplexed.

'Don't know that I know any Todds.'

'You'll know this one,' said Boxer, and produced the Walther P99 at waist height. The guy looked down.

'Oh shit,' he said. 'I don't have any money here, you know that?'

'We're not interested in money.'

'The product's not ready yet.'

'Show it to me,' said Boxer. 'We'll decide.'

The guy backed away down the hall as Boxer and Mercy came in. He put his hands on his head as instructed, told them his name, Leo, and kept going to a door on the right-hand side. He asked permission to open it, which Boxer granted. The door was thick with insulation. The light emanating from the basement was intensely white and there was the hum of extractor fans. Boxer made a gesture for Mercy to find the phone she was looking for while he and Leo walked down into a surgically lit environment with white plastic walls, an abundance of greenery, tubing, heat and humidity. From the powerful stench of hemp he realised they were looking at an urban cannabis farm.

'That big tree at the end,' said Boxer. 'What's that?'

'That's the mother plant. Provides all the seeds to grow these little guys,' said Leo. 'This is going to be the best crop of Super Lemon Haze grown in London, but it needs another couple of weeks.'

'And the lights. What kind of lights are these?'

'Metal halide,' said Leo.

There was a gurgling sound and a gentle thump followed by hissing, and a mist rose up amongst the leaves.

'I'm using hydroponic propagation with an advanced nutrient system.'

'And the power to run it?'

'I steal it from the grid.'

'You have to keep an eye on something like this.'

'That's why I'm here twenty-four/seven.'

'Got it,' Mercy shouted down. 'First floor.'

Boxer pointed Leo back up the stairs, told him to shut the door. Leo was confused. Not sure what this was about. The doorbell went. Boxer looked at Leo.

'The pizza you were supposed to bring.'

'You paid?'

Leo nodded.

Boxer opened the door. Domino's. Took the carton, handed it to Leo. They went up to the first floor and a room that had everything in it: desk, computer, TV, bed, cooker, gas bottle, fridge. It was a tip, too, with every conceivable fast food horror represented in empty box form with leftovers.

'Don't get out much,' said Boxer.

'Not allowed.'

'This place should stink with all this crap,' said Mercy, disgusted.

'I'd say that's a tribute to the chemical preservatives used in fast food production,' said Leo.

'Whose phone is this?' asked Mercy, pointing at the mobile on the desk behind the computer.

'Reef's.'

'Who's Reef?' asked Mercy. 'And is that a real name?'

'It's the only name he has,' said Leo. 'This is his farm. He's got maybe ten of these in London. Moves them around all the time. He's a specialist.'

'What do you do when this phone rings?'

'I answer it,' said Leo.

'Let's keep this moving, Leo,' said Mercy. 'We haven't got all night.'

'I listen to the request and call Reef, give him the message.'

'Who was the last person to call this number?'

'No names are ever used.'

'When did they last use this number?'

'This evening around seven.'

190

'What was the message?'

'"She's coming."'

'That was it?' asked Mercy.

'I can only tell you what was said.'

'Male or female voice?' asked Boxer.

'I'd say female but deep, bit of a croak in it.'

'She called before or was that the first time?'

'She's called a few times.'

'How do you get in touch with Reef?' asked Mercy.

'I call him.'

'Sounds easy.'

'Well, it is once you've got used to the protocol.'

'Which is?'

'He changes his number every day. I access it by running code through a website.'

'What code?'

'I have a program I run,' said Leo. 'The number changes every week as does that phone there on the desk. It's security. That's all.'

'What happens if you need to get in touch with Reef in an emergency?'

'No different. I just call him.'

'How often does he drop in?'

'Once every few days.'

'When did he last come?'

'Hasn't been since Tuesday, said he had something on.'

'Does he warn you?'

'Sends me a text.'

'Does he have a key?'

'Sure.'

'Let's have a look at your phone,' said Mercy.

'Are you going to tell me what this is about?'

'We're part of the Met's Drugs Directorate,' said Mercy, looking through the messages. 'But we're not interested in you.'

Leo looked at Boxer, then at the Walther P99, and scepticism was a mild form of the unease that passed across his face.

'What do you know about Reef?' asked Boxer.

'That he knows more about drugs than anybody else out there.'

'Is he a dealer?'

'More of a connoisseur, I'd say.'

'But he's not growing this for fun, is he?'

'Mostly, yeah,' said Leo. 'He's competing to produce the weed with the highest THC in the world. With some of his stuff he's hit more than twenty-five per cent THC content.'

'He still sells it, though.'

'Sure, but that's not the point,' said Leo. 'The point is to be the best—'

'Will you two shut up,' said Mercy. 'There's a message here, came through four hours ago from Reef. Says "Abt 12.00". What does that mean?'

Leo was hesitant. Boxer levelled the Walther P99 at his left eye.

'This isn't my gun,' he said. 'But I looked at the ammo the guy was using in it, and I can tell you, this would not leave much of your head for posterity.'

'You creep me out, you know that?'

'Tell her.'

'It means he's coming round here in about twenty minutes.'

'Well that's convenient,' said Mercy. 'And it means you won't implicate yourself.'

'You mind if I smoke?' asked Leo. 'Need to mellow myself out a bit.'

'You never had a gun pointed at you before?' asked Boxer.

'Sure, but not by someone like you.'

'What do you mean by that?' asked Mercy.

'He looks as if he doesn't care one way or the other.'

'There must be plenty of people like that in your business.'

'Not really. This isn't a gangster business. We're not looking for world domination. Just trying to grow a nice crop of weed is all. Now can I smoke?'

'Let the poor bastard smoke,' said Boxer.

Leo slowly opened a Tupperware box on the desk and removed a grey-green clump. He laid out a paper and sprinkled roll-up tobacco on it, then brushed some of the green clump on top. He rolled it up, lit it, inhaled deeply.

'You want to try?'

'No he doesn't,' said Mercy.

'Just a toke, won't do you no harm,' said Leo, holding it out.

'Don't,' said Mercy.

Boxer took the joint, drew on it, inhaled and held. Let out a small stream of smoke and a sigh.

'You lie down on the floor now, Leo,' said Mercy.

He sat down on the bare boards, lay back, crossed one leg over the other and smoked, yellow Converse nodding.

'Good stuff?' he asked. 'This is called OG Kush, won an award last year in the US, twenty-four-point-six per cent THC, medical-grade cannabis, earthy pine aroma, bit of citrus, very good for stress and anxiety. Perfect for your man, I'd say.'

Boxer pulled up a chair, sat astride it, gun resting on the back. Time passed.

'You're looking better already,' said Leo, holding out the joint. 'More human. And maybe, I don't know, a little sad.'

Boxer took another drag, gave it back. Long silence. Just the computer hum and the fridge chuckling. Leo carried on smoking. Mercy paced the boards. More minutes passed.

'I lost somebody tonight,' said Boxer. 'Somebody very important to me.'

Mercy stopped, turned, looked down on the back of his head, frowned.

'What happened?' asked Leo.

'She died in hospital,' said Boxer. 'The first woman I've ever really loved.'

Leo came up on to his elbows.

Mercy eased round to look at Boxer's face. Tears were falling silently down his cheeks. His body was still. She put a hand on his shoulder. He looked up at her.

'Isabel died tonight,' he said. 'She had a pulmonary embolism, fell down the stairs. They gave her an emergency C-section, but she died. The baby survived. He's this big.'

He held up his hand.

Mercy shook her head slowly, disbelieving, stroked the hair at his neck.

'When?' she asked.

'Seven thirty, something like that.'

'What are you doing here?' she said. 'You shouldn't be out. You're too—'

'I had to do something. I couldn't sit there doing nothing, just thinking of what I'd ... of that. It was too much.'

Leo sat up, cross-legged, lotus position.

'You lie back down,' said Mercy, pointing a long finger at him.

Leo opened his hands above his head: no foul. Lay back down.

Mercy took Boxer's head into her hands, pulled him to her stomach, stroked him. The tears poured relentlessly down. She felt them, hot on her palm.

And that was when they heard the key in the lock.

Boxer's head snapped away from Mercy's hands. He stood and held a finger to his lips, pointed at Leo. The front door closed. Footsteps down the hall and up the bare wooden stairs.

'Hey, Leo,' said Reef. 'There's a crack of light at the window, man. This supposed to be an abandoned house.'

No answer. Leo obeyed the powerful finger.

'Out of it again. Jeez. You got to stay the course, man.'

Reef pushed open the door and walked straight into Boxer's outstretched arm with the Walther P99 in it.

His blonde hair had been recently cut to a uniform brush, the goatee was gone. His bright blue eyes took in the brutal aperture of the gun.

'Come in and lie down next to your friend, face to the boards, hands on the back of your head,' said Boxer.

Reef got down on the floor. Boxer told Leo to roll over, do the same. He pulled the joint out of the back of his hand, crushed it into an aluminium tray with some rice in it. He grabbed hold of the back of Leo's waistband and lifted him away from Reef so that there was space around. He stood astride Reef, bent down and touched his head with the Walther P99, screwed it in, making an impression.

'Let's talk,' he said. 'Quick answers. Don't even think about them. Right? The longer you think, the more painful it gets.'

Reef nodded into the floor.

'Who are you working for?' asked Boxer, straightening up.

'I work for myself?'

'I'm not talking about your drug farm.'

'That's all I do?'

'What about this special phone that your friend Leo answers for you?'

Silence.

'Siobhan called on that phone tonight, and according to Leo, she said, "She's coming",' said Boxer. 'So let's try again. Who are you working for?'

Still no word.

Boxer raised his foot and kicked out so that the heel made contact with the back of Reef's head. His face smacked into the boards and blood poured from his nose.

'Next time it'll be harder and I'll break it,' said Boxer. 'Who do you contact when you get a message from this phone?'

Still no word. Boxer checked the kettle was full, remembered how effective that had been with the Ukrainian, turned it on. The roar of it filled the room.

'Know what that's for?'

The back of Reef's neck was shaking. Boxer bent down and ripped his jacket off, tore the jumper over his head taking the T-shirt with it. Reef's evident musculature twitched. The kettle clicked off. Boxer beckoned to Mercy to bring it. She shook her head, was appalled at the prospect. Held up a hand. She'd been thinking.

'Did you know Siena Casey before you met her on Tuesday night?'

Boxer reached over, picked up the kettle. He put his foot on the back of Reef's head and poured water on the boards in front of Reef's face so that it splashed back. Reef tried to jerk his head away.

'You want some of that down your back?' asked Boxer.

'Jesus Christ,' said Leo. 'Give it up, man.'

Boxer turned and yanked up Leo's jumper. Revealed his skinny back.

'What do *you* know?'

'I don't know fucking anything. I'm just telling him to tell you.'

'You hear that, Reef,' said Boxer. 'Maybe you'd like to hear your friend scream first, just so you know what it's going to feel like.'

Mercy had her hands clamped to the sides of her head in horror. Never seen anything like this in the man she'd once loved to distraction. Couldn't square it with the humanity she'd seen in him just a few minutes ago. The coldness, the anger.

She threw herself down on the floor, got her eyes level with Reef's, saw the wild fear in it.

'Tell me about Siena,' she said. 'I know it was you. That guy, remember him, Jerry? He was with Siena the night you took her. You had long hair then, tucked behind your ears, and a goatee.'

Reef squeezed his eyes shut, gritted his teeth as he felt Boxer's foot pressing down on his neck and heard him counting.

'Five, four, three, two, one ...'

'OK,' said Reef. 'OK. Let me breathe. I'll talk.'

'Thank fuck for that,' said Leo.

Mercy sat back on her heels. Boxer's foot relented. The kettle was put back on its stand. Boxer looked at Mercy, saw the fear in her eyes. He pointed to his chest and she nodded.

'Let's start at the beginning,' he said, straddling Reef's prostrate form with the chair. 'This is not the body many people would associate with a drug dealer.'

'I do yoga.'

'Since when do bullets fly in yoga classes?' said Boxer. 'You've got a wound under your armpit, left side. You an army boy? How old are you?'

'Thirty-four.'

'Gulf War vet 2003? Afghanistan, Helmand Province?'

'40 Commando Royal Marines.'

'So you've been in both.'

Reef nodded.

'Did you get the job of kidnapping Siena Casey from one of your marine, army or intelligence contacts?'

'I worked closely with a military intelligence officer in Helmand Province in 2006. We kept in touch after I quit the marines. She saved me and my unit's arse so many times in Helmand I couldn't ... I mean, I owed her big time. She freaked me out by knowing about all my drug interests, said she'd been following my career very closely for the last five years. Made out I was the perfect candidate for the operation. Told me Siena was a real coke whore and psychonaut. I've got a line into a Mexican who can deliver almost pure cocaine and I got this guy in a lab up north who engineers pills for me from different source materials. I found her at this party, called myself Joe, tempted her in with the coke and knocked her out with some kratom-based 7-hydroxymitragynine.'

'How did you deliver her?'

'I put her in a waiting car.'

'Where did that car go?'

'I don't know. He dropped me off at my place in Whitechapel.'

'What else did you know about the operation you were involved in?'

'Nothing until the driver and I got talking and he told me that Siena was the fourth person to be kidnapped that night and there would be two more. One in the morning and another the following day. That was it.'

'Now this is going to be a difficult one,' said Boxer. 'What's the name of your friend, the military intelligence officer?'

'I can't tell you that.'

'Can't or won't?'

Silence. Boxer stood, flicked the kettle back on. The roar filled the room once more. Leo's legs twitched as if he was going to pee his pants. Mercy put her hands over her ears.

'I'm going to tell you something that I hope will be persuasive,' said Boxer, as the roar reached its highest pitch, the water rumbling in the kettle's belly. 'This group your friend is working for, they've kidnapped our daughter and they're holding her lover and torturing him. And as your friend Leo knows, I've just lost someone very important to me tonight and the last thing I care about is you, because you steal people and you peddle drugs. I will have no compunction about making you and Leo scream this house down to get the answer I want. You understand.'

The kettle clicked off.

'Tell him. For fuck's sake tell him,' said Leo.

Boxer leaned over, picked up the kettle, sat back down on the chair, put a heel into the back of Reef's head. Put the Walther P99 to the small of his back so that he knew it was there.

'Five, four, three, two, one, zero.'

The water trickled down on to Reef's bare back. He screamed.

'Stop it!' roared Mercy.

'Now it's Leo's turn,' said Boxer, cautioning Mercy with a look that told her this was how it had to be.

Reef's back already had a long blistered streak down the middle.

'For fuck's sake, Reef.'

'This'll go on all night,' said Boxer. 'One to the other. All night. I only stop when there's no water left in the tap. The gun is pointing at your leg, Reef.' He stood up, moved over to Leo. 'You move and you'll lose your knee. I've already told Leo what sort of ammo there is in this gun, and it's not nice. Hollow points. You know what they are, don't you, Reef?'

Mercy was hyperventilating.

'Five, four, three …'

'For fucking hell's sake, Reef!' roared Leo.

'… two, one, zero.'

The boiling water trickled down. Leo squealed and wriggled under Boxer's foot. He kicked him in the head.

'Keep still.'

He turned back to Reef.

'Stop this, now!' said Mercy.

'You want to see Marcus alive?' said Boxer. 'This is the only language these people understand.'

'I can't be doing with this,' said Mercy. 'This is not—'

'Then leave,' said Boxer. 'Reef, you roll over. I'm going to pour this boiling water in your ear this time.'

'Her name is Jennifer Cook,' said Reef. 'But she's known as Jeff. Jeff Cook.'

'Thank you, Reef … for your co-operation.'

20

It had been getting more and more difficult for Jess to keep her distance from the Ford Focus since they'd edged out towards the Olympic Park around Stratford. There just wasn't the traffic. She'd found herself slowing down, leaving hundreds of metres between them, begging cars to overtake, in the hope that she wouldn't be too obvious. Then Todd had abruptly headed south on a busier road and she'd felt more comfortable amongst the traffic until he'd turned into a complex of blocks of flats.

She'd held back until the last moment and had seen him pull up at the end of a street that according to her sat nav was a dead end leading down to the Royal Victoria Dock. She parked opposite some modern terraced housing, got out of the car. She wanted to see where he was going, to get the exact block of flats he went into.

Todd set off on foot towards the dock. Jess grabbed the only weapon she had from the glove compartment: a folding knife with a four-inch blade. She followed him down the mews, which kinked at the end and came out on to the dock. Lights from the Crowne Plaza Docklands and the Hotel Ibis flickered in the vast expanse of water close to the ExCel Exhibition and Conference Centre.

She ran up some steps and tracked the dockside path from behind a hedge, trying to follow Todd, but he'd disappeared. She slid down the bank on to the walkway, crouching, looking left and right, but there was no one. The lights from the flats showed the old grey dock cranes with their jibs pointed skyward into the dark night like gargantuan saluting warriors awaiting the return of their leader. Jess decided on retreat. Feeling alone and exposed, she headed back towards the car. And that was when Todd reappeared in front of her: short, wide, a powerful, immovable presence. She eased the knife from her pocket, opened it behind her back, held it with the blade up her sleeve slightly behind her right thigh.

'So it's you,' said Todd, a little surprised, but not as surprised as she'd expected given her return from the dead.

'Thought you'd killed me off, Todd?' she said.

'Yeah, as it happens, I did,' he said. 'Glad I didn't teach you too much about how to follow a car. Been aware of you for the last half-hour or so. Had to see who it was. You want to tell me what's going on?'

'You want to tell me why you sent that fucking Ukrainian round to kill me?'

'That's kinda obvious,' said Todd. 'Yours ain't. I'm interested. Somebody had to help you deal with that guy. You wouldn't have been able to handle him on your own.'

'I thought we had something going,' said Jess, the fear tearing through her, desperate for a passer-by, but it was hopeless out there in the wind-whipped darkness, the water roughing up the edge of the freezing dock.

'We did,' said Todd. 'You were a terrific lay, but – and don't take this badly – not the best.'

'You didn't have to have me *killed* for that, did you?'

He grunted a mirthless laugh.

'I got to hand it to you, Jess,' he said. 'I like a chick with humour under stress.'

'And why didn't you kill me yourself?'

'Well, first of all I don't want to be seen going into or coming out of a flat where a dead body is going to be found, and yeah, you're a hard little bitch, maybe a bit masculine for my taste, but I kinda liked you. And you had the sense of humour. I dig that in a chick.'

'My mum was always telling me I had talent,' she said, nearly sad now.

'Just tell me what's going on and I'll finish it.'

She wondered if she could outrun him, but outrun him where?

Back to the car? Around the dock? Her heart was leaping in her chest.

'Nothing to tell.'

'Somebody helped you,' said Todd, pointing a finger at her now. 'You tell me that name and I won't hurt you. You don't and you'll learn something new about pain. I fuckin' promise you that, little girl.'

Anger flashed through her at those words. Todd ducked low and came in for the kill. She hopped up, sending out a kick that landed on his cheekbone and stopped him in his tracks, dropping him to one knee. She followed it with another swiping kick from her right foot, but he was quick enough to catch it and she had to turn and drop on to her hands while twisting and hammering her left heel into the side of his head. It was a good contact and she heard him moan with its concussive power. It meant he let go of her other foot. She wheeled round on both feet and was shocked to find him still conscious. Either of those blows would have dropped a normal man, but Todd Bone was still standing.

'Didn't know you were so handy with those feet,' he said, just to let her know he wasn't fazed.

She feinted with her right foot and brought the left round in what she hoped would be another swiping knockout blow, but this time he ducked and the foot flew over his head with such speed that she lost her balance. She rolled across the tarmac to the grass verge. He was on her in that fraction of a second, his full weight descending, crushing on to her chest, and she remembered his pectorals and shoulders and knew that he must have been bench-pressing all his adult life. She felt herself fading under his closing power and with one last effort swung her hand round and drove the knife into his side.

He went rigid and gasped as the sliver of steel ran in between his ribs. He knew then what he had to do, and before she had time to withdraw and stab again, he'd grabbed her by the ponytail, pulled it hard one way while ramming her chin with the ball of his palm in the opposite direction. The snap of her neck was audible. Everything went out of her. She deflated underneath him. There was a sigh as her last breath fled across the cold water, her mouth slackened and the glint in her eye dulled.

He extricated himself as if from a complex and shuddering sexual climax. The pain sliced through his innards. He had to squeeze his eyes shut, take shallow breaths to get through it. He came up on to his knees and with superhuman effort hauled Jess across to the water's edge. He fell back with the excruciating pain in his side, saw the knife still in her fist. He worked it out and threw it as far into the dock as he could. Then he kicked her over the edge with both feet.

There was a gust of fiercely cold wind and a splash. He rolled on to his good side, got messily to his feet and staggered back to his car.

Boxer had secured Reef and Leo with spare wire and tubing left over from the hydroponic and nutrient system. He and Mercy were in the corridor on either side of the stairs with the door open so that he could keep an eye on them. He sensed a change in her towards him.

'What are we going to do with them?' she asked.

'We can't afford to have them out there,' said Boxer. 'Reef, especially, has to be taken out of the game.'

'You don't mean ...'

'What I mean is we call your boss and get the drug squad in,' said Boxer, shaking his head. 'Reef's the one who kidnapped Siena Casey and he's running cannabis farms all over the capital. They'll want to talk to him, find out all his connections. It will take some time. Ryder will be mad keen to take him apart. MI5 and the CIA will want to parse him to pieces. He's your first coup of the campaign. It deflects a lot of future attention ... if you know what I mean.'

'How are we going to explain your ... I mean, *the* interrogation technique. Given that you're not supposed to be here.'

'It wasn't a technique, just an unfortunate spillage whilst making coffee during questioning.'

'I don't know how you can *be* like this,' she said, in a voice so low he almost didn't hear her.

'You asked me here. You told me to come armed. You made a very difficult request of me earlier today and I said I would help you in any way I can. We have to remember that we only care

202

about Marcus and Amy. And we've got another crucial lead from this scenario. It didn't come free. These things never do. Reef had his loyalties. I admire him for that.'

'Thanks for reminding me about the request,' said Mercy.

'Are you withdrawing now that you've seen the cost?' asked Boxer. 'People ask these things of me, but not many actually see what it takes. I can understand if you ...'

He petered out. Silence in the stairwell.

'Ask these *things* of you?' she said, peering at him in the darkness.

'Answer the question.'

Mercy stared down into the pit of the abandoned house.

'No,' she said.

'Then call your boss and the drug squad,' said Boxer. 'We've got more work to do. There's going to come a time when they feel our pressure and they'll come back at us, threaten us with pain and suffering for Amy and Marcus. So let's get moving. I'll talk to these boys and make sure they keep quiet.'

Mercy went downstairs to make the calls. Boxer sat with the two boys. Leo was grunting under the discomfort of his binding, ankles connected to wrists. Reef was calm, forehead resting on the floorboards, doing some yogic breathing.

'I'm sorry we can't release you,' said Boxer. 'I got nothing against what you're doing here, Leo. But you, Reef, you kidnapped someone. That's a heavy-duty crime. Not the sort of thing I expect from an ex-marine. You're going to have to pay for it. You're going to have to answer a lot of questions. During that questioning I don't want you to talk about me or the interrogation I just put you through, OK?'

'What's in it for me?'

'I won't come after you.'

'Now that you put it like that ...' said Reef.

'The same applies to you, Leo. You with me?'

'I'm with you,' he said, grunting with pain.

'You need to take up yoga like your friend,' said Boxer. 'You're in poor shape. I'm going now and I don't want you to make me come after you.'

Mercy came back up the stairs, beckoned to him.

'They're on their way.'

'OK. I'm out of here.'

'How am I going to explain being able to overpower two men and tie them up?'

'You'll think of something, but don't waste time on it. We've got to maintain momentum. This woman Jeff Cook, we have to find her. She could be anywhere by now.'

At 01.25, an email arrived in the central communications office in the kidnap unit. It was addressed to DCS Oscar Hines.

We will only talk and negotiate with one kidnap consultant for all six kidnap victims. That consultant will be 'Colonel' Ryder Forsyth. He must have the power to act on behalf of all the victims. We will not be drawn into conducting negotiations separately. We know this goes against all the principles of extremely wealthy individuals, who believe that they and they alone are the world's most important people, but this is a lesson in how the rest of the world has to live under their colossal capital power.

They have had a substantial amount of time in which to put together the expenses payment we asked for when their children were taken. This £25 million per hostage is a non-negotiable amount and does not represent a ransom payment in any way. It only allows the victims' parents to remain in the game with the knowledge that their offspring are alive and well. However, failure of any one family to make their payment will result in a punishment to the whole group of hostages. The punishment will be arbitrary and random, but will involve considerable pain and distress to all victims, who will witness each other's agony. All we can guarantee is that it will not result in death. If this punishment does not bring forth the required payment then it will result in the death of one of the hostages but not necessarily the child of the parents who have withheld the payment. We realise that this is not fair, but we're not in a fair world, as many of you have now come to understand.

Once we have received your agreement to these basic terms, we will give instructions as to where and when and in what denominations that £150 million in cash is to be deposited. Your reply is expected by 01.45. Failure to respond in the affirmative will result in punishment being administered to one hostage every minute that you're late until a consensus has been reached. We are willing to provide webcam evidence of the punishments. All your efforts at negotiation should be between the hostages' parents and not with us. We will not negotiate. We await your response.

Hines was immediately woken from sleep on a camp bed in his office. He ordered the email to be forwarded to MI5 and the CIA representatives as well as the kidnap consultants, from whom he demanded an immediate reaction from the parents.

The first response came from Uttam Sarkar, who was still in Mumbai and who absolutely refused to be 'browbeaten' by this gang of 'bloody kidnappers'. He proceeded to reveal that not only had he made no efforts to raise the £25 million for 'expenses', but also that he would have nothing to do with Ryder Forsyth nor even the consultant appointed by Oscar Hines. He had his own man who would fly in with him later this morning, a retired intelligence officer from the Indian equivalent of MI6, the Research and Analysis Wing, who, he said, would take over from the 'temporary' consultant on arrival.

Hines began to realise just how long the following eighteen minutes were going to be, but since the meeting in Thames House that morning, a lot of measures had been put in place. The first of them being to find the closest contacts to the wealthy individuals concerned, who had the greatest powers of persuasion over them. In the case of Uttam Sarkar, it was his brother, the Minister for Commerce and Industry, Manish Sarkar.

The brothers knew each other very well, and the first thing that Manish Sarkar had done when he'd been approached that morning was to talk to his close friend the finance minister, who had agreed to make £25 million available in London in the event that it was needed. The most complicated aspect of this negotiation was how the money would be repaid if it was lost. The Sarkars didn't pay out money unnecessarily, and after protracted discussions with Sarkar's chief financial officer, it was agreed that they would forgo a tax break on a bauxite mining project in Tamil Nadu.

Within minutes of receiving Oscar Hines's call, Manish Sarkar had digested the email and phoned his brother, who, in preparation for his flight later in the morning, had moved up to his Juhu Beach complex and was now striding about in a rage at the kidnappers' demands, while his mistress sat on the sofa sipping tea and waiting for him to burn out. She knew it was his brother who was calling because Uttam was immediately becalmed and sat down smacking his lips as if a dummy had been put in his mouth.

Seven minutes later, Oscar Hines received a call from Manish Sarkar saying that his brother had agreed to all the demands and that the £25 million was ready and available at the State Bank of India.

Sergei Yermilov refused to accept the kidnappers' demands. There would be no circumstances he could foresee that would make him accept an American-led negotiation of his son's release. Especially not one supported by the CIA with a British kidnap consultant of dubious background. That was the end of the discussion. Hines contacted the British Embassy in Moscow and asked the British ambassador to negotiate with the president's banker, in the hope that he would be able to bring pressure to bear on Yermilov. This was not going to be easy: from the outset of the conversation the banker revealed that he was in total agreement with his friend. They would not accept an American-led negotiation. That was the end of it.

DCS Hines decided to take it to another level. He called Ken Bass and asked him if he would be willing to speak to his friend the vice president of the United States to see if he would be able to intervene at a higher level than the president's banker. Three minutes later Bass called to say that the VP was now talking to the Russian Foreign Minister.

Hans Pfeiffer had immediately acquiesced and had already arranged with UBS in Zurich for the sum of £25 million to be made available in London.

Wú Dao-ming was not quite so straightforward. She was staying in Pfeiffer's house but had retreated to her rooms on the third floor before the kidnap consultant assigned to her had even arrived. He had been sitting there alone with no means of communicating with her for the entire day. Wú Dao-ming had locked herself in, turned off her mobile phone, drawn up a chair to the window and was looking out over Carlyle Square, listening to the rain falling on the bare trees outside. She was in a state of trauma at the disappearance of her only child. She had no one to talk to in London. Her parents were long dead and her husband had died from a stroke after a heavy *baijiu* drinking session six years ago. She was estranged from her politburo brother and the remaining few members of her family, as well as the many members of her husband's family, who all loathed her on account of the vast sum of money she'd inherited after his sudden death.

Having achieved an agreement from Pfeiffer, DCS Hines had asked him if he could help the consultant make contact with Wú Dao-ming. However much Pfeiffer and the consultant implored her in all languages from outside her room, she would not open the door, would not answer, would not even leave the window. This was partly because she blamed Karla Pfeiffer for leading her son astray, taking him to nightclubs when he should have been working at his degree. In her mind she had already withdrawn from the investment opportunities shown to her by Hans Pfeiffer and was excluding the Deal-O supermarket chain from the perfect sites she'd assigned to them in Shanghai, Beijing, Chengdu and Guangzhou. She was now in a state of focused fury, which despised all things Western.

The consultant knew that she had not seen the email and had not made any financial arrangements for the 'expenses' and decided that the only course of action was to break down the door. It took six kicks, bouncing back and forth between the corridor wall and the door, until finally a panel gave way and they were able to gain entry. Wú Dao-ming hadn't moved. The consultant asked Pfeiffer to stay outside. He pulled up a chair alongside the Chinese heiress and looked into her face. Tears filled her eyes and rolled down her flat, smooth cheeks. He gave her a handkerchief. She wiped her face and dabbed her eyes while the consultant told her about the email. She looked at him. He was young, in his mid thirties, and although he was only half Chinese he was good-looking and reminded her a little of her son. He was also respectful – something her son was losing as he'd imbibed London culture. A slight thaw occurred in her demeanour, which enabled the consultant to impress upon her the need for action.

After minute fourteen, Wú Dao-ming finally agreed to the kidnapper's demands and made a single thirty-second phone call that resulted in £25 million being made available at ICBC in London.

Anastasia Casey, who was now airborne in a first-class cabin on an Emirates A380, had left instructions for such an eventuality and was woken by the steward.

She was livid. She didn't like being woken up in the night, even though she'd ordered it. She liked it even less when the steward handed her the satellite phone and she listened to what Brian Horton, the executive director of Casey Prospecting, had to say to her about the email.

'Tell 'em to fuck off,' she said. 'I'm not having some fuck-arse kidnapper telling me what I can and can't do. The fuck does he think he is? And what are those Poms doing about it? Fuck all. Getting us to kiss arse to make their fucking lives easier. You tell 'em: Anastasia Casey says to fuck right off.'

'Just so you know, Ani, we've got six minutes before they start hurting people, so let's concentrate on what we want to happen. First off I've made arrangements for the twenty-five million to be made available to you at Westpac in the City.'

'We're not going to need it. That money's going nowhere.'

'The second thing is that they've caught the guy who kidnapped Siena,' said Horton. 'They've got him under interrogation now. The early reports are that he knows fuck all about the main operation. He was just hired to kidnap Siena, which was a piece of piss given her predilection for drugs.'

'That girl ...' said Anastasia. 'And this guy has no idea where they're holding her?'

'The interrogation has barely started,' said Horton. 'My advice to you is to agree to the terms. We don't have time to do anything else.'

'Who's to say they'll hurt Si first?'

'There's only six hostages, so within five minutes we know they'll have started hurting her.'

'Might do her some fucking good.'

'Come on, Ani.'

'You know what I mean, Brian. She's been nothing but trouble for the last couple of years. And anyway, what the fuck is this?'

'What?'

'This process,' said Casey. 'I mean, it's an engineered process. We're being forced into a situation.'

'My reading of it is that we're being given a lesson in powerlessness.'

'And what the fuck do I need with something like that?'

'You're a person who wields an enormous amount of power, Ani.'

'You telling me I don't deserve it?'

'Maybe we should talk about this later. We're into the last two minutes.'

'Has everybody else agreed?'

'Not yet.'

'Who's left?'

'The Russians and the Americans.'

'Fucking typical,' said Casey. 'Back to the good old days. I'll agree when the Americans come off the fence. Tell 'em that.'

With forty-five seconds remaining before the 1.45 a.m. deadline, the Kinderman Corporation agreed to the kidnappers' demands on the advice of Clifford Chase, the London CIA chief. This information was relayed to the US vice president, who was still in a three-way discussion with the Foreign Minister and Sergei Yermilov. He reiterated that Yermilov was now the only parent who hadn't agreed and that he was putting his own son and all the other children in grave danger. It made no difference to the Russians. They wanted a Russian negotiator not just involved, but in direct contact with the kidnappers.

At 01.45 the deadline elapsed and the central communications office received a second email.

It is no surprise to us that we have not received your confirmation of acceptance of our conditions to proceed. Lots have been drawn to see who will be the first hostage to be punished. The short straw has been drawn by Karla Pfeiffer. You will be sent a webcam recording of her punishment. The next on the list is Sophie Railton-Bass and then Yury Yermilov. Let us hope that you will have come to your senses before Sophie and Yury have to suffer.

21

At 1.30, the news came through from the insider in the communications room that Reef had been captured. This initiated the next phase of the operation. Karla was brought blindfolded into a room, pushed down into a metal chair, wrists and ankles taped to the arms and legs. Wires had been connected up to the chair's frame.

'When you hear this noise, Karla,' said the voice, pausing for an audible click, 'I want you to convulse. I want you to imagine that there's two hundred and forty volts going through that metal chair you're sitting on. And you scream. All right? Do you understand?'

The blindfolded girl looked around her, totally bewildered. The voice repeated it in her ear, close up, reassuring.

'I understand,' she said, 'but I don't know what it means.'

'That's good because it's not important what it means. It's important that you do as you're told. If you don't, we'll really have to stick two hundred and forty volts through the chair and you wouldn't want that, would you?'

'No,' she said.

'You're going to be on camera, so do your best. Ready?' said the voice, standing back from her now.

There was the click and Karla suddenly leapt up as if trying to get out of the chair. She let out a piercing scream, shuddering and convulsing until the chair finally tipped over and she lay on her side still twitching. Another click. The camera went in close on her face: spittle had gathered at the corners of her mouth and her tongue lolled.

'Cut,' said the voice. 'Excellent, Karla. Beautifully done. Are you sure you're not an actress?'

'I did theatre studies at school.'

'Bloody marvellous,' said the voice. 'Let's have the next one.'

Karla was led stumbling away and Sophie was brought in blindfolded, looking pitiful in her Francis Holland uniform, clutching the rag doll frog.

'All right, Sophie, now we're going to play a game.'

'That's not fair. How can I play a game when I can't see?'

'That's the good thing about this game,' said the voice. 'You don't have to be able to see. What's important is that people have to be able to see *you*. Do you get it?'

'No.'

'This is about acting the part. What we're going to do is lie you down facing up with your head over the edge of a sink just as if you were having your hair washed.'

'My mum always washes my hair with my face *down* in the sink.'

'Well this is going to be a little different, OK?' said the voice. 'When you're lying down and comfortable, we're just going tie your arms down by your sides and put a wet towel over your face. But what we're also going to do is sneak a little pipe into the corner of your mouth so that you can breathe. Then we're going to pour water over the towel and we want you to pretend that you're drowning. Do you know how to do that?'

'Oh yes, I nearly drowned in my friend's swimming pool up in Hampstead.'

'Well that's what I want you to remember to do when you feel water being poured on to the wet towel on your face.'

'Oh, OK. Sounds kind of weird.'

'It is a bit weird, but it's fun too,' said the voice. 'At the end we're going to pull the towel off your face and the pipe will come out of your mouth with it. And you've just got to lie there gasping like a fish out of water.'

They strapped the girl down on to the board, tucked the rag doll frog into her pullover so just the head was sticking out and moved her over the sink. They slipped the pipe into her mouth and laid the wet towel over her face.

'Ready?'

She nodded.

They started pouring the water over the towel. Sophie writhed, twisting her head so that a pair of hands came in and viced her around the ears. Her little chest strained upwards as if she was desperately struggling to breathe. Even Zach's red mouth was wide open as if trying to suck in air. They kept it up for thirty seconds and then pulled off the towel. Her face was red, she gasped and gulped and did her best impression of a goldfish she'd once seen flapping and mouthing amongst the broken glass of its bowl.

'Cut,' said the voice. 'Beautiful, Sophie. Loved it.'

They wiped her face down, wrapped a dry towel around her head and led her away.

Yury was next. They brought him in blindfolded, still in his Danes Hill school uniform, sat him down and introduced him to the elephant: a gas mask with a concertinaed breathing tube, which they let him touch.

'Now, Yury, we're going to put this over your head, OK?' said the voice. 'It's going to be a tight fit. The game is that when you feel me pinch the tube, you kick out with your feet as if you're short of air. Don't worry, we'll be piping oxygen into the mask from the back so you won't really feel out of breath. You OK with that? It's just a bit of play-acting. Some fun.'

'OK,' he said, afraid, uncertain.

They strapped him into the chair and put the mask on. When he felt the tube being crimped, he lashed out as instructed, the chair rocking back and forth with his efforts. At the end they lifted off the mask. His hair was all over the place, his face flushed.

'Cut,' said the voice. 'I think that should do it. What time is it?'

'How did that go?' asked Boxer, as Mercy got back into the car.

'No problem. DCS Hines is otherwise engaged. He was happy that we'd captured one of the kidnappers. He's got some kudos from that. But he's involved in some crisis that needs an agreement on procedure from all six of the victims' families within fifteen minutes.'

'And billionaires are always such agreeable people,' said Boxer. 'Where to?'

'It might be time to make a house call to Martin Fox in St George's Square, Pimlico.'

Mercy tapped the address into the sat nav, pulled out, drove past the house just as they were bringing Reef and Leo out.

'I'm thinking it's no accident this kidnapping has happened in London,' said Mercy, her mind on the driving. 'There are more billionaires here than in any other capital city in the world.'

'Even New York?'

'New York's third. Moscow's second with forty-eight and London's top with seventy-two.'

'Good to know we're top at something.'

'Pure accident. We've got the perfect time zone for both east and west. We're politically stable, with a nice gentle tax regime for non-doms, who can throw their money into property and walk away doubly rich. It's like free membership to the casino where the house is at a disadvantage.'

'Is this a theory?' asked Boxer.

'Not yet. I'm just telling you something,' said Mercy. 'The UK billionaires have a net worth of more than three hundred billion. That's over fifty billion more than they had last year.'

'By the way, does Hines know that we're both looking for Conrad Jensen?'

'Did you hear me?'

'Fifty billion more than last year. And?'

'That's the problem. Since the credit crunch back in 2008, we don't know what a billion is any more. It's become an ordinary number. How long is a million seconds?'

'For Christ's sake, Mercy.'

'Eleven and a half days,' said Mercy. 'And a billion seconds?'

'I don't know. A decade?'

'Thirty-one and a half years. A whole generation,' said Mercy. 'These guys sit on their backsides and become richer to the tune of fifty thousand million pounds, that's one and a half millennia, in a year. Is that a hell of a lot of money, or what?'

'In the hands of very few people ... dangerous, too.'

'And to answer your question: no. Hines only knows that *I'm* looking for Jensen. You don't feature, sorry. I'm the star of the show,' she said.

Silence as Mercy drove, interrupted only by the gentle Irish brogue of the male voice on the sat nav.

'You scared me back there in the house,' said Mercy.

'With someone like Reef you've got to mean it,' said Boxer, staring straight ahead. 'Leo, you cuff him round the head a few times and he'll cough it up through his tears. Reef's been there and back.'

'I meant how it came out about Isabel.'

'I was stoned. It just fell out. I don't seem to have much control over what's going on inside me,' said Boxer, looking across to her. 'You told me Amy'd been taken and it just went in. I can't react. I don't feel anything.'

'And that's terrible about Isabel. I'm so sorry, Charlie. I can't imagine ...'

'I don't want to think about it now,' said Boxer.

'You did the same with your father.'

'I was a kid. A seven-year-old kid.'

They were at a very long traffic light to get on to the East India Dock Road. Mercy hung on to the steering wheel, looking out into the night, shaking her head.

'I can't believe it,' she said, and sighed as a huge wave of grief tore through her. She dropped her head on to her fists and wept. Boxer rubbed her back.

'Why are you comforting *me*?' she asked.

'Because I feel the same way,' he said. 'I almost don't believe it's happened, even though I saw her.'

The lights changed. Mercy stalled. Restarted. Turned right into the City.

'Was Alyshia at the hospital?'

'She was devastated. As was Deepak,' said Boxer, nodding. 'I arrived after the ... event. There'd been a mix-up. They thought she was in ICU, but she didn't make it through the emergency C-section. She'd kept herself alive to deliver the baby and then died.'

'Don't you want to be there with him?'

'I can't ... I have to *do* something. I can't just stand there watching him struggle for life in an incubator surrounded by nurses, doctors, machines, monitors. What would I *do*?' said Boxer. 'And why wasn't I there with Isabel? If only I'd been there ...'

'Is *that* what you're thinking?' asked Mercy. 'Really?'

'What?'

'Guilt. You're feeling guilty because you weren't with her every minute of the day.'

'She was pregnant because of me ...'

'No,' said Mercy. 'No. Two people make a woman pregnant. And no woman in the history of the world has had the father of her child with her twenty-four/seven for the entire term of her pregnancy. So forget that as a line of thought. You should *not* feel guilty, Charlie.'

'But I do.'

'I can see where you're headed.'

'Tell me,' said Boxer. 'I'd like to know.'

'Complicated grief,' said Mercy. 'Look, Charlie, something terrible happened. Isabel flew back from Mumbai, some sort of blood clot formed during the flight, she fell down the stairs. It's just ... fate. None of that is your fault.'

'I think she knew before she went to Mumbai,' said Boxer. 'What woman wouldn't know that she was eighteen weeks pregnant?'

'Why would she do that?'

'To talk to Alyshia.'

'There are phones for that sort of thing. She went because she wanted to go.'

'I'm responsible,' said Boxer. 'In some way, I'm responsible.'

'You've lost her, which is bad enough. Don't make it worse.'

'Let's not talk about it then.'

'OK,' said Mercy, slowing down for some roadworks, looking over her shoulder to get into the right-hand lane. 'Why are we going to see Martin Fox?'

'He's in this somewhere, I know it ... I just don't know where,' said Boxer, taking out his smartphone. 'When Siobhan came to see me and asked me to find her father, she knew things that she shouldn't have known.'

'Like what?' said Mercy.

'That I kill people,' said Boxer, 'who deserve to be killed.'

'Jesus Christ,' said Mercy, slamming on the brakes for a red light. 'You can't say that sort of thing to *me*.'

'What do you mean?' said Boxer. 'You know it too now.'

'I didn't *know* it. I *guessed* it,' said Mercy. 'I guessed that you were going to kill El Osito because you thought he'd killed Amy.'

'You knew, which was why you asked me to deal with Marcus's kidnappers.'

'I didn't *know*. You only know with irrefutable evidence.'

'Suit yourself.'

'So why does that make you think that Fox is involved?'

Boxer didn't answer. He'd been going over his conversations with Siobhan and now he was looking things up on the internet.

'Now that's interesting,' he said. 'Did I ever tell you what Pavis means?'

'As in Fox's company Pavis Risk Management? No.'

'It's Latin for "shield",' said Boxer. 'Siobhan told me that around the time of Conrad Jensen's disappearance, three of her father's companies had paid money into three other companies in the same territories called Xiphos, Hoplon and Kaluptein.'

'Fascinating.'

'Listen to this. Xiphos is a double-edged sword used by the ancient Greeks. Hoplon is a circular *shield* used by Greek infantrymen. And Kaluptein is ... the root of the word "apocalypse" and it means "to cover".'

'And you want me to bring Martin Fox in for questioning on the basis of that evidence?'

'No. We don't even know if he owns any of those companies and it might be tricky to find out, but it's an indicator.'

'We've got people who can look into that.'

Boxer told her which of Jensen's companies had paid money into Xiphos, Hoplon and Kaluptein. Mercy told him to put it in an email and gave him an address to send it to.

They'd just gone through the Limehouse Link and were now tearing down the Highway heading for St Katharine Docks and the Tower of London. Mercy had put a blue light on the roof. Boxer sent the email, took hold of the security strap above the window.

'When are we going to get an answer to that?'

Mercy punched a number into her mobile, put her finger to her lips. The communications centre set up for the kidnaps answered. Mercy asked if they'd received the email, which they had. She told them she needed an answer in ten minutes.

'Where are you?' asked the female police constable.

'You don't need to know,' said Mercy, and hung up.

'That was a bit brutal.'

'Somebody in the unit is watching me. Since I've been operating on my own, I haven't had any threatening calls.'

'Maybe they're too busy with this procedural crisis you were on about.'

At 1.47, Irina Yermilov was pacing the living room, constantly checking her watch, knowing that the deadline had passed because of Sergei's intransigence. They were already at two minutes past and closing in on three, which would mean, if the kidnappers were sticking to the letter of their threat, that Yury would be punished. She could barely tolerate Sergei's presence in the room. His power play disgusted her. The old politics. He had thrown the Metropolitan Police kidnap consultant out of the house as soon as he'd arrived in the middle of the afternoon. Now he stood with his cronies at the other end of the room yabbering away to Moscow on his mobile phone, drinking vodka and smoking a Cohiba cigar.

The computer gave its little ringtone to signify that an email had arrived. It was entitled 'Karla'. She called out to Sergei and the men lumbered across the room like a family of bears.

Irina opened it and clicked on the QuickTime symbol. It lasted twenty-three seconds, in which time all the strength went out of Irina's legs and she collapsed on the floor, holding her hands over her ears to block out Karla's screaming. When it was over, she came up on one elbow and vomited on the pristine carpet. The men looked down on her without moving. She was covered in a cold sweat. She got herself on to all fours and crawled unaided out of the room, washed her face in the kitchen, couldn't find a bucket, didn't know her own house. Found a dustpan and brush.

The men were standing around the computer talking. Not one of them was in the slightest bit moved by what they'd seen on the screen. Their faces betrayed no concern, pain or emotion.

The computer gave another ringtone and Sergei raised his head, indicating to one of the men to open it. It was called 'Sophie'. They watched as the little girl was waterboarded. No one said anything. They sipped their vodka. Men so used to violence it made no impression on them to see an innocent girl suffer in such a way.

Irina couldn't stand it. Something came into her eyes, a great rush of furious black blood that crowded her vision, and she flew at her husband and beat him over the ear with the brush, brought it down on his stupid fat head again and again and again until finally Sergei pushed her away with such a shove that she cannoned backwards, flipping over the back of an armchair and landing heavily on her bottom on the floor. The wind was knocked out of her and she slumped to one side, grunting.

Sergei made the call that Irina had been wanting him to make since the gang's ultimatum came through. He nodded as if his point had been righteously made and slipped the mobile into his pocket. Blood trickled down the side of his face, which he cleaned up with a handkerchief given to him by one of his cronies.

Thirty seconds passed in total silence. Irina didn't move from her position on the floor. The computer gave another ringtone. Sergei ordered one of the men to open it. In a thickly accented voice he read out the email.

"'Too late, Mr Yermilov. Sorry.'"

This time the short film didn't even require a click to start it. The video rolled. Some of the men in the room who'd seen action in Chechnya knew what the elephant was as soon as it appeared. They tried to stop the film but it wouldn't respond. Yury's head disappeared into the mask and they saw his struggle. Finally one of the men ripped the plug from the wall.

Irina, who had been facing away from the screen, went upstairs to the bedroom and stripped to her bra and knickers. She put on a pair of jeans, a T-shirt, a jumper and some trainers. She packed a small case and went downstairs. She seemed to change her mind at the kitchen door and put her suitcase down. She extracted the largest knife from the wooden block on the work surface and went into the sitting room. Sergei was on all fours, weeping into the carpet, roaring with pain and rage. She knew she had to act quickly and she ran at him with all the remembered athleticism of her youth. The only thing that saved him was her vomit, which she'd failed to clean up. She slipped as she ran and fell short of her target, and the knife went into the calf of one of Sergei's cronies. One of the other men stepped forward and, with an open-palmed blow, knocked Irina into unconsciousness.

Todd Bone wasn't seeing things very well. The lights were blurring and doubling in his vision. He felt light-headed, dizzy, sick. The pain in his side was creeping deeper into his middle and up to his armpit. His stomach was swelling and very painful. His extremities were cold. He knew these were the symptoms of an internal bleed but didn't want to go to hospital.

'Stupid,' he said aloud. 'Stupid way to go. All that time in Africa. Iraq, Afghanistan. Fucking Taliban. Suicide bombers in your driveway. Shit. And then some dumb broad in nice old London town sticks it to you. What an asshole!'

He pulled up messily on to the pavement just before some kind of footbridge; had no idea where he was any more. Just been driving to get away from the scene. Trying to contain the pain, keep his thinking straight. He looked around him, saw cranes, a building whose top he recognised, and HSBC emblazoned on the block next door to it. He looked out the other side and realised it must be a station of some sort, but no name was visible. He called the emergency number.

'What is it?'

'It's me. I'm hurt. Been stabbed. Got an internal bleed.'

'Where are you?'

'On a road next to a station. Not strong enough to get out. On the other side is the HSBC building in Docklands. I need help.'

'Throw away your phone. We'll be right out there.'

He hung up, turned the engine back on to get the window open and threw the phone into some bushes. It took everything out of him. He collapsed over the edge of the window, an arm and his head hanging out in the cold night.

A black cab pulled up behind. The driver thought that maybe the car had crashed, or at least come off the road, especially when he saw the guy hanging out of his window, the engine still running. He got out, went over.

'You all right, mate?' he asked.

No answer.

He touched his face. Still warm, but unconscious. He called the police and an ambulance.

At 01.53, another email arrived at the central communications unit. It was sent straight out to all concerned.

Hello Ryder,

We're glad your group has finally come to their senses and we're sorry that it took some unpleasantness to get them to that point. We hope the next element will not be so troublesome because this time we're talking about a commodity that your people understand very well. Money.

This is how we want the money for expenses to be put together and delivered. We are going to make this very easy for you. You have all day until close of business (17.00 hours) to arrange the funds. They must be loosely packed, not sheafed, and the only denomination we will accept is £50 notes.

Each block of £25 million should be wrapped in clear plastic. Each package will measure 1.56m x 0.85m x 0.665m, configured in stacks of 10 x 10 and will weigh 605 kg. Six of those will come to 3.63 tons, so you will need a truck capable of a minimum load of four tons. The truck must be open, with a crane for off-loading and the cargo visible at all times. The packages of money must not be on pallets.

Now that you have seen what we are capable of, we are confident that you will not attempt to cheat. Remember, this is not the ransom payment. This is merely for expenses. What we can guarantee is that the children's release will not require any additional payment to us.

Failure to achieve this task by 17.00 hours today will result in the hostages drawing lots again and being punished along the same lines as before. We have no doubt that your group of billionaires can raise this kind of money in the time allotted. The only question remains: can they part with it?

At 02.27, DCS Oscar Hines was knocking on the door of 31 Wilton Place. The man in the blue suit didn't take him into the lower living room but straight up to the top one, where Ryder Forsyth was waiting, sipping orange juice on the rocks and wishing it was bourbon. He was standing by the window looking out into the pitch black of the rear garden while computer and recording equipment blinked in the corner of the room. The two men shook hands, sat down simultaneously, eyeing each other warily.

'What do you make of this?' asked Hines.

'If I was them, I would only want to deal with one person. Nobody wants to handle six separate negotiations. The time it would take, the possibilities for delay. No gang would want that,' said Forsyth. 'As for the money. That's very interesting. Nearly four tons of loosely packed notes on an open truck. The delivery of that sort of cargo is going to be very demanding on their resources. I don't know how they're going to get away with it.'

'And it's not the ransom,' said Hines. 'But then they add that strange guarantee: "that the children's release will not require any additional payment to us".'

'I think the idea is to get us feeding off their riddle. I don't think we should be distracted.'

'Another thing. "Hello Ryder" for a start. The targeting of the Kinderman's CEO's daughter, which they knew would mean you'd be handling the kidnap consultancy. It struck me that these are people who know you.'

'Or know *of* me.'

'I was looking at your CV before I came here. There's a bit of a black hole for eight years or so after you left the Staffords and re-emerged in the United States. I understand that to start with you were in Africa. Can you tell me what you were doing in that time?'

'I was a mercenary. I trained fighters in the Democratic Republic of Congo – or Zaire as it was then – Guinea-Bissau, Liberia and Sierra Leone. I was an adviser in Angola and Mozambique. I also, I might add, advised the British military on insurgency and guerrilla tactics in Bosnia and Kosovo. You might want to check that out.'

'And presumably you came across and even worked with other mercenaries in these areas of conflict?'

'Inevitably,' said Forsyth. 'It's a big leap to think that they would have anything to do with what's going on here. Most of that stuff was twenty years ago.'

'Before you surfaced in the USA, you were working in South America. I understand from our CIA partners that this was your training ground for the kidnap work you eventually became involved in. And that resulted in your big coup for Kinderman and your permanent post with them.'

'You seem to be implying something there, DCS Hines.'

'I don't think so.'

'I started off working for a number of private military companies, as we call them in the US. It was strictly security-based operations: film crews, teams of engineers, technicians, sometimes politicians, especially when FARC were targeting them. When I started working in South America, FARC were responsible for nearly three and a half thousand kidnappings a year; by the time I finished, it was less than a thousand.'

'You say you worked in various PMCs in the US. Do you remember any colleagues there who particularly bore a grudge against you, for whatever reason?'

'A lot of people didn't like me,' said Forsyth. 'That includes my employers as well as colleagues. I have my way of doing things and people sometimes disagree with me. I put my point of view very strongly. People don't like that. All I can say is that my record speaks for itself. I never lost anyone when I was running a security operation. None of the hostages I was employed to rescue have ever been killed.'

'These people we're dealing with here. What do they sound like to you?' said Hines.

'I understand you've already captured one of them, an ex-marine, a vet of Iran and Afghanistan. I don't know his role because I haven't been able to speak to him, but I would imagine it was peripheral. That to me is an indicator of the quality of personnel we're dealing with.'

'The sort of people you used to work with?'

'Let's be clear about this, DCS Hines,' said Forsyth. 'I'm English but I've adopted some American ways, meaning I prefer it when people say what's on their mind.'

'You've pissed somebody off and they want to teach you a lesson,' said Hines.

22

'Xiphos is wholly owned by Julius Klank, Hoplon by Martin Fox and Kaluptein by Boris Bortnik,' said the police constable from the central communication centre on speakerphone in the car.

'Do you have any information on those people?'

'Julius Klank runs a US-based private security company called SureSafe. Martin Fox runs a London-based PSC called Pavis. And we haven't been able to find anything out about Boris Bortnik other than in a 2009 *Guardian* newspaper article he was mentioned as someone trying to help the Russian arms smuggler Viktor Bout when he was arrested in Thailand in 2008. We've run the name past MI5 and they've had an initial reaction from MI6 saying they believed he had been an SVR agent but weren't sure what he was doing now.'

Boxer left Mercy in the car. As he headed for Fox's front door, Mercy's phone rang. The voice.

'What are you up to, Mercy?'

She gave him a recap of the night so far.

'That's good. Just what we want. The important thing now is that you tell Ryder Forsyth all of this first. He's going to appreciate it. He'll let you in to his deeper thinking, and that's what we want.'

Boxer turned as he got to Fox's door, saw Mercy on her phone. He was hoping there'd be a more open discussion with Fox without her presence, although nothing was guaranteed where Martin

Fox was concerned. He called him, knew that Fox always slept with his mobile close to his heart, closer than his wife.

'Jesus Christ, Charlie, it's two o'clock in the bloody morning,' said Fox, whispering hoarsely.

'I'm outside your door. We need to talk.'

'I'll be down,' said Fox, suddenly awake.

Fox let him in wearing a paisley dressing gown, striped pyjamas and slippers with a gold crest on the toes. Boxer followed him into the kitchen, where Fox made builder's tea in mugs.

'I'm going to say one word that I hope will stimulate an open and frank discussion about what the hell's going on here,' said Boxer.

'Go on.'

'Hoplon.'

The mug stopped on the way to Fox's mouth. He shook his head in dismay.

'Well that's a start,' said Boxer. 'We've had it confirmed that Conrad Jensen's company Ferguson Consulting Ltd in Bermuda made a payment to your Hoplon company. Do you want to tell me what services you were supplying?'

'How the hell did that get out?'

'I think Conrad Jensen keeps the people around him in the dark, so nobody knows what's important and what should be kept secret. Jensen paid three companies, one of which was Hoplon. I found out that Hoplon was a type of ancient shield, and after our chat a few days ago, I naturally thought of Pavis.'

'And the other two?'

'You might be able to help me on that,' said Boxer. 'Xiphos, owned by a guy called Julius Klank ...'

'I know him. He does what I do, but in America.'

'I'm assuming you mean he supplies personnel for work that might not be entirely legal.'

'He's an ex-Gulf War vet from 1991. He was one of the poor bastards who didn't react well to being vaccinated against chemical weapons. He runs a sideline to his main security business employing disgruntled vets from various US military campaigns who are prepared to act in, how shall I put it, unconventional ways.'

'We're still trying to get more information on the third

participant who received money from Jensen. His company is called Kaluptein …'

'Strange name.'

'It's the root of the word "apocalypse" and it means "to cover". And Xiphos is a double-edged sword,' said Boxer. 'Who came up with these names?'

'Conrad Jensen.'

'Kaluptein is owned by a guy called Boris Bortnik. Know him?'

'Heard of him but don't know him,' said Fox. 'He's ex-SVR and has teamed up with a mafia outfit in Moscow called Dolgoprudninskaya.'

'Any idea why Jensen would contact him for this series of kidnaps?'

'Series?'

'There've been five kidnaps and six victims, all billionaires' kids. One of them is a Russian guy called Sergei Yermilov.'

'Yermilov!' said Fox, startled, scared even. 'Why's he tangling with Yermilov and co.? They're lethal, those guys. The connections they have go deep inside the Russian military and intelligence establishment. But yes, I can see why they might want advice from Bortnik on that. Yermilov is with Solntsevskaya, and there's no love lost between them and Dolgoprudninskaya. The SVR are going to be crawling all over this.'

'Let's get back to what you were supplying to Conrad Jensen, and for what purpose.'

'Well, going back to our earlier conversation,' said Fox, 'Jensen wasn't interested in anyone who'd kill people, and certainly not children, even the entitled, privileged children of the massively rich.'

'What about killing people who were protecting the entitled children of the massively rich?'

'Is that what happened?'

'The Yermilov boy was under armed guard. The kidnappers were disguised as police. They stopped traffic in both directions and killed the driver and bodyguard.'

'Were they the only casualties?'

'As far as I know,' said Boxer. 'Now tell me what Conrad was interested in from you.'

'He wanted two people. The first was a very specifically described driver who could speak some German. He had to be a certain height and build with a defined head shape and preferably blonde hair cut in a certain way. He also had to be someone prepared to work with a team of people he wouldn't know and not averse to committing or witnessing violence. The second was someone fairly young who could supply high quality drugs.'

'And you knew people who could do this?'

'The first one, yes.'

'You got a name?'

'I'm not sure how much use it would be to you. He operates under so many aliases ...'

'How do you pay him?'

'Cash.'

'How do you make contact with him?'

'We have a dead drop.'

'OK, we'll need to make use of that.'

'It won't work.'

'Why?'

'He never does consecutive jobs. He will only work for me with at least six months in between. He completely keeps his distance, wouldn't even answer a dead drop from me now.'

'OK, what about the other guy? The drug dealer type.'

'I couldn't access him direct. I had to source him through someone else.'

'Would that be through Jennifer – Jeff – Cook?'

Martin Fox nodded.

'Tell me about her.'

'She's an active officer in British Military Intelligence in Afghanistan. She's left wing and hates the way the American military operates.'

'Have you used her before?'

'No. I know her sister. She's given me useful information.'

'So why did you approach her?'

'The last time she was back here we were talking about how soldiers coped under the pressure of being in Helmand Province, and drug use came up. She talked about a marine she knew who could supply, who'd now left the army. I made a mental note, and when this approach came from Jensen I told him about it.'

'So how did it work?'

'I don't know, because Jensen said he would only deal with Jeff direct,' said Fox. 'She refused a fee and I arranged a payment for the ex-marine in cash.'

'How can I get in touch with Jeff Cook?'

'Probably have to go to Afghanistan,' said Fox.

'So when did you set all this up?'

'Over Jeff Cook's Christmas leave.'

'Do you think she met Jensen?'

'She must have done.'

'When did *you* meet Jensen?'

'Last November, in Dubai.'

'Did Jensen mention kidnapping?'

'No. He said he just wanted to recruit people for an experimental project.'

'How did he describe it?'

'Not as kidnapping. Something along the lines of finding a way to make people look at the same world differently. In fact he said it was more of an artistic enterprise rather than having any criminal intention.'

'So what did you think when I started talking to you about Conrad Jensen's disappearance back there in Green Park?' asked Boxer. 'And more to the point, what about Jensen's daughter Siobhan? How did she know about my special service, and why?'

'I thought Jensen had disappeared to start his weird project.'

'Why would he send his daughter to find me?'

'Good question.'

'They used Siobhan to get close to Amy and now they've kidnapped her as well.'

'With what intention?'

'Difficult to say, except they know I'll come after her.'

'So they want you too … I don't get it.'

'Nor do I.'

'As for your special service, I've no idea how they knew about that, but it wasn't from me,' said Fox. 'Jensen is mixing at all levels of social strata. He speaks lots of different languages, some human and some technological, and he operates in a highly connected world. He could have found out from any of the people you've done that sort of work for.'

'There've not been *that* many.'

'Maybe it was the Russian, Marat Zarubin, whose boy you rescued from the Ukrainian gang. Jensen seems well connected in Russia. Speaks the language.'

'Text me Zarubin's number,' said Boxer. 'Where did you see Jeff Cook when she was here?'

'She has a flat in Hackney.'

'Text me her mobile number as well.'

'I'm pretty sure she's in Afghanistan.'

'This is just me at the moment. No police involved. If you and any of your people want it to stay like that, then you'd better be co-operative,' said Boxer. 'At the moment, your standing with Simon Deacon is safe, but don't push me, Martin. It's galling to hear him speak so highly of you and your spotless reputation.'

'You know as well as I do, Charlie, that there are two worlds. The one we all see and the one that's carefully hidden from us. All I can tell you is that the one that's hidden is a lot bigger than the one we see and the rules are not the same. I have to operate in both to make a living.'

By 01.55 three short films of the punishments given to Siena Casey, Rakesh Sarkar and Wú Gao were finished. After each film the hostage was taken back to their cell and given a sedative.

At 01.59, a specially insulated forty-foot container arrived at the warehouse in south London and was backed into an old loading bay. Two men opened the doors to the container and three layers deep of flat-screen TVs were removed to reveal a wall with a door in it.

Beyond the door was a narrow corridor, which opened out into a space with a table and chairs. On each side were three sleeping pods with glass windows, which could be locked and seen into but were opaque from the inside.

The two men opened up the six pods and switched on the ventilation system. In the corner were a couple of emergency oxygen cylinders. There was also a drawer of medical supplies and a fridge holding IV saline drips and blood products. The men prepared the sleeping pods by laying down clean sheets, duvets and pillows.

Meanwhile a doctor went into the cells containing the hostages, who were already asleep from the drugs administered earlier, and gave them a quick medical check. As each one was passed for travel, the two men came in and removed the hostage to a sleeping pod. Within half an hour all the hostages were comfortable and the two men, who were trained nurses, locked themselves into the room inside the container. The TV units were reloaded and the doors shut.

At 02.34, the container left the loading bay and started its journey down to Portsmouth to catch the ferry to northern Spain.

At 02.36, the comatose forms of Amy Boxer and Marcus Alleyne were loaded into a white transit van, which also left the premises. The remaining team went through the warehouse and bleach-cleaned the cells where the hostages had been held. By 03.14, the premises were empty of any human trace.

At 03.10, Boxer was sitting in the car trying to call Jeff Cook. There was no response from her mobile.

'Martin said she was in Afghanistan.'

'There's one way of checking,' said Mercy. 'It's not as if we don't have the means.'

'I know, but it will take things away from us.'

'There's nothing we can do about her on our own if she's out there.'

'Are you going to call Hines?'

'I'm not sure. I was thinking of telling Ryder Forsyth directly.'

'Any reason?'

'The people holding Marcus told me to make Ryder love me.'

Mercy sent Forsyth a text to ask if she could talk to him and got an immediate reply. They drove to Wilton Place.

'By the way, I asked Ryder if he knew you and he denied it. I could see he was lying but he didn't care.'

'That's crazy. We were on missions together into southern Iraq. We argued a lot, drank a lot…we even had a fight once, which I lost,' said Boxer. 'We had grudging respect for each other. I thought he was impossibly arrogant, but at least he was right most of the time.'

'So why the denial?'

'Just the way some people are,' said Boxer.

'Bullshit.'

'All right, if you have to know, I stole his woman. Or rather, she left him to be with me.'

'Was that another one of those really long relationships you had back in the day?'

And with no warning, Boxer found himself turning to the window and crying at his half-reflection.

'Oh Christ, Charlie, I'm sorry. I didn't mean that.'

'Not your fault,' said Boxer. 'Just came from nowhere.'

They drove in silence. Boxer recovered almost as quickly as he'd gone into it. They arrived at Wilton Place. Boxer stayed in the car. Forsyth answered the door himself and led Mercy up the stairs to the living room, where she told him about Reef and Leo and the connection to Jennifer Cook and where she was serving.

'You told anyone else about this? Like DCS Hines?'

'Not so far. I thought you should be the first to know.'

'Do you mind if we keep it like that for a few hours?'

'Any reason?'

'We'd like to be the first to talk to Jennifer Cook,' said Forsyth. 'It's always better to interview people when they're unprepared. Just give me a minute.'

Forsyth left the room. He was gone for ten minutes. There was no sound in the house and he startled her when he returned.

'How did you get to Reef and then Cook?' he asked, sitting down again.

'By pursuing the Conrad Jensen lead.'

'I tip my hat to you, Mercy. Sorry I doubted your instinct. That means Jensen is involved in this.'

'Yes, but in what capacity I'm not sure. I know that he and his daughter are in it,' said Mercy. 'The lead I got was from a contact phone number left in the flat his daughter was renting. I had that traced and it led to Reef. What I'd like from you is to find Walden Garfinkle, as he was one of the last people to see Conrad Jensen when he was at the Savoy.'

'I'll see what I can do.'

'Do you know a man called Julius Klank?'

Forsyth nodded.

'He received a payment from Conrad Jensen into an account under the name Xiphos in Belize.'

'For what?'

'That I don't know,' said Mercy. 'But I imagine it's for supplying men or services to this project.'

'Project?'

'The other name who received money from Jensen, into an account called Kaluptein in the British Virgin Islands, was Boris Bortnik.'

'Don't know him,' said Forsyth, making notes now.

'He works for a mafia outfit in Moscow called Dolgoprudninskaya.'

'Maybe Sergei Yermilov can help with that.'

'Anything happened here? How's Emma taking it?'

'I made sure she didn't see what they did to her daughter,' said Forsyth.

'Which was?'

'Part of a brutal demonstration by the kidnappers to establish a single line of contact for all the hostages,' said Forsyth. 'They waterboarded her.'

'My God.'

'Electric shocks to the German girl and they put the Russian boy in a gas mask and cut off his air supply,' said Forsyth. 'And it happened absolutely when they said it would, within minutes of the deadline.'

'What about the demand for expenses?' asked Mercy. 'Anything happened with that?'

'We've been given all the delivery details for the money except time and place.'

'And is that going ahead?'

'None of the victims' parents have raised any protest so far.'

'Do you know Conrad Jensen, by the way?' asked Mercy.

'No,' said Forsyth. 'Why do you ask?'

'It's interesting that they wanted you to be the lead negotiator. Normally they'd want to maintain the connection with the parents, where they would get the maximum emotional leverage. And most gangs prefer to talk to civilians even if they know there are professionals in the background. But to cut them out and make you totally responsible seems odd. They're also saying that the expenses demand is the last they'll make. What's that all about? This isn't a ransom, but we don't want any more money.'

'I've got to say, it's very confusing,' said Forsyth. 'But the other thing the victims' families have access to is power. And that worries me, having seen the lengths the kidnappers were prepared to go to establish a single line of communication. What will happen if they start asking for really complex political or financial manoeuvres that demand agreement from others? I wouldn't like to be the one to test their ruthlessness.'

'And the money. Have you ever known such a quantity of money to be delivered in this fashion in a kidnap?'

'Never. I'm not sure how they're going to be able to get away with nearly four tons of loosely packed money in plastic wrapping,' said Forsyth. 'That's quite apart from how they'll have to expose themselves in order to pick it up and where they will have to take it. I can't see how it's going to work.'

At 05.44, Captain Jennifer Cook was on her way to Camp Bastion. She was in a convoy of just two Foxhound vehicles, as the road from Forward Operating Base Sterga 2 to the south-west of Lashkar Gah had been very well secured and constantly checked for IEDs. They were aiming to get to Camp Bastion at sunrise, just after seven o'clock.

She had just completed a circuit observing the dismantling process of Main Operating Base Price, north-east of Lashkar Gah, followed by a training mission by the Afghan special forces units in Lashkar Gah itself, and finishing with a briefing of British troops at what would be, in a few months' time, the last remaining forward operating base at Sterga 2. She'd also filmed a survey of opium poppy growing in these two areas and was dismayed to find a 50 per cent increase in land under cultivation for opium over the last year. None of their initiatives had worked. She still cared about it, but it was now beyond British control and the power brokers in Afghan politics would have their way.

She was pleased because all she had to do now was file this report and in less than three months her last tour of duty would be over. She would be retiring from military intelligence, leaving the army and taking six months off to get married to her girlfriend and go on an extended honeymoon around Argentina. On her return she was finally going to use her Cambridge law degree and was starting a job with a law firm specialising in human rights. She was as happy as any soldier could be under the circumstances that prevailed in Afghanistan.

They were the lead vehicle, travelling at forty miles per hour on the completely flat desert terrain. The tarmac road was taking them into what had become the new HQ of British forces in Helmand in August last year after they handed over Lashkar Gah to the Afghan troops. There were some lights up ahead on the road. Cook's driver slowed and radioed back to the vehicle behind.

'What's all this about?' he asked.

'Fuck knows,' said Cook. 'But it won't be the Taliban out here and it's too early in the year for the opium growers.'

'There's an American flag,' said the driver. 'You think they're in trouble?'

'OK, let's stop, see what they want,' said Cook. 'Tell the others to keep their distance for the moment.'

An obviously American-looking soldier in full combat uniform was holding up his hand in the middle of the road and swinging a light in front of him. The driver pulled up. It was cold, maybe just below zero, and the soldier's breath was visible in the light. From behind him came five men also in combat gear.

One man went to the driver's side while two came to Cook's window, which she rolled down. The others continued to the vehicle behind.

'Can I help you, gentlemen?' she said, knowing how formal Americans, even soldiers, liked to be.

'Is your name Captain Jennifer Lucy Cook?'

'It is.'

'Would you step out of the vehicle, please, ma'am?'

'Only if you tell me what it's about.'

'The opium trade.'

'What exactly do you mean?'

'The CIA are currently interrogating a warlord on the growth of opium crops in Helmand and Nimroz provinces and we have been advised that you could provide substantial background material that would enable us to prosecute this man.'

'That might be true, but do you have to stop me in the middle of nowhere? Can't it wait until I've got back to Camp Bastion and had a shower and cleaned up? I've been on the road for a week.'

'This is urgent, ma'am. My orders come from Colonel Mark Rodgers of the CIA. We have a helicopter waiting to take you to Camp Leatherneck.'

'Here? Now?'

'That's right, ma'am.'

'And presumably you have permission from my commanding officer in Camp Bastion?'

'From Brigadier Martin Jenkins himself,' said the soldier.

Cook looked at her driver, who knew that the soldier had not given the correct name, and suddenly there were two rifles in the cockpit of the vehicle, inches from their noses.

'Out of the vehicle, ma'am.'

Cook eased herself slowly out of the now open door. Two of the soldiers marched her off into the darkness. There were shots, and the two British vehicles sagged on flat tyres. Two further shots finished the radios.

The Americans withdrew. Their vehicles took off into the night. Some time later, the British soldiers heard the sound of a helicopter.

'I'm very sorry you had to watch that footage of your son,' said Forsyth. 'How is your wife?'

'She has gone to the hospital,' said Yermilov. 'She fell over and hit her head when she saw what they were doing to my little Yury.'

'I hope she's all right.'

'Just a slight concussion. She will be under observation for the night.'

'I wanted to ask if you knew a guy called Boris Bortnik, who works for a Moscow mafia—'

'I know of Boris Bortnik. What has he got to do with this?'

'We believe that this kidnap gang is being run by a man called Conrad Jensen, and we understand that he made a payment to

Boris Bortnik into an account in the British Virgin Islands called Kaluptein.'

'Send me an email immediately,' said Yermilov, waving at his men to go to the computer. 'I will look into this.'

'We don't know how much money he received or what it was for.'

'We will find out,' said Yermilov, with a finality that chilled even Forsyth's hot blood.

Yermilov hung up and called two of Solntsevskaya's most brutal enforcers in Moscow and told them they had an hour to find Boris Bortnik. Then he called his sponsor, the president's banker, and asked him to investigate the Kaluptein account in the British Virgin Islands.

23

Jennifer Cook was kept face down, gagged and hooded, hands cuffed behind her back, on the floor of a Russian-manufactured Mil Mi-17 helicopter, which touched down in Camp Leatherneck twenty minutes after she was taken on the road to Camp Bastion.

A strange thing happened on landing. Rather than being marched from the helicopter, she was wrapped in a sheet, picked up bodily and carried by what felt like six men, who put her in the boot of some kind of personnel carrier and secured her arms and ankles. Having been scared before, she was really terrified by this development, as she realised now that she'd been brought in covertly. She still wasn't even sure whether this was Camp Leatherneck or that these were bona fide American soldiers.

The vehicle moved off and a few minutes later they started going through the procedure of leaving the camp, the men signing themselves out but making no mention of her. When she'd been on the road to Camp Bastion and guns had appeared in the cockpit of the Foxhound, she'd been unnerved. Once she was in the helicopter and landing in what she thought was Camp Leatherneck, she'd got a grip. But now that she knew for certain she'd been unofficially kidnapped, she had to make a conscious effort to control her terror.

They drove for an hour in total silence. Only part of the journey was on tarmac road; the rest was on what felt like desert *piste*, with the noise of loose stones clattering against the bottom of the vehicle. They slowed and stopped. She was lifted from the vehicle and taken indoors, where she was unwrapped from the sheet and dropped on the floor. Hands picked her up, threw her into a metal chair and strapped her in. She was left alone, a wooden door slammed shut. She was still hooded and gagged, panting with fear.

After some minutes she realised she was not alone in the room. Somebody was watching her. She listened, turning her head this way and that, and heard the chewing of gum. There was a rush of air and contact was made with the side of her head. So hard that blue lightning flashed across her brain and she keeled over on to her left side. She was immediately righted. More silence followed. Another rush followed by a terrible slap on the other side of her face, which made her neck crack and toppled her backwards so that her head flicked back on to the hard ground. She was righted again. Disorientated and shuddering, she didn't know where the next—

A boot thudded into her chest and she cannoned backwards, hitting a wall as she went down. This time she was left on the ground, lying on her right side, her wrist trapped painfully underneath her body, winded. She was rolled on to her back. The tie at her neck was loosened. A hand came under the hood, pulled out the gag. The hood was lowered and retightened around her neck. More silence apart from her own grunting as she relearnt how to breathe.

The sound of a plastic water bottle top being ripped off, someone drinking from the neck. Then water was splashing onto the thick material of her hood so that it was quickly sodden and sticking to her face. The water kept coming so that air was difficult to come by and she started to panic at the lack of it. Hands clasped the sides of her head and the water kept coming and she knew she was dying, could already feel a deeper darkness encroaching. The wildness of the terror that rose in her throat infected her brain, which was shot through with sadness at such a pathetic ending.

The water stopped. She was pulled upright, the hood drawn back above her mouth and nose. Her lungs tore at the air, ripped it open, sucked in the oxygen.

'What the fuck do you want from me?' she asked.

'Nothing.'

237

'Nothing?'

'This is the new interrogation technique for military intelligence officers,' said the voice, southern US accent, maybe Louisiana. 'You invent your own questions. Give us the answers. We don't like them. You go back under the hood and the water.'

'But I don't know—'

'That's the point. You *do* know.'

'What do I know?' she said. 'I only know what you know. We're allies, we share information, don't we? You're Americans ... I liaise with INSCOM via Captain Rick Hewitt of the 297th Military Intelligence Battalion ...'

'This is nothing to do with MI in Afghanistan.'

Silence from Cook, blinking under the hood, the panic rising in her throat. Suddenly she felt a face close to hers; the chewing gum breath worked its way through the wet cloth.

'You gettin' me now, Jeff?'

'I don't think so.'

Bang! She was on her back again. Her head smacked into the earth floor, whose wetness she could now smell. Nausea rose from her stomach. Hands were at her waist, undoing her buttons, tugging down her trousers so that involuntary squeaks of terror and humiliation creaked in her throat.

'We know you,' said the voice. 'We know you're a commie piece of shit and you don't like cock.'

She was shuddering inside now, her guts quaking with vulnerability and the knowledge that this was something completely out of control; that if these were American soldiers, they were behaving a long way outside all normal procedures.

'I don't know what to say to you,' she said, and she didn't.

'This is about London,' said the voice. 'Think about that while I give you some more water.'

The water splashed down on her face, plastering the hood to her mouth. Immediately the air wasn't there any more. She struggled against the horrible sensation of drowning, felt the storm-cloud darkness of dread creeping in. She wanted to kick out with her now bare legs, but they were strapped down and there was nothing in them anyway, gone to rags.

Just as she found herself on the brink of asking for help from

238

God, the water stopped. The hood came up to her nose. Light shimmered beneath her eyes. She tried to lap it up, her chest working like a bellows, her ribcage stretching the skin to splitting point.

'You had time to think now, babe,' said the voice. 'Let's hear your shit. Come on.'

'About London,' she said gasping. 'I'm ... trying ...'

'No need to try,' said the voice. 'You *know*, babe. There can be no doubt in your mind why you find yourself in this position. Now start comin' through, kiddo. You don't and this waterboarding is going to look like chickenshit. I got some hungry guys out there, haven't been with a woman for some months. They'll take it in turns, all together, every which way. You don't want that, do you, babe?'

'Oh Christ,' she said. 'What have I done? I don't know what ...'

'Don't ask *me* that question,' said the voice. 'Ask yourself and let's have the fuckin' answer. You got thirty seconds. Then I'm calling in the guys.'

She swallowed. Couldn't believe she'd found herself on the brink already. In training she'd been the most resistant to interrogation, but this guy had her on the edge after twenty minutes. She tried to remember how she'd got through it: by imagining a steel bar in her middle that she could grip so that nothing could shift her. But this was different. No rules here. Just as there wouldn't have been any rules with the Taliban, except that these people weren't the enemy.

'Twenty seconds.'

Or were they?

The thought of her lover came into her mind. Carmen. Her sweetness. The sheer ghastliness of war had never reached her. They would lie together in the sunshine after a picnic and it was an immense relief to Jennifer that Carmen's mind had never been bruised with anything like the bloody aftermath of an improvised explosive device. Its acronym, even its real name, didn't communicate any of the horror of discarded limbs, random offal, seared flesh.

'Ten seconds.'

Could she allow herself to be brutalised? What purpose would it serve? Was it going to save the world? She quelled a rush of disgust at the prospect of her utter defilement; didn't want it to get in the way of her pristine logic. It occurred to her, too, that they wouldn't kill her. They knew she wouldn't reveal anything to her commanding officer. All she had to do was balance the ethics in her mind. What was more valuable to her future? Carmen or what exactly?

'Five seconds.'

She searched herself for a sense of duty, until she realised that this was different.

'Four.'

She wasn't betraying anybody but herself.

'Three.'

The personal weighed more than the political.

'Two.'

Her love mattered more than any belief.

'One.'

'I met a guy called Conrad Jensen.'

'How?'

'You don't need to know that.'

'I don't need to but I want to. Everything. Let's have it, Jeff.'

'I know a guy called Martin Fox who runs a British PSC in London called Pavis. Jensen approached him wanting some unusual personnel for a project. Fox remembered a conversation we'd had about the opium trade in Afghanistan and drug use in the military. He asked me if I knew someone who was trained, no longer serving, into drugs and could perform a straightforward piece of work. I said I knew a couple of people, but I wouldn't talk to just anybody. I had to know the nature of the project and the person running it.'

'Why would Fox even approach you with something like that?'

'He makes it his business to know about people who can help him in the real world,' said Cook. 'Fox knows my elder sister. They went out with each other before he got married. My sister knows me very well. I have never denied my left wing beliefs and I've always had a subversive streak since I was at university.'

'Why join the army?'

'Perversity. I vehemently disagreed with the war in Iraq and I

240

wanted to see things for myself from the inside. I was a committed socialist. I did not approve of Tony Blair. I had the misguided notion that I could make a difference.'

'So you met Conrad Jensen through this Martin Fox guy?'

'Not exactly. Jensen didn't trust Fox. He didn't want to work through him. He only wanted direct contact with me.'

'How did you meet?'

'We set up a dead drop. He was able to observe me and satisfy himself that I wasn't working some other agenda. We met in St James's Park in London.'

'And he managed to persuade you that his project ... I don't know why you're calling it that. He's a fucking criminal. I mean, did he say you'd be participating in the kidnap of children?'

'No, he didn't. I wouldn't have agreed to that. He told me he wanted to use my contact to kidnap a known adult drug user.'

'You're a lawyer,' said the voice. 'What the fuck're you playing at?'

'He said he couldn't tell me his precise plan because it would be too dangerous to have me out in the world with that knowledge. His vision was to create a fairer society and to do that meant bringing about some sort of revolution. He said the difference with his revolution would be that it would not be started by the poor with nothing to lose rising up and violently attempting to assume power; rather it would come from the top down.'

'Sounds like bullshit to me.'

'He said he would not be seeking to make money out of the kidnap.'

'The guy's asked for a hundred and fifty million; he's tortured children and he's shot two guys so far. That sound like the velvet revolution to you?'

'How do I know you're telling me the truth?'

'There's nothing more we can do now,' said Mercy. 'You should come back with me. You shouldn't spend the night alone.'

She drove south, telling Boxer about the meeting with Forsyth. Boxer had nothing to say. They continued through Victoria and down to the river.

'What are you thinking?' said Mercy. 'I don't like it when you're silent.'

'I'm trying to work out why I don't feel anything.'

'It's normal, just the mind's way of coping with trauma. It puts you into a kind of emotional coma until you're ready to take it. You function, but you don't feel.'

'That's straight from the manual, isn't it?'

'Don't expect to be able to apply the manual to yourself. You're in shock. Nothing makes sense.'

Silence again. They crossed the river at Vauxhall. Boxer stared out of the window at the light playing on the black water, the MI6 building with its antennae towering into the orange night.

'You never spoke to me about Isabel,' said Mercy.

'I didn't speak to anyone about her, not even Amy.'

'Why?'

'It was private. Nothing to do with anybody else.'

'Not even the people who care about you?'

'Not even the people who care about me.'

'You've told me about all the other ones.'

'They didn't matter,' said Boxer. 'I told you about them because I could see why and how they were coming to nothing. I couldn't speak to you about Isabel because, although it was good and intense, so much of it was a mystery to me. I didn't understand how she could love me and why I loved her. All I knew was that it started the moment I first saw her. And I think you know what I'm talking about.'

'Why?'

'Because you've never spoken to me about Marcus,' said Boxer. 'You've asked me whether you should talk to your colleagues about his criminal life, but you've never told me anything important like ... *why* you love him, or he you. And I don't need to know, because as soon as you put it into words, it doesn't sound like anything special. Along the lines of "He's everything to me." We just don't have the vocabulary for it. We need poets, and even then it's not quite ours, it's still theirs.'

'What about now? Do you want to talk about Isabel now?' said Mercy. 'It's what people do. Talk them back into life. To make it feel as if they mattered.'

'The thing about her, the most important thing, was that for the first time I'd met someone who had the capacity to make things better. And I think it was because she understood where I was coming from after years living with Frank D'Cruz.'

'Did she know ... anything?'

'About what I'd done?' said Boxer. 'No. She knew I'd probably killed people in war and she knew there was something dark locked inside me. I wouldn't have wanted her to know about it, though. I mean the really black stuff.'

'You told me once she'd seen into Frank D'Cruz and hadn't liked it,' said Mercy. 'Did that scare you, that she'd see inside you and run a mile?'

'Frank was in love with himself. It was all about him. When she got inside, there was nothing there. He had to get what *he* wanted. Nothing else mattered. Not Isabel and not his second wife, Sharmila, either.'

'And you?'

'Isabel knew I loved her. That was the big difference.'

'You know what I always felt about Isabel?' said Mercy. 'We spent an evening talking together that time when we thought that Amy had been murdered in Madrid. She wanted to know about you. And I did my best ... not knowing what I know now. But I left her the following morning feeling that there was something missing in her.'

'Missing?'

'What it was, I've no idea. I'd have had to spend more time with her.'

'Yes, there probably was something missing,' said Boxer. 'For a start, she had no sense of belonging anywhere. Half English, half Portuguese. A diplomat's daughter. Then married young to Frank and living a weird life in Bombay before pitching up here. She always said the anonymity of London suited her.'

'She'd have recognised the same in you,' said Mercy. 'In a lot of us. That's why we're here.'

'Maybe that was the attraction. We both had something missing and thought we could provide the vital piece for each other,' said Boxer. 'Don't all lovers think that?'

'You've always known what's missing,' said Mercy.

'My father, you mean?'

Mercy shrugged, hands on the steering wheel: obvious.

'Yes, I think that was what I hoped she would do,' said Boxer. 'Heal that particular wound.'

'And what would you do for her?'

'I'd have loved her,' said Boxer. 'But you've got me thinking now. Maybe that was the mystery that I wanted to solve but never could. What did she want? What was missing?'

They pulled up outside Mercy's house. She fixed him, arms braced against the steering wheel.

'What are you going to do about the baby?'

'I don't know.'

'Have you thought about it?'

'Not beyond the fact that he's going to have to stay in hospital for another couple of months at least.'

'Maybe you should spend some time thinking about that. It being a more positive thing,' she said. 'You know what I mean? A reason to keep living.'

They got out of the car and went into the kitchen. Boxer checked his phone, saw the text from Martin Fox with Marat Zarubin's number, called him from the living room.

'Hello, Charlie, what you want?' said Zarubin, cheerful; it was just before seven o'clock there.

'You ever come across a guy called Conrad Jensen or his daughter Siobhan?'

'I do business with Conrad. He write computer programs for me,' said Zarubin. 'Why you ask?'

'Did you tell him anything about me?' said Boxer. 'What I did for you?'

'We talk about my son being kidnapped, that's true,' said Zarubin. 'He wanted to know every detail.'

'Did you tell him how you got the lead to the Ukrainian gang who did it?'

'A friend of mine in Moscow.'

'That wouldn't be Boris Bortnik, would it?'

'That's right. It was him. He work for mafia group in Moscow. They have contacts in Kiev. He found the gang. Better than police. I never bother with police now.'

'And you gave Jensen Bortnik's contact details?'

'He asked for them.'

'You might want to warn your friend that people might come looking for him.'

'Why's that, Charlie?'

'Did you tell Jensen I tracked down the Ukrainian?'

'Yes. I'm sorry, was that wrong thing to do?' said Zarubin. 'I only tell Jensen because I trust him. We work together for years. I tell him it's private ... not for broadcast. I say you don't do it for money. I tell him about the LOST Foundation. I think maybe he get worry about making so much money.'

'Making money ... how?'

'Energy. I don't know how, but he has very good connections in Lukoil, Rosneft and Surgutneftegas,' said Zarubin. 'Russian government looking to diversify, so they like Mr Jensen very much. Make his life easy.'

'Was there ever any relationship between Jensen and Sergei Yermilov?'

'Yermilov is very dangerous man,' said Zarubin, without thinking, knee-jerk.

'Did Jensen know him?'

'Of course. Yermilov very close to the president. Nothing happening without him knowing. He's friend with the president's banker,' said Zarubin. 'What this all about, Charlie?'

'You don't talk to anybody about this, Marat. And don't talk to anybody about me again,' said Boxer. 'You hear me?'

'I hear you,' said Zarubin. 'One thing, Charlie, Mr Jensen, he know you already. He know the name Charlie Boxer, he know what you do, kidnap consultant, your career in army, everything, before I talk about you.'

Boris Bortnik was on his way back to his flat near the Tretyakovskaya Metro on Boshaya Ordynka. He had been to his favourite nightclub, Soho Rooms, where he was always guaranteed to find the best women. One of them was with him now. He didn't know her name. They'd had something to eat and drink, but he hadn't got round to asking her name. They were alone in the back of the limousine. The driver and bodyguard were shut away in the cockpit. All that came through the heavily tinted windows was a dim version of Moscow by night. No noise penetrated the cabin. The only sound was the heater blasting hot air against the outside temperature of -18°C.

They were on Bolshaya Pirogovskaya, heading for Zubovskiy and the bridge across the Moskva river. The girl had been fellating him expertly. She had just removed her underwear and was now straddling his legs and lowering herself down on to him. The car slowed and stopped. Bortnik didn't care. He was concentrating. What broke his concentration were the two sharp thuds that penetrated the heavily insulated unit where he was sitting. They were recognisable to him as shots from a silenced firearm. Panic shot through him.

There was a gun in the armrest and he ripped it open, throwing off the girl just as the car door opened and a Makarov pistol with a fat suppressor attached swerved into his line of vision. The girl was squeaking with fear, legs flailing, dress around her waist, crabbing across the floor, pressing herself against the far door. She'd heard of this sort of thing happening from other girls. Never to her.

'Hands,' said the voice behind the Makarov.

Bortnik showed his hands. The girl started screaming, which was too much for the gunman, who shot her twice in the chest.

He leaned in and pulled Bortnik from the car, walked him to another vehicle in front, past his dead bodyguard and driver slumped into each other, past the roadblock that had been set up and the blue flashing lights of a police Lada. They laid him across the back seat of a black Toyota Land Cruiser, frisked him for weapons, took his mobile phone and the other contents of his pockets, wrapped some tape around his eyes, wrists and ankles and rolled him into the footwell. They climbed in, rested their feet on his trembling body. The car pulled away.

No words were exchanged between the four men in the car. Occasionally the men in the back would grind their heels into whatever body part they thought would cause most discomfort to Bortnik below them.

The journey took more than forty minutes and Bortnik thought they must be going to the very outskirts of Moscow, or even leaving the city. Finally the car pulled up. The men grabbed him by the ankles and hauled him out so that his face smashed into the ice. They dragged him over the snow and ice and down some steps into an enclosed room, where they gave him a severe kicking on the concrete floor. They left him bleeding in the brutal cold of the unheated room.

Bortnik tried to gather himself. Tracks of blood from his bleeding head and face had already frozen on his skin. He was shivering uncontrollably. The alcohol in his system from a night's drinking was making him feel the cold more profoundly. He was finding it difficult to focus. The only reason he could possibly be in this position was because of a rival gang, but he couldn't think what he'd done to warrant such action. Killing three people in the process. This had the stamp of Solntsevskaya. Only they could have such control over the Moscow streets.

Half an hour leaked past. The cold seemed to be more intense. Just as he'd got to the point where he was fighting to stay awake, the door to the cellar opened. There was the sound of gas. A lighter flickered and the roar of space heaters filled the room. The relief was immediate. His chest loosened. His muscles creaked back into life.

They cut the tape around his ankles and wrists, stripped him naked and strapped him into a metal chair bolted to the floor. They tore the tape from around his head and he shuddered under the bright lights of the grim room. He was aware of people but not of how many.

'We can make this short,' said the voice, 'or very long, protracted and extremely painful for you.'

Bortnik nodded, gasping against the pain as his returning body heat enlivened his bruises and wounds.

'You received two payments, one of two hundred thousand dollars and another of fifteen thousand dollars from a company called Sunbeam International Ltd into a company owned by you called Kaluptein in the British Virgin Islands,' said the voice. 'We want you to tell us who paid you that money and what for.'

The heat in the room had defrosted the blood tracks on Bortnik's face and he stared at the drops striking his bare thighs as he tried to marshal his thoughts to develop some kind of negotiation.

'I'm willing to tell you what you want to know,' he said.

'That's good.'

'In return—'

'There's no "in return" in this case,' said the voice, and Bortnik heard the roar of the space heater behind him get a little closer. 'You don't talk and you'll get this.'

The space heater was put near his leg; the room immediately filled with the smell of singed hair. He yelped as it started to sear the flesh on his leg. Then it backed off.

'You understand,' said the voice. 'You are not in any position to negotiate. You are only in a position to persuade us to give you some mercy.'

Bortnik didn't want to, but he started crying. He wasn't sure whether it was emotional, because he'd never been one to express or feel anything other than extreme lust. He put it down to the thaw induced by the space heaters.

One of the men in the room stood in front of him and beat him about the head until he brought himself under control.

'I was asked,' said Bortnik, 'to supply research on Sergei Yermilov.'

'How did you accomplish that?'

'I found someone close to him and paid him.'

'Name?'

Bortnik named Irina Yermilov's younger brother, Anatoly Drugov. He'd stayed with them in Weybridge and hated Sergei only marginally less than Irina did herself.

'How do you know Drugov?'

'I was friendly with Irina's old tennis coach. He knew him. I asked for an introduction.'

'What else were you paid for?'

'They wanted a bilingual English/Russian-speaking special forces guy who was prepared to work in a team and kill on foreign soil,' said Bortnik, and named him too.

'Was that it?'

'Then he called me later and asked for someone who would carry out a small hit, not significant,' said Bortnik. 'That was the fifteen thousand.'

'And who paid you this money?'

'His name is Conrad Jensen.'

'Did you ever meet him?'

'No. We were supposed to meet in Dubai one time in November last year, but he pulled out.'

'Do you know why he wanted you to research Sergei Yermilov?'

'I thought perhaps he might want to kill him, but he never told me.'

'Does that mean you had permission from a higher authority to conduct this research?'

'Of course.'

One of the men left the room. The others stayed behind and smoked, passing a bottle of vodka between them. Ten minutes later, the man returned and nodded. Two of the men put their cigarettes into the corners of their mouths and reached down for the space heaters, while another stuffed Bortnik's socks into his mouth and taped it shut. Bortnik's eyes grew wild as the men settled the space heaters in front of him. They turned them up and the blue gas flames shot out towards Bortnik, who struggled violently in his immovable chair. The men in the room smoked and watched and sipped on the bottle of vodka they passed from hand to hand.

24

Amy Boxer came to in the dark, confused by a dream where she'd been on a beach, a man walking towards her but never getting any closer. She'd started walking and then running towards him because she had a great need to see his face, but as hard as she ran, the man's features never became any more distinct than a blur.

'You've been dreaming,' said a voice from the darkness.

Siobhan.

'You're watching me.'

'My favourite pastime.'

'What it is with you?'

'That kiss …'

'Shut up about the kiss. It was nothing. You were just drawing me in to fuck me over.'

'That might have been the idea … then.'

'And look where I am.'

'But it's changed. I've changed.'

'Yeah, right. That's why we're walking off into the sunset.'

'Would you like that?' asked Siobhan. 'I'd like that.'

She sat next to Amy, whose wrists were secured by cuffs threaded through the metal bed head. The only light was from a crack under the door. Siobhan's features were black; only the outline of her hair was visible.

'Where am I?' asked Amy.

'London.'

'Is Marcus here?'

'Yep, he's fine. Still out of it. You were drugged and moved out of the warehouse. Got to keep ahead of the game.'

'And the hostages?'

'Not here. And before you ask, I don't know where they are. Nobody does.'

'Can you release one of my wrists?'

'Don't have the key,' said Siobhan, stroking her leg.

'Don't do that,' said Amy. 'It's not fair.'

'Fair?' said Siobhan, suddenly flaring. 'What's fair? Nothing's fucking fair in this world. You think it's fair that I was born like this?'

'Easy up, Siobhan. I just meant you're taking advantage of me. It wasn't a comment on ... the world.'

'You think I wanted it to be like this?'

'I don't know. You brought me in.'

'It was the plan. It was my job in the plan.'

Silence while Amy weighed that line for tone.

'What?' asked Siobhan.

'You're lying,' said Amy. 'I know you a bit by now, Siobhan, and you're fucking lying. What's it all about?'

Siobhan's black outline stared down at her.

'All right,' she said. 'I *persuaded* Dad it was a good idea.'

'Why?'

'Because I like you. Thought we could get to know each other under more ... relaxed circs.'

'Relaxed?' said Amy. 'So why did Conrad want my dad to come looking for him?'

'You've asked me that before.'

'And you didn't answer me.'

'Because I don't know. He doesn't tell me everything. Most of the time he tells me shit. He wanted him involved ... that's all I know.'

Silence.

'So they bought into your idea of bringing me in?'

'Dad did. As usual, having come round to it, he thought it was *his* idea.'

'And where's your father now?'

251

'Look, stop trying to find things out,' said Siobhan. 'I know what you're doing. Be a bit more subtle, for fuck's sake.'

'OK, so what else?' said Amy. 'If you don't have the key to these cuffs, who does?'

'A guy downstairs ... with a gun,' said Siobhan. 'Tell me about your boyfriend.'

'I don't have one,' said Amy.

'Would you like one?'

'Not any old one,' said Amy. 'I'd like to choose.'

'Do you think you could choose me?'

'I don't know. These circumstances are pretty unusual.'

'A kind of reverse Stockholm syndrome where the kidnapper falls in love with their hostage.'

'And what?'

'Won't release them for any ransom, not even a king's.'

'You're too weird.'

'I'm just playing,' said Siobhan. 'I don't like the guy downstairs. He doesn't say much, keeps cleaning his gun, then closes his eyes, strips it down and puts it back together again as if he's in some dumb action movie.'

'We're all doing the same shit,' said Amy. 'Telling stories to make ourselves more interesting.'

Silence.

'Maybe that's what I've been doing all my life,' said Siobhan. 'Coming up with stories better than my own. I've spent my whole life doing what my father tells me to do. All this spy shit. Now look at me. Don't know who I am. You know I said he'll fuck anything? That wasn't true either. I just wanted him to look bad. It's me who'll fuck anything. The lies just keep pouring out of me. It's what I've been taught. Pretend my life away. Why do you think I'm dressed like this?'

'Because you like it?'

'So nobody knows who I really am. I'm a walking identity crisis.'

'Aren't we all?'

'You want to know something else?' said Siobhan, teetering now that she'd brought herself to the brink.

'Go on,' said Amy, compelled by Siobhan's sudden intensity.

'He's not even my father.'

'Who? Conrad?'

'I just got into the idea of it. Told myself that story.'

'What is he to you, then?'

'He's nobody. He just looks after me,' said Siobhan. 'He got me out of a bad situation.'

'Like what?'

'I was a contractor like him, except I was being ... used. Know what I mean?'

'Not really.'

'I had to fuck people so they would tell me their shit or be caught doing it so that pressure could be applied to make them ... turn.'

'People?'

'You know, people that might be close to important players who could then be used to give information.'

The door opened. The guy from downstairs was silhouetted. He had a gun in his right hand.

'Everything all right in here?'

'We're talking,' said Siobhan. 'You got the key? She wants one of her hands released.'

'Why?'

'More comfortable,' said Amy.

He gave Siobhan the key. She released one hand and cuffed the other to the bed head, returned the key. The guy leaned forward to make sure the cuff was secure.

'You don't trust me or something?' said Siobhan.

'I'm checking the black guy now,' he said, and left the room.

'Not exactly sweetness and light, is he?' said Siobhan.

Amy took hold of Siobhan's hand, squeezed it.

'Don't,' said Siobhan. 'Don't fuck with me.'

'I'm not. You just told me something true. That means a lot to me.'

Boxer barely slept. He'd drunk some whisky and gone to bed in Amy's room but woke before dawn. He stared at the ceiling. Isabel filled his mind but no feeling came to him. No sorrow. No pain. He imagined his son in the incubator, looked at his hand, remembered the softness of his head on the palm, but couldn't raise any emotion for him. He felt perplexed, guilty, removed from life. The strange thing was the black hole, the one that in the past had opened out in him whenever he'd been rejected or suffered loss. He'd expected it to be there, expanding inside him, but he had no sense of it unless – and the possibility of this was disturbing – it had occupied him totally. He cast his eyes around his daughter's room. Her books: Javier Marias, Haruki Murakami, Jennifer Egan. He didn't know any of these writers. Did he know Amy? Her fascination with Siobhan, was that just a crush? A rush of worry penetrated the numbness and he started thinking how he was going to generate another lead.

He jerked himself out of bed, wrote Mercy a note, left it in the kitchen and departed silently. He took the bus to Brixton, the tube back to Belsize Park. At home he put the gun on the table and turned on the radio. He took a shower, changed his clothes and sat at the table with the Walther P99 and the Betamax cassette from his father in front of him. He realised he was in no mental condition to do anything about the tape now, as the possibility of destroying it resurfaced in his mind.

A news package on the radio caught his ear because of the name, Jessica Peel, and the description of the young woman who'd been found dead in the Royal Victoria Dock that morning. Her neck had been broken. There were bloodstains nearby, but the girl had not been wounded and it was assumed she'd managed to hurt her assailant, probably stabbed him. Divers were preparing to search the dock for clues. Police were asking for anybody who saw or heard anything to come forward.

Boxer called Glider, checked that Jess's surname was Peel. He confirmed it. Boxer told him what he'd heard on the radio, hung up.

The nearest hospital with an A&E to the Royal Victoria Dock was the Royal London on Whitechapel Road. He called Mercy and asked her if she could make a police inquiry about anyone being admitted last night with a knife wound, and if so where he'd been found. He set off for the tube. Mercy called back just as he was crossing the road to the station.

'The Royal London's confirmed that a man was admitted with

a stab wound to his left side last night. He had no identity on him, no credit cards, nothing, just a clip of money and some change. Not even a phone.'

'Did they say where they found him?'

'He was picked up from a car outside Poplar DLR station after a phone call from a cab driver who'd seen him awkwardly parked and hanging out of his window.'

'Do you know what's happened to that car?'

'It's undergoing forensic examination.'

'What state is the guy in now?'

'He's stable in ICU. He was unconscious on admission and hasn't spoken yet.'

'Have they linked it to the murder of the girl found in Royal Victoria Dock?'

'I've only talked to reception at the Royal London,' said Mercy. 'You want me to go deeper?'

'They should analyse the blood samples found at the scene near where Jessica Peel was killed and compare them to the mystery guy admitted to A and E last night,' said Boxer. 'If they find a gun in that car or on his person, they should compare the ballistics with the rounds they'll find in the body of a dead Ukrainian who's weighed down in the water of the Regent's Canal underneath the Caledonian Road.'

'You get around,' said Mercy. 'Should we put a police guard on the ICU?'

'Might be an idea.'

'Where are you going now?'

'Poplar DLR station,' said Boxer. 'I'm looking for a lead to find out where Siobhan's taken Amy.'

'What are you expecting to find at Poplar?'

'If he's who I think he is, then he should have had a mobile phone,' said Boxer. 'Can you tell me the position of the car before it was removed by the police?'

Mercy called the communications centre, asked the question. Told Boxer she'd text him the detail when they got back to her.

'I'll need your help when I find the phone,' said Boxer. 'There'll be numbers to trace.'

255

'I've got a meeting at Wilton Place with Ryder Forsyth, just the two of us, before DCS Hines shows.'

'That's good,' said Boxer. 'It means he trusts you.'

'Text me with any numbers you need traced and I'll put them through to the communications centre.'

Boxer took the tube to Bank, changed on to the DLR out to Poplar. A text from Mercy came through giving the exact position of the car, which had been on the pavement twenty-two metres to the east of a footbridge over Aspen Way.

He went up on to the bridge to check the scene. There was a lot of thick evergreen vegetation between the station and the road, and on the pavement a man and a woman were looking it over. The man took out his phone, thumbed it and put it to his ear. The woman ran her fingers over the bushes as she walked slowly down the road, listening.

'How's Emma?' asked Mercy.

'Under doctor's supervision, on medication,' said Forsyth. 'It's not just the loss of her daughter but Conrad Jensen's betrayal too. She's devastated.'

'I'd like to talk to her again. Find out how serious it was between her and Conrad.'

'Sure. She's a bit out of it, though,' said Ryder. 'She told me he'd been very supportive over the break-up with Ken. And he had a good relationship with Sophie.'

'Have you played her the tapes of the calls you've received from the gang?'

'None of them are Jensen, if that's what you're asking.'

'I'm beginning to think he's masterminding this remotely,' said Mercy. 'He's using well-trained people—'

'I just heard from Yermilov, by the way,' said Forsyth, cutting in. 'Seems Jensen researched the two more complicated kidnaps very carefully. He didn't just get up close and personal with Emma; he also used Boris Bortnik to persuade Irina's brother to get inside the Yermilov household.'

'I don't fancy his chances of survival.'

'Or Irina's,' said Forsyth. 'Jennifer Cook's been interviewed too. So far she's the only one who's actually met with Jensen. She tried to persuade our interrogators that this project, as she kept calling it, was some kind of socialist conspiracy to bring about a fairer world from the top down.'

'And that doesn't wash with you?' said Mercy, surprised at Forsyth's new openness.

'I reckon she's in denial,' said Forsyth. 'In my experience, if your intentions are philanthropic, you don't steal people's kids and murder a couple of guys in the process, demand vast sums of money, then torture the kids when you don't get an immediate agreement on protocol.'

'Socialists can be ruthless too. Got to break eggs to make an omelette and all that,' said Mercy. 'Any decisions made about using the media to locate Jensen?'

'DCS Hines and the Joint Intelligence Committee are having a meeting about that later this morning.'

'You had any more thoughts about this money?'

'I had a conference call just now with four active kidnap consultants. We discussed it to death. Can't see how they're going to make it work,' said Forsyth. 'For someone who's clearly very sophisticated when it comes to money, with all his business interests, global connections, offshore accounts, to be taking delivery of a huge amount of cash in this way doesn't make any sense.'

'But presumably you're thinking the handover is going to give you your best opportunity for targeting the kidnappers.'

'The fact that they've demanded a truck with lifting gear suggests they'll be transferring the money to a number of smaller vehicles,' said Forsyth. 'Obviously we'll have a tracking device built into the truck just in case they're crazy.'

'And in the money?'

'Sure,' said Forsyth. 'They're pretty sophisticated now. Super thin, undetectable. The latest from the CIA.'

'What's the current thinking about the hostages' whereabouts?' asked Mercy. 'Because the kidnaps took place over an extended period and different locations, it probably means that, at least for a time, they gathered them together.'

'We've studied the punishment videos and they all took place in the same location.'

'Has Reef revealed anything more under interrogation?'

'Only that he accessed the telephone number to call by running a decoding program through a website. We've tried to do the same, but no result. We reckon that now they know Reef's been arrested, they've rendered the website useless.'

'If they know Reef's been arrested, they'll move the hostages,' said Mercy. 'In the meeting at Thames House, the CIA said they were going to go through all contractors used by all PSCs in the USA and suggested we did the same here to see if we can find a pattern. I haven't heard anything about their findings, have you?'

'It's a slow process. First of all he must have a core of people he's known for some time, who will be expert at disguising identity, being in two places at once, that kind of thing. Then there are the people he's hired, but they seem to be on the periphery even if, like Reef, they pulled off one of the kidnaps. I don't think it's going to be fruitful working through thousands of contractors, and even if it is, it'll probably be too late. You know the game. We've either got to find the hostages or Jensen.'

'And we haven't even talked about the ransom yet.'

'We're having a brainstorming session on that later this morning with all concerned, including representatives from the various embassies.'

The woman, wearing a black mac, collar up, handbag slung across her shoulders, stopped and jutted her chin into the bushes. The guy listening on the phone nodded her in. She darted sideways and disappeared into the vegetation. It was almost comical. Her head reappeared and she wound her finger round so that the guy on the pavement thumbed his phone again. Listened. She moved to her left, ducked down again and then came up as if for air. This time her thumb was raised. She emerged with her hands in her pockets.

There was no access to the DLR station from that side of the road and no obvious place to park a car on a busy six-lane highway. The couple crossed the road, climbing over the central reservation. Fortunately there was no way into the Docklands at that point and their options were to either walk down Aspen Way and turn right, or climb up to the footbridge where Boxer was standing.

They chose the footbridge.

Boxer preceded them into the DLR station. He recharged his Oyster card keeping an eye on them. They went to the platform in the Canary Wharf direction. It was after rush hour, but there were still plenty of people. Boxer got up close and took a good look at them. They both had the lean, hard, purposeful look of trained operatives. Both were wearing coats that could easily have hidden firearms.

Boxer knew he needed backup for this kind of work. The couple could split up. The phone might already have been exchanged between them when they'd been behind him on the footbridge. He wouldn't know who to go after.

They boarded the train. Boxer went into a different carriage. The couple sat opposite each other, behaving as if separate. They went through Canary Wharf and out the other side into Greenwich. The train was practically empty. Boxer was glad he'd taken a different carriage. The couple didn't speak, didn't even exchange glances.

The train continued to Lewisham, the last station. They went out on to the main road, under a railway bridge, and walked alongside a small river into a modern estate of three-storey blocks of flats. It was an almost impossible task to tail them in daylight with so few people on the street.

The man was speaking on his mobile phone. The woman walked alongside but didn't look around. Boxer realised they were not expecting to be followed. They were taking no precautions. They walked in a continuous progression. They didn't stop or walk back in the direction they'd just come from or take a circular route. Maybe they were trained, but not in spycraft. They walked under a railway bridge and came out into some residential streets.

They turned up a road with cars parked on either side in front of Victorian terraced houses and a block of seventies flats. They went into a pebble-dashed house about halfway down. The only time they looked around was when they opened the door. Boxer was lucky. He'd teamed up with a young mother pushing her baby in a buggy. As he walked by, he saw that the terrace had a break in it, and set back down a passage were two wooden doors leading to the gardens behind the houses.

He had to act quickly before they set about destroying the phone. He let the woman with the buggy stride away from him. He crossed the street, walked back to the house and slipped down the passage, past the bins. There was a low wall. He jumped on to it and vaulted over the wooden door into a heavily overgrown garden, which backed on to flats in the next street. A cat on the roof of a decrepit shed slipped away. A crow took off into the gunmetal sky from a stone birdbath trussed in weeds.

The kitchen had open venetian blinds. It was empty. A door with a large glass panel led out into the garden. The key was in the inside lock. There was no time to think this through. Boxer ducked under the window, went to the door, took out the Walther P99 and used the butt to smash the window. He put his hand through the shattered pane and let himself in with the key. Gun in right hand, he marched into the front room, which was the only other place the couple could be. He flung the door open and introduced them to the Walther P99.

The phone was on the table with its rear panel removed, along with an open laptop. Both the man and the woman were on their feet. The guy had a Beretta 92 Compact Rail in his hand. The woman had nothing.

'I suggest you put that down,' said Boxer. 'I've got the Met kidnap unit outside and four members of the Specialist Firearm Command front and back.'

The man's eyes flickered towards his companion, which was all Boxer needed to know that he'd got the psychological advantage.

'Lay it on the table and both of you put your hands on your head.'

Another glance from the man to the woman. She nodded, did what she'd been told. The man put the Beretta down on the table and clasped his hands on his head too.

'Move over there, stand next to her.'

Boxer tucked the Beretta into his coat. He took a wallet out of the guy's back pocket, searched his jacket and found his mobile.

'Backs to the wall, sit on the floor.'

They slid down the wall. Boxer rearranged the furniture and sat in front of them. The woman's handbag was on the floor by the chair where she'd been sitting. He told her to kick it towards him. Inside he found a Beretta BU9 Nano. He pocketed that too. Put her mobile with her partner's on the table. Found her wallet, opened it: credit cards in the name of Louise Rylance. He opened the guy's wallet. His name was Michael Rylance.

'These your real names?'

They nodded.

'This your house?'

They nodded again.

'What's your story?' asked Boxer. 'Army?'

'Iraq vets,' said Rylance.

'How do you know Conrad Jensen?'

'We met when we were on honeymoon in Dubai.'

'What were you then? Freelancers?'

They nodded.

'What did you do for him in this job?'

'We acted as policemen in the kidnap of Rakesh Sarkar.'

'How much did he pay you?'

'A hundred thousand.'

'Sounds generous.'

'It's the first time we've done anything illegal,' said Louise. 'We haven't been working, needed the money.'

'So how did this part of the operation work?' asked Boxer. 'Who asked you to pick up this phone?'

'We got a coded text that meant looking at a website and receiving instructions.'

'What do you do now?'

'We've already sent a message saying that we've been successful.'

'Are you supposed to destroy the phone?'

'I don't think they're taking any chances. Somebody is going to collect. They'll advise us of the time.'

'Do you know where any of the hostages are?'

'We haven't seen anyone since the night of the kidnap.'

'Where did you take Rakesh Sarkar that night?'

'We took him to an old warehouse out west. Hayes. The Old Vinyl Factory.'

'Was that where the other hostages were taken?'

'I think so, but I can't be certain. There was a set-up there. But

Rakesh Sarkar was the first kidnap of the night. We delivered him and left.'

'Did you know whether the hostages were going to be moved?'

'We weren't told anything. We performed our task, that's all.'

Boxer sent a text to Mercy about the Old Vinyl Factory and said he'd need to speak to her when she was available.

'And is that it?' he said. 'You're not doing anything else for your hundred grand?'

'We picked up the phone,' said Louise.

'But that must have been extra. A guy got stabbed and chucked his phone. That wasn't planned,' said Boxer. 'So what else has Jensen asked you to do?'

'There are two other hostages and we've been asked to do a twenty-four-hour stint guarding them.'

'Where?'

'We don't know. We're waiting for those instructions.'

'In London?'

'That's what we were told. It might have changed.'

'When will you know?'

'We're supposed to take over sometime this afternoon.'

'Do you know who you will be taking over from?'

They shook their heads.

'Does he know you?'

'No,' said Rylance. 'He only knows our names and that there are two of us, a man and a woman.'

'How's that going to work?'

'They'll give us a line of code.'

Forsyth took Mercy up to Emma's bedroom and asked her to wait outside. She was amazed at Forsyth's transformation and unnerved by what his openness had revealed. His terminology when talking about Jennifer Cook being 'interviewed' had been threatening, and this had been backed up by the 'interrogators' he'd referred to later. And putting tracking devices in the truck and money was against the expressed instructions of the kidnappers.

'Don't be too shocked by her appearance,' said Forsyth, holding the door closed behind him. 'It's the medication.'

He left Mercy to it. Emma was dressed, but lying on the bed apparently asleep. She certainly wasn't the same woman. Her hair looked thinner. There were bags under her eyes, her skin had lost its tautness and her face looked slack. Her right hand trembled occasionally.

Mercy sat on the bed and took Emma's hand, stroked it and looked out of the window over the rooftops. Emma squeezed Mercy's hand to get her attention and put her finger to her lips. She got up with surprising agility and put a pillow gently but deliberately down on the dressing table. Mercy frowned at her.

'Don't think me paranoid,' said Emma, 'but they've miked the room. I saw them do it. They debugged it when they first came in and now they've rebugged it with their own.'

'What's this about doctor's supervision?'

'That's why he's left us alone this time. I'm supposed to be drugged up to the eyeballs. I don't take them. I just act completely out of it.'

'Why?'

'They didn't like what I said about Ken the last time we spoke,' said Emma. 'The next thing I know, Ryder's arranged a Kinderman doctor to see me, who prescribed some heavy-duty antidepressants.'

'Ryder said you were upset about Sophie's kidnap *and* Conrad's betrayal. You were devastated and—'

'I am, but I don't need an oral cosh, which is what they've tried to give me.'

'Why stay and be a prisoner in your own home?'

'I want to know what's going on. I'm not going to take myself out of the orbit of the people who are supposed to be saving my daughter.'

'Supposed to be? They *are*, Emma,' said Mercy. 'Conrad got involved with you so that he could kidnap your daughter.'

'I don't think it was just that,' said Emma. 'Ever since I heard about Conrad's involvement, I've been going over all our conversations in my head. It was protracted, over a period of months, but now that I think about it, he was mostly interested in Ken, and not just the reason we'd bust up. I mean, that's how it started, him wanting to know why and being sympathetic. But then it continued about Ken's politics, the people he socialised with, his close contacts, his wider network. It was as if he was trying to piece together a picture from a jigsaw of names.'

'So what are you saying?'

'I'm not sure. I keep thinking and listening and I'm very careful about what I say or react to in front of people. Especially Ryder. It's got easier since I'm supposed to be knocked out. I've heard names in the last twenty-four hours that have rung bells with me because I remember Conrad wanting me to go over them again in some of our talks. I mean, that's what Conrad and I did. We just talked. Something that Ken and I hadn't done for the last five years we were together.'

'What were these names?'

'Ray Sutherland and Clifford Chase.'

'They're both senior CIA officers,' said Mercy. 'Sutherland is running the CIA operation for this series kidnap and Chase is the London chief of the CIA.'

'Both of them, as Conrad pointed out to me, are intimately involved with Ken and Kinderman. And, as he later found out, hold extreme political beliefs.'

'And that wouldn't be to the left of centre, I take it?'

25

'First of all, I want everybody here to confirm that the preparation of their contribution to the kidnappers' demand for expenses is in process,' said DCS Hines. 'We've just heard that we will be given instructions for delivery of the money at 16.00 hours and that it must be in position by 18.00, which corresponds with the height of London rush hour. Ideally we would like each individual contribution ready by lunchtime so that we can bring it all together in one place with time to spare. It's going to be a high-security operation and we are going to need every minute of those two hours to position the money.'

'Where is the central collection point going to be?' asked Ken Bass.

'We've decided on New Scotland Yard. It's secure, and centrally located for all the banks and for wherever the kidnappers decide they want it sent,' said Hines. 'If anybody is having trouble putting together their twenty-five million, we should know now. Can we have a show of hands from anybody experiencing difficulty?'

Hines sensed an atmosphere of subterranean belligerence from the billionaires around the table. Uttar Sarkar and Sergei Yermilov had their arms firmly folded and their chins tucked into their chests. Ken Bass, in a white shirt and sports jacket, no tie, was looking around trying to find another person at the table as intelligently frustrated as he was. Pfeiffer, in three-piece suit and tie, was staring into the highly polished dining room table tapping a pen up and down through his finger and thumb, which was annoying the sizeable figure of Anastasia Casey, hair down to her shoulders as wild as a pro wrestler's, who had the edge of the table gripped in both hands as if she might be about to turn it over. Only Wú Dao-ming, who was sitting very still, hands folded in her lap, looked in any way forlorn.

'I think everybody's agreed here,' said Bass, 'that, having seen the brutality of the kidnappers, we should do everything in our power to comply with their demands.'

'You should know,' said Hines, 'that the way the kidnappers have asked for such a quantity of money to be delivered is very unusual. We've consulted around the world on this matter and none of the current experts have been able to work out what's going on here. The kidnappers will necessarily have to expose themselves, and that will give us an opportunity, which we are well prepared to take.'

'But not at any risk to our loved ones,' said Bass. 'I think I'm speaking for everybody here when I say that we are very happy with the way Ryder Forsyth has been handling the kidnappers, but what we need to know is how the Metropolitan Police are doing making progress with finding our children.'

'We were hoping for a free flow of information between ourselves and the CIA,' said Hines. 'As it happens, that has been one-way traffic. We have given all the information we've gathered, which, I might add, has been quite considerable. Colonel Forsyth's working relationship with our special investigator DI Mercy Danquah has been excellent by all accounts. We have captured one kidnapper and another is presently wounded and under armed guard in the ICU of the Royal London Hospital. I also understand that a British army intelligence officer, who DI Danquah identified as being involved in some way, is currently being interviewed after an incident in Afghanistan. Despite our extremely assiduous investigations and all-round effective communication, we have had precious little – in fact nothing – in return from the CIA. So perhaps your fellow American, Ray Sutherland of the CIA, would like to take the floor and explain that to us.'

DCS Hines sat down feeling righteous, expecting to see the CIA crash and burn in front of Ken Bass. Sutherland, though, was looking surprisingly cocky, which was at odds with how he'd been feeling on the inside since the name Conrad Jensen had been associated with this series kidnap. Had he been given the floor half an hour ago, it would have been a pitiful sight. As it was, earlier this morning he had been furnished with a photograph of the injured man being held in the Royal London and they had been able to identify him. It didn't make him feel any easier, but at least he wasn't going to look foolish.

'We have been conducting extensive research into the personnel used by US PMSCs and in that process we have been able to narrow down the number of operatives who could possibly have had associations with Conrad Jensen to fifty men and women. When we received the photo ID of the wounded man, we were able to immediately identify him as Chuck Powell.

'Chuck Powell and Conrad Jensen worked together in an interrogation team in a black site just outside Rabat in Morocco from 2003 to 2006. Obviously that was not continuous employment and there were changes of personnel in that team over those years. What we do know is that Jensen and Powell always worked together and we deduce from this that they were close friends as well as associates. We think Powell would be part of the inner core of this kidnap gang and we would urgently like to interview him.'

'He's still unconscious,' said Hines. 'He had a massive internal bleed from a knife wound. The doctors won't commit as to when we'll be able to talk to him.'

'As a result of focusing our attention on ex-colleagues of Conrad Jensen and looking at dates given to us by the UK Border Agency, we have now been able to identify three other possible suspects who were in the UK at the time of the kidnappings.'

While Sutherland handed out a sheet with mug shots of the three suspects, Hines glanced down at his mobile phone. A text from Mercy told him she was on her way with a team from the kidnap unit and Special Firearm Command to the Old Vinyl Factory in Hayes, believed to be where the hostages were held, but from which they had probably now been moved. Hines took great pleasure in announcing this to the gathering. The buzz amongst the police and intelligence officers left the victims' families bemused.

'Can somebody tell us the significance of this announcement?' asked Uttar Sarkar.

'Moving hostages is a very difficult thing to do,' said Hines. 'The gang is opening themselves up to maximum exposure. It enormously increases our chances of finding where they're keeping them. We're also hoping that their exit from this hiding place was as a result of our outside pressure and that they will have left evidence and therefore clues in their rush to vacate the premises.'

Ray Sutherland sat back, glad to feel the spotlight retrained elsewhere.

Mercy and Papadopoulos were on their way to the Old Vinyl Factory in Hayes. She called Boxer, who filled her in on how he'd come by the information.

'We need to talk to them,' she said.

'I don't think that's a good idea,' said Boxer, and told her about the Rylances' additional task later this evening.

Mercy glanced over at Papadopoulos, who was driving, following the convoy at high speed through west London.

'OK, how's that going to play out?'

'I'm going to handle it,' said Boxer. 'I'm going to deal with the situation as you asked me to do.'

'Do you think that's strictly necessary?'

'You'll never work again if I don't.'

Mercy closed her eyes at the thought of what she was sanctioning.

'Where are they now?'

'Sitting on the floor of their living room,' said Boxer, gun in one hand, glancing into the room from the corridor.

'Does anybody else know about this?'

'I only know about it because I listened to the news this morning and I knew things from what I witnessed last night,' said Boxer. 'When I saw them searching the site for the phone I thought I was going to hit a dead end, then I got lucky.'

'The injured man has been named by the CIA as a PMSC operative called Chuck Powell.'

'Doesn't mean anything to me, but the Rylances might know something.'

'I'll let you know what we find in the Old Vinyl Factory.'

Mercy hung up as they arrived at the factory site.

'Who was that?' asked Papadopoulos.

'One of my informers.'

'I realised that.'

'This one's deep cover. Nobody knows about him. And it's going to stay like that.'

The local police were pointing them away from the part of the factory earmarked for redevelopment, down to the other end of the eighteen-acre site. Police presence was even stronger there, and ID had to be shown. They parked up. The Special Firearm Command Unit were looking at a map of the site and deciding how they were going to go in: two through the main entrance and two via the old loading bay.

The men went in. Mercy and Papadopoulos sat on the car bonnet, watching, along with thirty or more silent policemen. A cold wind was blowing, buffeting the huddled figures with fierce gusts. Mercy sank into the collar of her coat, rammed her gloved hands into the pockets. Everybody flinched and ducked as they heard two distinct but muffled explosions. Mercy and Papadopoulos stood up from the car and ran towards the building

'Call an ambulance,' shouted Mercy.

As they reached the entrance, they met the men coming out. They were all relaxed, brushing themselves off, shaking their heads and laughing nervously.

'Take a look,' they said.

They went into the high-roofed warehouse with its rusted triangular steel beams. It was like being on the inside of a snow globe. The air was full of white feathers. In the middle of the floor were two boxes with their lids blown off.

'What the fuck?' said Papadopoulos.

'Very seasonal,' said one of the officers.

'They're taking the piss now,' said Mercy. 'Not sure we're going to get anything out of this.'

She walked through the space to the line of offices at the far end, stripped off her leather gloves, put on latex and opened a door. There was a smell of bleach. Sitting in a chair was a rag doll frog, legs crossed, looking pleased with itself. Sophie's Zach, thought Mercy. There was a note pinned to his chest: *Proof of life?*

In the other offices were personal items from each of the hostages: a piece of jewellery, a neck chain, a bracelet, an engraved watch, a personalised mobile phone. Mercy told Papadopoulos to collect them up and have them delivered to Wilton Place, where the meeting was still going on.

'We've got our work cut out trying to find anything under this lot,' he said.

'It wasn't just a joke,' said Mercy, tearing off her gloves. 'You know what to do.'

'You're leaving me with all this shit?' said Papadopoulos.

'That's what happens. I get the nice jobs, you get the ... not so nice jobs,' said Mercy. 'You could start by finding out the type of feathers and who could supply that sort of quantity.'

'And what are you going to do?'

'Pursue other lines of inquiry.'

'With that informer?'

'Could be.'

'Why all the secrecy?' asked Papadopoulos. 'We've hardly done any work together on this one. What's going on?'

Mercy went up to him, looked him hard in the eye, piercing right the way through to the back.

'Mercy?' he said, frowning.

'Nothing,' she said. 'Just checking. I'll take the car.'

His eyes followed her all the way. She nodded to him as she got in, reversed out of the parking space. At the first set of traffic lights, she texted Boxer for a postcode and street number. He sent it, asking her if she thought it was wise to come. She ignored the question, tapped the postcode into the sat nav and drove.

She writhed at every set of lights and at times found herself close to tears. What had happened to her? She'd always been so sure of herself, or at least so sure of that one thing about herself. She knew she had great potential to be an emotional mess; the darkness in her childhood, her broken, downcast mother, the cruelty of her father had all contributed to that. But the one thing that had held her together through all the years of neediness with Charlie, the uncertainty of Amy's paternity, the terrible conflict with her daughter, the endless battle of the job, was that at least she had something inside her cast in steel. It was possibly the only thing that she had taken on board from her father: an unshakeable morality.

And now?

The way she'd given in so easily. Sitting there with Charlie in the café with all the comfortable people sipping their espressos and telling him, yes, do it, kill them all. But now they're real, sitting on the floor of a living room in Lewisham, waiting for the word. So that she can carry on working in the kidnap unit? So that nobody finds out that she's having an affair with a known fence from Brixton?

And how had it come to pass that she'd accepted the unacceptable about Charlie? Had she gone through some process of justification without being aware of it? She remembered lying in bed next to him after he'd come back from Iraq, knowing that he'd killed people: soldiers as innocent as him who just happened to be on the wrong side. She'd asked him how he coped with it and he'd shrugged and said:

'You step over a line when you join the army.'

What line had she just stepped over?

She parked in an adjacent street and walked round to the address Boxer had sent her. She had plastic cuffs with her as requested. Boxer opened the door, let her in, stepped back quickly to keep an eye on his captives. She gave him the ties and he cuffed the Rylances together, lying down with linked arms behind their backs.

Boxer handed over the mobile phone.

'Any numbers on there you need traced?'

'It's been remotely wiped so you're going to have to recover the data, but I'm sure you've got people who can do that,' said Boxer. 'Somebody from the kidnap gang is due here to collect it.'

'And?'

'And what?'

'You're going to deal with him – or her – too?' she said, under her breath.

Boxer looked at her steadily.

'I'll spell it out for you if you like,' he said.

She nodded.

271

'These two are due to take over the supervision of two hostages who I'm assuming are Marcus and Amy. As soon as the kidnap unit hears that, everything is out of our hands. They'll find out about your relationship with Marcus and why he's being held. You'll be finished. The person who comes to pick up the phone—'

'OK, that's enough.'

'Stealing people is wrong,' said Boxer. 'Remember that. These two kidnapped Rakesh Sarkar. They didn't even know why. I've asked them. Was it for money? How did they know that Jensen didn't want to torture and kill him because he hated the guy's father? No, they stole him, handed him over and took a hundred grand for the work.'

Mercy stared into the wall of the corridor, where they were standing by the front door.

'The guy who ordered Marcus's kidnap is the one who's been knifed in the Royal London, Chuck Powell,' said Boxer, glancing in on the two captives. 'Jess, the girl he asked to arrange the gang, is dead. He broke her neck. I met the two guys who actually performed the kidnap last night. They run cigarettes out of a warehouse in south London owned by a white Bahamian.'

'Oh God,' said Mercy, making a fist against the wall, putting her forehead to it. 'You mean there are even more people involved. And Chuck Powell ... we can't do anything about him.'

'He might not survive that stab wound.'

'He's stable in ICU. They won't let him die.'

'So what's it to be?'

'Let me talk to them.'

'It'll be more difficult if you decide you want me to deal with them.'

'I can't ...' she said, and tried to brush past him.

'You'd better take this,' said Boxer, and gave her Rylance's Beretta. She put it in her coat pocket and went into the sitting room.

As soon as she saw them lying there on the floor, these two pitiful trussed-up human beings with fear in their eyes, she knew she wasn't going to allow it. What had she been thinking?

'I'm DI Mercy Danquah from the kidnap unit,' she said, and held her warrant card in front of their noses.

272

The relief spread through them. Boxer sat down at the table by the window.

'These are their phones,' he said, pushing them towards Mercy.

'Right, let's start with the names and numbers of everybody you've had dealings with in the kidnap gang,' she said.

Louise gave her four names: Conrad Jensen, Chuck Powell, Mark Lee and Jim Ford. The last two had been their fellow coppers when they'd stopped Rakesh Sarkar for drink-driving. Mercy went through the mobiles. Only the last two names had numbers.

As she was searching, a message arrived on one of the mobiles.

'The guy who's coming to pick up the phone will be here in seven minutes,' she said. 'Is there a procedure for this?'

'He knows my face,' said Rylance. 'He'll come to the door. I'll hand over the phone. He'll know its make and model number. He'll check it and leave. That's it.'

'Where will he take it?'

'That I don't know.'

'How do you want to play it?' Boxer asked Mercy. 'Hand over the phone and follow, or pull him in?'

'Not enough manpower for a tail,' said Mercy. 'You can't do that on your own and the phone's too important to lose.'

Boxer knelt down, released Rylance, recuffed his wife to a piece of furniture. He took the mobile phone, put it in Rylance's hand, walked him to the front door.

'This is how it's going to happen,' he said, seeing the fear in Rylance's eyes. 'When he calls, you open the door just to the point of your left shoulder, give him the phone with your right hand, keep your right shoulder to the wall. There'll be a gun on your spine. That's all you need to know.'

They went back to the sitting room, sat him down in an armchair. Mercy continued to interview Louise.

'Tell me what happened after you kidnapped Rakesh Sarkar. Where did you take him, who did what?'

'Mark Lee took the Porsche and parked it in Sarkar's street somewhere. Mike was driving the police car, Jim Ford was in the passenger seat. I was in the back with Sarkar. We dropped Jim off somewhere around Chiswick.'

273

'And when you delivered Rakesh to the Old Vinyl Factory in Hayes, what did you see there?'

'We just told your friend that ours was the first kidnap of the night. We reversed into a loading bay and two men came and took Rakesh away. We left. We didn't speak to anyone and we only saw those two guys.'

Footsteps shuffled along the pavement. Boxer checked the time. Too soon. They carried on past.

'You were in a police car,' said Mercy, 'and in uniform. What did you do with those things?'

'No, of course, you're right,' said Louise, struggling under the stress of the situation.

'Come on, Louise. Let's get this straight in our minds now. Don't hold things back.'

'That's it,' she said. 'We had to leave the car. They needed it for another kidnap. A driver took us back into town.'

'And the uniforms?'

'We had to take the uniforms off.'

'Where? In the loading bay?'

'No, they took us into a room and we changed into paper overalls.'

'So who picked the car up in the first place, before the kidnap?'

'Mark Lee. He was the driver. He was supposed to drive us back that night but he wanted a go in the Porsche.'

'And where did you meet to put on the uniforms?'

Louise blinked, staring into the floor, then glanced up at her husband, who nodded once.

'Always easier to tell the truth,' said Mercy. 'You don't and I'll have you in knots.'

'We met in Mark Lee's flat. He'd given Jim the keys. We changed there.'

'Let's have that address.'

'Longlands Court, just off the Portobello Road. Jim met us at the tube and brought us there.'

Rylance watched his wife lying on the floor. She had the look of an animal trussed for slaughter. He could see, even as she answered Mercy's questions, the future playing out in her mind. Prison. For a long time. There was the fatigue of regret in her voice, even in her strong, desirable body. It made him sad that they'd given in to the money. He hadn't thought they were like that. She sensed his gaze, looked up at him, and he saw the permission given in her eyes.

More steps. This time they turned up the path to the front door. There was a knock. Boxer pointed at Rylance, raised him to his feet with his finger. They went silently to the door. Boxer stood behind it, put the gun to Rylance's left kidney, nodded. Rylance opened the door, gave a sideways glance to the man outside as he made to hand over the phone, and then smacked the door hard into Boxer's face.

The blow knocked the gun away from his kidney and it slammed into the wall, jolting Boxer's trigger finger. The shot tore into the floor. Boxer fell back, eyebrow split, blinded by blood in his right eye, ears ringing from the deafening shot in the confined space.

The man outside knew instantly what he had to do and threw himself at Boxer's gun hand. Rylance vaulted over him, ran into the living room and launched himself at Mercy. The gunshot had been all the warning she'd needed. She had the Beretta out. Louise screamed with alarm. Mercy fired twice, hitting Rylance in the chest. He went down face first as if his feet had been kicked out from under him.

Boxer was dazed from the front door cracking into his forehead. The man had wrestled the Walther P99 from his slackening hand.

Mercy took four strides to the corridor to find the Walther P99 pointing up at her from the floor. She didn't hesitate and shot the man in the head. Blood sprayed against the white corridor wall. Two more steps and she kicked the front door shut.

'You all right?' she said. 'You're bleeding.'

Boxer nodded. He was lying with the man's weight across his chest.

'I'm fine,' he said, pushing the body away.

Mercy went back into the living room. Rylance was still alive. He'd reached out a hand to his wife, who was staring at him wide-eyed with horror.

'Sorry,' he said.

'You're an idiot,' said Mercy. 'A bloody idiot.'

And those were the words that Rylance took with him to the other side.

Louise blinked hard, as if this might alter the terrible image scored into her mind.

Mercy looked up at the ceiling, gathered herself, closed her eyes, trying to shut out what she'd just had to do. She took a deep breath and called DCS Hines.

'There's been an incident at 38 Algernon Road in Lewisham. It's quite possible that there will be reports of gunshots from neighbours. This is a continuing operation and it's imperative that no police come anywhere near the house.'

'Has anyone been hurt?'

'Two kidnappers have been shot dead,' said Mercy. 'You will get a full report just as soon as the operation is completed.'

Hines tried to ask more questions. Mercy was having none of it and hung up.

She looked down at Louise, who stared back at her with an implacable hatred.

'You've got no cause to look at me like that,' said Mercy. 'If he'd done as he'd been told, he'd still be alive.'

Boxer came in with a butterfly strip, found in the bathroom, over his eyebrow. He checked Rylance for life. He knew from the hole in the back of the other guy's head that he was dead. He knelt down beside Louise, who closed her eyes.

'Tell us about this line of code you need to take over the hostage supervision this afternoon.'

Louise said nothing.

'You know I'm going to stop at nothing to get this information out of you,' said Boxer. 'I'm not under the same constraints as my friend here. So make it easy for yourself.'

Louise slowly opened her eyes.

Rylance's mobile went off. Mercy reached over.

36 Arran Road SE6 at 16.00.

Then Louise's mobile flashed and vibrated.

Punish the innocent.

The first £25 million arrived at New Scotland Yard just after two o'clock. The bank had followed the instructions precisely. The money had been loosely stacked on a large plastic sheet, which had been folded around the notes to the dimensions laid down in the kidnappers' demands. Ray Sutherland had told DCS Hines that he had the agreement of the hostages' parents to install 'undetectable tracking devices'. A member of the kidnap unit's technology department was present as a CIA operative inserted the device supplied by the CIA. It was the size of a fifty-pound note and about as thick as three of them stuck together. They tested the device and taped up the plastic sheet.

Over the next hour and a half the remaining £125 million arrived. Tracking devices were inserted into each batch and they were loaded on to the open truck.

At 15.38, DCS Hines was informed that all the money had arrived and had been loaded on to the truck. An email was sent to the kidnappers, who responded.

At exactly four o'clock the truck will leave its present location at New Scotland Yard fully loaded with all the money. Each parcel of money should be loaded in such a way that it can be easily lifted off the truck. We suggest ropes connected to a central hook that can be attached to the truck's lifting gear. There will be no escort for this truck from police or otherwise. There must be no air cover. The only person in the truck will be the driver, who will have a mobile phone and you will give us that number. We will direct him to a place where he will drop his own phone and pick up our disposable one. This must be the only device he carries. We are making the assumption that you have not been foolish enough to try to plant tracking devices on the truck or in the money. If any such devices are found, it will result in the death of one of the hostages.

DCS Hines made a recorded call to Ray Sutherland, who confirmed that he had seen the kidnappers' email and reiterated that he had been given permission by all the parents to install the devices.

26

Mercy was driving to Catford. Boxer sat in the back with Louise, who no longer wore the cuffs. She rubbed her wrists occasionally where the plastic had chafed. Mercy parked in a street parallel to the one where they believed Amy and Alleyne were being held.

Mercy asked Louise to stay in the car while she told Boxer what she'd learnt from Emma about Jensen and his interest in Ken Bass and the CIA officers, Ray Sutherland and Clifford Chase. She also mentioned Ryder, and what he'd revealed about Jennifer Cook's interrogation.

'There's a political dimension to this that I don't get,' she said.

'Well, it seems to be left versus right,' said Boxer. 'We just don't know who's facing off, where the battlefield is or what they're fighting for.'

Boxer and Louise set off for the four o'clock rendezvous at the house. He was no longer carrying the Walther P99. To be consistent with what had happened in Lewisham, he'd agreed with Mercy that he should carry Michael Rylance's Beretta 92 Compact Rail.

'I'm sorry for your loss,' he said as they walked. 'You know that.'

'You're what?' asked Louise, looking across at him, astonished.

'I lost somebody important to me yesterday,' he said, thinking, *Was it only yesterday?* 'I'm sorry for what happened back there today.'

She stared at him. He had to pull her to one side out of the way of a lamp post.

'How long were you married?' he asked.

'Nine years. We got married as soon as we came back from Iraq in 2005.'

'No kids?'

'I couldn't have any. I got a piece of shrapnel in the gut from an IED outside Basra and they took everything out.'

Boxer was surprised at his interest. For some reason he had to know, or at least talk about it.

'Did you love your husband?' he asked.

Louise didn't answer at first, had to get used to the surreal situation. This man, who'd come across earlier as a psychopath, was now revealing himself as human.

'It was strange,' she said. 'I didn't think I did love him when we got married. I wondered whether I was doing the right thing, my friends, too. Michael and I had grown very close in Iraq, but that was a weird, intense scenario. I had no idea how we'd be in the real world. Then three weeks after we'd done the deed, I realised I couldn't live without him. He suddenly made sense to me.'

They turned into Arran Road, checked the house numbers and went right.

'Did you work for Conrad before this?' asked Boxer. 'Or see him at any time in the last nine years?'

'No, he just contacted us out of the blue. We were desperate for money, behind on our mortgage repayments.'

'What did you make of Conrad?'

'I really liked him. He was charismatic without being arrogant, generous without demanding anything in return. He listened. You know what rich men are like? They use false generosity to get you to do their bidding, but they don't care what *you* want, they're really only focused on what *they* want. Conrad wasn't like that.'

'Was that why you were prepared to do something illegal for him?'

'We trusted him.'

'Did he ever tell you why he was doing this, or mention any political motivation?'

'Nothing political, and he said it was better we didn't know. He made it clear that the mission could be dangerous, but his intention was not to hurt people.'

'One last thing,' said Boxer, as they arrived at the house. 'Your motivation to co-operate. The hostages held here are my daughter and Mercy's lover. The kidnap unit doesn't know about either of them and Mercy wants to keep it that way. If we come out of this unhurt, you'll walk, I guarantee it.'

He opened a wrought iron gate. They crossed a paved-over front garden to the door of a shabby Edwardian house.

'Better I do the talking here,' he said, and rang the bell, which made the sound of a gong in the depths. Feet made their way to the door, where they paused as someone checked through the peephole.

The door opened. An unsmiling, physically impressive man said nothing, waited. He had hair cut *en brosse*, blue eyes with long lashes, and biceps straining against the tight sleeves of his black T-shirt.

'Punish the innocent,' said Boxer.

The guy nodded, let them in. He tucked a Glock 17 back into a shoulder holster under his left arm as he led them down the hallway.

'Fancy a cup of tea?' he said, south London accent. 'Before I show you around.'

'Sure,' said Boxer.

'I'm Gav, by the way.'

'Michael,' said Boxer. 'Mike.'

Gav put the kettle on, tea bags in the pot, laid out mugs, sugar, milk.

'You come far?'

'Just down the road, Lewisham,' said Boxer, keeping to the story in case this was a vetting process. 'Where are you off to?'

'Wimbledon for tonight. Then I'm off early to Brize Norton to get a flight out to Afghanistan. Embassy security in Kabul.'

'You on your own here?'

'It was supposed to be just me and a single hostage, but there's another one, young woman, mixed race, don't know her name, and this bird Siobhan, who seems to be her chaperone. I haven't seen anything of her, spends her whole time up there in the bedroom. Bit fucking weird, you ask me. My attitude has always been don't get involved. You never know what you might have to do. Right?'

'Right,' said Louise.

He poured the tea, talked about Afghanistan, Iraq and a hair-raising job he'd done in Chechnya. He'd clearly been starved of company and wanted to chat. But he was boring and uninterested in what either of them had to say, except when he asked Boxer what weapon he was using. He was not impressed by the Beretta 92 Compact Rail. He didn't say anything, but Boxer could tell he'd gone down in his estimation.

'OK,' he said. 'I'll just go for a piss and give you a tour of the facilities.'

After he'd left the room, Louise leaned over.

'Be careful of him. All this friendliness is bullshit. He's very watchful but unstable and he likes to use his gun.'

Boxer nodded, glad that she was conspiring with him, felt her come onside.

Gav took them round the downstairs rooms, where he pointed out the computer set-up and the email protocol.

'Do you know any of these guys?' asked Louise.

'Nah,' said Gav. 'Just follow the instructions, take me money.'

He led them upstairs. Opened the door to a bedroom.

'This is Marcus,' he said.

Marcus Alleyne was lying on the bed, ankles crossed, sleeping mask over his eyes, wrists cuffed through the metal bed head. Calm.

'And this,' said Gav, holding up a key, 'is for when Marcus wants to go to the toilet.'

'What's for dinner?' asked Marcus.

'You don't need to ask,' said Gav, handing Boxer the key.

'Not frozen burgers *again*.'

'We can do better than that,' said Louise. 'You up for a goat curry?'

'Oh, finally a woman after my own heart.'

'Please yourself,' said Gav.

They backed out of the room.

'Now you're going to meet Siobhan,' whispered Gav, pointing Louise to another door across the landing. She stretched out her hand to open it.

'What's that?' said Joe, pointing at the chafe marks on her wrist.

The Beretta 92 Compact Rail was in Boxer's hand, hanging down by his side as the door eased open. The bedroom was in darkness. When Louise didn't reply, Joe lunged forward, grabbing her other wrist, and saw the chafe marks there too. He glanced at Boxer, saw there was something wrong in his eyes, and pulled Louise into the room, his left arm round her neck. He had the Glock 17 out and was pointing it at Amy on the bed, intuiting from the instant tension that this was something to do with the unknown hostage. Louise slashed on the light hoping to distract him.

'No,' shouted Siobhan, seeing the gun in Joe's outstretched hand. She threw herself across the room at the bed.

Joe fired, startled by the light and the sudden movement. The bullet thumped into Siobhan underneath her armpit. She fell over Amy, bounced back and ended up on the floor propped against the wall, her hand reaching for the hole in her side. Boxer swung the Beretta round on Gav, shot him through the temple. He went down, crumpling at the knees, dragging Louise with him.

Boxer shoved the gun in his pocket, knelt down and grabbed hold of Siobhan's shoulders.

'Look at me, concentrate, don't go under.'

She looked up into his face, blinked once, desperate to comply, but a slow wince of pain crossed her mouth.

'Oh shit,' she said, eyes opening wide.

Blood surged from behind her teeth down her chin. She slumped to one side, eyes rolled back.

Amy, still with her wrist cuffed to the bed, came up on one elbow and looked down on Siobhan. She saw that she was dead, and was surprised as a rush of sadness shuddered through her.

Boxer felt for a neck pulse, dropped his head. Amy flung her free arm around his shoulders, buried her face in his neck. He hugged her to him, kissed her, stroked her back. Louise unlocked Gav's arm from around her neck and got to her feet. She searched his pockets, found the other key, gave it to Boxer, who released Amy. He crossed the landing to Alleyne's room, saw that he was suffering a paroxysm of fear and told him it was all OK. He flipped up the sleeping mask, unlocked the cuffs. Marcus grabbed hold of him, hugged him round the shoulders and wept.

'Thought that was it, man,' he said. 'Thought I was done.'

Boxer patted his back, told him Mercy was outside and called her. He helped Amy downstairs, sat Louise down with her and opened the front door for Mercy.

Alleyne was shakily making his way downstairs, unused to being upright. Mercy's car skidded into a parking place outside. She vaulted the front wall, pushed open the front door and saw him at the foot of the stairs; went straight to him, walked into his arms. They stayed like that for minutes, breathing each other in.

Boxer came into the hallway, shut the front door.

'Amy's in here,' he said. 'We need to talk.'

Mercy eased herself out of Alleyne's arms, went into the living room and kissed and hugged Amy, who looked dazed and in a state of shock.

'You're going to be all right,' said Mercy.

'She took the bullet meant for me,' said Amy.

'Who did?'

'Siobhan,' said Amy, shaking her head, tears welling. 'Why'd she do a thing like that?'

'Instinct,' said Boxer, bringing sweet tea in from the kitchen. 'She saw Gav point the gun, felt responsible for you.'

'We connected,' said Amy, staring into space. 'I thought she'd just been playing me, you know, to pull me in. But then she told me something and ...'

She drifted off. Mercy brushed her tears away with her thumbs.

'I think we should drive them to your place. I'll get one of my doctor friends to come and look them over,' said Boxer.

'What have we got here?' said Mercy, back in professional mode.

'Two dead bodies upstairs,' said Boxer, and explained. 'Let's go in the kitchen.'

'Have you got a story for me?' asked Mercy. 'Because I'm in no condition to think one up.'

'This is what I've come up with so far,' said Boxer. 'One of your informers directed you to the Rylances' house. You went there, overpowered them and took Michael Rylance's weapon from him. They told you about the guy coming to pick up the phone. Rylance and the visitor tried to overpower you during the exchange and you had to shoot both of them.'

'It's a start, but even I can see the holes in that one,' said Mercy. 'Their body positions aren't going to look right with just me as the shooter. And what about here?'

'Rylance had already told you he was meeting Gav, one of the other kidnappers, in this house at 16.00.'

'Why?'

'Gav's leaving for Afghanistan in the morning and Siobhan needs help with some logistics. You turn up with the code word and are admitted.'

'But I'm not a white male called Michael Rylance. I'm a black woman. He'd know that.'

'All right, then we have to stage a break-in. The fact is, once you know about Siobhan being here, you're desperate to talk to her. Since you heard about her in the Savoy, you think she's the link to Conrad Jensen. There's a confusing situation, which we'll have to choreograph, and Gav tries to shoot you but kills Siobhan by accident. You shoot Gav.'

'Not much better,' said Mercy. 'And what about Louise? She knows everything.'

'The thing about Louise,' said Boxer, 'is that if you want an outside chance of holding on to your job, you're going to have to let her disappear into the night.'

The truck set off from New Scotland Yard, heading for Victoria Embankment. It made a small detour, during which the driver dropped his own phone and picked up another from the roof of a parked car. The truck continued past Westminster Abbey, the Houses of Parliament and Big Ben, following the river going east.

DCS Hines sat in the communications centre in Vauxhall, looking at the signals being sent from the tracking devices on the truck. Dusk came and went as teams of plain-clothes officers in unmarked cars stationed themselves all around the capital. They were being fed the signals via the communications centre.

There was also a microphone in the cab of the truck, which was sending back voice signals from the driver, who was being called by the kidnap gang at regular intervals, giving him new sets of directions each time. One moment he was due to head north from Blackfriars Bridge, the next they asked him to cross the bridge and

284

go south of the river to Waterloo, Southwark and Borough before re-crossing the river over London Bridge. The driver repeated the instructions each time so that the communications centre had a double check on his position.

As the truck neared London Bridge, the driver was asked to turn right and continue to Tower Bridge. After crossing the river and going around the Tower of London, he was directed on to Lower Thames Street, heading back the way he'd just come. The traffic was getting heavier, rush hour was building. The truck was grinding slowly forward under a railway bridge that took trains into Cannon Street station. Just after the turning to Southwark Bridge, the driver was told to take a left turn down a cul-de-sac and pull up.

From the dark recesses of the dead end came a man in a black balaclava, who got into the cab. He held a silenced pistol to the driver's head and ran a scanner over the dashboard, which located the microphone. He ripped it out. In the meantime, four men climbed on to the back of the truck and scanned the money, while two others ran scanners along the sides and underneath. The process took three minutes. The men disappeared, leaving the driver shaken.

A minute later, Ryder Forsyth, who was in Wilton Place watching developments on screen via a link to the communications centre, received a call.

'Ryder,' said the voice, 'we told you not to put tracking devices on the truck or in the money and you've done both. We also warned you of the consequences. Lots will now be drawn and one of the hostages killed.'

'Wait.'

'We told you. We were absolutely clear.'

'I know you were and I appreciate that. Whoever put those devices on that truck did not advise me or the hostages' parents.'

'But they knew the consequences of their actions. We were clear. It was in an email that went to the communications centre so that everybody would have seen it,' said the voice. 'We located one of the devices in the money and it was a state-of-the-art super-thin undetectable CIA appliance. Except that, unfortunately for you, every tracking device has to emit some electronic signal, however small, and we have the technology to pick it up.'

'It was done without our knowledge. Had we known, we would have—'

'Ryder. It doesn't matter. Whoever did it knew what they were doing and what would happen. We're drawing lots.'

'Look, how about this? I will talk to the people who did this. I will make sure that all tracking devices are immediately removed. I will get names. They will never work again.'

'I don't think you understand, Ryder. We had an agreement. That agreement has been broken. We have kept our word throughout. When we told you we were going to do something, we did it. When you complied with our wishes, we stopped. You were told of the consequences.'

'What would it take for you not to kill one of the hostages?'

Silence.

'You wouldn't be able to make it happen.'

'Try me.'

'We're assuming that this decision to go ahead with tracking devices was a CIA-inspired action. Is that correct?'

'I'd have to check.'

'You find out who was responsible and we'll start drawing lots.'

The phone went dead.

Ryder Forsyth knew immediately what he had to do. He called Hines.

'They're drawing lots to kill a hostage,' he said. 'Whose decision was it to retain the tracking devices when the kidnappers had expressly forbidden it?'

'As far as I know it was a CIA decision in consultation with Ken Bass representing the parents. I did not agree with it.'

'None of the other parents consented to any representative,' said Forsyth, who asked for an immediate video conference call between Hines, Sutherland and himself.

He shouted down to Ken Bass, who was in the other living room, told him to get upstairs.

'They found the tracking devices,' said Forsyth. 'We're going to have a video conference call with Hines. You've got two minutes to get your story straight with Ray.'

Bass said nothing, went to the corner of the room and called Sutherland. He was back in two minutes to take part in the call.

'Who ordered the tracking devices to be installed?' said Forsyth.

Silence. The men stared into the cameras. Hines and Sutherland looked serious on the split screen.

'They're drawing lots to kill a hostage,' said Forsyth. 'I have to get back to them with who was responsible. Only then do I have a chance at negotiation.'

'Like what?' said Sutherland, aggressive. 'Negotiate *what* with these guys?'

'No, Ray, they have always been very clear. They told us precisely the consequences of such an action. I have a chance of reversing it, but only with the truth. I have to know who took that decision. They were CIA devices, so I know you supplied them. Was anybody consulted?'

'No,' said Bass.

'Jeez, Ken, that's such a crock.'

'There was no consultation between you and me, Ray.'

'I told you—'

'But I did not agree to it with you,' said Bass. 'There was no formal agreement.'

'But you knew,' said Forsyth, 'and you allowed the devices to be planted without consulting any of the other parents or me?'

'I did not give permission. I was only told that these "undetectable devices" were available. Ray was well aware that I was not in any position to allow him to plant the devices.'

'Did you assume that he was going to do it?'

'There was no agreement.'

'You're not answering the question, Ken,' said Forsyth. 'I know these people by now. If we try to sell them some shit, they won't tolerate it and somebody's child will die. It could be yours. They're drawing lots. Now. Do you understand me?'

'I understand you perfectly. I reiterate that I was told of the availability of these undetectable devices, but I was not consulted and I did not give permission.'

'This is such bullshit, Ken. I cannot believe you're saying this,' said Sutherland.

'I'm only telling the truth.'

'Look, buddy,' said Sutherland, pointing into the camera, 'you and the truth were never even in the same goddam room in the whole of your fuckin' life.'

'Calm down, Ray.'

'I choose my words carefully,' said Bass. 'Your problem is you don't listen.'

'If we're not going to get the precise truth, then we should agree on a statement that is acceptable to both of you and hope they'll buy it,' said Hines.

'The problem with these guys,' said Forsyth, 'is they won't *buy* anything.'

'So tell them the CIA deployed the devices without consulting the parents,' said Sutherland. 'What they gonna do? Come after us? Fuck 'em.'

The video call ended. Forsyth sent an email to the kidnappers telling them what Sutherland had said. He sent Bass downstairs. The kidnappers called him back.

'That took a long time to decide,' said the voice. 'Do the parents have a spokesperson or do you have to speak to each one individually?'

'They're all billionaires,' said Forsyth. 'None of them would consent to having a spokesperson.'

'The CIA and the Kinderman Corporation have very close ties. I think it unlikely that the CIA would do anything without at least letting Ken Bass know.'

'He says they didn't and the CIA have confirmed that they planted the devices. They had the technology.'

'All right. Because you took so long, we have already drawn lots. The hostage who will be killed is Sophie Railton-Bass.'

'I did what you asked. I found out what happened. You told me—'

'Keep your hair on, Ryder. We won't follow through with the threat if you do two things. The first is to remove all the tracking devices right now.'

'And the second?'

'We'll tell you once you've confirmed the devices have been removed. You've got ten minutes.'

The phone went dead. Ryder called Hines and Sutherland. A tech team was sent under police escort to where the truck was parked and all the devices were removed. It took twenty-seven minutes. Forsyth confirmed the removal by email.

The kidnappers called him back.

'The second thing is that the CIA must agree to a press conference in which they fully reveal the extent of their manipulation of the weapons of mass destruction data in co-operation with the demands of the Bush administration, which resulted in going to war with Iraq. They also have to name who was responsible.'

Silence from Ryder.

'You still there, mate?'

'Yeah, I'm here. But you know that's impossible. Nobody's going to agree to that.'

'Then tell them that Sophie Railton-Bass will be executed in fifteen minutes,' said the voice. 'In the meantime, we'll get the truck on the move again.'

Forsyth shouted down to Ken Bass and made another conference call, told them the news.

Ken Bass immediately called the vice president of the United States. Hines disappeared from the camera and told the communications centre to alert all units to report any sightings but under no circumstances to follow the vehicle.

The truck reversed out into Upper Thames Street. The driver followed instructions. They took him on the same circuit over Blackfriars Bridge, south of the river and then back over Tower Bridge, but this time they sent him east on the Highway towards Limehouse.

'That sounds like it's going to be very difficult to achieve in the time frame given,' said the vice president.

'Remember they only have to agree to give a press conference. They don't actually have to do it,' said Bass.

'It's a complicated issue, the politicisation of intelligence data. It's not something easily condensed for a short press conference. It was the subject of the Senate Report on Iraqi WMD Intelligence in 2004 and 2007. I mean, what exactly are they looking for?' said the vice president. 'And what happens if this is an extended scenario? Your daughter will still be in danger ...'

'But she won't be executed in fifteen minutes' time,' said Bass. 'That's the point.'

'Leave it with me,' said the VP.

Bass called Sutherland on his secure line, told him about the naming of names. There was a long silence.

'Ray?'

'I'm still here.'

'Do you know what's going on?'

'I've got an idea.'

'Are you going to tell me?'

'I'm going to have to talk to Clifford Chase first,' said Sutherland, and hung up.

The truck descended into the tunnel of the Limehouse Link. As the driver reached the halfway point, he was told to slow down and stop with his warning lights switched on.

DCS Hines was given a report that the truck had gone into the tunnel but hadn't come out.

'Get me a CCTV feed from the Limehouse Link,' he said. 'Inside and all exit routes. Fast.'

Three minutes eased past.

'Do you think they're unloading in there?' asked one of the constables.

'It's high enough.'

The CCTV came up on a monitor. They searched through the cameras and found the truck stopped with warning lights deployed and all the money still on board. As they watched, it started moving again.

'I think that was a test,' said Hines, 'just to make sure we weren't following.'

The truck took the Westferry Road exit and joined the West India Dock Road. One of the plain-clothes teams spotted it cutting across the busy Commercial Road heading north.

Ten minutes had passed since Ken Bass's conversation with the vice president and Ray Sutherland. Bass was pacing the floor of the smaller living room downstairs, couldn't bear any company. He hadn't told Emma anything about the tracking devices or the negotiations. Since the revelation about her affair with Conrad Jensen, they'd reverted to their pre-separation state of not speaking, not making eye contact. Finally the vice president called him back.

'Well I've gotten an agreement from the CIA that, under the circumstances, they are prepared to give a fifteen-minute press conference on this subject. I've primed a journalist from the *Washington Post*, who's mystified and wants to know the bigger picture.'

'There's a media blackout at the moment. We can't say anything,' said Bass. 'What about the naming of names?'

'It's not as clear-cut as that, but they've come up with four names that won't stretch credibility. Two of them are dead, one is in a home with pre-senile dementia and the fourth has disappeared in South America.'

Bass went upstairs and rejoined the video conference call, gave his news.

'Can we have an email to that effect?' asked Ryder.

Sutherland, still connected through the conference call, glanced at his computer.

'Sure,' he said. 'I've just had confirmation. I'll forward it.'

As Forsyth sent the email to the kidnappers, the truck crossed the Mile End Road and continued north. Beyond the street lights to the west was the darkness of parkland leading down to the Regent's Canal. The squally wind, sometimes full of rain, was thrashing through the trees.

Hines was summoning unmarked cars from other parts of the city and stationing them along the route the truck appeared to be taking. He had a sighting from a car on Roman Road. Another, parked just down from the Crown pub, saw the truck cross the roundabout, maintaining its northerly direction on a road that bisected Victoria Park.

It was a couple of officers in the crowded Royal Inn on the Park who reported the truck heading into the western section of Victoria Park.

Hines told them to pursue the truck in their car, but not into the park; they just had to maintain a visual. He called the officers who'd made the two earlier sightings and told them to proceed to Victoria Park. He wanted both sets on foot: one to approach from the Regent's Canal side and the other from the north-west.

'You don't think they're going to use the canal, do you, sir?' asked a constable.

'I've no idea,' said Hines. 'It would be a slow process if they off-loaded it on to a boat. There's got to be ten locks between Victoria Park and Limehouse Basin.'

The car pursuing the truck from outside the park called in to say they'd seen it heading towards the canal. Minutes later, the officers stationed on a bridge over the canal said that they could see the truck, but that it had left the tarmac path and was heading into the flat open parkland.

It came to a halt after about a hundred metres.

'Keep your distance,' said Hines to the officers on the ground. 'Just tell me what you can see. Don't take any action.'

'The driver has left the vehicle and seems to be preparing to unload the first package. Yes, that's what he's doing. He's hooking the ropes up to the lifting gear. Now he's off the vehicle and operating the crane. He's lifted the first package off and he's being very careful about its position.'

'Is there anybody else in the park?'

'Nobody. And there's no light. He's using spotlights on his vehicle to see what he's doing. And it's bloody windy out there. In fact, yes, I can see it now. There's some kind of fluorescent tape marking the ground and he's positioning the package within the frame.'

'Get me a report from Battersea heliport,' roared Hines.

'We've already done that, sir. Nothing's been allowed to take off for the last two hours due to the weather.'

'What the *fuck* is going on?' said Hines, swearing savagely for the first time in his professional life.

'The second package is down now. He's starting on the third.'

Hines stared at the map.

'Right, I want two cars stationed on every road around Victoria Park. I want people on foot down by the Regent's Canal. There's a block of flats overlooking the park opposite the London Chest Hospital. Get some men on the roof looking down. I want

292

constant reports on what they can see. Get a camera up there. There's a boating lake in the park. Is there something on that? Tell me anything and everything.'

'The third package is on the ground now, sir.'

'If any vehicle approaches the park, you must allow it to enter,' said Hines. 'Do you hear me? Give any vehicle free access.'

Minutes passed. The fourth package was offloaded. A report came from the roof of the block of flats where they were setting up a camera to give a feed into the communications centre.

'There's a frame of fluorescent tape on the ground about five yards by four, I'd say, and all the packages are being positioned within that space. That's all we can see. There's nothing else in the park. Nothing on the boating lake, not even a pedalo. The weather's so horrible there aren't even any joggers out.'

'And on the canal?'

'There are some narrowboats moored near the park. It's clear there are people in them because they have lights on and smoke coming from the chimneys, but nothing unusual. I can see some of our officers down there and they're not in the least bit concerned by any activity. The fifth package has just been landed. Last one to go.'

The communications centre picked up the feed from the camera on the roof, which was focusing on the unfolding scene in the park, and relayed it to Hines's screen. The driver hooked up the last package and jumped off the back. The crane took the weight and slowly lifted the package and positioned it in the final slot. The driver used the remote to fold the crane back into its park position. He listened to the mobile phone, went into the cab, came out with something in his hand and did something to the top of each of the packages. He got back into the cab, manoeuvred the truck, churning up the sodden ground, so that the spotlights were on the packages of money. He left the vehicle, walked out of the park.

'We've got a van that's gone into the park via the Gore Road entrance,' said one of the officers. 'It's approaching the scene. It's a ... it's Sky News.'

'A BBC outside broadcast van has just gone in through the Grove Road entrance.'

The men on the roof watched as the newsmen set up their

cameras, while the presenters ran a test on their microphones.

An email came through to Hines from the kidnappers.

Are you ready?

One of the constables in the communications centre turned the television on to Sky News. Kay Burley stared into the camera and announced that they were going live immediately to Sky reporter Rhiannon Mills for a special broadcast from London's East End.

'Here we are in Victoria Park, otherwise known as the People's Park, on an extremely blustery night, for what we have been told is going to be one of the most spectacular events to take place in London since the opening ceremony of the Olympic Games,' said Mills, with her blonde hair whipping across her face. 'What we have been promised is one of the greatest disappearing acts in the history of illusions. Bigger than David Copperfield's promise to make the moon vanish. We have been advised that at precisely six o'clock, what you see in the background will miraculously de-materialise. We do not know what is in these six packages that you can see spotlit behind me, but we have been told that it weighs nearly four tons and is valued at one hundred and fifty million pounds. Only as it stunningly transmogrifies will we be told what was contained in the packages, and we have been assured you will be utterly astounded by the feat. We are just fifteen seconds away from … Hold on a moment …'

Mills put her finger to her ear.

'It has just been leaked exclusively to Sky News that what is contained in the packages behind us is one hundred and fifty million pounds in cash. An extraordinary amount of money, which belongs to—'

Mills ducked at the sound of a colossal explosion as all six packages were lifted more than forty feet into the air, spilling their contents into the gusting wind, which took the loose money high into the thermals and scattered it over the East End.

Mills snatched at the air above her and caught hold of a fifty-pound note, which she held up to the camera.

'There it is. A fifty-pound note. The air is full of them.'

The camera cut to the night sky, which was full of fluttering notes and the remnants of plastic sheeting towering and twisting, rolling and yawing in the gusting wind.

27

Mercy had thought long and hard before she called in the two homicide teams to look at the crime scenes in Lewisham and Catford. She'd decided that an anonymous informer would have to be involved in the first crime scene. The explanation of the bodies' positions wouldn't work without another person having been there. The second scene was more demanding as it involved Alleyne and Amy, who she didn't want anybody to know about. In her own mind she'd already approved of the idea of Louise Rylance disappearing. It was just explaining how Mercy herself had gained entry into the house, gone upstairs to witness Gav shooting Siobhan and then killed Gav in self-defence. This fiction was proving more difficult to frame into a believable story.

In the end she decided that the informer would have to be used to gain entry. That the kidnapper was expecting a white male and Michael Rylance had given them the code phrase was the key. Gav had admitted the informer, who in turn had let her in. She'd been hoping to make an arrest and interview Siobhan. On gaining entry into the house she'd heard them in discussion upstairs and drawn the weapon she'd taken from Rylance. Suspecting a conspiracy with the informer, Gav had attempted to use him as a shield. The informer had tried to wrest the weapon from Gav's hand and in the confusion it had gone off, killing Siobhan. Mercy had then shot Gav. It was messy, but that was the nature of these scenarios. It wouldn't have been the first time that somebody was killed under the stress of a kidnap situation with weapons involved.

She'd tried to call DCS Hines to give him a verbal report, but he was embroiled in the unfolding scene in Victoria Park and didn't want to know. So when Arran Road was clear, she took everybody back to Lewisham. They stayed in the car while Mercy studied the scene and Louise cleared her limited possessions into a large suitcase. Mercy called the first homicide team to the Lewisham house only after she'd dropped them all at the railway station to get a taxi.

The cab took them back to Streatham. Boxer called one of his doctor friends to come and look over Amy and Alleyne. They were both exhausted after days of living on the edge and went to lie down upstairs. Boxer sat with Louise, asked her if she knew how to disappear. She didn't. He made a call and left a message.

'He'll call back,' said Boxer.

'I'm not sure I want to do this,' she said.

'Nobody's ready to walk away from their own life,' said Boxer. 'It's the alternative that makes you do it.'

'It's like a betrayal,' she said. 'It's like I'm betraying Michael. Leaving him dead. Walking out on our life together as if he never existed.'

'Did your husband have any family?'

'He was an only child. His mother's still alive but in a home in Sussex with dementia.'

'You?'

'I've got a big family. Both parents and two grandparents alive, two sisters and a brother, nieces, nephews. Aunts and uncles. But they're an alternative bunch. Most of them are vegans and live in the rural depths of Devon and Somerset, some are in Wales and there's one in Patagonia. They never approved of me going into the army and they didn't like Michael. They called him a mercenary.'

'You won't be able to contact them ... ever.'

She nodded.

Boxer couldn't speak. He'd been suddenly consumed by a sense of loss that had risen up from nowhere and was so acute he didn't think he'd be able to contain it.

'The first time I saw you, I thought you were a psycho, a hit man,' said Louise. 'You looked dead behind the eyes. Michael could see it too. I was afraid of you. I thought you were capable of anything and it wouldn't matter one way or the other. And then on the way to that house in Catford you threw me by asking me ... by being so human. Don't take this badly, but you need help.'

'Help?' said Boxer, still struggling.

'Psychological help.'

'I'm beyond help,' he said, looking away. 'There's no cure for what I've done.'

'That bad?'

'Killing people,' said Boxer. 'Always bad people, but it's still killing other human beings and that's not so easy to admit to some shrink in Hampstead.'

'I know a woman, professional and discreet, who used to be in the marines. She's seen her fair share and helped a lot of post-traumatic stress guys,' said Louise, writing a name and number down on a card. 'Try her.'

Boxer didn't want to take the card.

'It won't get better on its own,' she said. 'You need someone objective who can trace it all back, find out where it went wrong, work out your ... motivation.'

'My motivation?'

'Why you've ended up doing what you do,' said Louise. 'Maybe you've got a personality disorder. All too human one moment, psychopathic the next.'

The doorbell rang. Boxer, still shaken, let the doctor in, took her upstairs. They'd met playing poker. She gambled on everything: cards, horses, sport, even the weather. She examined both patients, who'd been sleeping, and gave Boxer sedatives for them, but only if they developed anxiety or insomnia. She charged seven hundred pounds cash, which Boxer didn't have, but she knew he was good for it.

Back in the sitting room Louise was crying. He left her to it, waited in the kitchen until he heard the tears run out and went back in.

'You got money?' he said, sitting opposite her. 'I should have asked.'

'I've got the hundred grand, all offshore. No record of it in this country. I can access it.'

Boxer's phone rang. He took down an address. Hung up.

'This is where you go,' he said, handing her the paper. 'I'll walk you to a cab. Best not to call one here.'

They left the house, Boxer wheeling her suitcase. He had the strange sensation of saying goodbye to someone he'd known for a long time. He hailed a black cab, put the suitcase in the back. She kissed him on the mouth, held his face close to hers.

'Am I allowed to see *you* again?' she asked.

'Best not,' he said, but with the feeling of her lips on his.

'It could have been interesting,' she said.

He watched the taxi drive away on the black and gleaming road, confused, and wondering at how life never stopped coming at you.

Mercy had answered the questions as best she could with the first homicide team and then left to go to the Catford house. She had to clean all evidence of Amy and Alleyne from the house. She stripped the beds and bagged the linen, which she put in the boot of her car. She hoovered around the beds and wiped down the surfaces. She hated this. She hated subterfuge and lying. There was nothing more difficult than to keep track of a pack of lies. She'd broken too many suspects through their pathetic lies.

She called the second homicide team and gave her report when they arrived. She explained that she'd handed over the weapon used in this shooting to the first team and then excused herself, said she had to keep up with her special investigation into the six kidnaps.

It was a terrible night, with the wind buffeting her car and rain slashing across the windscreen as she made her way back to the Vauxhall office. She listened to the news and heard a full report of what had happened in Victoria Park. She went straight in to see DCS Hines and handed over the evidence bag with Chuck Powell's mobile phone. A member of the tech team came in to retrieve it, took down the details and left. Hines debriefed her on the afternoon and evening's events.

'Anything from the kidnappers since the big giveaway?' asked Mercy.

'An email. I quote: "We don't want to give you the impression that this is a mere redistribution of wealth. As you know we called this money 'expenses'. We believe that this is the minimum amount that these individuals would have had to pay if they hadn't enjoyed tax-free or non-dom status and been taxed at the same level as ordinary people.'"

'Probably right,' said Mercy.

'I'll make that our official quote for the press conference,' said Hines. 'I heard you had to kill three people.'

'My informer and I were attacked during the handover of the phone.'

'Which informer?' asked Hines. 'And why are you using informers for this kind of work? I'd have thought Papadopoulos would have been up to the task.'

'First of all I don't reveal the names of any of my informers,' said Mercy. 'And secondly, I was using this one in a slightly more inventive way than usual because I was concerned that the kidnap unit might have been compromised.'

'What makes you think that?' asked Hines, sitting up.

'We made significant inroads into the kidnappers' organisation but they always seemed to be ahead of the game,' said Mercy. 'We arrested Reef. They knew immediately and acted: cleared the hostages out of the Old Vinyl Factory and left a little booby trap to make us look stupid.'

'Somebody in the communications centre?'

'That would be the obvious place, the hub of all information,' said Mercy. 'But then again, they've been responsible for circulating that intelligence and it's gone everywhere, not just to our officers in the field, but to MI5, MI6 and the CIA.'

'There was a leak to Sky News about the cash, too,' said Hines. 'But what worries me more is that we're dealing with an organisation that doesn't appear to be motivated by profit. I mean literally blowing a hundred and fifty million is the ultimate demonstration of the ideologue. We might as well be up against religious fanatics.'

'How did the parents of the victims take it?' said Mercy, deciding to keep Emma's revelations to herself.

'All of them were stunned, some of them were very angry.'

'Angry?'

299

'Rich people care about money: not the status it confers by having lots of it in the bank or visible assets, but the physical presence of cash,' said Hines. 'And to see it thrown away like that was infuriating to some of them, especially Uttar Sarkar and Anastasia Casey. Apparently it wasn't even Sarkar's money. He'd done a deal with the Indian government and they'd supplied his twenty-five million in exchange for some tax break. It did not diminish his fury.'

'They think differently to us,' said Mercy.

'Wealth is like drinking seawater. The more you have, the thirstier you get.'

'And we haven't even got to the ransom yet,' said Mercy. 'But if you're right about Conrad Jensen being an ideologue, it looks like what they demanded of the CIA is going to be the name of the game. Announce this, declare that, name names.'

'We have to find these hostages,' said Hines.

'Any reports of movements in or out of the Old Vinyl Factory?'

'We're not hopeful in a run-down industrial zone with little night-time activity.'

'The lengths they went to in order to retrieve Chuck Powell's phone show how important he is. Has he come round?'

'Not yet and it's going to be a while before he's strong enough to talk. In the meantime we've got to look at all possibilities.'

'Are the hostages still in this country?' asked Mercy. 'Are we looking at the ports? The Channel Tunnel?'

'There's a limit to what we can achieve without intelligence,' said Hines. 'Trying to check every container leaving the UK might be a bit of an ask.'

'I interviewed Rylance before he attacked me. His phone had the names of two of his partners, Mark Lee and Jim Ford, who he worked with on Rakesh Sarkar's kidnap,' said Mercy. 'He gave me the address of Mark Lee's flat where they met up to change clothes for the kidnap.'

'Let's bring him in, both of them if we can, but they'll probably be peripheral like all the others we've caught,' said Hines. 'The people exposed by doing the kidnap work don't seem to know what's going on in the centre. We need to find someone who was in the Old Vinyl Factory when they moved the hostages.'

'After the kidnap, Rylance delivered Rakesh Sarkar to the factory. He maintains he didn't see anything. He left the police car, changed out of uniform and was driven back into town,' said Mercy. 'Reef delivered Siena Casey to a car, which must have at least gone to the Old Vinyl Factory if it didn't come from there. Siena was out of her head and it's unlikely they would have let her travel unsupervised in a highly drugged state. Reef must have gone with her. And he must have had some way of recognising the car he was supposed to deliver her to.'

'So who are you going to talk to first?'

'I think I should try to find Mark Lee.'

Boxer felt acutely alone after the strange connection he'd made with Louise. He went to sit in Amy's room, left the door open so there was a little light from the hall and watched her sleeping. It reminded him of when she'd been small and, on the few occasions he'd been in the country, coming back from work and going upstairs to watch her. The memory, tied up with the evening's odd liaison and the terrible sense of loss, brought on a crying jag. Tears streaked down his face as he breathed in, shuddering against the emotion. He tried to remember the last time he'd cried and had to go right the way back to when he'd first been told that his father had gone. He'd cried then, but only once.

'Is that you, Dad?' said Amy, from the bed. 'Are you … are you crying?'

He nodded, wiped his face with the back of his hands and told her what had happened to Isabel, and about the baby lying in an incubator in the Chelsea and Westminster Hospital. And then Amy was crying too, and she pulled him over. He lay down next to her and she clasped him to her in the dark.

'What a life,' he said.

'What are you going to do with the baby?'

'Your mum asked the same thing. And I don't know. I haven't got that far. I'm in a strange state. I've just lost Isabel, but she's left me this little life that I'm going to have to fit into my own and I'm not sure how.'

'I like the idea of a half-brother.'

'You'll have to go and see him,' said Boxer. 'It was one of the strangest things that's ever happened to me. To see Isabel, but to find her totally absent, and then to be introduced to this struggling, quivering life in a Perspex box.'

'Hang on to that, Dad, it's a good thing.'

He held her close, kissed her head and relaxed.

'I've been thinking about Siobhan,' said Amy.

'What happened there?'

'I don't know. I just got drawn in by her ... charisma – or his; she was more of a guy than a girl. Fucked up as she was, she had the force with her. She didn't care. I suppose that was it. She didn't give a damn. It got her into trouble, but she experienced life. I admired her for that. I can't get over her taking that bullet for me. Did you know I wasn't part of the original kidnap plan? Taking me was her idea and Conrad liked it and approved it.'

'Did Siobhan know why Conrad involved me?' asked Boxer. 'Why did he get Siobhan to hire me to look for him? I don't get that. It's the last thing he'd want to happen: to have people on his trail.'

'She didn't say. She was obsessed with Conrad. She called him her father, but he wasn't, you know. She told me that. He'd rescued her from a shitty situation, which was why she did all his dirty work for him and took no thanks for it.'

Boxer got to his feet in a single sudden movement and stood in the middle of the room, staring into the dark.

'What?' asked Amy.

'Are you and Marcus going to be all right on your own?' he asked. 'The doc said you were OK, just exhausted. She gave me some tranks if you need them.'

'I'm fine. Marcus might like them for recreational purposes. Where are you going?'

'I've got to go home to get a phone number and make a call.'

He left a note for Mercy, went back to his flat. He found the encrypted file on his computer and the number of Dick Kushner, who ran a rehabilitation centre for war veterans close to Worcester, Massachussets. He raised money for this centre by finding work for able-bodied vets and he had an encyclopedic knowledge of the best and the worst of types that operated for American PMSCs. Boxer had his secure number, which was the only way Kushner would talk about anybody in the business, and he was one of very few people Kushner trusted with it.

Boxer called him and went through the usual apologies for not having been in touch. He gave him as detailed a description as he could of the London kidnappings and concluded by asking him about Conrad Jensen and Chuck Powell.

'I know the names and I know they worked together on interrogation teams in black sites during the extraordinary rendition programme. I don't use Chuck Powell because he has an ugly rep. He's very strong and he kills people. As for Jensen, he's disappeared off my radar since those bad old days. Haven't heard anything about him in the last five years.'

'I heard through a friend of mine in MI6 that Jensen worked in a black site near Rabat in 2005.'

'There was one in Temara so I don't doubt it, but I don't know it.'

'What I need to know is whether he and Powell worked in any other black sites and if there was any other person they worked with regularly who could be described as a close personal friend,' said Boxer.

'I can't tell you that off the top of my head, Charlie. And anyway, I thought you said the CIA was involved in this,' said Kushner. 'They must be able to help you with that stuff.'

'I'm not officially in this business,' said Boxer. 'I'm just trying to find Jensen and the hostages and I'm not sure how friendly the CIA are.'

Kushner said he'd get back him.

They pulled into the parking area amongst the blocks of flats off the Portobello Road. The squad car that had followed stayed outside. Mercy was back working with Papadopoulos. She didn't fancy tackling Mark Lee on her own with no weapon. On the way to Lee's flat she'd filled him in on the reason for the visit. Papadopoulos hadn't said a word. There was an uncomfortable atmosphere of distrust.

Papadopoulos got out of the car and checked the address, pointed to the flat, which had a balcony with a short drop to where they'd parked. Mercy beckoned him back to the car.

'We can't work together like this,' she said.

'Hey, look, Mercy, you were the one who gave me the accusing look back at the Old Vinyl Factory. What was that about?'

'I'm sorry. I was nervous.'

'Of me? What did you think?'

'That somebody was feeding info to the gang.'

'And you thought it was *me*? We've haven't even worked together on this job.'

'I know, which is why I'm going through the process of reconciliation,' said Mercy, feeling terrible, having only just got out from under her own obligations. 'Once something's in your head, everybody's a potential suspect.'

'It's been a trip, this investigation,' said Papadopoulos. 'I thought I was going to get fired, then I was ostracised, accused of spying and finally brought back into the fold. All I need now is to get shot.'

'Don't say that.'

'Why?'

'It's bad luck.'

'Yeah, you're right,' said Papadopoulos. 'Things have been piling up on me.'

'The mortgage you and Josie just signed up to?'

'I've been meaning to tell you,' said Papadopoulos. 'She's pregnant, too.'

'Put it there, partner,' she said, and held out her hand.

They shook hands. Mercy leaned over and kissed him on the cheek. The contact seemed to make things better in the car.

'It happens to all of us,' said Mercy. 'Everything comes at the same time.'

'The convergence of shit, I think you call it.'

'Except that's not shit. It's joyful. You've moved into a new home, the first one you've owned together ...'

'With the bank in the spare fucking room.'

'And now you're starting a family.'

'Don't tell anyone,' said Papadopoulos. 'It's not been three months yet.'

'It's great news. Now cheer up and let's decide how we're going to play this,' said Mercy. 'Just looking at the way the flat is laid

304

out, maybe I should go in there on my own to start with. He might take one look at me and do a runner. It's not much of a drop from that balcony and God knows how many ways out of this warren there are.'

'What about the lads in the squad car? Can't we spread them around?'

'These flats back on to four different roads.'

'Two on the corners, two in the car in case of pursuit?'

She radioed the squad car, told them the plan.

'Are you going to call me in?'

'I'll set up a text and send it when I want you to show.'

They got out of the car. Papadopoulos stood at the foot of the balcony. Mercy went to the front door of the block, rang a bell, said she was police and asked to be let in. The door was buzzed open. She hammered on Mark Lee's door.

'What's up?' asked a male voice, through the closed door.

'Police,' said Mercy. 'I want a chat.'

'About?' he said, opening the door.

'Crime in the area. Can I come in?'

He beckoned her in. Mercy went into an open-plan kitchen/diner and living room with the balcony to the left and bedroom and bathroom to the right.

'We don't get much trouble up this end of the Portobello Road,' he said. 'Down Westbourne Park Road and beyond is where you want to be. Cup of tea?'

'Thanks. I was thinking more about crime in these blocks of flats.'

'Nah, they're all good people here.'

'In this flat in particular.'

He turned the kettle on, looked at her from the kitchen area.

'There hasn't been any. I've lived here nearly ten years and never had a break-in. Even with this balcony. Like I said, they're good people.'

'I was thinking more about *you*.'

'Me?'

'You are Mark Lee, aren't you?'

He nodded.

'Where were you just after midnight on the fifteenth of January?'

He poured boiling water into the cups, squashed the tea bags, lifted them out, added milk. Thinking all the time.

'Sugar?' he asked.

She shook her head.

'Never been asked that question,' he said, handing her the mug. 'Surprisingly difficult to answer. That was a Tuesday night, wasn't it?'

'You'd remember, because you were in here changing into police uniforms with Michael Rylance and Jim Ford.'

Everything in the room was audible in the silence. The kettle cooling. The fridge gurgling. The pipework moaning.

'I know what happened that night,' said Mercy. 'Rylance told me everything before I had to shoot him. You kidnapped Rakesh Sarkar. He last saw you overtaking him in Sarkar's Porsche.'

'Michael Rylance?' he said, puzzled. 'I'm not sure I know a Michael Rylance.'

'And Jim Ford.'

'Draws a blank too,' he said, getting up, going back to the kitchen with his mug. 'These guys told you I was involved in a *kidnap*? That's interesting, because that night I *was* working but not kidnapping people. I was at my regular job as the night concierge at the Flemings Hotel in Mayfair. You want a phone number you can check that …?'

He turned, and this time he had his arm outstretched with a Ruger SR9 in his hand.

'I don't think that's a good idea,' said Mercy. 'I'm not here on my own.'

He opened the sliding door to the balcony, looked out towards the Portobello Road; saw nothing. The squad car was out of sight. He backed up to the railing, which he gripped with his left hand, and in a stunning acrobatic movement fell backwards into the night. He held on momentarily with his left hand and then dropped out of sight. Mercy ran out.

'Armed man, George!' she roared.

There was a grunt and then the sound of a gunshot.

Mercy called the squad car, told them that Lee had a gun.

Lee sprinted up the ramp towards the Portobello Road. As he came up to street level, the squad car reversed towards him. There

306

was another shot and he toppled over the boot, roof and bonnet of the car and finished up on the ground. The gun skittered away from him.

'George!' roared Mercy, looking for him over the balcony railing.

She saw his feet.

The police driver was looking down at Mark Lee, who was moving, holding on to his leg.

'Man down!' shouted Mercy, pushing herself away from the railing as the uniforms came running down the ramp.

She sprinted out of the flat, down the steps to where George was lying under the balcony. He was up on one elbow.

'Shit, Mercy, I don't believe it,' he said. 'I got shot.'

28

B oxer was pacing the floor of his flat with the Walther P99 in his hand. Its weight was comforting. He stopped occasionally to look at the news, which was full of roving cameras shooting footage of people all over the East End of London rushing around with supermarket plastic bags collecting fifty-pound notes from gardens, trees, shop doorways, car windscreens, park benches. At times even the cameramen found the booty irresistible and the screen was suddenly full of a recycling bin with a bunch of notes plastered inside and a hand reaching for them.

'I got seventy-five fucking grand already,' said one wild-eyed, pierced and shaven-headed thug, who immediately ran out of shot.

'My mum always used to tell me that money doesn't grow on trees, you know, and here it is ... bloody hell ... it's growing on trees,' shouted a hysterical girl with pink hair and tattooed legs, hands clawing down her cheeks.

'My dad heard this bang, he threw open the window to see what's happening. Thought it was a gas explosion. And you know what? The house was suddenly full of all this money. We're still counting it. Hundred and twenty-five grand so far.'

The news package showed pandemonium around Hackney Wick station as commuters on the steady trudge home had been infected with money-grabbing madness. Fights had broken out with running battles on the main street. The presenter was being shunted around by shoals of people as he announced the possibility of riot police being called out.

It was no better in Stratford. A shot of the station alive with fluttering notes, and some bizarre CCTV footage of the whole of the Westfield Centre emptying in a cattle stampede as if a bomb had gone off, followed by footage of people running wildly, jumping in the air and clutching at elusive notes, their faces distorted with effort and greed.

It reduced Boxer to a gawping standstill. He wondered if this had been Conrad Jensen's intention: to show that, much as these people might despise the wealthy, when it came down to it they were all just as rapacious.

At least the wind had been gusting from west to east, he thought. It would have been intolerable for the money to have been blown into Hampstead, Knightsbridge, Kensington and Chelsea.

Kushner finally called back just before eleven o'clock.

'I've been talking to a CIA retiree,' he said. 'A Democrat. A guy who was at the forefront of the War on Terror until he quit the agency because he was so disgusted by extraordinary rendition and ... other things. He knew the name Conrad Jensen, but it was nothing to do with the black sites. He was an IT expert, wrote – or had written – a whole bunch of software for them. He knew nothing about Rabat. But he did know Chuck Powell. Or rather he was friendly with Chuck Powell's buddy, a Texan called Evan Rampy. They were both agency-trained. Chuck left after the Iraq invasion of 2003 because he saw a way to make money doing what he was already doing but for a PMSC. That's how he ended up on the interrogation teams in black sites. Rampy stayed until 2010 and then went to work for a guy called Julius Klank at a PMSC called SureSafe.'

'Conrad Jensen made a payment to Klank into a company called Xiphos in Belize. We don't know what for, but we assume personnel services.'

'Klank has a good reputation, but in my view he's dubious. The agency still use him. I wouldn't.'

'What can you tell me about Rampy?'

'I'll send you a shot of him. He's an operations and logistics expert. He can get people to the right place at the right time with the right equipment to perform their tasks,' said Kushner.

'Doesn't that sound like somebody Jensen could have used for his series kidnap?'

'Because of the Kinderman Corporation's involvement we're supposed to be working with the CIA, and yet so far they only managed to identify Chuck Powell *after* his capture and they've given out no other names,' said Boxer.

'They're embarrassed. They train all these high-quality people and then they go out into the world and do bad things. Some of them change on the job. Find themselves doing things way beyond their normal moral boundaries: extraordinary rendition. I mean, taking people off of the streets of their home towns, illegally moving them across borders to black sites in other countries where they can be tortured, all in the name of the War on Terror. That's got to do some permanent damage to your morality. And not only that,' said Kushner. 'One of the reasons my retiree quit was political influence of the wrong kind.'

'What did he mean by that?'

'Infiltration by the extreme right wing,' said Kushner. 'You want to find out what's really going on in the world, don't read the *Wall Street Journal*. Talk to your guys in the agency. And then you take the next step, which my guy really couldn't stomach: shaping intelligence to the outcomes you desire.'

'Interesting,' said Boxer. 'There's a definite political dimension to this series kidnap, which we haven't been able to piece together. Does your CIA retiree know what Rampy has been doing since he quit the agency?'

'He knows he served in Iraq, Afghanistan and Pakistan, that he speaks Arabic and has developed a love for the Arab world. He owns a property in Marrakesh. They haven't had any contact since he left.'

'So we have the name Evan Rampy, who looks a likely candidate, but how can I locate him?'

'He's got to be in Chuck Powell's phone.'

'I'm not sure I'll have access to the contents of that phone.'

'From what you've said, the kidnap's all over: the gang's dispersed, the hostages have been moved. If Rampy was on that job, he'll be long gone. Maybe to his place in Morocco?'

*

The squad car had a good first-aid kit and they got some packs on to George's gunshot wound, which was in his left side. Mercy was keeping him awake, talking to him. He was in shock and trembling; his lips had blended into the same colour as his face. He blinked and concentrated on Mercy's eyes.

'Don't tell Josie. I don't want her to worry. You know, and something happen to the baby.'

'You just concentrate on staying awake. Don't worry about Josie.'

The ambulance arrived and took Papadopoulos to St Mary's, Paddington. Mercy followed in her car, trying not to cry and failing. She ran in to A&E to find that he'd already been taken in and rushed to the operating theatre. There was nobody who could tell her anything.

She called the squad car and asked where they were taking Mark Lee.

'Notting Hill police station on Ladbroke Grove.'

'So he's not hurt.'

'Battered and bruised, but nothing a good kicking won't sort out.'

'Book him in. I want an interview as soon as possible.'

She knew what she was doing, putting off the moment when she had to call George's partner, Josie. They all had their next of kin's number on their mobiles. She went back to the A&E reception, showed her warrant card, begged the frantic staff for information, told them she was going to phone the man's wife. A young black guy took pity, left the desk and went down to the theatres for her. Fifteen minutes later he was back.

'They're operating on him now, but they wouldn't commit themselves on his condition. He's alive and they've got the bullet out, that's all they'd say.'

'Did it hit any vital organs?'

'No idea, I'm sorry.'

She called Josie.

'Josie, this is Mercy.'

'Oh, Mercy,' she said, in a voice of restrained panic at the instant realisation that Mercy had never called her.

'I'm at St Mary's Hospital in Paddington. We've just brought George here.'

'Oh Christ, what's happened?'

'He's been shot. They're operating on him at the moment. They haven't been able to tell me anything about his condition yet.'

Josie dropped the phone. Mercy heard her shunting her chair back and chasing after it.

'What I'm going to do, Josie, is send a patrol car round to your flat and they'll bring you here. Do you have someone who can come with you?'

'Yes, my sister, she'll come with me. I'll call her,' said Josie. 'Is it …?'

'All I can tell you is that he was still talking to me when they put him in the ambulance and he was taken straight into theatre as soon as he arrived. The bullet has been removed, that's all they've said.'

Mercy told her what had happened as best she could, keeping it level and calm, and Josie took it as well as could be expected. They hung up. Mercy arranged the patrol car and went to Notting Hill police station.

Mark Lee was brought up to an interview room. He was limping and had a black eye and a grazed face that had been treated. He took one look at Mercy's hardened expression and started bleating.

'It was an accident. I dropped to the ground. The guy grabbed me. The gun went off. I had no intention …'

'You had a gun in your hand. You threatened me with it. Your intention was to get away and you were prepared to kill to do it. That's my reading of what happened.'

'I'm sorry. Was he your partner?'

'Yes, he's married with a pregnant wife, and if you've killed him …' said Mercy, and just shook her head.

'OK,' said Lee, squeezing his eyebrows and pinching the bridge of his nose. 'Whatever it takes. Just tell me what you want to know.'

'How many times were you in the Old Vinyl Factory?'

'Four times.'

'And what did you see inside the factory when you went there?'

'I was picked up at Hayes and Harlington railway station by a guy who didn't give his name. He took me to this building, which we entered via a loading bay. There were two squad cars. He gave me the keys to one and that was it. I drove out of the loading bay the way I'd come in. I didn't see any other activity. The second time was a bit different. The same driver took me to the loading bay and told me to follow him. We went past what looked like some old offices. The door to one of them was open and I saw a girl, twenties, lying on a bed with a mask over her face. I was taken into an office where there was a bunch of computer and telecommunications equipment and I was presented to this guy. No names used. He laid into me for sending Rylance to bring the squad car back. Said that I should always follow the instructions given.'

'Describe him. Was he English? Did he have an accent?'

'No, he was an American. I don't know much about American accents, but he seemed to be from the south. Maybe Texas, I don't know. He had long blonde hair and a beard and really piercing blue-green eyes, and he was built. I wasn't going to argue with him. Something like six foot three, sixteen stone, but none of it fat. He wore jeans and a big floppy roll-neck sweater under a winter parka, gloves and thermal boots. I mean, it was cold, but not *that* cold.'

'How was the beard?' asked Mercy. 'Full, wispy, trimmed, shaggy?'

'It was full, not shaggy, but it didn't look as if he fussed over it too much.'

'Was that the only time you saw him?'

'No. I was taken to see him again after the Weybridge job. I'd dropped the two shooters off in south London and brought their uniforms and weapons back with me. He wanted to know what had happened, whether I'd seen everything clearly. I told him about the shooting. He asked if the guys in the boy's car had been armed and I said yes. He seemed annoyed that there'd been some killing, but the two shooters were up for it. They were pumped, as if he'd specially selected them to do just what they did. And that was it. I didn't see him again.'

'How did you get this job?'

'I'm a driver. I know London backwards. That's what Jim said they wanted.'

'How did Jim get the job?'

'Jim's ex-army, like the Rylance guy. He works all over the world in security. He heard about the job, I don't know how, said it paid well.'

'How do I get hold of Jim Ford?'

Boxer couldn't stomach any more news: the traffic jams around the City because of cars heading east to pick up on the bonanza, the clogged M25 because of all the people piling in from Kent, Surrey and Sussex. The endless interviews with a vast range of Londoners, some appalled by the behaviour on display and disdaining to pick up even a note of what was clearly dirty money, while others were nearly insane with an ugly rapacity that was reminiscent of the looting during the London riots.

He was on a mission now after connecting with Louise, the talk with Amy and that call from Kushner. He'd always had a powerful motivation to bring victims back to their families, to fill the terrible gap left by the missing. And he was aware that he had a huge need to fill his own black hole, but this time it was different. He was maddened by what Conrad Jensen was doing.

Gangs kidnapped people mainly for profit, sometimes for political purposes, occasionally for revenge, often for family reasons but never for a game. Conrad Jensen, the ideologue, was enjoying himself by torturing a select group of billionaires who, in the age of super inequality, were already a popular target for communal anger. He was indulging in this Robin Hood act of stealing from the rich and redistributing to the poor to demonstrate that everyone was as bad as each other, that they'd all relish being rich, disdain the poor and be greedy for more given half a chance. That was fair enough as a discussion over a pint in the pub, but you didn't taunt parents, even massively wealthy parents, by torturing their children. And as part of the game you didn't kidnap the investigator's child and lover.

That was when he realised he felt an immense hatred for Conrad Jensen and knew with certainty that he was going to do what Siobhan had hired him to do: find him. Then he was going to do what Mercy had asked him to do: kill him. First he was going to find Evan Rampy, and he was going to do it on his own. No Mercy this time. The kidnap unit was infected with spies; the

CIA had proved to be suspect and unpredictable and, according to Kushner's contact, politically infiltrated.

Mercy was driving to St Mary's. She'd asked Hines to arrange the pickup of Jim Ford. She wasn't taking that risk again and she had more than enough proof of his involvement to arrest him. She stumbled through the doors into A&E and was struck by the terrible randomness of life and death. How she'd spent the last days in paroxysmal bouts of fear at the thought of Marcus and Amy being hurt and of herself losing the work that held her together. As for the possibility of Marcus being killed, she hadn't been able to even go there. And now here she was looking a completely different tragedy in the face.

Josie and her sister were not in the A&E waiting room. She asked at reception. A different shift. She showed her warrant card. Asked after Josie, tried to remember her surname: Wentworth, that was it. A porter was called for, a young Pole. He took her to the family room near the ICU, where Josie was sitting staring straight ahead while her sister held her hand and looked at her as if waiting for seismic shifts.

Mercy introduced herself, sat on Josie's other side.

'Have you had any news?'

'He's lost a kidney and he can't feel his legs. They're not sure why. It might be trauma or it might be damage,' she said. 'But he's alive.'

'Have you spoken to him?'

'Just briefly when he came round after the surgery. Then he went under again. He's been sleeping since.'

'Do you mind if I go and have a look at him?'

She shrugged, emotionally exhausted.

Mercy went to ICU. The nurse took her to the bedside.

'It doesn't look it, but he was very lucky. The blood loss was nearly catastrophic. A minute later and we'd have lost him.'

Papadopoulos didn't look good. He was grey. The only thing about him that still looked like George was his thick Greek hair. Everything else about him was in negative form.

He opened his eyes, saw her, closed them again. He raised his index finger from the sheet in a salute.

Boxer was going to follow Kushner's lead: Rampy had a house in Marrakesh. He didn't know anybody there but he had a contact in Casablanca who would know how he could be supplied with a weapon and would point him in the right direction for some intelligence. The number was in the same encrypted file on his computer as Dick Kushner's.

Omar al-Wannan was somebody he'd met through Simon Deacon. It was only later that he'd found out that al-Wannan already knew about him from a consultation he'd done whilst still at GRM for a Jordanian whose daughter had been kidnapped in Oman. Al-Wannan was a businessman and family man, but he enjoyed the excitement of the other life, the feeling that he was making things happen in another dimension. He provided intelligence for MI6 and the Spanish CNI on potential terrorist threats, but he'd taken a liking to Boxer and had let it be known that he could be of service, as he put it.

Boxer called al-Wannan, who said he would have to call him back, which he did.

'I'm sorry, Charlie, I've had some security issues recently. I have to be more discreet. What can I do for you?'

Boxer gave him a rough outline of the kidnap scenario that had unfolded in London, and how he'd come to believe that Evan Rampy was an important connecting piece. He also told him he would need something for his protection while in Morocco. Al-Wannan said he would make enquiries and call him back.

While waiting for the return call, Boxer tried to relax, but lying down was impossible. He poured himself a Famous Grouse on the rocks, paced the room again, trying to analyse what was making him so anxious. Obviously the loss of Isabel was a contributing factor, but to find that he couldn't access an emotional response was more disconcerting, rather than distressing. This was like being uncomfortable in his own head, in fact his whole skin.

The boards creaked under the fitted carpet as he paced from side to side. He remembered being mesmerised by a jaguar in a Mexican zoo and his incessant loping of the length of his cage as if planning killing sprees after his release.

And it was at that moment, when he was almost outside himself looking down, that he realised it had been the stranger, Louise, who'd got under his skin. What was it she'd said?

Yes, he'd almost ignored it, let it wash over him, the fact that she'd seen the psychopath in him and then later been disorientated by his unexpected humanity. It was strange to be seen back to front. Most people thought him human. Of course they did. Why wouldn't they?

Louise had seen him for what he was. She'd used words about him that nobody else had dared to: personality disorder, psychopath.

Then it came to him, and not for the first time, that scene in a loop in his head that had taken place in Madrid a couple of years ago with the Colombian drug trafficker El Osito. The way he'd looked at him, this man, the epitome of evil. He'd called him his *compañero*: a hideous concept that he could even be thought of as that man's partner. The effect had been powerful. Later, in his hotel room, after he'd failed to carry out his revenge – to bludgeon El Osito to death with a baseball bat – he'd looked in the mirror and seen the unacceptable truth. On the integral scale of evil, he was much closer to El Osito's end.

Was it possible to be this aware and yet psychopathic? Did humans have the capacity to be selectively psychopathic: the vigilante psychopath who felt no remorse as long as he was killing bad guys? Was this what Louise called a personality disorder?

He reached into his pocket, pulled out his wallet and the piece of paper she'd given him with the number of the psychologist from the marines. He needed help. What had she said? With his motivations? But did he? He knew very well why he was doing this. He blinked at the intensity of that belief.

The phone rang, jolting him. Al-Wannan. He tucked the paper back in his wallet.

'Your first point of contact should be by ferry to Ceuta. That is the least conspicuous way for you to come in. You ask for a woman called Mercedes Puerta at the Bar Madrid and she will look after your entry into Morocco. She will take you to see a contact in Tétouan who will supply you with what you need. Afterwards she will bring you to see me in Meknes and I will give you a car and the information you require for travelling south. Just let me know when you will be able to arrive in Ceuta.'

29

Mercy woke up late, dazed to find herself in bed with Alleyne, the adrenalin still kicking in and then dissipating as she realised the real horror was over. He was sleeping. She lay there staring at his back, willing herself to get up. Fear was still seething in her head as she contemplated the possibility of her exposure. Would there be a problem when Rakesh Sarkar was released and he revealed that there'd been a third kidnapper involved? Only if Louise hadn't successfully disappeared.

She showered and dressed, dropped in on Amy, who was completely unconscious. She saw Boxer's note and had another burst of adrenalin at the thought of what he might be doing. She double-locked the front door, paranoid about leaving Amy and Marcus alone in the house, and drove to the office. She was due at a meeting with all the special investigation teams working on the kidnaps. DCS Hines called her into his office before she could get there.

'What's going on?' she asked.

'Total silence from the kidnappers is what's going on,' said Hines, handing over a file of paper. 'This is the rescued data from Chuck Powell's phone. You'll probably want to get your teams working on it, but you might be disappointed.'

'Hasn't he come round yet?'

'We're having a little battle there with the CIA, to the point where the FO is now in conference with the White House.'

'But it's a murder investigation. His blood has been matched

318

to the site of the dead girl in the Royal Victoria Dock. He has to answer questions.'

'That's true, and he will have to answer to the homicide team investigating that. It's just a question of who gets to talk to him first, and the CIA don't want it to be anybody else but them.'

'Seeing as they've been so helpful throughout?'

'They've got something to hide,' said Hines. 'When we look at all the people involved in this kidnap, we quite quickly realised that most of them are disaffected allied ex-military personnel who served time in Iraq and Afghanistan. I assume they know things that the CIA would prefer not to be aired or that the CIA would like to control. I am getting a lot of pressure from all sides letting me know that if we do find Conrad Jensen, the CIA, especially this guy Walden Garfinkle, don't want anybody else but them to interview him.'

'I never did get to speak to Garfinkle.'

'And I don't think you ever will,' said Hines, 'because we're being told in no uncertain terms that Jensen is CIA property. The reason we're getting precious little intelligence from them is that they want to get to him first.'

'So what are my orders regarding intelligence on the whereabouts of Conrad Jensen?'

'If you get any, call me, and by then I might know what the official line is.'

'Why will I be disappointed by the rescued data from Powell's phone?'

'A lot of names have been blacked out.'

Boxer had slept fitfully. There were dreams that woke him and left him on the brink with no memory of their content. Finally he lay awake staring at the ceiling with tears leaking down the side of his face and a sense of loss so vast that he was unsure how his body was containing it. This time it was for all his losses; not just Isabel, but his father as well, the belief that Amy had been murdered, even Louise disappearing into the night to be restarted in a different future. He wondered if there was some transference going on with Louise. That having lost Isabel, he'd just shifted a whole bunch of feelings with nowhere to go on to someone who was at least alive. He didn't think so. Too fleeting. And she was gone now and there was no reeling her back from where she'd vanished. The guy he'd sent her to was very thorough.

He got up, turned on a single lamp in the living room and went to work by its low light. He put fifteen thousand in a mix of pounds and euros with twenty thousand Moroccan dirhams in the false bottom of his case, along with a passport in the name of Christopher Butler for when he went into Morocco. He packed clothes on top.

In the bathroom he turned the light on over the mirror and prepared to shave. He was drawn in by his own bright green eyes, wanted to see if he believed in them any more, if he could work out what was going on behind them. There was no difference: still Charlie Boxer going about his business. But this time the business was going to be killing. He leaned in closer. No deadness. No psychosis. In fact, a slight pinkness from his earlier crying. He was so human.

He left the flat. His flight wasn't until midday, but he needed to be on the move. He took the tube and a bus up to the Chelsea and Westminster Hospital, listened to a couple of Brazilians discussing the hideous cost to their country of staging the World Cup.

At the hospital, he went to the neonatal ICU. The nurse on duty remembered him but he had no recollection of her. She told him that Alyshia and her partner had been there for hours yesterday. She asked him to wash his hands and put on a gown before she took him to the incubator.

The little frog looked different, or his memory was playing tricks. He asked the nurse if that was possible, and she said it was.

'He's growing all the time.'

He gave a little kick with his legs as if to prove he'd just added a micron in length to them. He was wearing a sleeping mask to protect his eyes from the light. He was on a ventilator, as his lungs were not quite as mature as they'd first thought. A range of drips from saline to antibiotics were running into his arms. There was a whiteboard behind him:

Name: ? Boy
Date of birth: 16 January 2014
Weight: 812 grams.

Mother: Isabel
Father: Charles

Boxer stared down at him, put his hand into the Perspex cabinet and touched the perfect round head. How was he going to fit this into his life? The boy needed a mother. He shook his head at the impossibility of what Isabel had left him. He found a chair and sat down, got to eye level with the baby. What a way to start your life, he thought. He remembered locals in the Ivory Coast telling him: '*La lutte continue*.' The struggle continues. And yet life for this boy hadn't officially even started and he was already in the midst of a tremendous battle for survival.

'We're very confident,' said the nurse. 'He's a fighter.'

'How do you know?'

'You can see it in them. The ones with a real will,' she said. 'Your son dances. He wants to get on with it.'

She moved away to keep an eye on another even smaller life. A tiny mahogany-coloured baby with feet about half the size of a little finger. This provoked an existential lurch in Boxer. What was he doing here? His mission was to find and kill. Only yesterday he'd seen all manner of destruction. While these nurses were fighting to keep these tiny lives going long enough for them to survive on their own, he was snuffing others out. There was a terrible disconnect. It was madness for him to be here. He stood to leave, shrugged off the gown and made for the door, which he opened on Alyshia.

'Charlie,' she said. 'I'm so glad you're here. I've been worried about you.'

'I just came to see him,' he said. 'I have to leave the country in a few hours' time. I thought ...'

'He's so beautiful, isn't he? I love him. I can't stop looking at him. I was here all day yesterday. Deepak came too. We're addicted. Have you been all right?'

Boxer swallowed at the footage ripping through the gate of his mind: the gun jumping in his outstretched hand, the bullet slamming into Gav's temple behind Louise's head.

'I've been OK,' he said. 'Are you all right, Alyshia? I know what she meant to you.'

Alyshia looked off down the corridor as if she might see her mother coming out of room 574.

'I don't know what I'd do without the baby,' she said.

Mercy had her meeting with the special investigation teams. She flicked through the printout of Powell's phone data as they made their presentations. Hines was right. A lot of names had been blacked out. Even the email traffic seemed minimal, as if plenty had been withheld. She did her best to maintain morale by linking all the personnel who'd been arrested or killed to the various kidnaps the teams were investigating.

Hines dropped in and asked her to come to a meeting at Thames House with all the parents, Ryder Forsyth and the representatives of the intelligence agencies, which was to take place at 11.00. They crossed the river from Vauxhall to Millbank.

'I don't want you to take this badly,' said Hines, 'but I think it better that we don't say anything unless we're addressed.'

'Meaning?'

'If we try to find out what game the CIA are playing, we're not going to do ourselves any favours.'

'Is that some political advice from above?'

'The Metropolitan Police Commissioner in a personal phone call.'

They went up to the meeting room on the third floor. The atmosphere there was one of latent aggression. Sergei Yermilov and Anastasia Casey looked particularly poisonous. Ken Bass appeared to have inside information. There was something comfortable about him that the other parents didn't like, and there was a little distance between him and the rest.

Mercy assumed from what Hines had said to her, and the seniority of the intelligence community present, that they were expecting trouble. Mike Stanfield made the opening statement about what had happened to the £150 million last night. Ray Sutherland was accompanied by a disturbingly hirsute man who, she was later informed, was the mysterious Walden Garfinkle. Clifford Chase, the London CIA chief, had the look of a righteous preacher.

Stanfield finished his presentation by saying how little of the money had been recovered and revealing their current belief that the hostages had been moved outside the UK and that the gang had now dispersed.

'So what makes you think our children aren't in the country any more?' asked Casey. 'That's a serious leap.'

'MI5 has a comprehensive network of agents and informers right across the UK in all communities of all ethnicities. Given the level of alert in the post-kidnap phase, it would have been impossible for them to move the hostages to another location within this country without something leaking,' said Stanfield. 'From the arrests we've made, and the personalities we know are involved, we are talking about a team of people with deep knowledge of the global intelligence communities. They would have known what had to be done.'

'So how do you think they were moved?'

'A shipping container is most likely.'

'And presumably you manned all the ports?'

'Just over forty per cent of container traffic leaves the UK via Felixstowe at a rate of around eleven thousand containers a day. We maintain a significant presence at that port looking for drugs, illegal immigration, firearms and the like. But there's a limit to what you can achieve without very specific intelligence.'

'So where do you think they've taken them?'

'We think it's most likely to be a location in Africa. It's not a long sea journey, and corruption at all levels makes it easier to do things undetected and be protected.'

'And the ransom?' said Yermilov.

'The final communication from the kidnappers, which you've all seen, came a few minutes after the money was blown up in Victoria Park last night,' said Forsyth. 'I've heard nothing more from them.'

'What happened last night was the clearest demonstration I've ever seen of one thing,' said Casey. 'These fuckers are not after our money. So what's the game?'

'You're all powerful people with important government connections and companies that have global reach,' said Stanfield.

'Yeah, blah, blah, blah,' said Casey. 'We know that shit. We also know you're not telling us things. We think there's a bigger game and we're the pawns in it. We want to know what that is. Who's going to tell us about this guy Chuck Powell? What more have you learnt about Conrad Jensen and what he was doing for the US military? We're all right-wingers here, and capitalists, and we've heard about some kind of left-wing conspiracy. What's that? More bullshit to put us off the scent?'

Stanfield gave a long, hard look at the three CIA representatives across the table. Nothing came back.

'It's not as if nothing is happening, Anastasia,' said Forsyth.

'Ryder, you're on our side, I know that. The people we want to hear from are the ones protecting their arses at our expense. The kidnappers who've been caught are all vets from Iraq and Afghanistan. Do they know something? Are they unhappy about some covert action over there? They threatened to execute Ken's daughter and Ryder negotiated a way out.' Casey pointed at the CIA trio. 'You guys had to agree to come clean about the manipulation of intelligence in the run-up to the Iraq war. What does all that shit mean?'

'You're right, Ms Casey,' said Clifford Chase. 'The point about intelligence manipulation is a very complex one when a country is about to go to war. Some of the findings are exaggerated, others are played down. It would not be the first time. We're still in a long debate about Pearl Harbor.

'There's no doubt that there are some very angry US vets who feel badly let down by their country, and more specifically the Bush administration. A lot of them don't know why we went to war. They are attracted by the theories that we invaded Iraq because that's what big business wanted, that we were after oil and influence in the Gulf region, that the Saudis told us to go in there. None of that is true.'

'Are you sure about that?' asked Anastasia Casey. 'The Iraq war cost one point seven trillion dollars. Don't tell me that none of that found its way into American corporate pockets. Kinderman alone earned something like forty billion from Iraq war contracts.'

'We can go into a long discussion about that if you like, Ms Casey, but it will come at the expense of what we're trying to do in this scenario, which is to get your children back. And we'd like that to happen with as little distress to you as possible.'

'What we're getting from you, Mr Chase, is some diluted reassurance and fuck-all hard facts.'

'We are an intelligence agency and we necessarily have to be secretive. We cannot reveal modus operandi or give you reasoning that, if known in the world, might have an impact elsewhere. So we might appear to be obstructive, but believe me, we want to get your kids back safely. That is our objective.'

'You've clearly been to some kind of persuasive speaking school,' said Casey. 'Where I come from in Western Australia, we like people to talk straight with us. The bizarre situation we have here is that our so-called friends are withholding and the kidnappers are telling us how it is. We're just wondering who our real mates are.'

The truck and its forty-foot container rolled off the ferry in Bilbao at 8.30 in the morning and joined the queue for customs clearance. All the hostages had been put back under mild sedation after the crossing. At ten o'clock the container cleared customs and started the slow climb out of Bilbao and up on to the *meseta*, heading south to Burgos.

30

Boxer had flown into Seville on the morning of 18 January, taken an afternoon bus to Algeciras and caught an evening ferry to Ceuta. He'd stayed the night in the Hostal Plaza Ruiz, not far from the ferry terminal.

He wasn't sleeping well, and rather than lie in bed staring at the receding ceiling, he'd got up early and walked around the Spanish enclave on the tip of the north-west peninsula of Africa. It was a cold morning, and as he walked along the front, with the high palm trees and apartment blocks to his right and the port to his left, he didn't mind the mild feeling of deracination he always felt when starting a new job in a different country. This was his first time in Ceuta.

He walked up to the Parque San Amaro and looked across the straits to Spain. It was a clear morning and the Rock of Gibraltar was visible. He thought Ceuta a strange place: neither one thing nor the other, a chunk of Spain balancing nervously on the tip of the Maghreb, an anachronism that had never been righted.

The Bar Madrid was empty at this time. He ordered a coffee, and toast with olive oil and asked after Mercedes Puerta. The guy looked at his watch and rolled his finger round as if it would be a while before she showed. Boxer sat back with the *El País* newspaper and read about *la loteria del viento*, the wind lottery, that had taken place in London the night before last. The barman served his breakfast, saw the headline.

'Incredible,' he said. 'What's that all about? A hundred and eighty million euros blown all over London. Doesn't make sense.

The world's gone crazy. You think you've heard it all, but there's always something crazier.'

Boxer wanted to tell him just how crazy it was, but he was reading the article to see the extent of the media knowledge. It was scant. No mention of what the money was for, the kidnaps. The media blackout had been maintained for the moment. The barman nudged him and pointed at the news on the TV. They were showing footage of the madness on the streets. They'd even sent a Spanish crew, who'd found some young Spaniards, all graduates in their twenties, living in crowded accommodation, all holding down jobs in clothes shops and restaurants, who'd been in the right place at the right time and were waving fans of fifty-pound notes in the air and promising to send money home.

'What a world we live in,' said the barman. 'This is going to be trouble for us. All the Africans will see that and want to come over the fence again, get into Europe, where they throw money up into the wind for the poor people.'

Half an hour later, a woman in her thirties in jeans and a leather jacket came in and the barman nodded her over to Boxer's table. He stood; she kissed him on both cheeks.

'A friend of Omar is a friend of mine,' she said. 'You mind if I have some breakfast, or are you in a hurry?'

She called to the barman. They sat down. Mercedes Puerta was a *morena*: black hair, dark olive skin, brown eyes that weren't afraid to look you straight in the eye and beyond. He'd always liked that about Spanish women, the way they dared to question your soul.

The barman put a strong black *café solo* and a cake in front of her and withdrew.

'So I've made sure everything is going to run smoothly at the border this morning. There won't be any delay for us. I'll drive you to Tétouan and take you to see my partner, Ali Mzoudi.'

'Your business partner?'

She looked at him very carefully.

'Omar has told me nothing about you,' said Boxer. 'If you want to keep it like that, it's no problem for me.'

'I'll tell you in the car, not here,' she said. 'Let's go.'

It was a short walk back to the hotel, where Boxer picked up his case. Before he left his room, he took out €2,000 for the weapon he was going to buy and put it in a money belt around his waist. Mercedes drove him down to the border, which was in a constant state of uproar as Moroccans with vastly overloaded trucks, pickups and donkey carts attempted to get into Ceuta. She connected with her man, who quickly dealt with their passports, Boxer travelling now on Christopher Butler's documents, and inside half an hour they were on the road to Tétouan.

'My partner Ali and I traffic hashish from the Rif to Spain,' said Mercedes. 'That's why he has access to firearms. He will sell you one, but not if you are going to kill his Muslim brothers. He is very devout. If I had to describe him, I would say that he is not quite a jihadist but very close, very anti-Western. His default setting will be not to like you.'

'Thanks for the warning.'

'You will know from the price he gives you whether he finds you acceptable or not.'

Tétouan appeared at the foot of the Rif mountains. A tumble of white cubes rolling down the low hills to the sea. They drove into town, parked in the street outside a rough, battered hotel, where Mercedes paid a glum, cold-looking person in a burnous with hood up to look after the car. She reached into her bag, put a scarf over her head and led the way into the medina. They walked down narrow cobbled streets behind men pushing carts of fresh mint, turnips and oranges, past shops with spices piled in cones of colour and then deeper into narrower streets where people lived. Women, who didn't look at him, held staring children with fingers in their mouths. Mercedes made a call on her mobile and stopped at a wooden door painted blue, which was opened from the inside by an unseen hand.

They went upstairs into a low-ceilinged room with bare wooden beams where a bearded man with blue eyes wearing a white djellaba was sitting at a desk with a glass of mint tea. Mercedes introduced Ali Mzoudi, who put his hand on his chest and bowed his head and then shouted downstairs for some tea to be brought up and served. They spoke in Spanish.

'You're from London?' said Mzoudi.

'That's right.'

'I don't like London.'

'Not many people who live there do either.'

'Better than Paris,' said Mzoudi. 'They're all racists in Paris.'

'And the Spanish?' asked Boxer, looking at Mercedes, nearly amused.

'They don't know what they're doing. They think it's a joke to make monkey noises and throw bananas at footballers. They're children.'

Mzoudi carried on in this vein, going through most European countries before starting on America. Boxer sipped his tea and didn't allow himself to be drawn in. This was business, not social. He was patient. The culture demanded it. It took forty minutes and four glasses of tea for Mzoudi to get past his invective against the USA and, in a natural progression, introduce the word 'gun'.

'Why do you need this weapon?' he asked.

'I have to kill someone.'

That seemed to surprise Mzoudi who'd been expecting something more anodyne like: 'for my protection'.

'I might have to kill more than one person to reach the person I want to kill,' said Boxer. 'None of them will be your fellow Muslims. They are either British or American.'

'What have they done?'

'They have stolen other people's children.'

Mzoudi nodded. He went to the door and gave extensive instructions in Arabic down the stairs, but in a much softer voice than when he'd roared for the tea.

The servant brought two cases into the room and withdrew.

Mzoudi opened the first one.

'What are you looking for?'

'Something light that I can easily carry and hide, but it has to be powerful. I have a Belgian FN 57, which I'm very happy with.'

'Nothing like that here,' said Mzoudi, looking through the pieces. 'I've got a Springfield XD-S nine millimetre, which has been used, but not for killing people, I'm assured. It's light, flat, easy to carry but still holds seven rounds.'

Boxer held out his hand and took the gun, checked the magazine, which was loaded. It was still light. He put on his coat with the gun in the inside pocket. It didn't show. He liked it. He reckoned new in the US this would be around the $600 mark.

'Where did it come from?' he asked.

'An American trafficker who ran out of luck in the Rif.'

'What money do you want for it?'

'A clean gun like that with a box of ammunition ... a thousand euros.'

Boxer nodded. 'I'll give you eight hundred.'

Mzoudi was happy with that. Boxer counted out the money. He tucked the gun into his coat and put the box of ammo in his pocket. They shook hands. He went downstairs while Mercedes and Mzoudi concluded some business. After a few minutes she came down and they left.

The streets were busier than when they'd arrived. The Moroccan day was slow to get off the ground. People were out buying now. There was the smell of coffee, and boys holding trays of tea aloft.

'He liked you,' said Mercedes. 'And he doesn't like many Westerners. Doesn't really like people that much.'

'I could tell,' said Boxer. 'He must like you, though.'

'He needs me,' she said. 'He'd rather not be dealing with a woman. It's purely business, you know. I have an eleven-year-old son back in Ceuta.'

'And a husband?'

'He got killed.'

'Doing your work?'

'I took over from him.'

'Brave.'

'Or crazy maybe.'

'You're worried about your son?'

'Always.'

They got back to the car.

'Omar told me I could put you on a bus to Meknes, but I'll take you there if you want.'

'Only if you can spare the time,' said Boxer. 'It's got to be a three-hour drive or more.'

The truck with the hostages had arrived in Algeciras at 22.00 on 18 January after two changes of driver in Valladolid and Seville. It rolled on to the first ferry of the day to Tangier, which was at four o'clock in the morning. The crossing was two hours and thirty minutes and arrived at 05.30 local time. A large bribe had been paid to the customs officer of the day and the truck was given a cursory inspection, the papers were processed and it was out of the port heading south by seven a.m.

They drove from Tétouan to Chefchaouen, a town on the edge of the Rif with a reputation for quality hashish that was well known to tourists. After that they cut away from the mountains and went through Ouezzane on the way to Meknes.

Mercedes was questioning him about his life and was surprised to find he came from such a conservative background as the army and police.

'I didn't see anything of the ex-cop in you when you were dealing with Ali,' she said.

'I was buying a gun.'

'And what are you doing killing people?'

'I've done twenty years as a kidnap consultant, mostly in difficult places. We don't always take the most orthodox line. We're dealing with criminals. Sometimes the criminals are on both sides of the fence.'

'And killing people?'

'It's not ideal, but given the circumstances, it's the only way.'

'So you've done this before?'

'Only in countries where the rule of law doesn't stand up very well.'

'This may sound strange,' said Mercedes, 'but do you want a job?'

'A job?' said Boxer. 'I'm not a hired killer.'

'Not so much a job, more of a partnership,' said Mercedes. 'I need someone like you in my business.'

'It's not my line of work, drugs,' said Boxer, wondering now what sort of man she saw. 'No offence.'

'I had to ask,' she said. 'Too good to miss, a friend of Omar with the right qualities.'

'You must like your work,' said Boxer. 'You must have made enough money by now not to have to do it any more.'

'I do it because I'd be an idiot not to,' she said. 'I see all these good people, like my parents, working hard to survive, earning their money, paying their taxes, and then a lot of bad people doing nothing but feeding off corruption, getting fat from government money. So this is me redressing the balance. At least that's what I tell myself when I put my make-up on in the morning.'

Boxer laughed. Glad to find others who told themselves things in the mirror.

'Where are you going after Meknes?' she asked.

'Marrakesh, I think. But I'm not sure until I speak to Omar.'

'Do you want a driver?'

'What about your son?'

'My sister is looking after him.'

'I mean, it's not going to be without danger, what I'm doing.'

She shrugged, looked across at him with those direct Spanish eyes.

In Meknes they drove to the edge of the old medina and found the Riad Lahboul, where al-Wannan was staying. There was a message telling Boxer to call straight away on arrival, and they went up to meet al-Wannan on one of the roof terraces.

He was surprised to see Mercedes, but delighted too. They sat down for a light lunch. When they'd finished Mercedes left so they could talk.

'She's sorted you out, Mercedes,' said al-Wannan, in English. 'She's very good. A very strong woman. Not to be underestimated. You know her husband was murdered by gangsters in El Hoceima.'

'She only said he'd been killed.'

'She didn't tell you that she found the men responsible and shot them all dead.'

'No, she didn't,' said Boxer. 'She offered me a job.'

'You must have impressed her.'

'We get along. She's volunteered to drive me to Marrakesh.'

'She knows the place quite well, and some people there. I would accept her offer.'

'Have you got any information on Evan Rampy?'

'You're talking to someone who is a close personal friend of Colonel Ahmed Tsouli of the DST,' said al-Wannan, proud of his connections. 'That's the Direction de la Surveillance du

Territoire. Our MI5. He tells me there is no active file on Evan Rampy.'

'Did they know he was ex-CIA?'

'Yes, but that's no reason to open a file on him. The DST talk to the local police and ask for a report on his activities and if he is behaving like a normal citizen then they have no reason to bother with a file. He's a tourist. He has a riad in the old city where he lives for half the year. He doesn't even have suspect sexual tastes. This man Chuck Powell you mentioned has been to see him several times over the years. Nothing unusual there either.'

'Do they have a record of when he last left the country?'

'Of course. He has been here since the beginning of October, when he flew into Casablanca from London, and he hasn't left the country since.'

'And the photograph matches the one I sent you?'

Al-Wannan handed him a file, which included a passport photo that was recognisably Evan Rampy. There was his address and all known details.

'You look concerned,' he said. 'I'm sure any CIA agent would be able to get in and out of a country unseen.'

'Yes, but Morocco feels like a haven for Rampy. You'd think he'd want to keep his dirty business away from here, not bring it to his doorstep.'

'It's a big country with a lot of isolated places. The mountains. The desert. And it's the closest underdeveloped country to the UK. There are plenty of advantages.'

'I can see that, but it was a complex operation using a lot of people, with many opportunities for leaks, which is what happened,' said Boxer. 'The CIA are behaving very ... awkwardly. They are giving nothing away to the UK investigators. It seems they want to keep the lid on something. And from the kidnappers' side it's as if they've planned it like this, to draw us down here, as if there's going to be some kind of showdown.'

At 16.05, an email was received in the communications centre, arriving simultaneously on DCS Hines and Ryder Forsyth's computers.

333

The ransom demands are as follows:

Anastasia Casey's company Casey Prospecting will make an announcement with the backing of the entire Australian mining industry that after due consideration they have decided that the rights they have been granted represent a contract enabling them to mine a natural resource that is not theirs but rather belongs to all Australian people. To this end they have decided that they should pay a minerals resource rent tax amounting to 30 per cent of revenues, and these monies should be deposited in a sovereign wealth fund for current and future generations.

Hans Pfeiffer of the Deal-O supermarket chain will renounce his Swiss nationality and revert to being German. He will also announce that from now on, his supermarket chains will pay corporation tax on all revenues at the rate of the country in which they make their profits.

Wú Dao-ming will announce that in the spirit of communism, she will guarantee that 15 per cent of the units built in all future development projects will be for social housing. They will be built to the same standard as the rest of the development but will be given to families in need.

Uttar Sarkar will announce that the Amit Sarkar Group will make a one-off payment to a sovereign wealth fund of $8 billion, which represents the difference between the price paid and the market price for all the coal mines currently under their control. They will also join forces with all the other mining companies and commodities companies to announce that from now on they will pay tax of 30 per cent on all their revenues to a sovereign wealth fund.

Sergei Yermilov must openly declare the extent to which he, as a Russian mafia boss, is co-operating with the Russian state, the FSB, SVR and GRU in order to effect arms sales to Syria and Iran with the intention of destabilising the Middle East.

Ken Bass must reveal how the Kinderman Corporation was awarded uncontested contracts for rebuilding Iraq as well as running the entire extraordinary rendition operation on behalf of the US government, and the effect this had on the company's near bankrupt state prior to 2003. He will also release minutes of the meetings between the US government and the defence industry, which clearly indicate that the major source of pressure for a war in Iraq came from this quarter rather than any intelligence on Saddam's WMD.

We realise that these are complex demands, which will require substantial negotiation, and for this reason we are giving you three months to effect them. We guarantee the safety and health of all hostages for that term.

As each ransom demand is met, it will secure the freedom of that hostage, but no hostages will be freed until all demands have been met.

Failure of any one of these ransom demands to be met will result in the death of the hostage in question.

You will only hear from us again as each demand is met to our satisfaction.

We attach separate files that will give additional detail on what we consider to be a satisfactory outcome for each of our demands.

Any attempt to find and rescue the hostages will result in all their deaths.

DCS Hines called Ryder Forsyth as soon as he'd finished the email.

'You seen this?' he asked.

'I'd still be laughing if we hadn't seen such ruthlessness and determination to deliver on all their promises,' said Forsyth.

'I can't see any of these demands being met inside a decade's solid negotiation,' said Hines. 'And even then...'

'So what's it all about? We deliver the expenses to see them blown all over London and now we have a set of impossible ransom demands,' said Forsyth. 'I've never known a kidnap like it.'

'This will come out in the media.'

'I thought the black-out was still in place.'

'They're digging and we're leaking.'

At 15.00 hours, the truck with the hostages pulled into the Zone Industrielle Sidi Ghanem on the outskirts of Marrakesh. It backed into a loading bay in a modern warehouse. The TVs were removed and a coded signal was sent to one of the guards' mobiles. The door within the container was opened from the inside. The hostages were still in a state of mild sedation but were able to move. They were led out of the container and given shower facilities and a change of clothes.

At 18.00, two Toyota Land Cruisers left the warehouse and, skirting the centre of Marrakesh, headed out into the High Atlas on the N9 in the direction of Ouarzazate. There were three hostages in each vehicle, with a driver and two guards. The hostages slept using the guards' shoulders as pillows. They stopped for the night in a small village in the mountains. It was close to freezing. The men made food for the hostages. They spoke to each other in Berber but did not address their captives, who, for the first time, began talking to each other tentatively, exchanging names, finding out nationalities, where they lived, what they were doing and what their parents did.

They all slept on rolled-out mattresses in the same room in which they'd eaten. Siena looked after Yury who'd taken to her because she looked similar to his mother. Karla took care of Sophie, who was getting close to a full meltdown having been separated from Zach, her rag doll frog, for the first time in living memory. The German girl was glad of the company because Wú Gao had embarked on a long conversation about gaming software with Rakesh Sarkar. Two of the Berbers went outside, while two remained awake inside and two slept.

Boxer and Mercedes drove into Marrakesh at just after eight o'clock in the evening. On the way he'd told her in more detail what he was hoping to achieve there. Mercedes had called ahead to a friend of hers who had a large house in Zaouiat Lahdar in the middle of the medina.

She left the car in a parking zone and they walked across the huge square of the Djemaa el-Fnaa market, which at that time of night was full of people and stalls selling food. The smell of boiled goat's head, roast lamb and charcoal was in the air. She hired a boy for a few dirhams to take them to the house through the lacework of narrow streets.

Mercedes' friend, Françoise Lapointe, was a French-Togolese woman in her seventies who looked no older than fifty. She'd lived alone in this big house since her French husband had died seven years ago. She was happy to have company, and especially Mercedes, because then they could have a smoke. According to Mercedes, Françoise also enjoyed a good drink and occasionally liked to slip a little needle into her arm if she could get the heroin.

Françoise led them under horseshoe arches, *muqarnas*, and out into a central patio with two orange trees and an empty oblong tank with a stone heron fountain surrounded by terracotta pots full of greenery. Their rooms, up a narrow, uneven staircase, were decked out in a fantasy Moorish style and were opposite each other across a small bright yellow landing.

They had showers and changed and relaxed for an hour before going down for dinner. On the landing, Mercedes took Boxer by the arm.

'I've spoken to Françoise. She knows all the expats who have houses here in old Marrakesh, including Evan Rampy. She invited him tonight but he couldn't make it. He's asked if we'd like to go to his place for a drink after dinner and I said yes.'

'Is Françoise on our side or neutral?'

'She's with us, completely.'

337

31

They sat on cushions around a low table. A servant girl put couscous and a chicken tagine on the table and left with short, fast steps. Françoise served the food. Boxer poured the wine, a heavy Moroccan red. They ate with the concentration of the very hungry.

'Mercedes tells me you know Evan Rampy,' said Boxer. 'Do you know what he's doing here?'

'He's retired as far as I know. He used to be in the CIA, or so he tells me, but all the expats here have well-developed fictions about their lives,' said Françoise. 'These people and their houses are not so different. On the street they look like nothing. A door in a wall. Then you enter the labyrinth. Evan may have been an agent, I don't know and I don't care.'

'Do you go to his house often?'

'A couple of times a month, sometimes for dinner, other times for a little party with the other permanent residents in Old Marrakesh.'

'Have you ever met new people there?'

'Sometimes he has visitors. Mostly Americans.'

'Any English people?'

'Once or twice.'

Boxer handed her a photo of Conrad Jensen.

'Is that who you're looking for?' she said, handing it back, shaking her head.

'His daughter asked me to find him.'

They finished the main course and the wine. Françoise asked

if they wanted sweet and coffee. The girl came in and cleared the plates. Françoise spoke to her in Arabic. She returned with plates of pineapple, a small cup of coffee for Boxer and a bottle of Poire William from which they all took a small shot.

After dinner they filed out of the house into the empty street. Françoise took them on a confusing walk through the medina until they arrived at another door in a wall. She knocked. Boxer checked his watch: half eleven. An old Moroccan called Mohammed appeared and led them into the house.

Rampy, long-haired, bearded and massive in a white djellaba was standing at the end of a long corridor. Françoise introduced Boxer as Chris Butler.

'Welcome,' he said, and showed them into a room whose floor was overlaid with rugs, scattered with cushions of all sizes and carpeted around the walls to hip height. A hookah smoked quietly in one corner. There was an autumnal smell of apple in the room.

They arranged themselves on the cushions. Rampy sat cross-legged, sucked on the hookah, offered drinks. Mohammed took the order and returned with a tray.

'Sorry I couldn't join you for dinner,' said Rampy. 'A friend of mine was over to discuss a screenplay we've been working on and I'd promised to give him dinner.'

'What are you writing?' asked Boxer.

'A spy thriller based on a story from when I was an agent in the CIA,' said Rampy. 'I'm not sure it'll ever see the light of day.'

'Why not?'

'Too radical. Nobody would support it. If you want Hollywood money you've got to toe the propaganda line, and this script doesn't do that. An American audience is OK watching the CIA do bad things in the country's interest, but not to be a force for evil in the world.'

'Is that what you think they are?' said Mercedes.

'I'd like to tell you otherwise, but personal experience won't let me.'

'Like what?' she asked.

Silence from Rampy, who continued to smoke.

'Did you see that money blown all over London the night before last?' asked Françoise.

339

'Couldn't miss it,' said Rampy. 'I heard on CNN that some notes have gotten as far as Romania.'

The two women talked about it animatedly. Mohammed refreshed their drinks. Rampy sucked on the hookah and maintained a geniality about his person while looking unswervingly at Boxer, who returned his stare, unflinching. There'd been a distinct change of atmosphere in the room. Boxer had been unaware of some earlier tension until now, when it had suddenly relaxed. He realised that he was the main subject of interest in the room. The two women stood.

'We're just going to the ladies' room, if that's OK with you,' said Mercedes.

Rampy smiled. Boxer's eyes followed them as they left. He listened as their footsteps retreated down the hall and heard words exchanged with Mohammed. The front door opened and closed. Silence.

'You doin' all right, Mr Boxer?' said Rampy.

Boxer turned his head slowly, making direct eye contact with Rampy.

'Been waitin' for you a while now. Somethin' held you up?'

Rampy reached under a cushion and produced a SIG Sauer P228 but didn't go to the trouble of pointing it. He just rested it on the cushion next to him, took another puff from the hookah and blew out a cloud of apple smoke.

'Goin' to have to ask you to stand up now, Mr Boxer,' he said, raising himself in one easy motion from his cross-legged position.

Boxer stood. For a big man, Rampy was precise and cat-like in his movements. He frisked Boxer expertly, pressed down on his shoulder to make him sit.

'Understand from Françoise you lookin' for Conrad Jensen,' he said. 'That right?'

'Siobhan asked me to find her father,' said Boxer. 'It seems he's been busy with the same kidnaps you were involved in. So I came to find you, see if you could help. I've got a few questions need answers.'

'Like?'

'Why did Siobhan draw me into this scenario when there was no need for it? You and Conrad set up your elaborate series kidnap. You put pressure on Mercy to collaborate by kidnapping her partner. But then you bring me in, and my daughter, for reasons I don't quite understand.'

'I heard Siobhan got shot,' said Rampy.

'We were rescuing my daughter and your security guy let one off in her direction. Siobhan took it for her.'

'Noble,' said Rampy. 'Not always a word that's been associated with Siobhan. She must have had a thing about your little girl.'

'She did, but that doesn't answer my question.'

'Can't help you there. Not part of my remit. You'll have to take that up with Conrad.'

'I can see now that you've been expecting me.'

'Mercedes is one of ours.'

'And Françoise?'

'Just a good friend.'

'And al-Wannan?'

'No,' said Rampy, grunting as if that was highly unlikely, 'but we know the extent of his network and can introduce people into his orbit.'

'And tonight?'

'Just reeling you in, my friend,' said Rampy. 'We've got a long journey ahead of us, so much as I'd like to talk, we'd better get going.'

Mohammed appeared with Boxer's hand luggage and a hooded burnous. Rampy told him to put it on and led him out of the house into a different street to the one by which they'd entered. They walked out of the medina. Mohammed gave Boxer his case and headed across one of the main arterial roads to the car park. Rampy and Boxer waited by the roadside until Mohammed returned on a BMW F800ST motorbike. He dismounted, handed Rampy a helmet, took another off the back, which he gave to Boxer, and showed him the storage box for his case. Rampy put on the helmet, hitched up his djellaba and mounted the bike, told Boxer to get on the back. They set off at speed and within twenty minutes were heading out of Marrakesh and, under a brilliant starlit night, started riding the twisting hairpin road into the High Atlas.

Rampy was an expert motorcyclist and the BMW had plenty

of power even weighed down by the two men. There should have been some terror involved on the night drive. Rampy rarely slowed down and slipped between cars and trucks with wheel arches practically brushing their shoulders, but Boxer found himself strangely fearless riding pillion. Even though he'd lost control of the situation, he was accepting of fate. He wondered whether this lack of concern came from seeing Isabel lying dead on her hospital bed, and thinking that if she could pass over to the other side, then he could do it too. And with that thought he swallowed hard against a terrible pain, and braced himself against Rampy's enormous back.

It took them just over ninety minutes to get to Ouarzazate, where Rampy filled the tank and two jerrycans stowed in the rear panniers. They sat outside the garage with some truck drivers and drank coffee from a stall in the dark and cold.

'You going to tell me where we're headed?' asked Boxer.

'The desert, my friend,' said Rampy. 'Somewhere in the High Atlas that's clean, empty of people, dry, cold and with a terrible history.'

'What happened up there?'

'You ever read a book called *The Blinding Absence of Light* by Tahar Ben Jelloun?'

'Can't say I have.'

'It's the most extreme prison story ever told and it's based on the experiences of an inmate of an infamous Tazmamart prison near a small village called Er-Rich,' said Rampy. 'Enemies of King Hassan II plotted his assassination at his birthday party and ended up killing a hundred guests but not him. He sent some of them to this prison. They were kept on starvation rations in solitary confinement in underground cells of less than fifty square feet, with ceilings so low they couldn't stand, with just a small air vent, a hole for a toilet and absolutely no light. There were twenty-eight survivors of this ordeal. It lasted nearly twenty years.'

'Is that where we're going?'

'Not far from there.'

'And this is where you're keeping the hostages?'

'They'll be there.'

'Under those sorts of conditions?'

342

'A little more luxurious.'

'And will Conrad be there?'

Rampy didn't answer. He gave Boxer a jacket and a pair of gloves and put some on himself. They got back on the bike and headed east out of Ouazarzate through the Vallée du Dadès, Tinherir and Goulmina, where Rampy refilled the tank from one of the jerrycans. They had enough fuel to reach Er Rachidia, where he filled up again. They headed north. First light was coming up as they rounded the dam of Al-Hassan Addakhil and followed the course of the river, with deep greenery on either side and the mountains turning from violet to yellow to grey as the sun rose higher in the cold blue sky.

In less than an hour they hit the main road to Er-Rich, but Rampy turned away from the town, heading east. After twenty kilometres he came off the tarmacked road on to a graded surface, which turned into a rough track, and wound slowly up into the mountains until they reached a set of low cubic buildings set into rocks of exactly the same colour. These buildings were masked from the road by craggy outcrops and were only visible once Rampy pulled up in the courtyard in front of them.

They dismounted. There was a clear and empty view down the slope to the main road they'd just left. The wind was cutting through Boxer's jacket and the burnous. Rampy wheeled the bike into one of the low buildings. As he shut the door behind him, Boxer could see that there were a couple of all-terrain dirt bikes. Rampy beckoned him into an adjoining building. He opened the door and guided him in with his finger to his lips.

Sitting on the floor cross-legged in the middle of the room with his eyes shut was Conrad Jensen.

32

Rampy pointed to a space on the carpet opposite Jensen and went to a galley kitchen at the back of the room to make some mint tea. The main room had only a single window with a closed shutter through which two cracks of sunlight cast white bars on to the wall and ceiling. Boxer lowered himself to the floor, which was covered with overlapping carpets, and studied the perfect calm of the face in front of him.

He'd been a long time waiting for this moment and was surprised to find that the anger he'd readily summoned in London was now more difficult to come by. The distance from the turmoil of modern life, the presence of time and space, the cleanliness of the mountain air, the tranquillity of the room and the meditative serenity of the man before him were not conducive to extreme emotions.

Jensen's face was bearded, as it had been in the photo Siobhan had sent him, but perhaps a little leaner. The hair was longer. What had been missing from the photo was the overall impression of the man. He looked barely ten years older than Boxer. His body was taut, hard and exuded vigour even in his state of repose. He sat with his shoulders back, chest open, torso straight and chin raised. He had beautiful hands, which hung over his knees, the long fingers not quite brushing the floor. He looked heroic, like a man others would follow willingly into battle.

With a sudden intake of breath through his nose, Jensen's eyes opened and fell immediately on Boxer. In the light of the room they weren't as absolutely blue as Deacon had described,

344

but rather aquamarine, which somehow rewarded the man's face with an expression of curiosity and kindness.

'You've done us a great service,' he said.

'I have?'

'Bringing people out of the woodwork.'

'People?'

'Our erstwhile employers,' said Jensen, cautious, accepting mint tea from Rampy, who handed a glass to Boxer as well.

'You mean the CIA?' said Boxer. 'Is that what this has been all about? Some sort of industrial relations dispute?'

'Depends how you look at it,' said Jensen. 'People behave in strange ways when they feel power being taken from their grasp. Nobody ever hands that over without a fight. There's ugliness, a brutal reaction that comes from desperation. Our intention has been to arrest things before they got totally out of control.'

'So what's the big idea?' asked Boxer. 'Blow money back to the disenfranchised, force the club members of the elite to reveal all and co-operate?'

'That's the sideshow,' said Jensen. 'There always has to be some entertainment, some shock and awe, to keep the media and their catatonic population amused while we get on with the real business at hand.'

'Which is what? Arresting some kind of movement within the CIA?' said Boxer. 'I suppose as an ex-contractor you're in a good position to do that.'

'It's been a long time in the planning,' said Jensen. 'And it's not only about the CIA. They're just one of the instruments in the orchestra. Because we know their structure and how they work, we're using them to send a message to the conductor.'

'The conductor?'

'When the richest one per cent own forty per cent of a nation's wealth, and growing, it doesn't happen by accident. When the Democrats get into power and yet all their policies contribute to this expanding inequality, it doesn't happen by accident.'

'So, a right-wing conspiracy?'

'I don't think it's so much about politics.'

'Greed ... for money and power?'

'That's just human nature.'

'Then what?'

Jensen looked at him, his eyes now piercing, seeking out trust and deciding Boxer wasn't ready. He changed direction.

'A lot of servicemen were enraged when they thought that more than a hundred thousand civilians and four and a half thousand soldiers had died in Iraq so that a handful of people could make themselves rich. In the run-up to that war, something had happened to the mind and spirit of the American administration. Nobody even stopped to think what was taking place. Not even me … until a couple of years ago.'

'What happened then?'

'As everybody now knows, we were already spying on the world through activity on the internet. That had been going on for ten years or more. I wrote the software. Then we started spying on our friends. With my European contacts I was asked to recruit people close to Cameron, Merkel and Hollande, install phone bugs, take copies of minutes of top-secret policy meetings. And then the killing started.'

'The killing?'

'People who were considered to be obstructive to American interests, or rather the interests of those orchestrating the running of the US administration, were eliminated. They might be journalists researching major US companies that had avoided paying taxes; software developers who'd found a way of tracking laundered money; engineers who were investigating the long-term dangers of fracking, tar sands extraction or even culpability in a major oil spill. I pieced together the intelligence reports and their consequences, started drawing conclusions and decided it had to stop, not just in the US, but globally. This is the conclusion of phase one.'

'What is?'

'The reason we've drawn you down here.'

'Which is?'

'To smoke out the sons of bitches and bring them into the killing zone.'

'Who exactly are these sons of bitches?'

Jensen stared into him again with eyes even bluer and colder. Still he wasn't ready.

'A CIA cell of extreme right-wing infiltrators who want to have a powerful influence on government policy.'

Boxer woke up to find that the two bars of light on the wall had shifted around the room. Rampy and Jensen were sitting cross-legged on the floor, sipping tea and looking down on his supine form as if he'd been the subject of some analysis. He must have slept for a couple of hours and had no recollection of how it had happened. He'd been exhausted after the all-night drive from Marrakesh, but not even that would have been enough to over-whelm the adrenalin in his system. Had they drugged him? Boxer checked his watch – 11.00 a.m. Rampy poured him some tea and left the room.

Jensen stroked his beard with thumb and forefinger.

'You did well to find me,' he said.

'I don't think I can take much credit for that.'

'You followed the clues presented to you.'

'Did Rampy tell you that Siobhan didn't make it?'

'Her instructions were to take full responsibility for Amy,' said Jensen. 'She was the one who wanted her along for the ride, said it would make her happy, and she hadn't had much of that in her life.'

'She introduced herself as your daughter, but she told Amy something different.'

'Siobhan was a contractor to the CIA, who'd made rather unpleasant use of her,' said Jensen. 'Some marks have extreme sexual tastes and Siobhan was good at satisfying them. I suspect Amy was one of the few real people Siobhan had met in her life and she was probably ... enchanted by her.'

'As she was by you.'

'Enchanted is too romantic a word. I just looked after her. Gave her work that wasn't abusive, tried to help her make sense of who she was. She wanted me to be something more to her, a father, but I didn't think that was a good idea.'

'And Tanya Birch? Was she just a conduit into the arms of Walden Garfinkle?'

'She's on the team – an old MI6 agent who, like your friend Deacon, found herself complicit in extraordinary rendition. Some

347

were able to live with it, others weren't. She got out.'

'You've done a pretty good job of extraordinary rendition yourself, complete with waterboarding and other extremes.'

'We were far more concerned with introducing the notion of powerlessness to the consummately powerful,' said Jensen. 'And as you know, those who control the media take control of the minds watching it. We trust in so much of what we see. It's an affecting but deceptive means of communication. Of course, none of those punishments really happened, but the parents' minds were primed to believe it, so they did.'

'And blowing up the money?'

'A spectacular act of redistribution,' said Jensen. 'Have you been checking the world's media recently? We sent a press release to the leading newspapers about the ransom demands.'

'And you seriously think you're going to achieve any of those demands?'

'We're using the media in every possible way, this time to increase the pressure of public opinion to make things change,' said Jensen. 'The Norwegian government holds a sovereign wealth fund from North Sea oil with a million dollars per Norwegian in it. So it's not as if it's impossible.'

'But that wasn't the real point of the exercise, was it?'

'Just as kidnapping the kids and asking for money wasn't what we were after,' said Jensen. 'Our aim is to smoke out as many guys from this rogue cell as we can and remove them from the game. And, as we know, when extraordinary things happen in the media, it's to take our eye away from the really important matters that make a difference to the way we live. I enjoyed the irony of that.'

'Was that why I was directed to Walden Garfinkle?'

'Walden was already uneasy. You coming along with the additional information made him think that we were going to blow the whole thing open. He's had to mobilise and act. You don't know what's been going on behind your back in London, Ceuta, Tétouan, Meknes and Marrakesh.'

'Like what?'

'These rogue players have been taking our people out of the game.'

'Are you expecting to see Garfinkle up here?'

'That would be a result, but an unlikely one,' said Jensen. 'He's a very important figure in the control of personnel within the CIA. He recruits agents to the cause. So we need to get to him, and we will … eventually.'

'Does that mean you've got support from within the CIA to do this sort of thing?'

'Evan said you wanted to know why you're here?' said Jensen, ignoring the question.

'It seemed perverse for Siobhan to ask me to find you when you didn't want or need to be found.'

'But now you know you were instrumental in joining things up.'

'But why me? My foundation doesn't operate on that remit. I could easily have turned you down.'

'But you didn't. And if you had, we'd have found another way of involving you,' said Jensen. 'Think about it. Why did you go and see Martin Fox?'

Something cold flowed over Boxer's skin. He sipped his hot tea, looked at the bars of light on the wall and ceiling.

'And I'm very sorry about Isabel,' said Jensen, standing up, putting his hand on Boxer's shoulder. 'My condolences. That must have been a terrible shock.'

They looked into each other's eyes and Boxer saw a genuine hurt there for him. And he realised that since he'd been on the road, apart from last night riding pillion with Rampy, he hadn't thought about Isabel. She didn't belong in this life up here in the High Atlas with these strange men and their bizarre history.

'Thank you,' said Boxer, 'for taking the trouble to say that.'

'We're not very good at expressing our sorrow for someone's loss,' said Jensen, returning to his seat. 'Even in this era of new sentimentality.'

Boxer didn't miss the humanity and the irony. He could still feel the electricity of the man's touch on his shoulder. He couldn't help but be drawn to him.

'It sounds as if you want me to do something for you,' he said. 'That finding you was not the real purpose of the … mission.'

'Finding me has its importance,' said Jensen. 'I need people with talent that I can trust.'

349

'But you don't know me.'

'You've been observed at first hand during this mission,' said Jensen. 'You've done everything expected of you without wavering for a moment, and you've done it under the extreme duress of loss, but then that does have an odd way of focusing the mind.'

'Do you know why I came here, why I had to find you?'

'Probably you were angry and wanted to kill me. That would not be unusual.'

'Why should I believe you?' said Boxer, baffled by the ordinariness of that statement.

'You don't have to. You'll be able to talk to the hostages to verify the way they've been treated. You're also going to see the showdown. We're waiting for them to move in.'

'Who are "they"?'

'Ray Sutherland has access to highly sensitive intelligence in the UK, Europe and Russia. The way he's operated throughout these kidnaps is indicative of the man he is. He was responsible for installing the tracking devices in the money and on the truck without asking the parents, and knowing full well that it would result in the death of someone's child. He is the prime target of this exercise. We're hoping he won't be alone,' said Jensen. 'Ask Mercy how helpful Sutherland has been. Find out from your friend Simon Deacon what the CIA head of counter intelligence for the UK, Europe and Russia contributed to the meetings in Thames House.'

'Are you expecting some surprise guest appearances?'

'That's what we always hope for in these things,' said Jensen. 'We'd be happy if they sent Ryder Forsyth up here.'

'Ryder?'

'That would be a coup for us,' said Jensen. 'We're hoping that the lure of freeing the hostages and being the hero will be too strong for him to resist.'

'Ryder is with them?'

'That's why Kinderman positioned him at the centre of the kidnaps.'

'Did you know that I knew him from my time in the Staffords?'

'Just one of the reasons why we wanted you involved.'

'You avoided answering my question about the support you're getting from within the CIA for this action ...'

'You don't get to know that until you're on the inside,' said Jensen. 'This isn't something the agency can do themselves. They've had to employ trusted outside contractors. That's all you need to know.'

'But you can't just want me because I knew Ryder. There must be plenty of highly trained people out there who know him better than me and can do the work you want done.'

Boxer looked up to find Jensen's eyes on him, not just resting on the outside, but boring in.

'You're a good man who doesn't have a problem with killing bad guys.'

He wanted to question that, not just because nobody had ever described him like that before, but because he felt certain that Jensen had left out something crucial. Rampy returned.

'There's somebody out there,' he said. 'Just turned off the tarmac.'

Jensen beckoned Boxer outside and up some steps on to a flat roof where there was a telescope set up and some binoculars on a low wall. On the floor, resting on its case, was a sniper's rifle fully assembled with sights, bipod, suppressor and a small magazine inserted, with four others as backup. They kept their heads down. Rampy realigned the telescope and Jensen looked through it, nodding.

'The advance party,' he said.

'They're pulling up,' said Rampy, looking though the binoculars. 'They've seen the bike tracks on the dirt road. Let's see who we've got here.'

All Boxer could see was an approaching vehicle in a cloud of dust maybe four kilometres away on the painfully open expanse of the wide valley. It was winter light in a merciless blue sky. The valley was grassless and relentlessly grey, with only the occasional stubborn tree. The dust died down around the stationary vehicle. The passenger got out.

'Sutherland,' said Jensen.

'Who's he brought with him?' asked Rampy.

'I can't see the driver,' said Jensen. 'Sutherland's wearing body armour.'

'Not even I'd take a shot from two and a half miles away,' said Rampy. 'Anybody in the back seat?'

'Too difficult to see,' said Jensen. 'He's checking us out now.'

Rampy lay down on the floor, relaxed, silent.

'He's getting back in the vehicle. They're turning round.'

They stood up and went back downstairs, had tea and something to eat.

'Where are the hostages?' asked Boxer.

Jensen nodded to Rampy, who led him out and across to another building.

'We had to do this, you know, just so those guys didn't lay down some mortar fire and take us out. Believe me, they wouldn't hesitate. This way, they've got to come up and take us on face to face.'

Rampy unlocked the door to an anteroom with a basic kitchen where two Berbers were preparing food. He showed him into another room where the six hostages were lying and sitting around and left him there. There was no tension that the fear of the unpredictable would normally produce in a group like this. Siena Casey and Rakesh Sarkar were playing cards. Wú Gao and Karla Pfeiffer were lying on the floor next to each other, reading. Yury Yermilov and Sophie Railton-Bass were involved in some elaborate fantasy.

'My name is Charlie Boxer,' he said. 'I've come to get you out of here.'

They all looked up, disbelieving.

'Are any of you hurt?'

They shook their heads.

'Have any of you been mistreated by the people who kidnapped you?'

'We've been treated very well,' said Karla Pfeiffer.

'Better than at home,' said Siena, and the older ones laughed.

Sophie came up to him, gave her name.

'Have you spoken to my mum?' she asked.

'She's fine,' said Boxer. 'She's very worried about you, but she's doing well.'

She hugged him around the legs. He rested his hands on her head.

'All your parents have been doing everything they can to ensure your safety,' he said.

'Believe it,' said Rakesh Sarkar.

More grunts of laughter.

'There's not long to go now,' said Boxer. 'Whatever you hear going on outside you must always stay in here.'

Rampy called him out. He left the building and they walked back to where Jensen was waiting. Rampy went up on to the roof.

'Satisfied?' asked Jensen.

'Have you told them anything?'

'It's better they don't know what's going on.'

'And now?'

'We wait. Evan will tell us when Sutherland comes back.'

In the middle of the afternoon, Rampy came down to tell them Sutherland had returned. They watched from the roof. This time the vehicle was a covered pickup. It stopped at the same point where the graded road turned into dirt track, and turned round. Two bodies were rolled out the back and the pickup pulled away.

'Can't see who they are,' said Jensen. 'They're hooded.'

'You want me to go down there?' asked Rampy.

'Give it some time, then check them out.'

Fifteen minutes later, Rampy took a dirt bike down to the bodies. He laid one over the front and the other over the back and drove slowly back up the track. He offloaded them in the courtyard and put the dirt bike away. Jensen lifted the hoods. The first body was that of Françoise Lapointe; the second was Mercedes Puerta. Françoise had an eye put out and cigarette burns all over her face and back. She'd been shot in the forehead. Mercedes no longer had any fingernails, but ripped and bloodied stubs, and from the rope burn around her neck, she'd been garrotted or hanged. There was a note attached to her shirt, which Jensen read out loud.

'"You can still walk away from this. Just leave the hostages and clear out. We guarantee you free passage to the desert border south of Bouanane and you can take your chances with the Algerians. If you agree, put a white sheet on the rocks and we'll let you ride out under cover of darkness."'

'Anybody put their name to that?' asked Rampy.

'Unsigned,' said Jensen, who turned to Boxer. 'You think that's any way for the head of counter intelligence for the UK, Europe and Russia to behave?'

Rampy called out to one of the Berbers and they put the bodies in the basement of one of the disused buildings.

They left Boxer alone for the rest of the afternoon to think about what he'd just seen. Jensen and Rampy took it in turns to keep watch and sleep until the light started to fade and the cold descended.

'Earlier you talked about a conductor,' said Boxer. 'Do you know who he is? And if so, why don't you set about eliminating him rather than the foot soldiers?'

'We're not talking about one person,' said Jensen. 'They're a group of influential businessmen, politicians, religious leaders and thinkers.'

'A group with a cause normally has a name.'

This time Jensen was ready to come through.

'They call themselves the ARC – pronounced Ark. The American Republic of Christians. They like the biblical idea of being a safe ship in the flood. They're a radical group of fundamentalists who made a decision after 9/11 to ensure the integrity of the United States and the beliefs of the founding fathers. The only problem is that they decided it was best not to do it in a democratic way, but rather by stealth, by infiltrating organisations with the power to create or heavily influence policy. And like the Hydra, if you cut off one head, two more will grow. Our aim is to make it more difficult for them to operate within the intelligence community, and the best way to do that is by cleaning our own back yard.'

354

33

As dusk was falling, Rampy came down from the roof.

'We've got some activity out there now.'

They went upstairs. In the grey light, the landscape had become darker. Nothing was visible to the naked eye, but the telescope was fitted with a night sight and the covered pickup could be seen making its way up the dirt track.

'Let them come in,' said Jensen. 'We'll get armed up.'

In the carpeted room Rampy and Jensen opened a chest and strapped ammunition belts around them stuffed with spare 9mm magazines. They took two handguns each.

'You seen enough?' asked Jensen. 'Or are you still undecided?'

'No, I'm with you,' said Boxer, struck by Jensen's humanity, his insight, and sure that, wherever his loyalties lay, it wasn't with the people in the pickup.

'You don't have to get involved in the battle we're fighting here,' said Rampy. 'I see you've got your own weapon in your case but with limited ammo, so you might want something more for your own protection.'

'What happens if you two don't make it out of here?'

'You came here because of the hostages. You brought the ARC guys here through your own investigative talent,' said Rampy. 'As far as they're concerned, your motives are still good.'

'I mean if you don't succeed,' said Boxer. 'Is that the end of the road?'

'You remember Louise?' said Jensen. 'She disappeared, but not totally, and she spoke very highly of you. You'll hear from her and she will know what to do.'

Rampy handed Boxer his case and gave him another gun and some spare magazines.

'Stay in here for as long as you can. There's a back way out through that door.'

They switched off the light and went outside. The pickup's engine was audible. Boxer camouflaged himself with large cushions, which he propped up around him and sat by the window looking through the crack of the shutter. It was dark now. He could just make out the two men standing in the courtyard, waiting. As the pickup, with no lights on, rounded the corner, Rampy's hand twitched. Lights came on in the courtyard – an empty circle into which the pickup rolled and halted. The engine continued to run and then cut.

Silence.

A hand came out of the window.

'Are we free to come out and talk?'

'Sure,' said Jensen.

'Are we allowed to see you?'

'You show yourselves and we'll follow.'

Sutherland got out of the driver's side, stood under the light, his slightly closed eye making him look as if he was already taking aim. Clifford Chase climbed down from the passenger side with the righteous arrogance of a man with a higher power on his side. They were both wearing fatigues and flak jackets. Rampy and Jensen stepped into the circle of light.

'We're here to negotiate,' said Sutherland.

'What's there to negotiate?' asked Rampy.

'Your fees,' said Sutherland. 'That's why we've brought Ken with us.'

Ken Bass stepped out of the rear door, passenger side.

'We were already beyond that point even before you sent us Françoise Lapointe and Mercedes Puerta,' said Jensen.

'The Moroccans got to them before we could intervene,' said Sutherland. 'You know what they're like, Conrad.'

'I know you better.'

'What's it going to take?' said Sutherland. 'Ken has a satellite phone and he can make an immediate transfer. You just have to give me the numbers.'

'There are no possible numbers,' said Jensen. 'You must know that by now.'

'You've taken our money before,' said Bass. 'What's so different now?'

'You've gone too far,' said Jensen.

'What could go further than extraordinary rendition?' asked Sutherland. 'You didn't have a problem with that. You accessed excellent intelligence. You saved American lives.'

'We've already seen the Senate report due out at the end of the year,' said Jensen. 'That and Benghazi: blocking intelligence so our own people got killed in the hope of making the Secretary of State look so bad she'd be forced to stand down from running for president.'

'We were looking at sixteen years of Democrat rule. It would have changed America into a socialist state. Something had to be done,' said Sutherland. 'And Con, you've got no idea how powerful we already are. You think that by getting rid of us you'll be arresting the movement? Think again. We're everywhere, right through the system. If I was you, I'd take what you can and get out with your hide intact.'

Boxer glanced back as the door at the end of the room opened and somebody came in. From the cracks of light penetrating the room, he could make out a heavily built man, gun in hand, striding across the room. Somebody was up on the roof as well. Boxer crouched behind the cushions. The heavily built man paused, listened, and then ripped open the front door. He raised the gun to fire into the courtyard. Boxer stood and shot him twice in quick succession hitting him first in the shoulder so the man dropped his gun and following it with a chest shot.

Gunfire roared outside.

The two Berbers who'd been guarding the hostages left their building and ran into the darkness. Rakesh Sarkar wanted to follow.

'Remember what he said. We stay here,' said Karla.

The little ones were squeaking with fear. There was nothing to hide behind in the room. They retreated to the corner, pulling their mattresses with them, which they piled over their trembling bodies.

Boxer looked out of the door to see Rampy already face down on the ground, his upper half in the circle of light. Sutherland had been flung back on to the bonnet of the pickup with a gun still hanging from his slack hand, his cheek obliterated by a bullet taken in the face. Clifford Chase was lying on his back with a large burgeoning stain on the ground behind his head. No one else was visible. Gunfire continued around the courtyard. Boxer ran up the steps, keeping low, saw a slim blonde guy kneeling at the wall, both hands clasped around a handgun, shoulder jolting with the recoil. Boxer fired once. The man went down, holding on to his neck. Four more steps and Boxer was over him. Black blood was squeezing through the man's fingers. A single head shot finished it.

And then silence.

'You all right, Charlie?' said Jensen, from below.

'Everything's fine.'

'One more to go. Ken Bass.'

Boxer looked down over the wall. Three dead in the circle of light. He moved to the side of the roof near the steps, surveyed the night. Keeping low, he ran to the back of the building, thinking this was how the two men he'd shot had come in. There was a steep but climbable rock face, and halfway up it was a man on all fours, crabbing his way up to a ridge. Boxer tried to take aim in the poor light and let off a shot, heard it ricochet off the rock face. The man worked harder, faster, and disappeared over the ridge.

'He's at the back here,' shouted Boxer. 'Just gone over the ridge.'

'You have to kill him,' said Jensen. 'There must be no surviving witnesses from their side. This is unfinished business.'

Boxer threw himself off the roof, landed on the rock face and powered up to the ridge, put his head over the top. No light, just stars in a black firmament and a cold wind blasting across the rock. He scoured the landscape for movement, his eyes getting accustomed by the second. A twitch of the night off to his left and he saw Bass running and stumbling, not caring, crazed with fear, heading across a basin of rock and up to another ridge. Boxer checked the terrain and dropped down into the basin. Bass had reached the ridge and appeared not to like what he saw over the other side. He was jogging, falling over, clambering to his right now, heading for a pinnacle of rocks. Boxer changed direction and made for the other side of the pinnacle, got up there and started to work his way round. He could hear Bass coming towards him, unknowing. He waited, gun at his side, until Bass was within a few metres of him.

'Stop,' he said.

But an uncontrollable terror had already seized Bass and he immediately turned and ran, arms flailing, back the way he'd come. He hit the ridge, tripped and disappeared into the darkness with a protracted scream that was interrupted by two thuds as his body made damaging contact with the rock face, followed by a final crunch and then silence apart from the dry, cold, howling wind.

Boxer checked over the ridge but couldn't make out where Bass had landed. He went back to the hostages' building, found them huddled under the mattresses, told them it was all over, they were safe, but to stay put for the moment. He went back to the courtyard where Jensen had lined up four bodies in the circle of light. Rampy had been left where he'd fallen, only rolled over, face up. Jensen was checking the covered back of the pickup. He came round from behind the vehicle.

'Is Rampy dead?' said Boxer.

'He was unlucky,' said Jensen. 'He caught a ricochet in the eye.'

'Did you get who you wanted?'

'Ray Sutherland was the one we were after. He brought along Clifford Chase, the chief of the London office of the CIA, who we were not expecting. We were hoping Sutherland would bring Ryder with him for protection, but maybe he was told to keep him for another day. The other two are just soldiers.'

Jensen bent down and picked up the satellite phone that had fallen from Bass's hand, threw it at Boxer.

'Use that to bring in the cavalry. Maybe your friend from MI6 would be best for this.

'What about you?'

'I'll take my chances across the desert through Mauritania, lose myself in black Africa for a while.'

'And what do I do?'

'You'll have your hands full with the fallout from this for a bit,' said Jensen, moving off towards the building with the dirt bikes. He kicked open the door, threw his leg over one of the bikes, tucked the gun he'd used into his belt. 'And then you wait for Louise to make contact. We'll need you to deal with Ryder. I'll work out the details and she'll brief you.'

'But when?'

'When we're ready.'

'And why should I do this for you?' asked Boxer, surprised at himself, his sudden motivation to help this man in his strange quest.

'You're asking *me* that?' said Jensen, nearly amused.

'There was something you didn't tell me when you gave your reason for choosing me. I mean, there are plenty of good people out there prepared to kill bad guys, so why me?'

'I know you, Charlie.'

'I don't think so. I'd remember you if we'd met.'

'You *do* know me,' said Jensen, reaching back for the helmet.

Boxer looked at him hard, trying find him amongst all the faces he'd ever known.

'Where from?'

'I was the man you always thought of as your father, until I left you,' said Jensen. 'David Tate. Remember him?'

'I thought I did,' said Boxer, stunned.

Jensen strapped on the helmet, kick-started the bike.

'Why should I believe you?' roared Boxer, over the blat of the engine.

'Do something for me when you get back to London,' said Jensen, revving the engine. 'You're still in the flat which used to be the top floor of our family home. You remember the room I used as my study? Take a look under the floorboards. You'll find a tape there. All the answers are in it.'

He flicked the bike into gear, opened the throttle, took off out of the building, flashing past Boxer, round behind the back of the pickup, out of the circle of light and into the dark.

34

This was the day, ninety-two days after Isabel's admission for the emergency C-section, that Boxer took delivery of his son, weighing in at five pounds and three ounces, to bring him home. He'd called him Jamie. He didn't know why. He just liked the sound of Jamie Boxer. The baby had been breathing on his own since the middle of February, when he'd also taken to kicking his legs out as if he needed to make progress out of the aquarium of his incubator. Boxer had been to see him every day since he'd got back from Morocco.

It had not been easy to extricate himself from that mess. The first call he'd made on the satellite phone that Jensen had thrown him was to Simon Deacon. He was the only person he could rely on completely who could influence the outcome of his predicament. Deacon had taken the number and told him to await further instructions. Boxer then wiped the gun he'd used to kill the two CIA operatives and tucked it into Rampy's belt.

As soon as Boxer had straightened out the scene to his satisfaction he'd gone to see the hostages again and called them together. He stood amongst them, told them to hug each other and him. They began to cry at the release from shock and stress. He got the two girls to look after Sophie and Yury while Wú Gao and Rakesh Sarkar went with him to make mint tea. He made them sing and tell each other stories and stayed with them until they were all sleeping.

At dawn, two helicopters landed in the valley and four army

361

vehicles arrived and drove up to where Boxer was waiting for them on the roof of the main building. A man from the Moroccan secret service, the Direction de la Surveillance du Territoire, introduced himself as Youness Benjelloun. He said they were going to remove the bodies first and take them to a nearby military base. Boxer told him about the bodies of Mercedes Puerta and Françoise Lapointe and led him up the rock face behind the building to point out where Ken Bass's body had fallen a hundred feet below.

Once the bodies in the compound had been removed, the hostages were led out and driven down to the helicopters, which flew them to a military base on the outskirts of Marrakesh. Boxer was kept separate from them. Later he found out that a private jet had come in from London City airport during the early evening and taken them all back to the UK.

Boxer's debrief started on the night they brought him in. It was not as civilised as he'd expected. As Benjelloun set about breaking him down through a process of sleep deprivation with loud music, bright light, freezing conditions, no bedding, poor food, no washing facilities and constant interrogation, he realised that his role in the scenario was far from clear to the DST.

First Benjelloun wanted to know what he'd been doing up there in the High Atlas using a passport belonging to Chris Butler. Boxer didn't lie, he just omitted things: how he knew Mercedes, buying the gun from Ali Mzoudi, meeting al-Wannan. His story was looking thin. Benjelloun set to work on him. He wanted to know how he'd found out about Rampy's involvement and the Moroccan connection. He spent several days wearing down Boxer's considerable resistance to revealing that the connection to Mercedes Puerta had been Omar al-Wannan. He jabbed and poked him about his relationship with Françoise Lapointe, then hit him with the bombshell that they'd arrested Ali Mzoudi, who under heavy interrogation had admitted to supplying Boxer with a Springfield XD-S 9mm, which was one of the weapons found on the body of Evan Rampy. That opened up a whole new avenue of investigation, as Benjelloun now wanted his confession that his role had not been as passive as he'd maintained.

Boxer told him of his intention to kill Jensen and free the hostages, but with Mercedes and Françoise dead, he had no way of proving the one incontrovertible truth as to why he had been at the scene: Rampy had kidnapped him and taken his weapon. Before the hostages had been flown out they'd revealed that Rampy had brought Boxer into the room where they were being held, and he had told them he was going to get them out of there. This was a source of great confusion to Benjelloun. Whose side was Boxer on?

Benjelloun also didn't believe that Jensen and Rampy were straightforward kidnappers. The money blowing up in London, the organisation required to deliver the hostages to the High Atlas and the characters involved all led him to believe there was a subtext that Boxer was not revealing.

'You're not getting out of here,' said Benjelloun, 'until you come clean about Jensen and Rampy's objectives and your own role in this business.'

Boxer's second week in the military base outside Marrakesh was one of the most uncomfortable of his life. He still refused to admit that he had a hand in any of the killings, but realised that Benjelloun had to be thrown a bone. He told him Jensen's story: that he was acting for the CIA in order to wipe out a politically motivated rogue cell within the agency. Benjelloun asked him why he hadn't told him this before and Boxer said that it sounded too fantastic, that he wouldn't believe him.

'You're right,' said Benjelloun. 'I don't.'

On 8 February, Simon Deacon was finally allowed to see him.

'We've done everything we can from our side,' said Deacon, after they'd hugged and Boxer had apologised for his beard and high odour. 'But the CIA won't back up the story Jensen's fed you about this rogue cell. They say it's a complete fabrication.'

'Have they offered an explanation for Jensen's behaviour?'

'Only that he's an ex-contractor turned crackpot.'

'I suppose they have to,' said Boxer. 'Can't go around admitting the agency's been compromised. What did they have to say about the four CIA operatives and Ken Bass found dead in the High Atlas?'

'They were on a rescue mission to free the hostages.'

'What's your reading of it in MI6?'

'We're getting the same confirmation through our CIA

channels,' said Deacon. 'They were the good guys.'

'What about you?'

'I'm going to ask you a question as your friend,' said Deacon. 'What were you doing out there?'

'I've told Benjelloun a hundred times over: I went to kill Conrad Jensen and free the hostages. I got the lead about Rampy from Kushner and pursued it. Everything else that happened was out of my control once Rampy kidnapped me in Marrakesh. From that moment onwards I can only tell you what I saw and what I was told. But where does that leave me as the lone survivor?'

'I'll be honest with you,' said Deacon. 'You're in a deep hole, but we'll see what we can do.'

Three days later he was free. He wasn't sure what had happened but he could sense that Benjelloun wasn't happy about it, that the order had come from well above his head. On his arrival in London, five kilos lighter, Deacon met him off the plane. He too was reticent, said it had been the result of a combination of diplomacy and a cover story they'd invented about him acting for MI6. He was taken into Vauxhall Cross for two days of debriefing, staying with Deacon and not communicating with anybody in the outside world.

They released him in time for Isabel's delayed funeral on 12 February. The service was held at St Mary Abbots church, and afterwards there was a wake at the Orangery paid for by Frank D'Cruz.

It was the first time Boxer had seen Amy, Mercy and Alleyne since that night in Streatham three weeks ago. He was still physically weak and the emotional funeral, with more than two hundred people in attendance, followed by their reunion left him exhausted. Alyshia and Deepak Mistry came over to talk to Mercy, Amy and Marcus about the baby. They'd all been seeing each other during their regular visits to the neonatal ICU. Mercy took Boxer off for a walk in the cold, damp gardens where she told him about George Papadopoulos getting shot.

'He lost a kidney and he had some paralysis in his legs, but, thank God, that's cleared up. He took his first steps a couple of days ago.'

'Is he going to get back to work?'

'Not for a bit. A few months, I'd have thought, and then maybe not in the special investigations unit.'

'And Amy? How's she been?'

'I took her back to the shrink. That thing with Siobhan's changed her. Something ... intense went on in there,' said Mercy, tapping her temple. 'I thought she should talk to someone. She seems to be all right, but she's anxious. She wakes up every morning inexplicably edgy.'

'Two people got killed in front of her,' said Boxer. 'Siobhan took a bullet meant for her and her own father shot someone in the head. It'd be unusual if she didn't wake up anxious. How about you and Marcus?'

'What about us?'

'Still good?'

'That's not what you meant,' said Mercy. 'I know you.'

'Have you told DCS Hines about his criminal career?' asked Boxer. 'Or are you waiting for the next time?'

Mercy sighed.

'Hines is never going to let you go,' said Boxer, 'not now. You're his star performer. Probably the only woman who's ever impressed Ryder Forsyth.'

'Ryder and me,' said Mercy, smiling. 'You know, he invited me to Brize Norton to meet the hostages off the plane from Marrakesh with all the parents.'

'How did that go?'

'Very emotional. The six of them walked off the plane holding hands. Wú Dao-ming fainted when she saw her boy. I'd been talking to Anastasia Casey before the plane arrived. Ryder had told me how tough she was. All I saw was this great bruiser of a woman beside herself. And Yermilov. I didn't think Yury was going to survive the hug he gave him. Emma and I were already close. She'd told me she wouldn't have been able to keep going if anything had happened to Sophie. Her head was full of how she was going to tell her daughter she no longer had a father. The Germans were very un-Germanic. And the Sarkars turned up with about twenty family members, including the ambassador. It's good to see that even the super-rich are as vulnerable as the rest of us.'

'So you and Ryder…?'

'Inseparable,' said Mercy. 'I've even asked him why he'd denied knowing you.'

'Did he tell you?'

'He said he didn't want the personal to get confused with the professional.'

'Nicely done, Ryder.'

'I like him.'

'Simon's told me Ryder's come out of this thing smelling of roses.'

'You make that sound as if he should be stinking of something else.'

'Depends how wonderful you think the Kinderman Corporation is,' said Boxer. 'And don't think I haven't noticed that you still haven't told me what you're going to do about Marcus.'

'Let's talk about you, shall we?'

'Me?'

'You've got a son, remember?'

'Who needs a mother,' said Boxer.

'Don't look at me,' said Mercy. 'Amy'll tell you it's not my strongest card.'

'Not you.'

'Amy's not ready for anything like that.'

'Not Amy,' said Boxer. 'I was thinking of Alyshia.'

'Alyshia,' said Mercy, nodding. 'Are we talking adoption?'

'I think that would be the fairest way.'

'And you'd be all right with that?' said Mercy. 'What if she went to India … permanently?'

'We'd have to talk about that,' said Boxer. 'I'm just thinking about it at the moment. She loves the baby. She loved her mother. She and I have got closer over the last couple of years.'

'It's a big decision.'

'It came to me as I was flying back from Marrakesh,' said Boxer. 'I couldn't see myself looking after a baby in my flat in Belsize Park. The boy should have a family life, more of a family life than I had, with parents and other siblings maybe.'

And with those words came the flickering image of the Betamax cassette tape on his kitchen table, along with Conrad

Jensen's revelation to him in the High Atlas, and the other reason for giving his son away. It was something that had gripped him throughout his ordeal in the Moroccan prison: the bad seed being passed from father to son. Perhaps that could be contained or even reversed by nurture from a different parent. He looked at Mercy and in that instant thought, no, this was not for her, and realised that once again he'd become a man with secrets.

'Let's go back inside and have a drink,' he said.

Towards the end of February, Boxer was feeling stronger. He'd got his sleeping patterns back to normal and was eating properly. He spent some time turning the Betamax tape over in his hands but doing nothing about it, not even finding a player to view it.

He met with Simon Deacon regularly and they talked about what had happened in Morocco, and MI6's analysis of his debrief, which had not included the name of the group that Jensen was trying to extinguish nor the fact that he'd revealed himself as Boxer's father, and certainly not that he would be contacted by Louise and was expected to follow up on Ryder Forsyth.

'The first thing the analysts at the Cross still can't work out is why Siobhan employed you to look for Jensen,' said Deacon.

'Nor can I,' said Boxer. 'But Amy released those recordings of my initial interview with Siobhan, so I hope there's no doubting my word on that.'

'No, no, we don't doubt you, it just doesn't make sense.'

'I can't help you,' said Boxer. 'What's the second thing?'

'There was never any trace of Jensen out in the Mauritanian desert. Benjelloun informed the CIA of Jensen's intentions as soon as you told him. The Americans have very powerful satellite technology. I've heard it on good authority that he never showed up on any of their scans, and their field agents haven't picked up on him anywhere in west Africa.'

'Maybe he went off and became a tourist in Agadir instead,' said Boxer. 'Or maybe the CIA didn't really look that hard.'

'The third thing we're uncomfortable about is this rogue CIA cell?'

'I saw what I saw and heard what I heard. They offered Jensen money to walk away. That's why Bass had a satellite phone.

Sutherland confirmed their involvement in the Benghazi debacle. Nobody wants to believe me and I'm sure the CIA don't want anybody to believe me either.'

'Then there's the set-up of the kidnaps,' said Deacon. 'You know we brought Jennifer Cook back. She took quite a beating from those ... well we don't know who they were exactly. Anchorlight operatives reporting back to Kinderman, maybe?'

'Have they let you anywhere near those guys?'

'No, even though Cook was travelling with four other soldiers who've confirmed her story.'

'How helpful was Jeff Cook?' asked Boxer.

'Her left-wing conspiracy theory is interesting,' said Deacon. 'If we're to believe Jensen, then it fits our analysis at the Cross that this was a crucial part of his plan to draw out the extremists in the CIA. Socialism does something to extreme right-wingers' brains. The targeted threat of each hostage was important, too. Taking Sophie Railton-Bass was obvious, but all those other countries are places where extreme right-wingers want to have influence.'

'Even the Russian mafia?'

'That was one of the most interesting targets of them all: organised crime, banking, access to the Kremlin all wrapped up in one guy.'

'So you *are* coming round to my version of events?'

'We don't doubt you, we just lack corroboration,' said Deacon. 'We know that American politics has never been more polarised, but it's another leap to say that a right-wing extremist faction has been infiltrating the CIA. You can't build an intelligence strategy on rumour. We need facts, not pretexts.'

'Maybe that's why you'll remain one step behind the game.'

'But at least we'll be right,' said Deacon, laughing.

Boxer and Amy were on their way to see his mother, Esme, in her flat in Mount Vernon for Sunday lunch. They were walking up Haverstock Hill; it was raining and they were huddled together under an umbrella.

'How's it going with the shrink?' asked Boxer.

'Don't call her a shrink,' said Amy. 'It makes her sound like some African witch doctor who boils heads down to a manageable size.'

'They've always been called shrinks. I don't even know why.'

'Anyway, I'm not going to tell you about discussions with my analyst.'

'Why not?'

'It's about sex. It's private.'

'Does she think you're a lesbian, is that it?' said Boxer. 'I've got no problem with homosexuality, you know. It's just the way we are.'

'Dad? Just shut the fuck up. I told you, this is precisely the conversation I *don't* want to have with you.'

'All right,' said Boxer, changing tack. 'Can I ask you something about the baby?'

'Don't take the piss.'

'How would you feel about Alyshia and Deepak adopting Jamie?'

Amy stopped in her tracks, pulled him round to face her.

'Are you serious?'

'Can you see me bottle-feeding a baby up in that flat before flying out to Pakistan for three weeks to earn a living?'

The rain thrashed across the umbrella.

'No, I can't, you're right. You'd be hopeless.'

'You OK with the idea?' asked Boxer. 'He's your half-brother.'

They walked on, arm in arm, in silence for several minutes.

'I can't think of anyone better,' she said.

Boxer was with Alyshia. It was late afternoon and dark. They'd spent some time with Jamie and gone for a cup of tea in the hospital canteen, and were now heading back to the Neonatal ICU. Boxer pulled her over to the window and they looked out across the wet Fulham Road.

'I don't know how to put this,' said Boxer, 'so I'm just going to ask you straight. It's a big question, so you don't have to answer immediately. I wanted to know if you'd like to be Jamie's mother.'

Her head turned slowly away from the glass. She could see Boxer's face clearly enough in the reflection, but she needed to see him for real, to make sure that the offer she'd heard was genuine. She smiled.

'Did Mum tell you?'

'I don't know.'

'About Deepak and me?'

'All she said, when she asked if I wanted her to have the baby, was that it should be you not her having a child … that's all.'

'Deepak and I have been trying to conceive for over a year now. I'd just started IVF when Mum came over to Mumbai and we found out she was pregnant. It hit me hard. I was angry with her, envious, but I got over it, came round and got involved.'

'So you've already thought about this?'

'I've been hoping,' she said, 'waiting for you to ask.'

'And Deepak?' asked Boxer. 'It's not always easy for a man to have a child that's not his own in the house.'

'He's cool,' said Alyshia. 'We're still going to try for our own.'

'I'd want you to adopt him. That would be best. I'll be his god-father,' said Boxer. 'And by the way, I've spoken to Amy and she's hoping you'll agree.'

'Are you all right with us splitting our time between London and Mumbai?'

'Is that what you're planning?'

'Dad's reeled Deepak back into the fold,' said Alyshia. 'He wants him to build the electric cars in the UK plants. So if anything, we'll be more here than there.'

Mercy and Marcus Alleyne were eating groundnut soup in her kitchen in Streatham. It was Alleyne's favourite Ghanaian food. They'd just started on the second bottle of Malbec.

'I'm going to talk to DCS Hines about you,' said Mercy, out of the blue. 'Tell him that I'm in a full-blown relationship with a known criminal.'

'I'm not known to him, Mercy,' said Alleyne. 'I'm only known on the street.'

'You think?'

'I'm very careful.'

'People know about you, which means *we* know about you.'

'Then why aren't I in HMP Wandsworth?'

'Probably because you're the acceptable face of crime. You're not violent. You don't use firearms or knives. You keep a low profile. If we busted you, the replacement might be a lot nastier.'

'So you're being … kind?'

'You *could* think of it like that.'

'If you tell DCS Hines, maybe that kindness is going to run out.'

'I doubt it.'

'Before you talk to him, I got some news for you.'

'What's that?'

'I'm out.'

'What do you mean?'

'I'm selling the stock left in my flat and I'm out. No more fencing.'

'Why's that?'

'Got me into some scary shit, that's why,' said Alleyne. 'Don't want to go through that again. I told Charlie, I thought I was done for. That's no way to live.'

'How're you going to make a living?'

'I still haven't got the answer to that, Mercy. But I will find it. I guarantee.'

Alleyne put his knife and fork together, finished his Malbec and wiped his mouth with his napkin. He took a pouch out of his pocket and proceeded to roll a large joint, which he lit and smoked.

On the day that Jamie Boxer was due to leave the Neonatal ICU, the adoption process had still not been completed, so Boxer went to pick him up and bring him back to Isabel's house in Kensington, where Alyshia and Deepak were now living so that they were close to the Chelsea and Westminster.

There was a small party for his arrival of about twenty people standing around drinking champagne. Boxer made a very moving speech about Isabel, the adoption and Alyshia, who looked radiant holding the still very tiny bundle in her arms.

Deacon was there, and afterwards he gave Boxer a big hug and told him he'd made a great choice for Jamie. They went outside on to the small patio during a brief moment of sunshine.

'I haven't seen you for a while,' said Boxer.

'Been busy with a new terrorist group in Syria and Iraq,' Deacon said. 'You won't have heard of them yet but they call themselves the Islamic State.'

371

'You're looking at me in that questioning way of yours,' said Boxer, wondering if Deacon was teeing him up to ask about the American Republic of Christians.

'You've had no word from Jensen?'

'Me? Why would I have word from him?'

'There's still no satisfactory explanation for your involvement in that business back in January.'

'I can't help you.'

'You will get in touch with me if you ever hear from him?'

'Sure, but I can't think why he'd want to make contact,' said Boxer. 'It's all over now. What have I got to offer him?'

'We don't know,' said Deacon, looking at him hard. 'We never knew.'

'Does that mean I'm back on the suspect list?'

'It means we don't have an answer to a fundamental question,' said Deacon.

'Did you get anywhere with the CIA?' asked Boxer. 'Or ask Mercy to talk to Ryder?'

Deacon shook his head.

Esme came out of the house for a cigarette and the conversation changed to the Russian takeover of the Crimea.

The party was over by four o'clock and Boxer left to go back to Belsize Park. It was strange leaving the house under the circumstances, and he had a sustained pang of grief as he walked down the hill to the tube station.

Just as he started to go down the steps, he had a call from an unknown number. He took it. There was a beat of silence. A voice said:

'Hello, Charlie, this is Louise.'

ACKNOWLEDGEMENTS

This is the first book I've written since the death of my wife, Jane, and it could not have been done without the support of my family and friends from all over the world.

I would especially like to thank Bryony Spencer who looked after me in the immediate aftermath of Jane's death, taught me yoga and kept my head together. She left her life in France and came over at the beginning of 2014 to stay with me in Oxford while I got this book off the ground and then later helped me transfer to Portugal to finish it. Without her, my task would have been doubly difficult.

I would also like to thank Mick Lawson and José Manuel Blanco who kept me going with their phone calls of love and support from Seville. They were very close to Jane and that was enormously important to me.

Paul Johnston, my old Oxford pal and fellow crime writer, also phoned me regularly from Napflion in Greece, which was hugely helpful.

Jane's family: Michael and Marianne, John, Louise, Anna and Fenella, Annabelle, Geoff and Eleanor, Guy, Chantalle, Tyrese and Morgan, John Luke and Robyn all played their part in keeping my spirits up.

I'd like to thank my mother, who provided much-needed insight and love. My thanks, too, to my sister, Anita, and her husband, David, for being there for me.

I was also very lucky to have my old Oxford housemates, Peter and Monica Tudor, nearby as they often had me over and couldn't have been better friends in my hour of need.

It was strange, after all these years, to be living in Oxford, where I had also been to school, and to find friendship extended from that quarter. I'd like to thank Mike Stanfield, Chairman of the Board of Governors of St Edward's, and Chris Jones, who'd been my first 1st XV captain, both of whom were very warm and supportive.

My thanks to Kristian Lutze, my German translator, and his partner Anne Braun, for looking after me at the Cologne literary festival and being great friends.

Once I went back to Portugal to finish the book, I was brilliantly supported by Alexandra Monteiro, Manuel and Deb Pilar, Nucha and Miguel, Joris and Sandra.

With Jane's death I had not only lost the love of my life but also my first reader and editor. I was fortunate that Liz Wyse, who'd read all my books and knew me well, could step in and give me excellent advice and do it with love.

I am very fortunate to be a part of the literary agency Aitken Alexander Associates and I would like to thank everybody there for the support they showed me over that difficult year and especially Anthony Sheil, Lesley Thorne and Sally Riley.

I would also like to take this opportunity to thank everyone at Orion for sticking by me through that difficult time. They never put me under any pressure and I only ever felt total support from them. I would especially like to thank Genevieve Pegg who gave me the best editorial notes I have ever received on a book.

My thanks, too, to Anu Ohrling, who advised on the medical condition of one of the characters in this book.

Finally I would like to thank Lucy Maycock, the new light of my life, for being close but giving me space, for enlivening my mind and making me laugh, for opening my eyes to new experiences and making me happy. Lucy and her daughter, Tallulah, have made me feel that I belong again.